Cybil looked at the mayor. "Do you have any questions?"

"Just one," LaSalle said. "How big will it be?"

"The cloud or the fire?"

"Both. Either."

"It's a rough guess but I'd say that, assuming the entire contents of the tank vaporize, and assuming that the other tanks remain intact, the cloud will be about half a mile wide and five miles long."

LaSalle once again lapsed into silence, staring vacantly at his ██████████████████████ lmost closing. Cybil ██████████████████████ next question.

"One last thing ██████████

"Yes?"

"How do we stop it?"

"Stop it?" Cybil answered. "I thought you understood. You can't stop it. Nothing can stop it."

"THE PUBLIC NEEDS TO KNOW THAT SUCH A DISASTER, ON SUCH A MAMMOTH SCALE, REALLY IS POSSIBLE."
Dallas Morning News

THE DEADLY FROST

By Terrence Moan

BALLANTINE BOOKS • NEW YORK

Library of Congress Catalog Card Number: 78-64797

ISBN 0-345-28947-1

This edition published by arrangement with
Rawson, Wade Publishers, Inc.

Manufactured in the United States of America

First Ballantine Books Edition: December 1980

To Syble, Jeanne, and Althea.
For their love, language, and support.

Chapter 1

The gray-green waters of New York harbor shimmered in the oppressive August heat. The sharp white bow of the Coast Guard cutter *Apple Tree* cut through the oil-slicked sea, sending a spray of foul-smelling droplets into the air. Catching the morning sun, they reflected a spectrum of vivid colors before the advancing vessel.

On the foredeck, Cybil Yale leaned against the waist-high railing. Sweat plastered the blue-checked blouse against her body, cutting her figure in stark outline against the horizon. The matching coat to her pants suit was thrown carelessly across the rail, the sleeves hanging limply at its sides. The speed of the ship only stirred the sluggish air, making a humid mixture that heated rather than cooled.

"Nice," one of the sailors on deck commented, gazing at her trim figure. His voice was pitched conspiratorially low as he nudged his companion.

"Yeah," the other sailor agreed.

It wasn't because she was the only woman on board; Cybil was undeniably beautiful. She was small, five feet two, and well proportioned, with thick brown hair and large brown eyes.

Her presence on the *Apple Tree*, however, was due to her international reputation. At twenty-eight, she was one of the world's leading experts in low-temperature physics. Her papers were cited as gospel and her comments were sought by every major university from Boston to Moscow.

Two years earlier, Cybil had taken a leave of absence as a full professor from M.I.T. to join the newly created Department of Energy, and had been sworn in as Deputy Secretary by the President.

Now, technically at least, she was in charge of the *Apple Tree*. This was the fourth time she had sailed on the

1

cutter out to the Ambrose Light to inspect one of the LNG tankers that made their biweekly calls to New York to feed the growing demands of the American consumer for energy. Each trip to the mouth of the harbor was the same. Each tanker waiting there was different.

Liquefied natural gas technology was still in its infancy. New techniques, new materials, new designs only a few years, and in some cases only a few months, out of the laboratory were being applied on a massive scale. There was no time to test. No time to try out all the alternatives.

Every ship was a prototype. Each different from the one before. Each with its own ideas, problems, and solutions.

The growth of a technology is a slow process. No substance should be taken directly from a half-liter laboratory flask and transported in millions of gallons on the high seas. Cybil remembered what James Dillon used to say. "Some things cannot be extrapolated from the small to the large. Take an atomic bomb, for instance. You can examine a small piece of plutonium and nothing will lead you to expect an explosion if you add more. But just try it."

Dillon. James Dillon. He was one of the reasons she was here. The deck of the cutter was more than two hundred miles from Washington. Two thousand wasn't enough to escape the memory of James Dillon.

She had first met him in the Oval Office. The President had introduced them. Dillon's wit had been incisive. He seemed to calculate every angle of every question and every statement he made, even a simple hello. As she grew to know him better, she found out that it was true. Dillon had the mind of a computer.

And the heart to match.

Perhaps that was why he had been given the sensitive position of director of the National Security Agency, the top position in the U.S. intelligence community.

For two years they had been lovers. In bed, his steel-gray eyes softened to tender blue. His calculating mind stopped adding and subtracting long enough to feel. He became human, if only for a few minutes. But two years was long enough to love a machine. Two years was long enough to live under a microscope where each action, each emotion was weighed and catalogued for possible later use. She had had enough.

On the Fourth of July, Cybil walked into the President's office and asked to be relieved of her duties. She wanted to get back to the simplicity of her own laboratory, her own classroom. She wanted to get away from government, from Washington, most of all, from Dillon. But the President said no.

Instead, he asked her to take on a new assignment. Partially a vacation, partially work, he told her. And far enough from Washington to give her time to think. His southern charm worked.

She accepted.

The vacation never materialized. Work dominated everything. The deck of the *Apple Tree* was her Caribbean beach. And the LNG tankers were her picturesque fishing villages.

"Professor?"

Cybil squinted against the harsh glare of the sun. The spotless white uniform made her squint more. Although she couldn't see his face, she recognized the commander of the *Apple Tree* by his stiff, formal attitude.

At their first meeting Cybil had tried to be friendly but had found only hostility beneath his professional demeanor. Only when she began reading the Coast Guard manuals on LNG procedures did it become clear. The name Alexander Wade was on the front page of each one. He had been a lieutenant then, now he was a commander.

They had retreated into a shell of stiff formalities. He called her "Professor." She called him "Commander."

"Yes, Commander?"

"We'll be docking with the *Prometheus* in a few minutes. I thought you might want to watch from the bridge."

"Thank you, Commander. I think I'll stay here if you don't mind."

"As you wish." He casually saluted and returned to the bridge.

She could tell by his manner that he was hurt, but she couldn't worry about wounded feelings. There would be enough bruised egos before her job was finished.

Commander Wade mentally cursed himself as he returned to the bridge. As he automatically gave the orders necessary to bring the *Apple Tree* alongside the *Prome-*

3

theus, he thought about this woman who had turned his promising career into a dead-end job in just a few short weeks. Whenever she was around he felt both inadequate and angry. She had turned him into little more than a uniformed taxi driver and he hated it, and her, for it.

"Rudder amidships. Ahead dead slow. Keep her steady, helmsman." Wade was a career officer and proud of his service, his ship, and his skill. He was also a superb seaman, with an almost instinctive knowledge of the sea and her ever-changing ways.

"Right full rudder." More than three years ago he had been assigned to a Coast Guard study group to establish inspection and safety standards for the fleets of LNG tankers that were scheduled to flood U.S. ports carrying their cargoes of liquid energy. As the junior officer of the team, he had done most of the actual work. In fact, he was recognized within the service as the author of most of the regulations that were now standard operating procedures for the Coast Guard in New York, Los Angeles, Boston, Baltimore, New Orleans, and Houston. He was the Coast Guard's leading expert in LNG safety and had trained dozens of junior officers in his methods. A promotion to captain was in the offing.

At least, until the Department of Energy and Miss Yale, Professor Yale, Deputy Secretary Yale, stepped in.

"Back one third." The powerful engines of the trim ship revved as they answered the command. "Helmsman, I want her to just kiss the landing platform, not even nick the paint."

The cutter slid up to the *Prometheus*, an ant approaching an elephant. The *Apple Tree* was a medium-sized cutter, one of the Coast Guard's fastest and best ships afloat. Yet she was dwarfed by the mammoth gray shape she approached.

"All stop. Bow and stern lines ready." Nothing more than a taxi driver, Wade thought, as the *Apple Tree* executed a near-perfect landing. There was barely a noticeable thump as the heavily padded nylon bumpers cushioned the impact of the cutter against the side of the tanker. The steady drone of the engines ceased their throbbing as they cycled to idle.

On deck, Cybil felt the shadow of the *Prometheus* cover her. She looked up and her breath caught in her throat.

4

The tanker was mammoth. Despite the heat, Cybil shivered.

11:00 A.M.   *On Board the* PROMETHEUS

She was the reigning queen of the Greek LNG fleet. By size alone, nine hundred thirty-six feet in length and one hundred forty-four in width, the *Prometheus* was the unchallenged ruler of the harbor. Only the largest crude-oil supertankers could rival her in the sea lanes and, drawing almost three times as much water, they were exiled to artificial deep-water terminals. Anchored at the mouth of New York harbor, the *Prometheus* dwarfed the other, lesser giants of the sea as they slowly passed by, giving her the wide berth her size and cargo demanded.

In shape, she was unique. Even the rankest sailor could identify her the moment her silhouette cut the clean line of the horizon. She rode high in the water, her deck more than eighty feet above the waterline even when fully loaded, and her stern-placed superstructure rose one hundred feet to the bridge.

But it was the tanks that made her unmistakable. Five spheres poked through the plane of the deck, their geometric symmetry alien to the sleek lines of the ship. Each sphere was one hundred forty feet in diameter, roughly the same size as a twelve-story building. Painted a high-gloss white, they almost glowed in the harsh sunlight.

Val Paknis, first mate of the *Prometheus*, strode across the deck toward the Jacob's ladder. His eyes roamed unceasingly across the deck and the surface of the five domes, looking for anything out of order. He hated these mandatory inspections whenever they entered an American port. Unnecessary, he thought, as his eye picked up a slight discoloration on one of the tanks. Almost an insult to his ship, questioning whether she was seaworthy. Seaworthy. She was one of the safest ships afloat. Her hull had been inspected for defects with every device known to man. Her tanks had been inspected by sonar and X-ray. Her engines were tuned to the precision of the pitch of a concert piano. How could anyone challenge his ship?

Yes, his ship.

Even though he was only the first mate, Paknis had

been with the *Prometheus* ever since her keel had been laid, more than five years before. He had endured the bitter New England winters to watch the workmen as they turned soulless slabs of steel into the body of a living ship. He watched the engines being constructed in the dark recesses of the mammoth ship. And then, on one frigid afternoon, the sky a cloudless blue, he watched the first of the prefabricated spherical tanks lifted by the giant cranes and lowered into the body of his ship.

His ship. He knew every passageway, hatch, and piece of equipment in her. Even though she had another man as her captain, she had only one true master, only one mate. Val Paknis.

"Chief!" Paknis motioned the crew chief to his side.

"Yes, mate?" Stephen Dunn, the crew chief, an Englishman by birth but a sailor by choice, answered in his oh-so-casual voice. His insolence was second only to his ability to nurse any sick piece of equipment into instant health. A wizard with machinery, he had been kicked off a dozen ships until he met Paknis, one of the few officers who could tolerate him.

"The paint on the domes," Paknis pointed. "It's begining to yellow again. Get some men and chip it clean on our way out. I want it repainted by the time we make it back to port."

"Aye, mate, but I'm tellin' ya' . . ."

Paknis smiled and waved him into silence. "I know. I know. There's nothing that will stop it. It's the cold. You told me the last time. Just get it painted, chief."

"Aye, mate," was the half-sullen reply.

The metallic ring of feet on the Jacob's ladder announced the approach of the inspection team. Paknis motioned the reception committee into their places. The seven men lined up smartly and stood at near attention. Paknis reviewed them with pride. Although merchant mariners would never stand for the spit and polish of the military, the men of the *Prometheus* took pride in their excellence. They were the highest paid and best-trained men on the sea and they looked it.

When the men of the *Apple Tree* appeared, they were met by equally professional counterparts. Paknis accepted Wade's salute with a crisp one of his own. It barely faltered when the unmilitary figure in blue stepped on deck, her jacket casually thrown across her shoulder.

The commander introduced them.

At first, Cybil had eyes only for the tanks. They rose forty feet off the deck but looked larger. Each one held six and one-half million gallons of LNG. They dominated the deck. They dominated her view.

"Professor?" Wade's insistent voice penetrated her concentration.

"Errr . . . yes, Commander?"

"I was saying, this is Mr. Paknis, first mate of the *Prometheus*. I thought . . ."

Cybil stuck out her hand. "Mr. Paknis." She smiled. "Or should I call you 'mate'? I'm afraid that has certain modern connotations that . . ." The sentence was left hanging.

Paknis smiled. "Just call me Val. As first officer of this ship I get called a lot of things. From you, Val will be just fine."

Cybil grabbed the proffered hand. Despite the heat, it was cool and steady. Strength flowed from one to the other in the grip. A handshake of equals.

Cybil squinted to see his eyes. There was something familiar about the first mate, although she knew she had never met him before. His eyes, she realized with a shock. Under the shade of the uniform cap, they shone with a familiar intensity. An intensity born of intelligence and unrelenting determination. The eyes of James Dillon. Only, she realized slowly, somewhat different.

The corners were equally wrinkled. Paknis's wrinkles curled upward, Dillon's downward. The steel-blue color of the mate's eyes wasn't impersonal, merely strong. Dillon's had reflected strength without weakness, without flaw. The man who looked at her was human, more human than he wanted to admit. There were other similarities, Cybil admitted, as she looked at the man before her.

Paknis was tall. He towered at least a foot over her. His frame was square, the uniform concealing an inner strength that years of turmoil had lent his body. He had a certain grace that she couldn't define, something she had never seen before. A certainty of movement, as though he was conscious of every muscle, every tendon, every bone as he glided across the deck. He was the picture of confidence; confidence that came from knowledge of his environment. Paknis was a man of the sea. Dillon could survive with equal ease in a swamp or a desert.

Similar but infinitely different.

"Pleased to meet you, Mr. Paknis . . . Val," Cybil smiled at the Greek officer. "I'm looking forward to inspecting your ship. I've read so much about her, I feel as though I know her already."

Val grinned. "Ah, but I'm afraid that there's no way for you to have any real feeling for the *Prometheus* without seeing her for yourself. There's just no substitute for experiencing her personally."

Cybil noticed that the officer still held her outstretched hand. Reluctantly, she withdrew it. Her eyes fled to the dome behind his back.

"Mr. Paknis," Wade cleared his throat as he spoke. "I believe you have some papers before we begin our inspection."

The mate returned to his military demeanor. "Of course, Commander." He reached inside his coat pocket and produced a sheaf of folded documents. "Here." He handed them over. "I trust they are all in order."

Wade gave the papers a formalistic glance. He had seen photostatic copies the day before. Without these clearances, the *Prometheus* would have been stopped long before she entered U.S. territorial waters. He passed the packet to Cybil.

"Thank you, Mr. Paknis." Wade's smile carried no warmth. "If we could begin the inspection."

"Of course, Commander." Paknis waved to his crewmen. "We're waiting for you to do just that. My men will, of course, accompany yours." The men paired off. They had done this before. They knew their jobs. There would be no confusion.

Cybil flipped through the documents. She had seen them before. The first was a certificate from the firm of Stocton and Stocton, one of the most respected names in the shipping industy, attesting to the seaworthiness of the *Prometheus*. It was sealed by a bright blue ribbon that hung limply against the paper, as though pomp alone would ensure its accuracy.

The next was less gaudy, but as far as Cybil was concerned, all the more important. It was sealed by the U.S.

Coast Guard. It attested to the condition of the five tanks, the safety equipment, the safety shields, and the soundness of the outer hull. A scuba team had inspected the hull; their report was attached. The engines, the fittings, the electrical system, virtually everything that came into contact with the cargo had been checked and rechecked.

The date of the certificate was eleven months earlier. She was almost due for another full-scale inspection. Another month and she wouldn't be allowed into the harbor.

Below that there were a series of papers, ending in the bill of lading. It was in English since the cargo had been on-loaded in Algeria.

METHANE: LIQUID ***** 122,885 m³
−175C. (260 F.)
57096057 m. tons

Cybil looked from the bill of lading to the tank behind the mate. The sturdy white side of the dome looked innocuous enough. Behind that, another dome arched above the deck. And behind that another. Five, all told. Five domes. Five tanks. Thirty-three million gallons.

She carefully folded the papers and handed them back to the first mate. "Your papers appear to be in order." Their hands touched as she returned the documents.

"Would you like a tour of the ship, Miss Yale?" Val asked, returning the papers to his pocket. "I'd be more than happy to show you around."

"I'd love one," Cybil responded. She turned to the commander. "But I don't want to get in the way of the usual inspection. Commander?"

Wade shook his head, more than happy to get rid of her for a few minutes. "No, you wouldn't be in the way. The men have their assignments. You won't be interfering at all."

"In that case . . ." Val bowed slightly, pointing toward the superstructure at the stern. "May I suggest we start with the refrigerator units."

Cybil smiled, remembering the drawings of the *Prometheus* she had seen earlier. She pointed forward. "I think I'd rather start with the bosun's storeroom in the bow and work toward the stern, if it's all the same to you, Val."

"Of course," he said, nonplussed by the abrupt change in course. "Commander, would you like to join us?"

"No, thanks, I have work to do. I'll meet you on the bridge when you're through." He saluted and dismissed his men. They dispersed and left with their merchant marine counterparts. The voices blended into the friendly banter of sailors doing routine duty. Anything, no matter how inherently dangerous, Cybil thought, became routine when repeated often enough.

Paknis took her to the hatch that led into the dark recesses of the ship. A blast of cold air swept over them as he opened the hatch, startling her.

"It's only the air conditioning," he explained.

The hatch closed behind them with a hollow metallic clang that resounded through the empty corridor of the mammoth tanker.

11:30 A.M.   *Coney Island Boardwalk*

". . . and in the tenth day of the worst heat wave in the city's history there is little sign of relief. Temperatures remained above ninety-five for the tenth consecutive day. Eleven A.M. readings in Central Park were ninety-five percent. The air quality remains dangerously unhealthy and anyone with a heart or lung condition is advised to avoid unnecessary physical activity.

"The Air Pollution Advisory remains in effect for New York City and vicinity. All private vehicles are banned from midtown Manhattan between Fourteenth Street and Fifty-ninth Street until the advisory is lifted. The M.T.A. has assigned additional buses and subways to meet the increased demand and are running only air-conditioned cars on all routes.

"Con Edison reports that they have reduced power by an additional five percent in an effort to prevent a total blackout. The blackout affecting three hundred thousand customers in the Bronx and parts of Westchester is expected to end sometime this evening according to a spokesman for the utility.

"The official death toll attributed to the air inversion and heat wave has reached two hundred seventy-nine. Most heavily hit are the elderly."

"Isn't it the truth," complained Sadie Lazarus. "The old are always the victims. You remember Rachel Freedman, the one with the bakery on Sherman Avenue. She's in the hospital in an oxygen tent, with tubes and needles sticking into every inch of her body. And it's all because of the heat. I tell you, it just isn't worth growing old anymore.

"And Rachel isn't the only one. Old Mr. Shellmeyer is in Mount Sinai. He had a heart attack walking up those steps to his apartment on the third floor. I told him to move, but oy, the rents they charge nowadays. And the apartments! I tell you they should put those landlords in jail for what they charge for a tiny little one-bedroom apartment you can't even lie down in. Robbery! That's what it is! Stealing from the old."

The recipient of this incessant tirade was Rebecca Friedman, Sadie Lazarus's oldest and dearest friend. After ten years of widowhood, Rebecca had learned the value of human companionship. She endured Sadie's daily one-sided commentary for the sake of hearing another human voice. She didn't mind, really. In fact, it was rather pleasant to listen to Sadie without having to concentrate on the meaning. An occasional grunt or nod of agreement was enough to keep Sadie going.

The two old women, wrapped as always in black shawls despite the heat, had sat on the same bench on the Coney Island boardwalk every sunny day for the past seven years. They had become a fixture, an institution like the hot dog vendors and the Good Humor man. They took turns bringing lunch, making them both feel needed.

". . . and now for the Wall Street report brought to you by Merrill Lynch, the firm that is bullish on America . . ." blared a nearby radio. ". . . The weather seems to have affected the market as well as everything else in the city. Trading remains light and most market indicators are down . . ."

"How's the asthma?" Sadie asked suddenly, breaking off her normal stream of words.

"Not good, Sadie. Not good. I didn't sleep well last night. And to tell the truth, I don't feel so well either."

"Look," Sadie held up a half-finished bagel. "You didn't eat. How do you think you're going to keep up your strength if you don't eat? Next thing you know they'll put you in the hospital like poor Mrs. Freedman or Mr. Shellmeyer. Then they'll make you eat. So eat." She shoved the bagel at Rebecca.

"Maybe later, Sadie. Later."

"It's the air, Rebecca. The air. It's no good, what with all those chemicals and things they pollute the air with it's a wonder it doesn't poison us all. You rest now. And soon we'll go home."

Sadie leaned back, worrying. Rebecca was not a complainer and she always ate her lunch.

They actually occupied one of the nicest benches on the entire boardwalk. They were shaded by one of the few surviving trees, which kept the worst of the sun off them yet didn't block their view of the beach or the harbor. Both women loved to watch the ships come and go, their flags flying proudly in the breeze. It was activity. It was life. A reminder that the world still went on even though they had aged and slowed down.

It was one of the nicest spots on the beach and, consequently, the sand was always littered with bodies gleaming with Coppertone and Johnson's Baby Oil. Teen-agers gathered there, and it became a meeting place for young lovers, for groups of boys and girls anxious to meet one another. Both Sadie and Rebecca loved to watch the antics of the pubescent youngsters; each privately reliving her youth, while expressing "shock" over the way young people dress and make public spectacles of themselves. Neither one ever suggested moving.

The past ten days had brought out more people than ever before. The heat was unbearable and the beach, always crowded, was completely covered by blankets and towels. People had actually spent the entire night on the sand to reserve choice spots for the next day. The police, who were supposed to clear the beaches, looked the other way. It was just too hot to hassle anyone wanting to stay cool.

Rebecca had fallen into an uneasy slumber, Sadie noted with concern. She took the limp bagel from Rebecca's unfeeling fingers and carefully wrapped it in a paper napkin before storing it in her lunch basket. Maybe she'll want it later, she thought.

Sadie stared out to sea, looking for the lighthouse that

marked Sandy Hook. The pollution was too heavy and she couldn't see it. She clicked her tongue and shook her head, mumbling, "Poisoned air. It'll be the death of us all."

Chapter 2

12:00 NOON *Auxiliary Control Room on the*
PROMETHEUS

"The blue valve is the emergency manual override on the tank boil-off." Paknis patted a large blue wheel almost affectionately. "The computer constantly monitors the pressure in all five storage tanks and in the two auxiliary tanks in the engine room as well. When the pressure begins to drop in the engine room, as it does, for example, when we're traveling at full speed, the computer allows more of the boil-off to be diverted to the engine room. When that's full, the gas is cycled through the CO_2 refrigerator units, one for each tank by the way, and returned to the main storage tanks."

"So you operate on the waste product from the tanks, right." Cybil jotted something in her notebook. "Kind of like carrying your fuel piggyback. No wasted space. No wasted energy. Very efficient."

"Yes, it is. We're proud of her." He patted one of the valves. They were standing in the auxiliary control room just forward of the engine room. The room was a maze of dials all carefully labeled and marked in metric and English systems to prevent any possible confusion. They were standing next to a wall of multicolored valves—the emergency controls of the ship. They had never been used, but Paknis explained the use of each one without ever referring to the labels underneath.

"What would happen if there wasn't enough boil-off to meet the engines' demands?" Cybil asked.

"That hasn't happened, so far at least, but theoretically the computer would open the emergency gas reserve supply located in the engine room. Since LNG is constantly boiling it produces more fuel than we consume. Even on return voyages, when we carry only enough gas to keep the tanks at operational temperatures, there is enough. That's probably due to sloshing when the tanks are nearly empty. With more room to move around in, the LNG vaporizes faster and it more than meets our needs."

"I would think that the company would be a little upset that their LNG was being used to operate the ship. LNG isn't cheap."

He smiled at her, warming to his subject. "No, it isn't. But we only consume about one-hundredth of one percent of the total cargo. That's less than the standard tanker leaves clinging to the walls of the tanks. And that oil is wasted. It has to be washed out of the tanks, usually at sea when the Coast Guard isn't looking.

"With LNG, the word is efficiency. Not one erg of energy is wasted. Even the air conditioning is a free spin-off. Remember the gas that's used for the engines, the boil-off? Well, the average temperature is about minus two hundred and fifty-eight Fahrenheit. It has to be warmed to ambient temperature, about plus seventy-eight degrees, before we can safely mix it with air in the engines and burn it. That's over three hundred degrees differential. The water we use to warm the gas is then pumped into the air-conditioning system. *Voilà.* Free air conditioning.

"In the winter we just reverse the process. We hook up the heating system to the CO_2 refrigeration units that return the LNG to the tanks and," he snapped his fingers, "free heat. All part of the system. All necessary for the transportation of the cargo. As a result, we have the most comfortable ship on the Atlantic." Paknis beamed.

"I assume you use a closed system of seawater for your air conditioning-heating units. Or do you use a Freon base? That would prevent local freeze-ups."

"Seawater," he answered. "We thought about using the Freon chemical complex but decided that in the long run it wasn't worth the extra expense. Seawater is free and we don't have to worry too much about leaks, the way we would if we used Freon." Paknis was impressed. The woman's questions were not the idiotic ones he would have expected from some Washington bureaucrat. It was evident that she was not the normal visitor.

"Where next?" she asked, her eyes sparkling with interest. She closed her notebook with a snap.

"Well," Paknis ticked off the items with his fingers. "We've seen the refrigeration plant, the steering room, the engine room, and the secondary control station." He waved an arm to encompass the multicolored room they occupied. "Other than the storeroom and the mess hall, there isn't a lot more to see. The crews' quarters are standard," he smiled, "except for the air conditioning." She smiled back.

"How about the tanks? We haven't inspected the tanks yet. And I've only been on the membrane-type tankers before. This is my first time on a free-standing tanker."

The respect that had been slowly building suddenly plummeted. "But you can't . . ."

"Why not?" she protested.

"Because the temperature . . ."

"So. You have cryogenic suits on board. They're listed on your manifest and besides, they're required safety equipment on all LNG carriers."

"Of course we have the suits, but that's not the reason. It's regulations." He finished weakly. He never considered taking anyone, Christ, he never even thought of inspecting the hold himself while the ship was carrying a full load of LNG.

"Whose regulations?" she challenged. From the look in his eyes she knew she had him. "Not Coast Guard regulations. In fact the regulations specifically require the 'thorough examination' of any and all points of possible escape." Her voice took on a stentorian note as she quoted the regulations verbatim.

Paknis frowned. "You're right," he said slowly.

"I know."

"But if I were you, I wouldn't push it." He hesitated. "You probably have the right to go into the hold to inspect the tanks. And if you insisted, I would take you there. After all, it's your neck. But, as first mate of this ship, I'd advise against it. Not because there's anything to hide but because of common sense. Those tanks aren't anything to fool with. We're carrying more than thirty million gallons of LNG. For the safety of the ship, the crew, and, ultimately, the people in the communities surrounding the harbor, I'd advise against the inspection. If you want to check the safety of our tanks, do it the way any sane person would, by remote control. We have one of the most sophisticated detection systems in the world. Use it."

Cybil stared at the tall Greek officer. Her instincts told her to trust him. She linked her arm through his and smiled. "You win, Mr. Paknis. The course of discretion charted by an expert of the sea." She laughed. "Lead on, my captain. To the bridge."

1:00 P.M. *On the Bridge of the* PROMETHEUS

"How was the tour, Professor?" Commander Wade asked as they entered the bridge.

"Educational," Cybil replied. "How's the inspection? Shouldn't you have the results by now?"

"Results are just coming in. These things take time, particularly on a ship of this size. The others we inspected last week were only about half the capacity of the *Prometheus*."

"How much longer?" she asked, her impatience obvious.

"Another ten minutes, Fifteen at the outside."

On cue, the first white-uniformed sailor entered the bridge, carrying his clipboard. He was followed by a white-haired officer in the same uniform Paknis wore, only with an additional gold braid on his sleeve.

"Professor." Wade was glad of the opportunity to divert her attention. "I don't think you've met Captain Stratakis, master of the *Prometheus*." He introduced her to the aging captain.

The captain took her hand, held it with both of his, and met her brown gaze with his blue one. "My dear, if you're an example of what the Department of Energy plans to send on inspection tours, I'm sorry they didn't take over these duties years ago, while I was still young enough to enjoy your company." His blue eyes twinkled with grandfatherly mischievousness.

The captain did remind Cybil of the grandfather she only barely remembered from her childhood. He stood about six feet two inches, taller than the first mate and even thinner. His white uniform was neat and crisp, almost crinkling when he moved, and his face was weathered from years of exposure to the hardships of the sun and salt air. It looked healthy; the lines and wrinkles added character, not age, to the man.

"Captain, I thought you knew, American women prefer the more mature male." She allowed her hand to remain captive in his two warm, dry ones. She laughed, realizing that she had been utterly charmed by the man in only a few seconds.

"Ah, yes. I remember reading something about that in the papers in Athens. But I didn't pay much attention to it. You know how we seamen are, married to out ships. How do you like her? Isn't she beautiful?" He drew her to the vast forward window overlooking the deck. All Cybil could see was the tops of the five tanks. "One of the most beautiful ships that ever sailed." The captain sighed.

"Yes," Cybil agreed, moved by the sadness that the man exuded, "she is beautiful."

They stood in silence, each looking across the same deck, each seeing a different view.

"What do you think of the professor?" Wade whispered to Paknis as they leaned over the first of the reports.

Val shrugged. He looked at Cybil's trim figure as she stood next to the captain.

"I know what you mean," the commander said, following Val's glance. "She's something to look at but, ouch, don't get too close or you'll get burned. A freezer burn, like the stuff she studies. I swear, she's colder than LNG."

"You mean she gave you the cold shoulder?"

"Hell, no," he protested, raising his voice. He lowered it again as the enlisted men looked at them. "Well, to tell the truth, yes, but it's not just me." Paknis looked at him skeptically. "No, it's true," Wade insisted. "I hear it's the word on her. All around Washington. She's an iceberg. All looks but no heart. Just look at the way she cuddles up to the old man. What a waste. And what a brain," he added respectfully.

"What do you mean?" Paknis asked. They came to the end of the first page of the report and simultaneously flipped pages to the next sheet of the checklist.

"You mean you don't know? She's Yale, of M.I.T. Don't you remember studying Yale in your cryogenics course in Bethesda? The one on theoretical expansion and contraction formulae. And on the crystallization equations for cryogenic ice formation. And on . . ."

"Yale of M.I.T.? She's that Yale?" His voice took on the same tone of respect that the commander's had had a moment before. "I never imagined . . ."

"Yeah, that Yale. And we took that course, what was it, three, four years ago? She must have been a teen-ager when she wrote it. And remember how embarrassed the professor was when he couldn't even explain it? Well, she's the author. She's that Yale. The last word in cryogenics."

"Tell me," the captain asked, "has Mr. Paknis taken good care of you? Shown you all of his toys? His computers, his automatic gadgets, his scientific marvels?"

Cybil nodded. "Yes. I've had the Cook's tour of the *Prometheus*. Very impressive. Everything except the tanks. They're off bounds." She smiled. "At least temporarily, I intend to inspect them before I leave."

"Have you shown our guest your baby, yet?" the captain asked.

"Baby?" echoed Cybil, turning to Paknis. He blushed.

"Computer. An IBM Mark VII. The captain has nicknamed it my 'baby' since I spend most of the day at the console. The terminal is right over here, if you'd like to see it."

"A Mark VII. We only had a VI at the university. I didn't know you needed that much hardware."

"We don't really, but the owners decided to see whether they could automate some of the maintenance functions. We found out we couldn't, but the computer stayed."

Like a father showing his newborn infant to the world, Paknis led her to a padded chair in front of a small television set. He turned on the console. The screen flared briefly and flickered into life; a dot in the center of the picture tube gradually expanded into a line. The line grew to fill the screen with a pale green glow. The words "Hello, my name is Valenkia. How may I serve you?" appeared in glowing green letters.

Cybil laughed. "Valenkia. That's Greek for 'Little Val,' isn't it?"

The mate punched another key on the console. The

words were replaced by the more standard computer salutation: Ready. "That was somebody's idea of a joke. Someone bribed a company computer programmer during our last overhaul in Athens. If I ever find out who did it, I'll . . ." He scowled at the rest of the crew on the bridge, including the captain. The captain stared out the window, ignoring the mate. The rest of the crew seemed suddenly to become involved in an unusually large number of attention-consuming tasks.

"Some joker thought it would be a good idea. I've talked with the computer specialists on the radio telephone and they tell me that they can't eliminate it without tearing the whole thing apart when we're in for our annual inspection. Even then there's no way of telling how deep the responses go . . ."

"Something like this happened at M.I.T during my undergraduate days. Some hot-shot reprogrammed the computer department's new experimental multiphasic computer to answer all questions in iambic pentameter. When they cleared that program, it started answering in four-line meter. They cleared that and found the computer would answer only in limericks, usually of the graphic nature. It seems that one of the graduate students who was programming the computer was dating an English major and wanted to impress her. It was too expensive to try to debug all of the contingent programs he had put in. Apparently, the grad student had had a little too much to drink that night and even he couldn't remember all the programs he had written.

"Nobody cared too much because the computer operated perfectly otherwise. The grad student was some kind of a genius. Snapped up by IBM the next year. Last I heard, the computer was into sonnets. So I wouldn't feel too bad, Val. It could be worse."

"Not much." Val grinned. "Well, maybe," he admitted. They laughed. The captain seemed to have a coughing spell. He cleared his throat.

"Why don't you show me what Valenkia can do?"

Paknis grinned and almost rubbed his hands together as he sat at the second screen and keyed it into life. He deftly "slaved" her console to his and set up the first of his programs. Computer language is universal and Cybil had no trouble following his flying fingers as the instructions were mirrored on her screen.

```
VALENKIA.  *  READY
DISPLAY; LINEAR MODE:   X AXIS TIME (DAYS)
                        Y AXIS PRESSURE (P.S.I.)


Tank #1 thru #5;
X = O: 8–14
RUN.
```

The mate sat back, crossed his arms, and waited for "Valenkia" to display the information. Almost instantaneously the five graphs appeared. Each was as comprehensible as a graph of stock market activity, yet the mate seemed to be proud of the accomplishment.

"You see," he explained to Cybil, "the computer constantly monitors all ship functions, and takes appropriate action to ensure stability. These graphs represent only one of the hundreds of different variables that she has to correlate before making a decision. It isn't as simple as in a laboratory," his voice took on a condescending note, "where the only consideration is maintaining the right temperature and turning the compressors off when it falls below a certain point. No, the computer analyzes future needs based upon present reserves in the storage tanks and estimated consumption. Not only does she extrapolate from consumption rates but she also uses the course and routing information filed at the beginning of each voyage to project for entire trip consumption. She automatically accounts for outside temperature, tides, and other meteorological conditions that might affect the condition of the cargo.

"She's also the disaster control center." His voice became serious, losing the fatherly warmth that had crept in. It was easy to see why the officers and crew of the *Prometheus* had nicknamed the computer Valenkia.

"In the event any of the gas detectors in any of the restricted areas of the ship, and that is virtually everywhere, detects gas in any concentration above two parts per million, the computer automatically takes over all electrical systems in those areas and shuts them down. All sparking equipment is automatically shut off and the leak would be traced by the computer to its source. Temperature detectors pick up any sudden drop in temperature, and emergency lights and sirens would warn the crew in the affected areas. Flashing yellow lights mean cryogenic contamination. Red means gas.

"More than one hundred hypothetical leak or contamination conditions are contained in the memory bank along with procedures for limiting the spread of the leak. Some of the best minds the shipping industry could find have worked on the safety of this ship's operation."

Cybil nodded, impressed by his sincerity. He not only knew his ship, he knew his computer and the potential of both. "Let's see how good Valenkia is." Her hand poised over the control that freed her CRT console from his, giving her independent programming power. She waited for his approval. No computer expert would think of keying into a strange system without getting approval.

He nodded. She hit the switch. Her screen flickered for an instant, then returned to the five graphs the mate had ordered. She punched in her commands, her fingers flying over the keys.

VALENKIA. * READY
DISPLAY: AS ABOVE. CORRELATE ON Y-AXIS RELATIVE VAPOR PRESSURES OF LIQUID WITH FOLLOWING COMPOSITION: 0.95 METHANE; 0.03 ETHANE; 0.01 PROPANE; 0.01 BUTANE.
RUN.

The lines blurred for a second and then reappeared, noticeably flatter than before.

"You see," she explained, "your basic program was written by a programmer, not a chemist. The programmer thought of LNG as liquid methane, not a mixture of methane, ethane, propane, and some butane.

"Algerian LNG has an unusually high ethane component. That's why your computer was slow to react to changes in pressure and overcompensated when it was re-refrigerating the liquid. The model didn't match reality. That's why you had so many variations in your chart."

Paknis was impressed. He never would have thought

of that. He had always assumed that the computer was operating on the actual composition of the cargo.

He keyed control of the computer back to his console and punched in another set of commands. The words, HOW ABOUT DINNER TONIGHT? appeared on the screen.

She looked at the words glowing in green on the screen, not able to understand for a second. She thought he was still working on their last program. Then she realized that he was asking her out for a date. She turned on her console. IN FRONT OF VALENKIA? WHAT WOULD SHE THINK?

The screen was suddenly wiped clean and Valenkia answered, seemingly of her own volition, DOES NOT COMPUTE.

They both laughed out loud, attracting everyone's attention.

"What's going on there?" The captain ambled over, his hands clamped behind his back. "Don't tell me Valenkia has started to tell jokes now?"

Still laughing, Cybil answered, "In her own way, I think she has. Quite a little girl you have there, Captain. One you can be proud of. I know a couple of universities that would kill to get their hands on her."

The captain looked grave. "Kill eh. Well, if that's the case, I know a few members on our board of directors I wouldn't mind trading for. Just turn in a list of those colleges before you leave, Miss Yale." A Greek sailor entered the bridge and delivered a radio message to the captain. He scanned the paper briefly and excused himself from the bridge, leaving Paknis in command.

The commander joined them at Valenkia's terminals. "The last of the reports are in. You want to check them over, Professor?"

"No, thank you, Commander. I'll review them later."

"I trust everything is secure," ventured Paknis, casually turning off the computer and wiping Valenkia's last message off both screens.

"As usual, everything is in perfect order." Wade checked his clipboard, reading the list of categories inspected. "No gas detected anywhere in the ship. No unexplained loss of cargo en route. No unusual temperature or condensation pockets. Safety systems and detectors operating within acceptable limits. Environmental protection devices in place and secondary safety released battened down. Everything . . ."

"Secondary safety releases battened down?" Cybil echoed, her voice showing her confusion. "Why would you do that?"

"E.P.A. regulations. It prevents the discharge of unburned gas into the atmosphere. While in American ports, the tanker must rely on the refrigerators to maintain pressure," Val explained. "It was put into the regulations to stop the early practice of maintaining pressure by letting the boil-off escape from the flue. Unnecessary really, since LNG's too expensive to just allow it to drift off."

"I see. But I thought that the safety valves were a necessary back-up and that if anything went wrong——"

Paknis cut her off. "No need to worry there. The refrigeration units in the *Prometheus* are more than enough to handle the load. The only time we ever used the secondary systems was during a mid-Atlantic storm. We're not going to be needing anywhere near that much capacity. The compressors will barely be operating all the time we're in the harbor. It's smooth water all the way. Isn't that right, Commander?"

"Right. Regulations prohibit any movement of LNG carriers under less than optimum conditions. It must be daylight, flood tide, and less than a ten percent chance of fog, rain, snow, or any other condition that would reduce visibility or constitute a danger in the harbor."

"Good. The tide's coming in. It'll be flood conditions until four thirty," Paknis explained to Cybil. "We planned it that way. To arrive just about an hour before flood tide, allowing enough time for the Coast Guard to complete their operations. We run on a very tight schedule. Now the only question is the weather. How do we stand in that department, Commander?"

Wade pulled out a yellow telex sheet and passed it to the first officer. "Good. Very good," Val said. "Looks as though your heat wave is going to last at least another twenty-four hours, maybe longer."

"I don't think you'd find a lot of New Yorkers who'd agree that that was good news. People are dying from the heat out there."

"I guess you're right. I've been hearing about it while

we were crossing over. The worst in history. First you get hit with the heaviest snowfalls in more than fifty years and then the hottest summer. Somebody must be doing something wrong in New York. I hear it's called Sin City these days."

"Maybe so," Cybil admitted, "but this isn't the Apocalypse, it's an air inversion. A high temperature mass of air pollution that has parked itself right over the center of Manhattan. I don't think it's God's punishment for anything other than, perhaps, allowing Detroit to produce too many cars." Cybil glanced through the forecast. "Besides I see here that the low pressure area in Bayonne is turning into a storm. When the inversion does drift out to sea, we'll be in for a nice cooling shower."

"I hope it doesn't happen while we're unloading," Paknis complained.

"Why's that?" Cybil asked.

"It's a thunderstorm. We can't unload in a thunderstorm."

"Professor, are you ready to go?" Wade asked.

On earlier runs, she had always stayed with the commander, trying to see the shipment from his vantage point. She looked at Paknis and impulsively made up her mind.

"Not this time, Commander. I think I'll stay on board the *Prometheus*. I've never been on a tanker while it was docking before."

"Ahh . . . well, in that case I'll see you at Rossville, Professor."

Wade signed his name across the front page of his inspection report and handed a copy to Paknis. "You're cleared to enter the harbor."

1:00 P.M. *Weather Forecast for New York City and Vicinity*

TEMPERATURE:	98° F.	36° C.
HUMIDITY:	80 percent	
WIND:	South 0–3 knots	
PRECIPITATION:	5 percent probability	

SPECIAL CONDITIONS: The air inversion that has been covering the Metropolitan area for the past fourteen days remains intact. Unless the low developing along the North Carolina coast or the storm, which has remained stationary in Rahway, New Jersey, begins to move, the stagnant air condition will continue in the Metropolitan area. Severe pollution advisory in effect. Special warnings for elderly, infants, and anyone with respiratory or heart conditions. Dangerous levels of sulfur dioxide, nitrous oxide, and carbon monoxide have been recorded in Manhattan, Brooklyn, Queens, Connecticut, and Long Island. Driving is to be avoided, wherever possible.

NATIONAL WEATHER SERVICE
NATIONAL CLIMATIC CENTER, ASHEVILLE, NORTH CAROLINA

1:45 P.M. *On Board the* PROMETHEUS

"What do you think about all this?" Cybil waved her hand in front of her, encompassing the empty harbor, the tugs, and the Coast Guard cutter that fanned out in front of them. "Is it really necessary? Or is it just a show? Or maybe," her voice dropped to a near whisper, "not enough?"

"Are you asking me as a Deputy Secretary? Or as a woman?" Paknis countered.

"Why? Would there be different answers?"

"Certainly. The Deputy Secretary would get the official answer. The woman would get my answer."

"As a woman, then. What do you think?"

"Well," Paknis rested on his elbows, looking out the forward window. He was very conscious of Cybil's perfume and the slight pressure of her arm against his as they leaned side by side. "I guess you could say I'm a fatalist. I believe things happen in their own time. On the other hand, I also believe in doing everything possible to avoid accidents. Most accidents are someone's fault. Negligence. Bad planning. Stupidity. Incompetence. Alone or in combination.

"But as far as these preparations go, I'd say they're about the best in the world. In London, LNG tankers sail right up the Thames every week without anyone so much as batting an eye. And nobody has died yet. Sure, there've been a couple of incidents, but the safety systems have always done their jobs, just the way they were supposed to, and nobody got hurt."

"How about coming into New York harbor? Is it safe? Even with all of these precautions?" She didn't look at him. She kept staring out of the window, watching the tugs nudge the *Prometheus* into the harbor. On the left, Sandy Hook slid quietly by. It looked like a child's playground, unspoiled except for a standpipe that marked the point. She could see the tiny figures of fishermen as they cast their lines into the Atlantic surf. She couldn't imagine that any fish could live in the polluted waters near the mouth of the Hudson, yet they must. Otherwise, why the fishermen?

"Safe? Who can say? As safe as man can make it, I guess. The Coast Guard has tried. But safe? When you've been at sea you learn that the ocean is never safe. There's always the unknown. Worse yet, there's the known." He paused, almost hesitant. The droning of the harbor pilot who now commanded the *Prometheus* filled the bridge. He was ordering the tugs to begin their turn into the Sandy Hook Channel. The mouth of the channel was more than a mile away, but it took that much time to turn the mammoth ship and head her on a new course. It was the ancient problem of inertia, first discovered with the motion of a falling apple. The *Prometheus* with her cargo was a ninety-five-thousand-ton apple. Once set in motion she tended to remain in motion.

"Fact." Paknis ticked the points off on his fingers. "New York is the most dangerous harbor in the world. Ask any professional seaman. Most dangerous stretch of water known to man. It makes the Bermuda Triangle look like Disneyland. Collisions. Floating debris. Junk in the water. Did you know that over five hundred collisions occur in the harbor every year?"

Cybil shook her head.

"It's true. More than five hundred. More than one a day. And that's only counting the ones between ships. There's no accurate count of the collisions with floating shit, excuse me, floating debris, because the ship owners never report most of them. Only increases the insurance costs and they're already sky high. Every year the insurance companies pay more for collision damage than they collect in premiums in this damn harbor."

He pointed to the hazy outline of the Manhattan skyline. The silvery twin towers of the World Trade Center were barely visible in the pollution that hung over New York City. "You see the piers off Brooklyn?"

"No," she answered honestly. She barely knew where Brooklyn was.

"Between Manhattan and Brooklyn. The old Navy Yard. The other abandoned piers. And they're only part of it. Look over there," he commanded, pointing to the west. "The Jersey and the Staten Island piers. All built before the Revolutionary War. Your Revolutionary War. That's two hundred years ago. The damn things are falling apart every day. Disintegrating. Floating off into the channels and getting caught in the props of half the ships that come into the harbor. Damned lucky that you don't have a ship sink in the middle of the Ambrose Channel after one of those things gets through its hull. Probably will some day. And then you'll clean up the damn harbor."

"But those things couldn't hurt the *Prometheus,* could they?" Cybil asked. "The hull is heavy steel. Certainly a piece of floating wood couldn't hurt a ship like this." She hesitated. "Could it?"

"What do you think those other ships were? Schooners? Hell, no. They had the same type of hull the *Prometheus* has. Six inches thick. Carbon steel, Grade B. And still got holes knocked in them. Remember, it's not the strength of the material that causes the damage, it's the force of the collision. When a piece of wood shoots off a spinning propeller, the wood is traveling at maybe one hundred miles an hour, maybe more, within a few feet of the hull. Add that to the mass of the ship and you get one hell of a bump."

"But the tugs aren't near the ship." She pointed. The lead tug was more than a hundred yards in front of the tanker. "That couldn't possibly affect us."

"Not that type of accident, that's true. There are hundreds of others. Limitless other ways a ship can be damaged. There's grounding . . ."

"Now wait a minute. Grounding? You're in the middle of New York harbor, not sailing into an unknown port of some uncharted island. This is one of the best natural harbors in the world. You can't really be serious that grounding is a problem."

"Do you have any idea how many ships grounded in

New York harbor last year?" He waited. She said nothing. "Guess. Just guess."

"Fifty. And that's probably too high."

"More than a thousand. And that's only the ones that called the Coast Guard. Most harbor pilots," he lowered his voice so the pilot who now commanded the *Prometheus* wouldn't hear, "wouldn't admit that they got laid up on a sandbar or strayed out of the channel. Matter of pride. And most ship captains won't tell either. They can make up the time on the rest of the run so they don't antagonize the pilot.

"Besides, it's an entirely different problem with the *Prometheus* and most of the other LNG tankers. They all are deep-draft vessels. Our draft is thirty-six feet. The depth of the Ambrose Channel, the main channel entering New York, is only thirty-five feet at low tide. Sandy Hook Channel is designated thirty-five feet deep. Just a few feet out of the channel and it drops off into the teens. Fifteen, sixteen, fourteen feet.

"We can only enter the harbor during the last half of flood-tide, and then only for about three hours. High tide gives us an extra four feet of water. The Sandy Hook Channel we're in right now is only thirty-nine feet deep in some places. Only three feet of water between the hull and the bottom of the channel. So there's not much room for error. We've got to stay dead center of the channel. We've got to turn just right or our ass will be hanging out on a line to dry. And when the tide goes out, we'll be sitting there like a fish out of water.

"The damn channel's so narrow we can't turn around if anything goes wrong. We have to be towed out backward, not the easiest of jobs under the best of circumstances. Even after we unload at Rossville, we have to be towed down the Arthur Kill stern first until we reach a point where we can be turned around by the tugs."

Cybil gazed out the windscreen, looking at the gray waters of the bay. The shallows and the depths that Paknis described were only numbers that were written on charts. It all looked the same on the surface. "You make it sound terribly dangerous."

"Oh, it isn't really that bad. It's routine. These are problems that sailors have been coping with for centuries.

With good charts and a skilled pilot, the risks are acceptable. The course is cleared of everything that we could reasonably anticipate and everybody knows exactly when we're going to make a turn and how to do it. It takes meticulous seamanship and, in the final analysis, it's results that count. There haven't been any accidents with any of the LNG tankers since they've been afloat. That's a record that stands for something."

He paused while the tugs completed their turn, dragging the reluctant tanker behind them. Then he added, "Maneuvering a ship the size of the *Prometheus* is like driving a car on an icy road. Each turn is a controlled skid. She drifts, driven by momentum, rather than turns around curves.

"How did you ever get involved in this kind of work?" Val continued. "I mean, it just doesn't make sense to send someone with your qualifications to do what must be the lowest kind of field work. I read your papers on low-temperature crystal formation. Everybody at Bethesda did. Compulsory reading. I know I didn't understand half of it. I don't think anybody did. Hell, it was brilliant work. Why would they send someone of your capabilities to play shepherd to tankers in New York harbor?"

"Someone has to do it," she explained slowly, hands clasped before her. "Someone has to question the safety regulations that control all of these things, from nuclear power to LNG. It's been scattered among half a dozen federal, state, and city agencies for too long. Nobody took on the entire ball of wax. Important decisions were and still are being made by default. That's not a good way to plan for the future. It's bound to catch up with you one of these days and when it does, I don't want to be one of the one's saying 'I told you so.'"

"But there isn't anything safer . . ."

"Safer? We don't have enough experience in cryogenics to know whether anything is safe or not. It's an infant industry. Every time one of these tankers gets built it becomes the new prototype. The new standard of excellence and safety. Until the next one is built. They are experiments, very expensive experiments, each one progressing beyond the one before, based on the findings of the other. I'm a scientist. Science learns more from its failures than its successes. Only by seeing something fail can we discover its true limits. All the experiments have succeeded, with a few notable exceptions. We learned a lot from the exceptions.

"You want to know why I took the job? The true reason?"

"Sure." Paknis was fascinated.

"One day one of these things is going to blow up." She said it as though challenging him to rebut her. He took the bait.

"Impossible. Absolutely impossible. Not with all the backup . . ."

"Ah," she pounced, "I thought you were the one who believed in fate. That anything was possible."

"Sure, hypothetically. But as a practical matter—" She cut him off with a curt wave of the hand.

"As a practical matter, it's an absolute certainty. Not a probability, a certainty. With the number of LNG tankers scheduled to double in the next five years and then double again, one of these days one of them is going to end up as a large candle in the middle of a harbor. And that candle will be enough to burn any city, and I mean any city, from Boston to New Orleans to London, to the ground."

Paknis mulled over her argument, looking for some flaw. He couldn't find one. Her logic mirrored his own thoughts too closely. There were just too many tankers being built. It was like the supertankers ten years ago. People were terrified that one would spill millions of gallons of oil, ruining beaches and killing scores of wildlife. The oil companies countered with their safety record. More tankers were built. Then probability caught up with them and they started to break up. He vividly remembered the *Cadiz* that poured crude oil along the coast of Europe. She finally had to be shelled to get rid of the environmental mess she had created.

"But that still doesn't explain you. You could have sent someone else. You're too valuable. After reading your work, I'd say you were unique. You don't send the captain when a seaman can do the job."

Sadness entered her smile. A silence engulfed them.

"Hard left rudder," the pilot's voice filled the void between them. The tugs in front of the *Prometheus* strained against the six-inch hawsers as the tanker began her skid into the channel.

"I had my reasons," Cybil answered finally.

The *Prometheus* slowly slid into the mouth of the Sandy Hook Channel.

Chapter 3

2:00 A.M.   *Two Days Before; Hastings on Hudson*

An empty police car was parked on the tree-lined street, its siren silent, its red light discreetly off. The town seal of Hastings on Hudson was emblazoned on the front doors.

In the foyer of 37 Sherwood Lane, two uniformed officers confronted the owner of the house, Mayor Thomas C. Richardson. To one side stood the mayor's youngest son, Robert R. Richardson, number one in his class at the Hunt School, an exclusive New Jersey prep school that specialized in turning out Princeton freshmen. He was home on summer vacation. He was wearing faded Levi's and a sweatshirt. His hands were handcuffed behind his back.

The boy next to him was similarly attired and also handcuffed. Stephen Knight was a junior at Hastings High School. His father was the local judge. Both boys reeked of beer.

"Take those silly things off them," the mayor ordered, pointing to the handcuffs. "They're not common criminals. They won't try to get away."

"You should've seen 'em down by the warehouse, your Honor. They fought like hell when we hit 'em with the spotlight. Almost got away, too," the patrolman explained. The mayor stood silently while the handcuffs were opened. The two teen-agers stared at the expensive wall-to-wall carpeting, discreetly rubbing their wrists.

"We didn't know they was your and the judge's son, your Honor, or we wouldn't 'a been so rough on 'em

31

when we was tryin' ta' catch 'em. But like I said, they fought awful hard. Me and Harry here followed them right into the river. Almost got carried away in the current, too."

"Don't worry, Frank. You did just fine. As long as no one was hurt," the mayor answered, while dialing the phone.

"No, we wasn't hurt. Like I said, we didn't know—" The mayor held up his hand, cutting off the police officer. Frank respectfully held his peace, nervously fingering his hat. He had almost shit in his pants when he found out whose kids he'd caught vandalizing the municipal warehouse. All the way over to Sherwood Lane, he had been practicing his speech. He was particularly worried about the blood that decorated the front of Robert's white sweatshirt, completely obliterating the "H." He had given the boy a bloody nose just after being thrown into the river by the strong youth.

"Bob, this is Tom. Sorry to wake you at this hour. I hope I didn't wake Martha. Good. Listen. It's about Bobby and Steve. No, they're all right. Physically, anyway. They're standing right here. Along with our local constabulary. I think you ought to get over here right away. Good." He hung up. The judge lived next door.

Five minutes later the judge appeared and Frank nervously recited the charges: "Breaking and entering. Trespassing on public property. Destruction of city property. Resisting arrest and assaulting a police officer." He looked at Harry whose right eye was already beginning to blacken. "Two counts."

The mayor and judge excused themselves and adjourned to the library where each treated himself to a Scotch. They emerged a few minutes later. The judge spoke for both of them. "I really think we can handle this informally, don't you, Frank? Since nobody was really injured," he glanced at the bloodstained sweatshirt, "seriously injured. I don't see that anything would be gained by letting a little high school prank ruin these two boys' lives. Don't you agree, Frank?"

"Whatever you say, Judge."

"The mayor and I will pay for any damages. What did you say they broke?"

"They didn't break anything, your Honor; they lost it. A coupl'a utility poles. The big ones we were goin' to use to put up the new lights in front'a the junior high. They knocked out the wedges and rolled 'em into the river. By the time Harry an' me got there a couple had already floated away. We tried to round 'em up but they were just too big. That's how we got all muddied up." He'd be damned if he'd tell the judge and the mayor that a half-drunk teen-ager had thrown him into the river.

The mayor wrote out two checks, handing one to each cop. "That ought to take care of the costs of cleaning those uniforms. Or, if necessary, to buy new ones. I think they're ruined. You know what the Hudson is like these days." He waved aside the officers' protests, reminding them that he was, after all, the mayor. "And tomorrow, I'll write out a check for the full amount of those missing poles. Good work, Frank. Harry. Good work." He patted them on the back as he escorted them out the door. "I won't forget it. Everything's paid up and there's no damage done."

Before they even reached the car they heard the yelling begin.

The officers exchanged glances. Frank spat, carefully aiming away from the lawn. "Money. Whoever said it solved anything." He folded the check and put it in his pocket. "You notice the old bastard never said anything about the resisting arrest charge."

"Yeah," Harry agreed, as he examined the check. It was more than two weeks' pay.

The police car left the neighborhood quietly.

Everything was paid up. No damage done.

2:00 P.M. *On Board the* PROMETHEUS

"What the hell!" Paknis exclaimed suddenly. "What the hell is that tug doing?" The mate pulled a pair of binoculars out of a cabinet and focused on the starboard lead tug. "He's way off course." He watched for a second. "And he's going farther off. Pilot!" He called the harbor pilot over. "Take a look at that tug, he's wandering all over the harbor." He pointed at the errant tug.

The two officers watched the tug drift slowly back on

course. In the narrow channel, even a little variation could spell disaster. Then the radio sprang into life.

"Sea Maverick to *Prometheus . . ."*

The pilot picked up the mike. "What's going on, *Maverick?* You're way off course."

"I know, but we've had some trouble." The tug's captain hesitated.

"Trouble? What kind of trouble?" The pilot's tone became wary. He never liked piloting these tankers. They were just too big for the harbor. One mistake and . . . he never completed the thought.

"We . . . we hit something." The captain's voice was tinged with fear.

"Hit something?" the pilot echoed. "Hit what, man? Come on," the pilot demanded. "Speak up. Are you damaged?"

"No. At least, I don't think there's any damage. We struck it bow on and the hull's pretty thick there . . ."

"Go on, man." The pilot was plainly getting angry. His nerves were on edge.

"Well," he hesitated for a second. The pilot's knuckles whitened on the mike as he restrained his growing impatience. "It didn't come up."

"What didn't come up?" Puzzlement wrinkled the pilot's brow. His knuckles remained white.

"A . . . a pole. The thing we hit. It never came up."

"That's impossible," the pilot sputtered. "You must have missed it. It probably sheered off when you hit it and you just missed it . . ."

"No, pilot," the voice insisted. "We didn't miss it. I tell you we hit it dead on. It was lying directly in our path. There was nothing we could do to avoid it. We drove it back and down. If it had come up it would have come up right underneath me. I'm telling you that that goddamn pole didn't come back up. It's still down there."

The pilot looked at the captain who shrugged his shoulders.

"Okay. Make a note of it in your log. We'll look into this when we dock. And, *Maverick,* no more deviations from course. I don't care if you run into a damn mine. Stay on course. This channel's too narrow for you to be going off on a sightseeing cruise."

The pilot replaced the microphone in its holder and

took out a handkerchief to wipe his perspiration-beaded brow. He mumbled something about "goddamn tugboats" and made his way back to the captain, where he stood calmly looking out at the harbor. He could see that the leading tugs, their towlines linking them to the *Prometheus* like thin umbilical cords, were even. The *Prometheus* was on course, executing a slight turn to port as they rounded the curve of Sandy Hook.

"Could it really be dangerous?" Cybil asked, trying to keep out of Val's way.

"Probably not." Val quit pacing. They would pass over the spot in a few seconds. A knot of tension was growing in his stomach. "Happens all the time in this harbor. Usually it doesn't amount to anything at all. Just part of the job." He smiled. Cybil noted a nervous twitch in one corner of the smile.

An unnatural stillness settled over the bridge as the *Prometheus* ploughed ahead.

The first sign was a slight tremor. Almost too faint to notice. It was like hitting a small pebble on a highway while riding in a car with good shock absorbers. There was no feeling of being lifted, only a subliminal awareness that the normal smooth ride had somehow been interrupted.

Then a terrible screeching tore through the ship. It was the sound of heavy steel rasping against metal. The sound was transmitted by the metal framework of the *Prometheus*, amplified by the tanks that acted as huge sounding boards. Every piece of metal on board vibrated.

The ship shuddered. Once, twice, and then, after a pause, a third time. An angry buzzing began deep inside the computer console.

The mate picked up the microphone and called for the disaster teams to go to their stations.

Cybil stood frozen, her hands gripping the edge of the control board panel. She watched as the men on deck scrambled away from the railing and ran for the nearest hatches. They cleared the deck. Paknis's voice boomed out over the intercom, giving orders directing the men to different positions. In seconds, more men appeared on deck, wearing bright orange life jackets.

Someone turned the buzzer off and the sudden silence startled Cybil. She turned to look for Paknis and spotted

35

him hunched over the computer. His fingers flew over the keyboard repeatedly. The captain moved behind his first mate and watched as the computer spelled out the fate of his ship.

Cybil joined the captain. She put her hand against his tensed arm. He looked down, smiled, and patted her hand reassuringly.

The green screen glowed with artificial intelligence. Words magically appeared at the command of Val's flying fingers. One punch of the button and the words disappeared. Valenkia was "thinking."

The screen burst into life once again. Five boxes appeared, graphs, Cybil recognized, identical to those they had used before. Then it had been a game, now it was for real. She peered over Val's shoulder, straining to read the caption. "PRESSURE: ALL TANKS TIME TWO MINUTES." That meant that the screen was showing what was actually happening in the tanks right now and using the prior two minutes to establish a baseline.

It was the most sensitive indicator they had on the condition of the tanks. Where every volume of LNG represented six hundred volumes of vapor, the smallest change in tank conditions would result in sizable pressure changes.

Val punched in more information. A vertical line appeared on five graphs. The time of the collision, Cybil surmised correctly.

At first all five graphs appeared normal. The line remained steady. Then Val increased the sensitivity. The graphs seemed to leap out of the screen for a second before settling back to their respective places. The lines remained level.

Then, one of the graphs came to life. There was a small flick upward, then it dropped down again. It was so small that Cybil first thought it was a mechanical failure; then it was repeated. This time it kept on climbing.

The small print below the chart read: "TANK NUMBER TWO."

Another flurry of the keys. The computer noted that the refrigerator had switched on. The line continued to climb.

A blinking horizontal line appeared at the top of the graph. The rupture point of the tank.

The click of keys. Emergency valves opened and

drained off some of the pressure, channeling it into the other tanks where their refrigerators labored to convert it back into a liquid.

The graph on tank number two hesitated and then continued to climb.

Val tapped another command into the computer. A valve in the engine room opened and excess boil-off was drained into the ship's tanks.

The line continued its upward climb.

"Val?" the captain asked. His voice was steady.

Val leaned back, his eyes never leaving the console. "We'll know in a minute, Captain." His hands rested on the keyboard, poised for any command that would be necessary.

In the heart of the *Prometheus,* the computer-controlled machinery labored to absorb the massive swelling that was taking place in tank number two. All five CO_2 refrigerator units were functioning at full capacity.

The tank itself began to expand like a balloon, straining to contain the tons of pressure that were struggling to escape. Aluminum is one of the most flexible metals, even at cryogenic temperatures. Steel, even the hardest steel, would have shattered. But the aluminum held.

The line hesitated. It neared the blinking line that hung over the top of the graph like a ceiling and hesitated. Less than a few pounds per square inch separated the tank pressure from the rupture point.

The line flattened. A plateau on a mountain.

An inch below the ceiling.

"It's holding," Val said simply. "Not by much, but it's holding."

"What happened?" Cybil asked.

Val swiveled the chair so he could look at Cybil and the screen at the same time.

Val took a deep breath before he answered. "I'd say that we've been holed. Whatever that tug struck, we hit it too. Only I'm afraid that it broke through the hull. Judging from the signs," he nodded to the computer screen, "I'd say that the point of impact was somewhere near tank number two."

"Any sign of gas?" Cybil asked.

Val punched a series of queries into Valenkia. The answers appeared. He studied them for a second before answering.

"No. Any release of methane would have set off the automatic alarms, and klaxons would have been sounded all over the ship. As a safety precaution, Valenkia has cut all power to the hold. No sense in having sparks that close to the tanks, under the best of circumstances."

"Will we be able to make it to Staten Island to offload?" the captain asked.

Val nervously chewed his lower lip. "I'm not sure. The refrigerators are holding. The bilge pumps have been started automatically. The pressure seems to be steady. From up here it looks good. I'd say that we'd be able to take her in without too much trouble. I'd like to take a look at the tanks before we go in, though. Just to see for myself." He shrugged. "You never can be too careful."

Val stood up, wiping his hands on the pants of his immaculate white uniform. They left dark smudges in their wake. He motioned to another officer to replace him at the console.

"Captain?"

"Yes, of course. Be careful." Paknis turned and started to leave.

"I'm going, too." Cybil walked after him. He stopped and whirled.

"What do you mean, you're going? You're not going anywhere. You have no idea how dangerous it'll be down there."

"If that tank does go, it won't matter where I am. So I'm going with you. You need me to clear this ship into or, for that matter, out of the harbor. I'm the only one on board who can speak for the Department of Energy. Or have you forgotten that you're in a U.S. port?"

"Listen, Miss Yale," Paknis lowered his voice and put his hands on her shoulders. "I don't have time to argue. This is no place for a woman. There's a repair crew waiting for me. I have to go." He glared at her.

"Then I suggest we stop arguing and get to work. You can't move this ship an inch without me."

Paknis looked at the captain in silent appeal. "I'm afraid Mr. Paknis is right, miss. That hold is no place for a woman." She started to protest but he held up his hand, cutting her off. "Even a Deputy Secretary."

Cybil put her hands on her hips, her eyes flaming. "Captain, I'm telling you that you have no choice. You may be captain of this ship, but as long as you're in American waters carrying LNG, your ship is subject to our regulations. In time of emergency, control of the ship must be turned over to the ranking member of the department. This collision qualifies as an emergency. And I am the ranking member of the department.

"I could technically take over control of this ship, but it'd be better if I don't. All I want to do is inspect those damn tanks, and if I have to get the Coast Guard to board and order you to do it at gunpoint, well then, by God, I'm ready to do just that. I'm going into that hold to check the condition of that tank. Do I make myself clear, Captain?" She stared up at him, meeting his eyes directly.

The captain sighed. "All right, Miss Yale. Go ahead. But stay out of the men's way."

"I will." She turned and rushed past Paknis before he could protest. "Let's go. We've wasted enough time already."

The captain watched them disappear. He shook his head. "Damned stubborn woman."

2:05 P.M.   *On Board the* APPLE TREE

"Emergency. *Apple Tree* to base. I have a Code Two emergency. Put me through to the captain. Repeat. I have a Code Two emergency."

"Coast Guard Central to *Apple Tree*. Message received. Stand by."

The speaker was filled with static as the commander nervously juggled the mike in his hand. "Come on," he whispered. "What's taking so long?" He would have paced the length of the bridge but the cord kept pulling him up short. The deck of the cutter pitched as she cut sharply to circle the tanker. They were on the port side when the collision occurred and they had to come almost entirely around the ship in order to near the point of collision.

"Captain Bassil here, go ahead, Wade." The speaker crackled as the captain of the port came on.

"We have a reported collision, involving the *Prome-*

theus. I'm awaiting a damage report from her. They've sent a crew below to check the damage . . ."

"Any sign of fire?"

"No, sir. We're coming to the point of collision and there isn't anything visible . . ."

"Is there any sign of a gas leak?"

"No, sir. And the detectors on board the tanker don't report any sign of leak."

"Thank God for that." The captain's sigh of relief was audible. "Any injuries?"

"Not that I've heard, sir. The tanker's dead in the water. Whatever she ran into stopped her."

"She isn't aground, is she?"

"No, sir. We're in the Sandy Hook Channel, about two hundred yards off Sandy Hook and just off Flynn's Knoll. We should have a good four to five feet of clearance. No, whatever she hit, it wasn't a sandbar. One of the tugs reported striking a submerged object immediately before the collision. It was probably the same thing that the tanker hit."

"What the hell could stop a tanker like that? All right, Commander. Seems to be pretty routine, but keep a close watch on it. With these LNG tankers. . . . Say, isn't that Deputy Secretary from Energy with you?"

"Professor Yale, yes, sir. She's on the *Prometheus*. She decided to stay on board to watch the landing operation from there."

"Damn, this would have to happen when she was along. Well, stay close to it, Wade. And keep me informed of the situation. As soon as she's checked out, get her into dock right away. We don't want any unnecessary trouble stirred up about this . . . you understand what I mean?"

"Yes, sir." Wade did understand. If the newspapers got hold of this they would blow it all out of proportion. It was just one of those common harbor accidents that happen every day. But the sensationalistic newsmen would turn it into a scare story about a "near disaster." They were fortunate that the Coast Guard frequencies weren't monitored the same way the police channels were, otherwise the camera crews would be on their way out to the tanker already.

Wade paced the deck, free to roam across the entire expanse now that the restraining cord to the mike was gone. Damn bad luck that Yale had to be here when it happened. She would probably be terrified, he thought with some satisfaction, worrying whether the ship was going to sink or blow up. She wouldn't be taking it like a trained seaman.

Chapter 4

2:15 P.M. *On Board the* PROMETHEUS

Cybil was faster than Paknis in donning her cryogenic suit. Two other suited figures waited for them to finish. Impersonal hands checked her suit and seals professionally and quickly.

Externally the suit resembled a NASA space suit. In fact, it had been designed by the same company that produced the space suits for the astronauts, but to even more rigorous specifications. The insulation was doubled and then doubled again, particularly on the soles of the boots and in the gloves. The air connections were of the more simple clamp type rather than the screw types used by the astronauts.

The two men introduced themselves while Paknis struggled with his suit. The older one was the crew chief, Stephen Dunn. He carried a knapsacklike contraption over his shoulder. It looked heavy, but he carried it effortlessly.

The other one, Miguel Lopez, was little more than a boy, short but massive. He too carried a sack, strapped above his air cylinders.

Dunn handed her a black box shaped like a pack of cigarettes. "Have you ever used one of these?"

"No, never." She turned it over in her hands. It looked like a small SONY portable radio that might grace any beach blanket. "How does it work?"

He pointed to a switch on one side. "Here. Just press that and you'll be able to talk to the bridge. Hold it up in front of you faceplate and speak in normal tones. It'll pick up your voice. Let go of the switch and you'll be

41

able to hear. Works by induction. Normal radios don't work inside the ship, so they built induction lines into the detector circuits. As long as you're inside the hold she'll pick it up."

She hooked it onto her belt. "Good. Anything else?"

The chief shook his head. "No. Me and the boy here, we got all the equipment we need. You're just along for the ride."

"Let's go." Paknis opened the door of the hatch. Lopez entered first, shining his hand-held light before him. Then Paknis followed. Dunn bowed and waved a hand in an exaggerated flourish. "After you, ma'am."

He stepped through and closed the hatch behind him, spinning the wheel to seal them away from the rest of the ship. "Any idea where in number two?" Dunn asked as they made their way into the hold.

"No way of telling, Chief. I would guess on the starboard side, because that's where the tug was, but beyond that nothing."

They traveled in silence. The darkness was lit only by their tiny auxiliary lights. Inside the suit, Cybil couldn't feel the slightest hint of cold. Her air regulator brought her pre-warmed air. Her suit insulation, layer upon layer of specially created synthetics, kept the heat in. Any temperature loss would be made up by the tiny heating coils that lined the inner skin of the suit. It was a comfortable seventy-eight degrees, humidity forty percent. Perfect weather conditions for nudists, astronauts, or cryogenic engineers.

The silence was broken by the thundering of the refrigerator pipes, and the bilge pumps fighting to siphon the seawater out of the tanker. Below those constant noises, there was another sound. She struggled to identify it. Then it hit her. Running water. The sound grew louder as they advanced.

The lights appeared to be getting brighter. At first, Cybil merely thought her eyes had adjusted to the dimness of the hold, but then it began to cast strange reflections on her visor. She called out to Paknis to stop.

"The light. You notice it?" She held up her hand and it seemed to be lit from all sides. "It's different."

The men aped her actions, revolving their hands in front of their helmets. Dunn supplied the answer.

"Ice. Ice crystals in the air. Means water's nearby. Otherwise the ice wouldn't travel so far." His voice sounded grim. "Unless there's a lot of it."

"Let's go." Paknis took the lead. They carefully edged their way toward the sound.

As it got louder, the ice became thicker. Cybil wiped her faceplate, but it didn't dispel the fog. The ice was too cold to melt and stick against the insulated plastic. The tiny particles merely bumped and rebounded like hail against a car's windshield. Only in utter silence.

Colors sprang to life in the glow of their hand-lights. Water condensed and froze against every surface. Each drop of ice became a prism, breaking the light into rainbows of reds, blues, yellows, and indigos. Each prism refracted the light and scattered it in all directions. As they passed through different temperature zones, certain colors predominated. There was a breathtaking blue zone that made everything appear frozen. Then they moved into a red area that looked as though it were on fire. The air itself took on colors from the reflection of ice particles.

But they barely noticed the effects. After identifying the cause, it became part of the background; an annoyance that interfered with their main job of locating the leak. One corner of Cybil's mind silently recorded every phenomenon for future study, but those were only her scientific reflexes. Her attention was focused on following Paknis to the leak.

They reached the stairs leading to the lower level. Paknis halted at the top of the ladder and flashed his light around. A myriad of colors followed the once-yellow beam. He pulled the radio off his belt and held it close to his faceplate.

"Inspection team to bridge. Inspection team to bridge. We have reached the landing to the lower level. We are descending now." He clipped it back into place and stepped off the landing.

Underneath his insulated feet, hard nodules of ice crunched against the unyielding floor. That was good. As long as the temperature remained low, the ice would remain hard. Only when the temperature neared the freezing point would it become slippery. The tanks would never stand the pressure if the temperature got that high. He looked at the thermometer strapped to his wrist like a wristwatch. Minus two hundred and forty. High, but the refrigerators could handle it. As long as the water didn't touch the tanks directly.

The descent took a small eternity. He had to sweep his foot across to knock the drifts of ice off the steps. The rest crowded behind him, careful not to push into each other. A fall could mean death. Not from the height, but from a puncture in a suit. The cold would be fatal. Their hands grasped the railing firmly as they descended.

They reached the lower deck and gathered around the foot of the stairs, shining their lights on the walls and the floor. No sign of the leak. Visibility was bad. They were in a red area and Cybil automatically checked her thermometer. Red meant warmer. Blue meant colder. The information was quietly filed away.

"Well," Val said, his voice muffled by his suit. "There doesn't seem to be any sign of the damage on this level. That's a good sign." He pointed forward. "Chief, you and Miguel go that way. We'll go this. The first one who . . ."

"It's that way." Cybil pointed with her light.

"What?" Val was puzzled by the interruption.

"That way." Cybil repeated her motion. The air before her hung in a red haze. "The leak is somewhere over there. You can tell by the color. Where it's warm, it's red. Blue is cold. Over there it's red. Q.E.D. the leak is somewhere over there."

Val flashed his light in the indicated direction. A red wall arose where his light illuminated the darkness. When he flashed it behind them, a blue one took its place. "I'll be damned," he whispered. "Okay, Chief, you heard the lady. Forward it is."

The foursome trudged into the reddening gloom. They stopped before a plate that almost glowed amber.

The chief unslung his pack, dropping it to the deck. Miguel did likewise. A small flurry of red-tinted ice crystals scattered before the descending objects.

"Well, mate, I think we've found it," he rasped. "The breech should be right below us. If what the lady says is right, that is. Not that I'm doubting your word, understand. Just that I like to see for myself."

Miguel dropped to his knees and swept the deck clear of ice pellets with a carelessness that frightened Cybil. He uncovered what looked like a handle set deeply into the metal of the deck. With one inhumanly strong heave, he yanked the inspection plate loose from the deck and dropped it off to one side with a metallic "clang" partially muffled by the ice that cushioned its fall.

Without a word, Dunn dropped to his stomach and slid across the deck until his head and shoulders disappeared into the dark abyss he had uncovered.

"Yeah," the chief said, his voice muffled by the cavernous expanse his head now occupied. "I see it. Miguel, pass me the other light. The big one." The light and the hand disappeared again. A red rainbow surrounded him.

"It's coming through the starboard hull. Looks like it's about eight inches in diameter and . . ." He shifted his position, leaning farther over the edge. Miguel grabbed his legs. "Yes, the hole is a long gash, at least ten feet long." More of his body disappeared into the hole. Paknis joined Miguel, each holding one leg. "Okay. Pull me up."

Very carefully they pulled him back. All knew that any tear in the heavy cryogenic suit could be fatal. Val reached over and lifted, pulling the crew chief by the harness that circled his chest. He reappeared, sitting down heavily, panting from the exertion.

"Thanks . . ." He gasped between breaths. "It's bad. Real bad. Can't tell how big the hole is, 'cause it goes under the waterline and it's blocked by whatever it was we hit. But the water's rising, so it's gotta be pretty large."

"The pumps?" Paknis asked. "Can they handle it?"

"I don't know." Dunn shook his head. "The pumps should be able to handle almost any leak that didn't rip through the entire section of the hull. But, as I said, mate, the water's still risin'. I don't know what's wrong, but the pumps aren't holdin'."

"Could something be blocking the pump intakes?" Cybil asked, leaning over Paknis's shoulder.

"No, ma'am, I don't see how. They're designed to cope with just this sorta thing."

"How about ice?" she asked, pressing forward.

"Ice?" Dunn and Paknis echoed each other.

"Yes, ice." She pointed to the tank. "Don't you think that the tank absorbs enough heat to make a few cubic feet of ice? Where the hell did you think all that heat came from when the pressure began to skyrocket? From the water. And when you cool water, you get ice. Don't you have heaters on your intake valves?"

From the look of surprise on their faces Cybil could see that they didn't. "No wonder you have water backing up. It's freezing at the intake. Soon it'll be a solid cake of ice and then you'll have no pumps at all."

"But," Paknis objected, "we've never had problems with the bilge pumps before. And they're on the same level as these. I don't see how you would have gotten ice now, all of a sudden."

"It's simple, really," she explained. "Normally, the water never comes into direct contact with any cryogenic surface or even the cryogenic atmosphere. The only cooling that the bilge pumps would have to deal with is indirect cooling from the insulation on the deck. Given time, that would be enough to freeze the bilge solid, if it weren't for the convection currents that keep exchanging the cold water for warmer. The hull is warm because it's against the ocean, which has a temperature of about forty to sixty degrees. Any cooling by the tanks is offset by the heating from the ocean. Convection currents, which try to maintain a uniform temperature throughout any volume of water, make sure that the warm hull water is thoroughly mixed with the colder ballast water. So it never freezes.

"But when water is being sprayed into a cryogenic atmosphere, you have direct cooling. Heat is drawn off faster than the water can crystallize and you get what is known as super-cooling, cooling of a liquid below its freezing temperature. It will tend to stay a liquid until something touches it to begin the crystallization process. In this case, I'd say that the intake pipes in your bilge pumps acted as the 'seed-crystal' and started the ice formation just as the water was being drawn into the pipes.

"We're lucky the pipes haven't burst from the expansion of the ice. Probably would have except that the pressure is knocking out the ice formations before they get too large and block it entirely."

Paknis was silent for a second. "Chief, what happens if the bilge fills?"

"You mean before we sink?" He shrugged. "I'd guess that the water would begin to back up against the splash shield. It would be trapped between the hull and the shield."

"Would the shield hold?"

"Hold? Mate, that shield wouldn't last a second against a coupl'a tons 'a water. No, she wouldn't hold."

"Then what would happen?"

"If the shields went, the water would run into the drip pan, right below the tank. Water would rise until it reached the bottom 'a the tank. Then the whole thing would go. Tank, ship an' all."

"Would the refrigerators be able to compensate?" Cybil asked.

"No, ma'am," the chief answered quickly. "They're only CO_2-based refrigerators. Designed for small temperature fluctuations of one, maybe two degrees. It'd be like buildin' a bonfire under her. She'd never take it, ma'am. Never."

"Well then," Cybil answered, "we've got to find some way of stopping the water before it gets there, don't we?"

Paknis and Dunn stared at one another for a few seconds, the importance of the last sentence dawning on both of them.

"Any suggestions?" Val asked. His question was sincere.

"No. I'm a scientist, not a naval architect," Cybil responded. "Why don't you put Valenkia on it? She might come up with something."

"Good idea," Val agreed, as he pulled his communicator off his belt.

Cybil's attention wandered. She played her light over the sides of the tank. The air turned a healthy blue wherever her light touched. Any major defects would already mean an LNG leak, and by the silence of the ship, she knew that hadn't happened. Minor stresses would probably be too small to see without special equipment: infrared detectors, ultrasonics, and other scanning devices. But, as a scientist, she also depended on her most basic piece of detection equipment: her sight. Coupled with a trained mind, that could tell her a lot about the ship's condition.

She circled the tank, looking up and down, following the edge of the spray shield. The old gray glitter was gone. Probably masked under the layer of reflective ice crystals, she concluded. The blue lights were hypnotizing and she found herself staring up at the expanse of the tank.

Something was wrong, but she wasn't sure what it was. She tried to analyze what she saw. The scientific rules took over. Step one: observation; Step two: identification; Step three: classification; Step four: hypothesis; Step five: test and observe. Then start over.

She was seeing something important, but she couldn't put her finger on it. She was stuck at the second step. The blue haze. Her eyes were fixed on the blue haze that seemed to cling to the side of the tank. It might have been her imagination, but she thought she saw a pattern. No, not a pattern, but several patterns. Lines, like the lines left on a sandy beach after the tide has gone out. Regular patterns of parallel lines.

Not parallel, she realized as she moved along the shield, playing her light over the tank that rose eight stories over her head. But clustered. They seemed to radiate from somewhere over her head. Somewhere along the equator of the tank. She remembered, almost unwillingly, the significance of that. Pressure would be greatest along the equator in a rapid increase of pressure.

The lines were stress marks. They meant that the aluminum had flexed and, just like human tissue, separated.

The tank was deeply weakened. Any new stress, no matter how small, might be enough to crack the tank.

She hurried back to tell Paknis.

Val was still on the communicator with the captain. "Yes, sir. Someone should stay here and watch for any spillover into the pan."

She pulled on his arm.

"Wait a minute, Captain. Miss Yale has something to report." He lowered the communicator.

She took it and, holding it as the chief had shown her, she shouted into it, "Captain, Captain, can you hear me?"

"Yes, Miss Yale."

"You can't go any farther into the harbor, Captain. The tank has severe stress lines, indicating a change in the structural strength of the walls. Under no circumstances should the *Prometheus* go deeper into the harbor."

There was a moment of silence after she finished. It lengthened. "Captain?"

"Yes, Miss Yale. I'm still here. It's just that I'm afraid we have no choice."

"But you can't." She was shocked. "You can't without my okay, and I'm telling you that you can't move this ship an inch. Not into or out of the harbor. Not until we have a chance to examine the tanks. Not an inch, Captain. That's an order."

The captain's voice sounded sincerely sorry when he replied. "I'm afraid, Miss Yale, that not even the Department of Energy has yet become that powerful. The tide is coming in."

The *Prometheus* shuddered and the sound of rending metal once more echoed throughout the ship. The tank sang its resonant song of pain.

2:25 P.M. *In Hold Number Two of the* PROMETHEUS

Deputy Secretary Yale found herself in the first mate's arms. She didn't remember reaching out for him, but she could recollect the reassurance those arms offered when they encircled her while the ship shuddered. The sound and the need for the arms diminished equally. She extricated herself from Paknis, still aware of his strength and closeness.

"The tide," he explained. "Pushing us against whatever we hit. Chief, check it."

Dunn obediently dropped back to his stomach and looked over the edge of the inspection hatch. A second later he called back. "Worse. The water is rising faster than before." He pulled himself up. "Felt like we were being driven farther up on whatever we hit. I'd guess the hole is larger."

The mate put the communicator to his faceplate. "Captain! Can you hold her steady? I think we're drifting farther upstream. The water's pouring in heavier than before."

"I'm not sure," the captain replied. "We're doing the best we can, but between the tide and the currents it's impossible to hold the ship entirely steady."

Paknis looked at Cybil. "I know, but we have to have some time; anything you can do will give us a few extra seconds to think."

"We'll do our best," the captain promised.

"Thanks." The mate turned to Dunn. "Chief, what do you think? Should we try to back off or go on?"

Dunn looked off into space, visualizing the alternatives. Finally he spoke, weighing his words carefully. "If we back off, we'll run the risk 'a pullin' the thing outta the hole. It's actin' like a plug now an' that would be like pulling the cork from a bottle. Sure as sunrise, more water would come pourin' in. But at least the hole wouldn't be getting any larger. We might just be able to get somethin' else to replace it . . . but . . ." He shook his head. "More than likely not. On the other hand, goin' forward, we stand the chance of tearin' the guts outta her." He patted a nearby bulkhead affectionately. "If that happens, then there'll be no chance a' savin' her. You can't go forward and you can't go back. Death either way. Maybe."

The ship shuddered and groaned again, as though to emphasize his next words.

"And you can't stand still. I'd say go back, mate. You can't hurt her any more that way, at least. If only there was some way of draining this hold," he added wistfully.

"Any way to do that?" Cybil asked.

"Maybe you could string some hoses from here to tank number one. The entry hatch is just a little ways along an' if you could rig an auxiliary pump in between———"

"Impossible," Val interrupted. "The only auxiliary we have that could do the job is gasoline-powered. I don't know that you could even get it to run at these temperatures and if you could it would be too dangerous anyway. If one of those tanks leaked even the slightest trace of gas you could get a critical mixture in no time. No, absolutely not. It's too dangerous."

"Well then," the crew chief continued, "I guess that you gotta pull back an' pray for the best. I don't see no alternative."

"But maybe the thing we hit"—Cybil pointed into the hold that was rapidly filling with water—"maybe it'll break off when the ship goes forward?"

"Maybe," the chief admitted. "But if it don't then you got all your tugs in the wrong places to get you outta the harbor. It'd take time to relocate." He shook his head again. "No. Too risky. You gotta choose one or the other. Forward or aft. I say aft."

Paknis, whose thoughts echoed the chief's, concurred. "Aft. Too much risk the other way."

"But isn't there something else?" Cybil pleaded. "That almost guarantees that the ship is lost." Her voice sounded desperate, more desperate than the men who ran and loved the *Prometheus*.

"That's the way it is sometimes," the chief consoled her. "Sometimes there's no way to help a ship in trouble. It's up to the Lady herself. She's the one who decides whether she lives or not. I've seen many a ship come outta worse places than this. The *Prometheus*, she'll do her best."

Paknis informed the captain of their conclusion and advised that the ship try to back off the obstruction. The captain agreed and gave them five minutes to prepare. It would take that long for the tugs to get into position. Paknis ordered the crew chief to use anything he could find that might slow the rise of water in the hold. He rummaged in his pack and came up with something that resembled a blanket, a small can of foam spray. and what appeared to be a torch.

"Not that," Paknis objected, pointing to the last object. "But that's the only . . ."

"I don't care. I said it was too dangerous." He picked up the cylinder attached to the torch. "Acetylene. You know better than that." His voice was almost accusatory. "One mistake and . . ." He threw the bottle back into the bag.

"You won't stand a chance unless . . ."

"I said no! No fires. If there's even the slightest chance of a leak it would be suicide. Worse. Murder."

Dunn shrugged, the gesture almost lost in the cryogenic suit. "Okay."

"How about the foam?" Paknis asked. "Could that help?"

"No." The reply was fast and certain.

"Foam?" Cybil asked.

"A high-density polymer," Paknis replied. "Forms an insulated barrier on contact with just about any surface. It's used to control small leaks."

"Right," the crew chief continued. "Small leaks. Not

that mother." He pointed to the gaping hole. "Too big. The foam would never stretch across the width of the hole. I'm telling you, mate, the only way we've got a chance to control it is to try to weld a temporary plate across the hole. Or find some other way of draining the water off before it reaches that tank." He shook his head. "If only we could fix the pumps."

Val turned to Cybil. "You're the expert. What do you think? Any chance we might be able to break up the ice?"

"Well," she pondered. "Assuming that you could get someone to the intake point with something that could break up the ice, you might, just might, be able to do something. It would be temporary, and whatever good you do wouldn't last long. It might not be worth it. At cryogenic temperatures ice is as hard as steel. I doubt you could break it without powered drills, which you can't use in here anyway."

"Chief?"

Dunn smiled. "Mate, Miguel is one of the strongest men alive. I've seen him bend deck steel in his bare hands."

"Chief, this is serious," Cybil scolded. "It would be dangerous. Very dangerous. He could be killed."

"So could we all, ma'am, just standin' here. No, ma'am. I think he's got as good a chance as the rest of us. Miguel!" He called the young sailor over. "Miguel, you think you might be able to break up a little ice that's cloggin' the bilge intakes?"

The broad-shouldered youth nodded. *"Sí."*

"If anybody can do it, Miguel can," Dunn said, patting the boy on one shoulder.

Miguel unloaded his pack and carefully laid out its contents next to the access hatch. Cybil recognized only a rope, a wool blanket, another can of the foam, and a tool kit. He laid the wool blanket across the edge of the hatch, padding the sharp edges. In seconds it became rock hard as the water spraying from below saturated the material and froze in the cryogenic temperatures.

He attached one end of a new hemp rope to one of the supports of the spray shield and gave it a hefty tug to check it. The rope held. He coiled it near the hatch. With skill far beyond his apparent years, he quickly fastened a series of knots, leaving a loop in the line large enough for a booted foot. He withdrew a wooden mallet from the tool kit. Natural materials seemed to fair best at cryogenic temperatures without losing their normal properties. Synthetics disintegrated easily at such temperatures. He hefted it. It looked heavy but he handled it as though it weighed nothing. He looked up. All was ready.

"Chief." Miguel circled his waist with the end of the rope.

Dunn approached the young seaman and peered into his helmet. "You know what to do?"

"*Sí*," Lopez replied, firmly tying the rope in front of him. The knot wouldn't pull loose. It fit snugly under his armpits.

"When we begin to move, I want you outta that hole. No excuses."

"*Sí*."

" 'An I want you to keep the line on all the time."

"*Sí*."

Dunn rechecked the knot, tugging it hard against the boy's chest. It held. He seemed satisfied. "An' watch out for any sharp edges. One cut an' your suit's for shit, got that? Be careful."

"*Sí*."

He sat on the edge of the hatch, dangling his feet over the dark cavern. With a casual gesture, he waved and pushed off. It was less than a three-foot fall to the surface of the water bubbling below but it seemed like an eternity before the splash resounded in the frozen cavern. Dunn held the rope as the three crowded around the hatch waiting for the youth to bob to the surface. They shone their lights on the frothing surface. Nothing but the glimmer of the foam.

"His suit's like a diving suit," explained Dunn. "Ya can't drown till the air gives out. Not for another hour at least." His voice sounded reassuring in the cold darkness. But still the boy's head did not appear.

"Like a deep-sea diver. Doesn't need no oxygen, but what he carries on his back. He'll be all right, don't you worry none, miss. No need to worry," he repeated, as his light flashed across the water. "He'll be all right."

The silver head broke water. The chief's light found him first, the other two centered in shortly thereafter. He held up his hand, thumb and forefinger forming the traditional sign that he was all right. The water was chest deep.

"Took your time, boy," Dunn called. "What you doin'? Looking for shells? Get to work." The head looked up. Cybil could see the flash of a smile before the head disappeared beneath the waves.

Then nothing. Not even bubbles to mark his disappearance. Only the thin line of rope that broke the surface. Enough to show that there was life. It moved toward the hull.

Below the surface, Miguel fought against the current. The weight belt he had strapped around his waist was enough to give him negative buoyancy, but not enough to keep him from being buffeted by the current rushing through the hold. His light was strong and it cast a harsh yellow glow against the hull. It was a stark contrast to the red air that covered them above. He allowed the current to guide him.

In moments his fingers found the hull. They stubbed the hard, brittle metal. Pain pierced through his hand. He pulled back. With an odd sense of detachment he watched the bubbles in front of his mask turn red. Blood. His. The glove was torn between the thumb and forefinger, exposing the meat of the palm. Wisps of red colored the water. The throbbing that crept down his wrist replaced the pain. He ignored it.

He reached the hole. He was surprised to see it wasn't that large. But it was near the turn in the hull, almost at its maximum depth. That's what made it so dangerous. The water pressure increased exponentially as you descended below the surface. Thirty-five feet of water pressed against the hole, forcing water into the ship. Not large, but large enough to kill the *Prometheus*.

2:30 P.M. *On the Bridge of the* PROMETHEUS

"Tugs are in place, Captain." The pilot looked nervously out the stern windows of the tanker's bridge. Ever since the accident, the pilot had effectively relinquished his command of the *Prometheus,* deferring to the captain.

"Thank you, helmsman."

"Yes, sir." His voice shook with the tension of youth. He almost saluted, so great was his excitement.

"Notify the repair party that we are prepared to withdraw." He looked at his chronometer. "Tell them we will commence in two minutes. No more."

"Yes, sir." This time the boy did salute, an almost unheard-of act on a civilian vessel. The captain didn't notice. His eyes were focused in mid-air, giving him a look of supreme indifference.

The captain's mind, however, was far from indifferent. It was racing, faster than it had in years. He was trained for crisis. He was thinking of all the possible actions and reactions that he might make in the next few crucial minutes. The ship was a living entity, an extension of himself. He could almost feel the pain of the barb sticking in her side.

"How's the board, Mr. Belkin?" He didn't raise his voice above a normal conversational level even though the computerman was sitting at Valenkia's console on the far side of the bridge.

"All clear, sir. Temperature and pressure steady in all tanks. Refrigeration holding on tank number two. Bilge pumps running at full suction in hold number two. No gas and no temperature variations unaccounted for." The computerman's voice took on the tonal qualities of his instrument as he mechanically recited his report.

"Good. Automatic safety systems on and interlocked?"

Belkin tapped the keyboard for a few seconds. "Automatic systems locked in, sir."

The automatic safety systems put the computer in control of the electrical system and the engines of the tanker. If any of the more than one thousand gas detectors stationed throughout the ship detected the presence of methane, the computer would shut down all possible ignition points in the contaminated area. Human reflexes were too slow.

"*Prometheus* to *Apple Tree*." The captain used the bridge-to-bridge radio; normally the first mate's job.

"*Apple Tree* here. Go ahead, *Prometheus*."

"The tugs are in position. We will commence the operation in one minute."

"Understood, *Prometheus*. One minute." Wade hesitated before continuing. "How is your passenger?"

The captain had to think for a second before realizing the commander was referring to Cybil. "She's fine. She's inspecting the tanks with Mr. Paknis."

"What?"

"She insisted. As the ranking member of the Energy Department, she was quite insistent. Forty-five seconds until we commence." The captain cut off the radio phone. Turning to the pilot, he said, "I believe we should have the tugs begin as slowly as possible. That should give us maximum maneuverability should anything go . . ." He hesitated. Superstition demanded he not voice the worst. "Should we need it. Don't you agree?"

The pilot nodded.

The captain gave the necessary orders to the skippers of the four tugs now clustered off the stern. On his signal they pulled away from the *Prometheus,* their lines snapping out of the water, vibrating with tension as they pulled taut.

Slowly the mammoth tanker began to move.

2:30 P.M. *In Hold Number Two of the* PROMETHEUS

"Pull him back," Val ordered. "They're ready to tow. I don't want him in that hold when we start to move. There's no telling what might happen."

Dunn tugged on the rope that linked them to the young crewman. He shouted into the hold. "Miguel. Come back. Miguel." He applied more pressure on the line. It didn't give. "He's not coming, mate. Should I nip down an' . . ."

"No. Chief. One man is enough. Here, let me give you a hand." He grabbed the line behind Dunn and pulled. A second later, Cybil joined them, adding her weight to the task.

They stopped pulling. "Nothing, mate. Feels like he's caught on somethin'. You sure I shouldn't . . ."

"I'm sure, Chief. Keep trying and see if we can free the rope. Miguel will have noticed it's been caught and he'll be trying to get back on his own." They returned to the rope, alternating slack and pressure, hoping that it would somehow loosen.

Miguel had indeed become aware that the line was caught. Although the water wasn't more than neck deep, the current made it impossible for him to keep his footing and he had been forced to relinquish control over his direction to the forces of the current. Now it seemed stronger than before.

Suddenly his light caught something. At first, he didn't recognize the white lump as the drain. Then, as he slid closer, he saw it was ice. Ice surrounding the drain like the mouth of a volcano. As he drew nearer he entered the lee of the frozen wall and found himself suddenly free of the current.

The water was noticeably colder here. Cryogenic suits were not designed to withstand the effects of liquids. A liquid could absorb heat much faster than a gas, so the insulation strained under the unaccustomed heat loss. Miguel could feel the temperature difference. He glanced at his wrist thermometer. Twenty degrees Fahrenheit.

Within seconds, the ice mountain began to change, growing as new layers of ice formed on its sides. He pulled the mallet and aluminum chisel out of the sack he carried about his neck. They looked pitifully small against the side of the white slope, he began to pound into its base.

The swinging of the hammer became mechanical, automatically pacing the throbbing of the drain's pumps as they labored. He kept a firm grip on the chisel, shifting it along the edge of the ice as pieces of white rock broke free to drift to the surface. His mallet never stopped or hesitated as he brought his strength to bear against the ice.

Although as strong as steel, ice remains a crystal regardless of temperature, and Miguel was able to shatter it by striking at the vulnerable seams. After a few mis-strokes, he soon found the best places to strike. Inch by inch he moved deeper into the mountain of ice, until the first few squares of grill appeared underneath his chisel.

He stopped, not realizing what the pattern was. It was quickly recovered with a layer of white ice. After one feverish stroke, it reappeared. He could feel the drag against his hand as he held it suspended over the grill. It was working! He could clear the grill, if only he could free the entire surface.

With renewed energy, he pounded away at the white growth, revealing more and more of the regular squares. They were quickly recovered with another layer of ice, but one sharp blow would peel the layer off in large chunks. He concentrated on expanding the area he had liberated.

So great was his concentration that he didn't notice his safety line had become incorporated in one edge of the growing wall of white, just out of arm's reach. He didn't notice the frantic tugging that was his signal to return.

He noticed nothing but the flying chunks of ice that drifted away to the surface and the grill that appeared with every stroke of the mallet.

He noticed nothing until the ship began to move.

"Get back," Val ordered. "Away from the hatch. Get against the splash shield."

"But Miguel . . ." Cybil protested.

"There's nothing we can do for him now. He may be in better shape than we are if anything goes wrong. Chief," he shouted to Dunn, who lingered at the edge of the hatch. "Chief, get away from there. Come on. Move, man! There's no telling what might happen when she starts to move."

"But, mate, I just can't leave Miguel down there . . ."

He grabbed the seaman by the arm and pulled him around until their faceplates almost touched. "Chief, that's an order. Come over to the splash shield. No matter what happens we're going to need you before this is over." His voice softened. "You're the best in the business, Chief. The *Prometheus* needs you alive."

Dunn nodded unhappily, and went to join Cybil, who was already crouching against the overhang of the splash shield.

"Brace yourself," Val ordered. "Get a good hold on one of the struts, but be careful you don't get your suit caught in the bracing. It'll tear open against that sharp metal. Chief, get on Cybil's other side. I'll stay on this one. Keep her sandwiched in between us. That'll reduce the chances of getting hurt if there's any tossing around when the tugs start."

Cybil started to protest that she didn't want to be treated specially but he cut her off. "Listen, someone has to be in the middle, so it might as well be you. Besides, as you've pointed out a few times so far, you're an important person in deciding what's going to happen to this ship, so, like it or not, I've got to protect you."

He looked at his watch. "Brace yourselves. The tugs will be starting in five seconds. Four . . . three . . two . . . one . . ."

Nothing happened. Paknis's "one" hung in the frozen air waiting for something to fill the gap. Cybil realized she was holding her breath and exhaled noisily, after about fifteen seconds of silence. She almost let go when the first tremor shook the ship, throwing her against the crew chief. He pushed back, stabilizing her. The next tremor pushed her toward Paknis.

The sound of rending metal filled the hold. The three suited figures crouched against the splash shield. The sound was repeated, this time accompanied by another jolt that shook the deck. Then, silence.

"Chief, check the hold. See if there's any sign of Miguel. Cybil, check the tank. If you see anything, give a shout." Paknis plucked the communicator off his belt. "Captain, Paknis here. What's happening?"

Cybil didn't hear the answer as she rounded the edge of the splash shield. Everything looked the same. The red tint was fading more to blue, due to the nearness of the tank. It was quiet, almost silent compared to the space outside the shield. The sound of the pumps, ever present, was muted by the distance and the insulation.

She flashed her light against the side of the tank. It looked the same. There were the telltale stress marks, shining out against the side of the tank. They hadn't grown, she noted with relief.

The ship groaned again. The light showed the tank holding steady. Cybil was thankful they were well built. It looked secure at least. She returned to the other side of the shield to share her good news. Even before she reached Val's side, she knew his news wasn't good.

"Chief," he called, waving Cybil's remark aside before she could even begin.

Dunn was lying on his belly, his head lost over the side of the hatch. They caught the faint yellow streaks from his light as he flashed it toward the edge of the hull. His voice drifted out of the dark hole.

"Miguel, Miguel, where the hell are you?"

Silence, except for the ever-present beating of the distant pumps.

"Miguel," Dunn called again. The result was the same. He pulled back, resting on his heels. "Nothing, mate. No sign of him. Should I . . ."

"No, Chief. Maybe later when we know more. Are the pumps holding?"

Dunn looked into the hold. "Damned if I know, mate. Too many waves. Have to wait till things have quieted down before we can tell."

"How about the hole?" Cybil asked. "You should be able to see whether it's still blocked or maybe grown even larger."

"Good idea." He dropped back to his stomach. The yellow light flashed out once more. "Damn." The answer came floating back to them as they watched him half disappear into the hold.

"What is it, Chief?" Paknis asked.

"It's gone, mate." He pulled himself erect once again. "Clean as a whistle. Gone. Hole as big as your chest. Water is pourin' in like there's no tomorrow."

"The pumps, Chief. Are they holding?"

"No, mate."

"You sure?"

"Positive. Water's racing like a tide in the shallows. Pumps aren't holdin'."

"What do we do now?" Cybil asked.

Paknis remained silent, his mind, like the captain's, considering the possible alternatives. "How about the drip pan pumps? If they were put in series with the bilge pumps, would they hold?"

Dunn shrugged. "Who knows? I don't think so, mate, but maybe."

"But they're the last line of defense," the chief protested. "If the tank goes, even just a little bit, there won't be nothing left a' the ship if you take them away. No, mate, I'd say leave them alone."

"The drip pan pumps?" muttered Cybil. "The ones in the bottom of the drip pan? I thought they were for LNG. They lead back to the CO_2 refrigerators. They operate at below two seventy-five. You'd have more ice problems than ever before. Besides I thought that the lines led right back to each tank. Even if you could somehow keep the lines clear, you'd just be dumping the water back into the very tanks we're trying to keep it away from. Who's idea is that?"

"It's Valenkia's," Val explained. "Running the program you suggested, she came up with a plan for disconnecting the pan lines on the other side of the pump room, before they enter the refrigerators. The lines could then be dumped into any other part of the bilge or even dumped directly overboard. The only question is how quickly it could be done. And, as the chief said, it's the last defense against small leaks in the tank. If we divert the pumps to water, there's no way of using them for LNG if the tank begins to go."

"There's another question you haven't counted on, and it's not Valenkia's fault for not answering it. How do you plan to keep the water from freezing around the intakes in the pan? They'll be no more than ten feet away from the surface of the tank. It's impossible that it wouldn't freeze. The pumps wouldn't be of any use because they would be dealing with a solid, not a liquid. No, the drip pan pumps wouldn't be of any real use."

"Miguel!" cried the chief. "It's Miguel!" He rushed over to the hatch where the silver-suited figure clung to the side of the deck, obviously exhausted.

The chief reached out for the young crewman. He didn't respond. Together Paknis and Dunn pulled him on to the deck.

"His hands," Cybil cried, and rushed to the boy's side. The gloves were in tatters, revealing the lacerated flesh that had been exposed to the cryogenic atmosphere of the hold. Already the red blood had stopped flowing and turned into a whitish brown solid, covering his hands. He held them out in front of his body as though they belonged to someone else.

Dunn was no longer looking at the young crewman; he was staring at the uncovered hatch.

"Look," he pointed. Only a few feet below the deck the brown water of the harbor bubbled. "I don't think it matters much whether the pan's pumps can take the cold or not. They'll never be able to handle that much water."

It was true, Cybil realized. The level was rising much too fast to be controlled by the relatively small drip pan pumps. There was nothing they could do to keep the water from reaching the tank.

The *Prometheus* was doomed, she realized, as she cradled the injured seaman's hands in hers. Nothing could stop the rising water.

It was only a matter of time.

Chapter 5

"Coast Guard Central, patch me through to the captain." Commander Wade nervously fingered the mike. It was becoming slippery with sweat despite the air conditioner that throbbed in the corner of the bridge.

"Wade," rasped the voice of the captain. "Is everything under control? What's happening with that Energy woman? Have you calmed her down?"

"Well, Captain, it's not that simple. It seems there's a complication."

"Complication? Complication! What sort of complication? I thought you said that this was a routine . . ."

"No, sir," Wade insisted. "I never said it was routine. That's why I declared a Code Two."

"Don't quibble, Wade. Tell me, what's happening?"

"The captain of the *Prometheus* relayed a message from Secretary Yale. Things are apparently more complicated below than I first thought."

"Complicated? Don't mince words, Commander. What do you mean?"

"Well, this is all second hand, Captain, and I'm only relaying the tanker crew's reports of what Secretary Yale said."

"Yes, so what has she said, Wade? Tell me."

"She's denied permission for the *Prometheus* to proceed farther into the harbor."

"She what?" The captain exploded.

Wade took a deep breath. "She wants the tugs to tow the tanker out of the harbor. They've already realigned the tugs to tow the *Prometheus* out, but . . ."

"Well, Commander . . ."

"But, I'm not too sure how safe the withdrawal can be. The tanker is wedged between Flynn's Knoll and. . . ."

"I'm familiar with the present position of the tanker, Commander. And I believe that I'm sufficiently familiar with the Sandy Hook Channel to know when something is safe and something is dangerous. And I don't think you'd be calling me to remind me of any of those elementary things. So there must be something you aren't telling me. What is it, Commander?"

"Captain, I think the tanker is in imminent danger of breaking up."

Silence. The empty hum of an open line.

"What did you say, Commander?"

"Sir, I believe that the *Prometheus* is in imminent danger of breaking up. At least that's what the captain of the tanker says. He reports that the water level is rising and will soon reach the tank. Once that happens . . ." His voice trailed off.

"Commander, do you believe him? Have you heard from the Energy Secretary? What does she say about this? She's supposed to be some kind of an expert, isn't she?"

"Yes, sir. She's one of the world's experts in cryogenics, but I'm not certain she knows too much about ships. I haven't heard from her. She's still with the inspection party below decks and she's out of reach. I'm afraid that we have no option, sir; we have to believe the captain. It's his ship, sir, and if he says there's a chance she'll break up I don't see that we can afford to ignore it."

"No, I suppose you're right, Commander." The captain hesitated. The sound of drumming fingers could be heard clearly. "Well, as the on-the-scene officer, you're in charge. It's up to you to get that tanker out of the harbor and out to sea as fast as possible. How long do you think it'll take before you round Sandy Hook?"

"About half an hour. The tugs are in place and it's only a matter of building up speed and staying in the channel. The tide's against us, but that can't be helped. I've stationed the *Apple Tree* to the stern of the tanker. I think it would be a good idea if you ordered the ships out of the approaches to the harbor, just in case . . ."

"Right. I'll issue the orders right away."

"Captain?"

"Yes, Commander."

"Do you think we should go to a Code One status?"

The captain hesitated before answering. "No. Not yet. Code One is only for a major maritime disaster. As yet, there hasn't been any fire or explosion. Other shipping isn't in immediate danger, since the bay has been cleared. It's a bad situation, but so far we only have the captain's word on it. No, I think it would be premature to issue a Code One. That would only bring in the civilian authorities and, with them, the press. It might only complicate matters without serving any useful purpose. I'll call the fire commissioner myself to let him know unofficially what's up. I'm sure that will take care of it. All right, Commander, keep me informed of developments and, when you hear from the woman again, tell her I'd like to talk to her."

"Yes, sir."

Wade watched the massive tanker creep through the channel. Even with four heavy tugs, the going was slow. From his position astern of the tanker he could see how fast she was actually going.

Her wake was barely a ripple.

The commander drummed his fingers on the console, unconsciously catching the captain's rhythm. He wished that somehow he could get out and give the tanker a push.

2:35 P.M. *In Hold Number Two of the* PROMETHEUS

"Get me something for his hands," Cybil ordered, holding the youth's hands by the wrists. By the pasty white color she knew they were already frostbitten. She had seen cryogenic accidents before and knew that the boy would probably lose his hands unless they could get him to a doctor soon. If not, he would probably lose the entire arm as well. Gangrene was fast to set in when the frozen tissue began to thaw.

"Hurry." She looked at Val. "Don't you have a first aid kit?"

He looked at the unmoving hands. "Nothing that can do any good for that. We'll have to wait until we get out of here." He glanced at the boy's eyes. They were becoming glazed. Shock. They'd have to carry him out.

Cybil saw the shock setting in. "We have to cover them with something. We can't let them be exposed to the cold any longer. We can't afford to wait, he'll . . ." She checked the boy's face. He wouldn't understand her, so quickly was he losing consciousness. "He'll lose the arms if we don't do something. Is there anything in the pack that might . . ." She spotted the cans of foam.

"Chief, give me one of those cans, will you?"

Dunn brought two cans over. "You think he'll be all right, miss?"

She broke the seals and began spraying the foam over the white hands. "All right? No, not unless you call losing both hands being all right. But he'll live, maybe, if he gets good medical attention and soon. Cryogenic frostbite isn't anything to play with." The whipped-cream-like foam quickly hardened into thick white mittens. She sprayed above the hands, sealing the insulation to the suit. She inspected her work. One last spray and she was done.

"There, that's the best we can do here. Keep his hands away from his body," she said. "I don't know how strong that foam is and it might break off if he brushes against his suit."

"Come on," Val said, impatiently waiting for Cybil to finish. "Chief, take his other arm." He lifted one arm and carefully draped it over his shoulder, gripping it firmly just above the foam. Together they pulled the boy to his feet.

He groaned and tried to struggle free.

"It's shock," Cybil explained, examining the boy's face through the helmet. The face was slack, eyes closed. His breathing was heavy; she could see his lips move as he muttered in his coma. She knew that his temperature was dropping as the body's defenses became overloaded, but there wasn't anything she could do about it until they got him out of that suit. She hoped that there weren't any other leaks that she hadn't found. There wasn't time to give him a full inspection.

"We've got to hurry. He won't last much longer if we don't get him to a doctor."

"Neither will we if we don't get out of here before that tank goes." Paknis nodded at the water that suddenly appeared at the edge of the hatch.

Half carrying, half dragging the unconscious boy, they raced for the stairs. Cybil followed, pushing to help the two men lift Miguel up the stairs. She was light but strong and her help was necessary. Dunn's foot left the deck only seconds before water rolled around the base of the stairs. Miguel mumbled and tried to break free. They held onto him without much trouble; Cybil spoke soothingly to the boy and he quieted.

As the water reached the deck, it froze. Pushed by the increasing water pressure from below, the ice floated free and cascaded on the deck. The deck became ice-coated wherever the water touched. More water poured in, running now on the layer of ice rather than along the deck. The water moved farther and farther away from the open hatch in succeeding waves of growth. It finally reached the splash shields.

The splash shields were effective in preventing LNG from spraying directly on the exposed hull in the event of a failure of the aluminum wall of the tank. They were designed after months of careful computer simulations pinpointed the kind of force that could be expected. However, the computer had been programmed for pressure against the front of the shields. Now the pressure was coming from behind.

Ice covered the entire deck with a layer of white almost as strong as the steel it concealed. Above that ice, a river of water formed, seeking the lowest spot in the hold. The splash shields prevented the river from reaching its destination, the drip pan. Water began to back up behind the shields, fighting to pass.

The shields, made of a thin layer of steel and aluminum-covered balsa wood and styrofoam, at first withstood the pressure. But the water froze, it turned solid and expanded, pushing against the outer hull and the thin shield. Between these two forces, the shield crumbled, crashing into the drip pan.

The dammed-up water followed behind, freezing as it went. In waves, water came pouring through the hull, turning immediately to ice, only to be quickly covered by another layer of water.

"Hurry!" Cybil shouted as the rending sound of metal signaled the end of the splash shield. She pushed against the limp body, trying to make them go faster. The narrowness of the stairwell made it almost impossible to pass through carrying the boy between them.

"Give him to me, mate," the chief shouted. "We can go faster if I carry him alone. We can't make good time draggin' the lad between us." He reached up and pulled Miguel's arm from Val's neck.

"Sure you can carry him alone, Chief?"

"Sure we don't have no other choice, mate. You and the lady go ahead. I'll take care of the boy." He leaned forward as the mate draped the unconscious figure over his shoulder.

"No, Chief. I'll stay with you and the boy. We'll get out of this together. But you're right. Cybil, you should go on ahead." Dunn straightened, staggering a little under Miguel's weight. He wavered for a second, fighting for his balance, then, with one hand firmly on the railing and the other balancing the boy's weight, he took his first step forward.

"I got him, mate." He panted. "I got him. You go on."

Paknis tried to balance the boy but saw that he was only making Dunn's job more difficult.

"Okay, Chief, you got him. But hurry. The shield's gone and we don't have much time."

The chief didn't answer, saving his strength for the task of climbing.

The din of the pumps receded and the crackling sound of ice forming and contracting grew louder, echoing through the cavernous hold. The air, once blue with cold, now turned an angry red as millions of calories of heat were released by the freezing of the water. The tank absorbed the heat; all eight million gallons increased first one degree and then another. Pressure rose inside the tank.

The refrigerators were operating at full capacity as the computer switched first one, then another of the compressors into the circuit to try to control the pressure. All five CO_2 units were sucking in "warm" methane, cooling it back to two hundred sixty degrees below zero and returning it to the stricken tank. The computer again diverted some to the other four tanks in hopes of reducing the pressure to manageable levels.

But the water level grew, adding layer after layer of ice, until it finally touched the aluminum skin of the massive tank.

The chief labored under the dead weight of the unconscious crewman. Never for a moment did he consider leaving the boy behind. Dunn could feel the boy fighting for breath against his shoulder so he knew Miguel was still alive. While there was life, the bond of shipmates ran strong.

Cybil and Paknis had reached the next level, the equator of the tank. They reached out for him, offering him a hand. He ignored them, not out of pride, out of necessity. He couldn't remove his hand from the railing without losing his balance. Another step. He was nearly there.

The pressure in the already overstressed tank finally tore through one of the weakened seams, near the equator of the tank. Propelled by the combined pressures of weight and vapor, the cryogenic liquid spurted out in a heavy stream, vaporizing into a white cloud in a few feet.

The break occurred just below the two men. Even their suits could not withstand contact with a cryogenic liquid, and Dunn felt the wave of cold flash over them. It was enough of a shock to stop him, even before he heard the sharp crack of the bank giving way. He stood for an instant wavering, off balance.

The noise and the cold woke Miguel. His delirious dreams had been nightmares of frost. The cold, whipping across his prone body, made those horrors real. He fought to get free. Striking out, he pushed away from Dunn's body just as he fought to get his balance. They began to fall.

The split in the side of the tank grew as the pressure in the tank continued to grow. One wisp of frozen gas reached out and covered the two struggling crewmen, hiding them behind a curtain of frosty white. When the cloud drifted away, the men were gone.

Cybil stared, horrified. They were only a few feet away. If they had just reached out . . .

"Come on." Val put his arm around her shoulder, pulling her away from the edge of the stairwell. "There's nothing we can do for them now."

"But . . . we can't just leave them." She fought to get free of the restraining arm. "They're still alive. They might only be down a step or two. He was so close. So close."

"There's nothing we can do," Val repeated. "Nothing. The tank's beginning to go, we've got to get out of here. Come on." Again a gentle pressure.

"But—"

A shriek cut her off. At first, she thought it was one of

the two missing men, but then she realized that it was the sound of the tank. The sound of LNG spraying at incredible pressures into the air. It brought her back to her senses, now that she identified it scientifically.

"You're right," she agreed. "Let's go."

Grabbing her hand, partially fearful that she would turn away and run back to the stairs, Val led her to the exit that he knew was somewhere ahead. He began slowly, but they were soon jogging as fast as they could, hampered by their suits. Long after the need to hold hands had passed they continued to grab onto one another. Neither wanted to let go. Together they ran for the exit.

2:40 P.M. *On the Bridge of the* PROMETHEUS

"Captain!" the computerman shouted.

"Yes, Mr. Belkin." The captain's voice was deliberately calm and reassuring.

"Pressure rising in number two. The refrigerators won't hold. Pressure will enter red levels in about ten seconds."

"Divert additional refrigeration to tank number two, Mr. Belkin."

"Already done, Captain, and the pressure's still rising." The computerman's voice sounded desperate.

"Steady, Mr. Belkin," the captain whispered leaning down next to the man, staring at the green C.R.T. screen displaying the critical data on tank number two. "Any positive gas readings?"

"Nothing, Captain."

"Can we siphon off any of the gas into the engine room tank?"

"A little, sir."

"Every little bit helps, Mr. Belkin. Transfer as much as you can. Also instruct Valenkia to transfer some LNG into tanks one and three. That might help a little as well."

"Yes, sir." The computerman began punching in the instructions. He opened the valve for the engine room tank. That would take boil-off, and also immediately reduce pressure. He had just pushed RUN when the siren began screaming.

"Gas leak, sir," shouted Belkin as the computer's report flashed onto the screen. "In number two hold. Pressure increasing beyond the critical point. Hold temperature dropping. Ten, twenty, thirty degrees. Structural failure of the tank."

"Thank you, Mr. Belkin. Radio operator." The captain waved the junior officer to his side. "Notify the Coast Guard that we have a gas leak. Tank number two is undergoing structural failure. Recommend immediate . . ."

The captain's voice was drowned out by the deep reverberation of an explosion echoing in the heart of the *Prometheus*.

"I don't know, sir." Belkin stammered. "There was no preliminary . . ." Another message flashed onto the computer screen. "Here it is, Captain. Explosion in engine room. Pressure surge in gas storage tank. Release of one hundred thousand cubic meters of methane, estimated. Automatic program shut off all electrical and other ignition points in affected area. Temperature gauges indicate cryogenic temperatures in engine and generator rooms. All power is shut off. Emergency battery power switched on automatically for lights. Emergency generator started."

"Thank you, Mr. Belkin. See if you can shut off that damn siren." He turned back to the radio officer. "Amend that message to the Coast Guard to read: '*Prometheus* without power, both internal electrical and engine. Am ordering nonessential crew to abandon ship. Recommend you stand by to pick up survivors.' "

The siren died, wailing a final note that seemed to hover in the air for several minutes.

"Mr. Belkin, signal the crew to abandon ship. Have the computer shut down all electrical and other possible ignition points. The crew might as well have as much chance to get clear as we can provide. As soon as the computer is shut off, join me in the navigation room to collect the log."

The screaming of the Abandon Ship alarm wailed through the tanker. Men ran across the deck and began to lower aluminum boats from their davits into the warm waters of the bay. A recorded message continuously repeated the message "Abandon Ship" in three languages. The voice sounded inhumanly calm.

2:42 P.M.   *In the Hold; Tank Number Two*

The tank erupted like an overripe fruit, split apart by the forces growing within. The air, once an angry red,

turned icy blue and then white as the temperature of the
hold dropped one hundred degrees in as many seconds.
As LNG poured out of the tank, only some vaporized
immediately; the rest splattered against the hull and
slid toward the drip tank below.

Then came the first contact between water and LNG.
It was almost explosive. The LNG vaporized instantly.
Only the most sophisticated scientific cameras and equip-
ment could have caught the contact of the two liquids.
Both the LNG and the water disappeared.

The water became tiny ice crystals, only a few molecules
in diameter. The LNG became vapor. The vapor cap-
tured the crystals and the two became a suspension, far
finer than any mist that ever came out of an aerosol can.
The ice was suspended, drifting freely, apparently without
weight, almost indefinitely. The water and the LNG were
now one.

The tank cracked, a radical split that ran the entire
length of one side. LNG poured out, falling into the depths
of the drip tank, meeting and merging with the ice and
water below.

Pressure in the hold began to build. The water in the
hold was pushed back as the pressure of the gas fighting
to get out became greater than the pressure of the water
that fought to get in. Only the ice remained in the drip
pan and that was being eaten by the cascading LNG.

The hold was never designed to take that kind of
strain. Steel buckled. Explosively the steel dome covering the aluminum tank gave way, peeling back. White gas
billowed out of the opening, thrown hundreds of feet into
the air before gravity dragged it back to the deck of the
Prometheus.

Below decks, the water once more rushed into the
hold, now free of pressure to join with the LNG.

A giant white mushroom blossomed above the deck
of the *Prometheus.*

2:42 P.M. *On the Bridge of the* APPLE TREE

"Lieutenant, send the five-minute location and status
report," Commander Wade ordered. Since his last call
to the captain, he wanted to remain as calm and as quiet
as possible. Under a Code Two Emergency, he was re-

quired to report in every five minutes. That way, he smiled grimly to himself, they'll know if we've been killed within at most a few minutes. And, with the regular entries on the report, it'll look as though they were doing all they could. They knew that was the rationalization. He had written the regulation.

Actually, there didn't seem to be anything to worry about. The tugs were all in place, going as fast as they could in the Sandy Hook Channel, starting as they had from a dead stop. It would take a good half hour before they made it out of the harbor. He hoped they would make it. He was already planning to take the crew off the tanker and set her on a course out to sea. He could visualize it now, the hero's welcome as he steamed back into port, the survivors jamming the decks, the television cameras rolling, recording his moment of victory just as the *Prometheus* burst into flame far out at sea, forming a perfect backdrop for his greatest moment. A hero. And, shortly thereafter, a captain. Even the professor would admire him for his bravery.

"Commander?"

Wade shook himself out of his reverie. "Yes, Lieutenant." He hoped the captain didn't want to talk to him again. He didn't want the Old Man horning in on his glory.

"Something seems to be happening on the *Prometheus,* sir. They're lowering lifeboats." The lieutenant pointed.

Sure enough, the lifeboats were swinging out on their davits in preparation for lowering. "Lieutenant, see if you can raise the *Prometheus.* I want to speak to the captain."

"Yes, sir." The lieutenant turned to the radio and adjusted the frequency to the channel designated for communications with the tanker.

Impatient, Wade went to the door of the wheelhouse. Sensing he would hear what he feared most, he opened the door. There it was. The wailing of klaxons. Trouble. He had heard them before, just an hour ago when the safety systems of the tanker were tested. It meant that gas had escaped from one of the tanks. Probably number two. It was breaking up, just as the captain had predicted.

"No answer, sir," the lieutenant reported.

"Well, keep trying, Lieutenant. They have to have someone on radio watch at all times," the commander snapped. The lieutenant returned to the radio. "It's regulations," the commander muttered under his breath. "Regulations."

"Still no answer." The commander ignored him.

A new sound drifted across the intervening water that separated them from the tanker. A voice. He struggled to understand the words, distorted as they were by distance and by multiple repetitions from the dozens of loudspeakers on the tanker. It sounded foreign, a language he didn't understand. Then the echoes of English drifted across the water. It sent chills down his spine.

"All hands abandon ship."

"My God," the lieutenant breathed. It was a prayer.

The radio crackled into life. *"Prometheus* to *Apple Tree, Prometheus* to *Apple Tree."*

The commander grabbed the radio mike from the startled lieutenant. *"Prometheus,* what the hell's going on over there?"

The voice continued uninterrupted: *"Prometheus* is without power, without steerage. All electrical systems shut down by computer after a rupture of the auxiliary gas tank in the engine room."

"Without power?" muttered the commander.

"Have positive indication of gas in engine room and in hold number two. Entire breakup of ship imminent. Have ordered crew to abandon ship. Please stand by to pick up surviv——"

Just then the radio was drowned out by a loud boom that reverberated from the *Prometheus.* All eyes turned to the tanker.

Slowly, with the majesty that comes with size, a plume of white rose above the deck of the *Prometheus.* It climbed slowly into the heavens. Two hundred, three hundred, four hundred feet. It seemed to hang there for a moment, weightless against the sky, almost as though it had found some invisible hook to hold it there forever.

Then the illusion broke as the cloud descended, tumbling down in a white column, heading back to its source. It drifted lazily toward the now open tank, missing as the wind and the motion of the ship pulled it off target. Pieces of steel, the remnants of the protective dome covering hold number two, rained down on the *Apple Tree,* splashing in the water around her like shells from an unseen enemy. That was the commander's signal for action.

Instantly galvanized, he spat orders to one man after the other. "Lieutenant, issue a Code One signal to headquarters. Send the message '*Prometheus* explosion at,'" he checked his watch, "'fourteen forty-two hours. Am standing by to pick up survivors.' Helmsman, hard left. Stay clear of that cloud. If it's what I think it is . . . Just steer well clear of it. Stay upwind. Keep a watch out for survivors in the water."

In the background he heard the lieutenant begin to transmit his message. He ignored it just as he did the helmsman's change of course. "Spector!" he shouted into the intercom.

The crew chief's voice responded immediately. "Yes, sir."

"Pass out the life preservers and get the men on deck to help with survivor rescue. Oh yes, hand out the gas masks."

"Gas masks?"

"That's right, Spector. Gas masks. And tell the men to put them on."

"Commander?"

"Yes, Lieutenant? If it's the captain, tell him I don't have . . ."

"No, sir. But I think you ought to see this . . ."

"What?" He joined the lieutenant by the radio.

"There, sir. The tugs." He pointed. "They're leaving. They've dropped their lines and are pulling away."

"Son of a bitch!" the commander shouted. He took the radio and tuned it to the tugs' channel.

Despite all the shouting, cursing, and threats that Wade could muster, none of the four skippers could be coaxed to return. It was better to be alive without a license, they said, than to be dead with one.

Wade, defeated, tuned the radio back to the Coast Guard frequency. The angry voice of the captain of the port greeted him. "Wade, come in. Damnit, Commander, I want a full report . . ."

"Wade here, Captain."

"Wade," the anger and the relief were both evident in his voice. "What's happening? Why have you issued a Code One?"

"Yes, sir. Some kind of explosion seems to have blown

the protective cover off of one of the tanks. It looks like gas is escaping at a rapid rate."

"Any sign of fire?"

"No, sir. Not yet. The last report we had from the *Prometheus* was that the computer had automatically shut off all electrical and ignition points."

"Survivors?"

"So far we haven't seen any. They were beginning to ready the lifeboats just before the explosion." He peered at the silhouette of the tanker. "They seem to have abandoned them. Perhaps only on the starboard side. The wind, what there is of it, is coming from the south. They're probably using the port lifeboats. That's what I'd do if I were in that captain's position. I've ordered the *Apple Tree* to the port side to pick up possible survivors."

"Do you think it's safe to remain in the area, Commander?"

"No, sir. I don't, but then I don't seem to be the only one. The tugs have dropped their lines and high-tailed it for home." He paused to let the import of that sink in.

"You mean that the *Prometheus* is . . ."

"Yes, sir. She's a derelict. Might go up any second and there's not a damn thing we can do about it."

"And the gas?"

"The gas?"

"Yes, Commander, the gas. The cloud. What direction is it going?"

"North." Then, suddenly seeing the captain's point: "Toward Brooklyn."

2:42 P.M. *On Board the* PROMETHEUS

Val and Cybil ran silently, side by side, through the deserted corridor. Their only companion was the lonely wail of the gas alarm and the flashing of red lights at every turn. They held hands, one insulated glove firmly grasping the other. It had been this way ever since they had escaped from the hold.

They had been running for what seemed an eternity in the vast confines of the hold. The gas cloud was growing heavier, the mist growing denser with every passing second. The noise of the gas violently vaporizing as it touched the water and ice below was an incessant hiss, like a nest of angry snakes disturbed from a peaceful slumber. The hissing grew to a roar, echoing and reechoing around the chamber.

Finally, Val pulled them to a stop. In front of him stood the steel hatch linking them to the outside world. He dropped her hand to spin the wheel. It refused to budge.

"It's frozen," he grunted as he exerted his strength against the resisting metal. "Give me a hand, will you?"

Cybil leaned against the wheel, pulling down on one side with both her hands. She could see the wheel was covered with a layer of ice. It glistened in the yellow glare of their headlamps. She pulled harder. Nothing.

"Wait a minute," Val gasped. "Rest for a second and then let's try it together." He took three deep breaths. So did she. "Okay, ready?" He put his hands on top of the wheel. She placed hers beside his and nodded.

They both strained against the wheel. Blood pounded in her ears as she put all her strength to the task. Her teeth clenched with the effort.

The first thin lines appeared around the edges of the ice seal. They grew, spreading like spiderwebs across the face of the hatch. Then the ice shattered, sloughing off to lie on the floor in a heap of white particles. The sudden release of pressure tossed Cybil to the floor. She lay there panting as the mate spun the wheel as hard as he could until it banged to a halt against the stops.

"Okay. Let's go." He pulled against the door. It wouldn't budge. "Damn, don't tell me this is frozen too." He inspected the edges around the seal, testing them with a gloved finger. "No, no sign of ice." He rubbed two fingers together to demonstrate.

The answer popped into Cybil's head. "Pressure."

Val stared at her. "Of course. Damn, I should have thought of that. The pressure's holding the door closed. We're trapped."

"Val, what can we do? The tank's going to blow any minute." A deep crackling added to the general din now filling the hold. Cybil diagnosed it as the sound of the tank wall giving way. "We've got to get out!" she shouted.

Val looked around for anything he could use as a lever. There was nothing. The hold had intentionally been designed to exclude direct contact of metal on metal, to reduce the possibility of sparks.

The crackling noise grew until it drowned out the hissing. It seemed to be directionless. Cybil struggled to identify it. This time it was Val who found it first.

"Look," he pointed to the steel girder arching across the walkway. Tiny spiderwebs appeared along the steel member. "The temperature is getting to the steel dome. It's not designed to hold cryogenic temperatures. It's beginning to go." He joined her on the floor.

"Lie down. Flat!" He shoved her to the floor. "Hurry. I don't know how long the dome's going to last. It's our only chance. When the dome goes, it'll be murder if we're standing up."

She obeyed. They lay together, side by side, helmets touching. Cybil reached for his hand. She found his searching for hers. They grasped each other tightly. The pressure grew, forcing the suits flat against their bodies. Their eyes met.

With a half smile, Cybil said, "Val."

"Yes?"

"About dinner tonight . . ."

Her answer was drowned out by the hurricane force wind that beat over them. The first wave picked them both up and tossed them back, hard, against the walkway. Then the wind grabbed at their bodies, sliding them back toward the center of the hold. They held on to one another.

Val managed to catch the railing with his free hand and hold on. Cybil flailed her arms as he tried to hold her. She struck the railing and quickly wrapped her legs around it. Supported at two points she was secure. After an eternity, the gale diminished and disappeared altogether. Silence engulfed them.

Shaken, they reluctantly relinquished their grips on the railing. "Is it over?" Cybil asked, whispering as though fearful that any noise might reawaken the forces that missed them.

"Should be. Now that the gas has someplace to go it shouldn't build up like that again. Are you all right?"

"I think so," her voice quavered. "Thank God these suits are as heavy as they are. One rip and . . ." She had a vision of Miguel's pasty white hands just before she covered them with foam. "Oh, Val," she cried, turning back to the center of the hold. "The chief and Miguel. They're . . ."

He wrapped his arm around her, pulling her close so he could look directly into her visor. ". . . dead, Cybil. If the fall from the stairs didn't tear open their suits, the wind would have. They were in the center of the hold, right below the dome. They would have been tossed around like rag dolls in that hurricane. There's nothing we can do for them, now."

Cybil felt the tears stream down her face. There was no way to wipe them away, so their wet trails glistened for a moment before drying. "Okay. You're right. And I'm just acting like . . ."

". . . a woman?" he said gently.

"No," she sobbed, pushing her helmet into his chest. "A fool. A silly fool." She sniffed. "I'll be all right." Pushing herself away, she straightened. An old gleam came into her eyes. She was in control again.

"We have our own problems to worry about. We still have to get out of here."

His face darkened. "You're right. Let's see what the explosion did to the hatch. If it's warped, we're in real trouble."

Together they approached the hatch again. The hole in the top of the hold made their auxiliary lights unnecessary, so they extinguished them as they walked. The cloud still covered the interior of the hold like a determined ground fog and they stumbled against the hatch. It was hanging wide open.

"Well, that's one problem easily solved," Cybil remarked as she stepped across the threshold.

"True," agreed Val as he followed her. "When the dome went and the pressure dropped, it created a vacuum pulling the hatch open. I'm glad we weren't standing in front of it when it blew open."

"Christ, look at the room," Cybil said, pointing to the overturned lockers. "Looks like it was hit by a tornado."

"That pretty much describes it. Explosive decompression. If we had made it in here before the dome burst we would've been killed."

"I guess we were pretty lucky."

"Lucky? It was damn near miraculous."

"I wonder how the rest of the ship made out?"

"We'll soon see." Val was busy closing the hatch, spinning the wheel shut. He noticed Cybil's quizzical look. "Sailor's habit. Can't abide seeing a watertight hatch left open."

When they opened the outer hatch, they found themselves alone with the klaxons and flashing red lights. "Don't open your helmet," Val warned. "The red lights mean gas."

"I wasn't planning to," Cybil answered. "But thanks for the advice."

They passed through the maze of the ship's interconnected passageways, heading toward the stern. There was no sign of life. Every time they passed a cabin, Val would peer in before passing on. Cybil forced herself to look as well, always dreading the sight of a frozen corpse sitting at a table. But the ship was deserted. Not a living or a dead body to be found.

"Where are we going?" Cybil finally asked.

"To the bridge. If there's anybody still on board, that's where they'll be. It's the highest point on the ship and the gas will reach there last."

"Why don't you use the intercom?" She pointed to one of the square boxes set every few yards along the corridor. "It'll be faster than walking."

"Power's off. Automatically, whenever there's a gas leak the computer turns off all sparking equipment in the affected area. That includes the intercom. No choice but to go and check it out for ourselves."

They reached the bridge tower and made their way up the stairs, accompanied only by the faint echoes of their footsteps.

Near the top, they suddenly passed through the cloud that had surrounded them since exiting from the hold into the clear air. It was like emerging from a white night into a gray day.

"Well, that's good news," Val commented as they rested just above the bubbling cloud. "It means that there might be someone still alive on the bridge."

"But not for long," Cybil pointed out. The cloud was climbing. In a few seconds their feet were once again blanketed in white. They moved on.

The door at the top of the stairs was open. It led into a short corridor. Although there was no cloud, there were no people either. Everything was deserted. They passed the officers' wardroom where Val and the other officers had spent many a night warming their hands over a cup of espresso. The room was deserted. The table was littered with half-emptied demitasses. Val picked up one of the cups and sloshed it. The film of cream and coffee circled the cup in a yellowish brown slurry.

"At least the temperature hasn't dropped below freezing yet."

"Wish we could be as sure about the air as we are about the temperature."

Val nodded. One of the greatest dangers of methane gas was that it was totally undetectable: odorless, colorless, tasteless. A silent killer, slowly starving the brain of oxygen.

They hurried down the corridor. The door at the end was closed.

Val opened it and led the way in.

"Captain!"

Chapter 6

2:50 P.M.   *Captain's Office; Governor's Island Coast Guard Station*

James Bassil, captain of the port, stared into space. Drops of sweat glistened and dried on the black handle of the telephone which, until recently, had been tightly clutched in the officer's hand.

Except for his crisp white uniform shirt and the small battery of medal ribbons tacked to his right breast, Bassil looked like any middle-aged bureaucrat. He was bald, and the few remaining strands of gray-black hair were carefully combed across his forehead to cover the vast expanse of exposed skin. He was fat, but nothing that a few weeks of regular exercise wouldn't cure, he always claimed. The only anomaly was the deep reddish brown tan that covered his face and hands. That was a color that couldn't be found on golf courses or at swimming pools. It was the color of the sea.

Lying unseen in front of him were two folders. One was marked PROMETHEUS; its contents were spilled out across his desk showing schematics of the tanker and copies of the regular inspection reports. It was very thick, since it dealt with a very detailed subject.

The second folder was thin. It contained only one document with the crossed anchors emblem of the Coast Guard embossed on the top of the cover page. It was not detailed or specific. There were few numbers and no diagrams or schematics. The folder was unopened. Bassil didn't need to see the report. His signature graced the bottom of the first page. It was marked: LNG PRE-DISASTER PLAN.

Some internal stimulus roused him and he flicked open his intercom. "Sally, get Mayor LaSalle on the phone immediately."

Less than five minutes later the intercom began to buzz. "Yes, Sally?"

"I have the mayor's press secretary on line one, Captain."

"But I didn't . . . oh, never mind." He picked up the phone. "This is Captain Bassil, U.S.C.G., captain of the port. It is urgent, most urgent, that I speak with the mayor immediately."

"Sorry, Captain, but I'm afraid that he's tied up in a very important meeting and can't be disturbed. This is Abe Newfeld, his press secretary. Can I help?"

"No, I'm afraid not. This is something that doesn't involve the press, at least not yet. I must speak with the mayor immediately." Bassil hated dealing with civilians, particularly politicians. They were so . . . undisciplined.

"Listen, Captain. You gotta give me a good reason to break into that meeting if you wanna speak to the mayor. If you don't, then call City Hall an' leave a message with his secretary. He'll call you back later this afternoon or maybe tomorrow. It's no skin off my back either way. You wanna give me the story or you wanna wait?"

"All right, tell the mayor that I've just declared a major maritime disaster and have closed the harbor to all traffic. I must speak with him to discuss what might be a terrible disaster."

The press secretary whistled between his teeth. "You

ain't shittin' around, are you, Captain? Close the port? That could cripple the economy of the city in a couple a' weeks. How long you say the freeze was goin' to last?"

"I didn't. Maybe a couple of hours. Two, three at the most. But . . ."

"Well, that's different. Nothin' a few hours a' overtime couldn't cure."

"It's not the port that's in trouble. At least not in the way you think. It's the *Prometheus*."

"The who?"

"*Prometheus*." He spelled it for him. "She's sinking in the harbor. In Sandy Hook Channel, and she's leaking cargo. Oh, hell, Newfeld. Can't you just tell the mayor that it's a matter of life and death and if he doesn't come to the phone right away he's going to be responsible for the death of maybe thousands of people?"

The press secretary whistled. He said nothing for a few seconds.

"Newfeld?"

"Yeah, I'm still here. Just thinkin'. Can you be at City Hall in, say, ten minutes? No, we're getting into rush hour, make it twenty."

"Yes, I'll be there. Just have the police clear the parking lot for a helicopter landing."

"A helicopter?"

"Yes, and also I suggest having the fire commissioner and the police commissioner there as well. I've already called the fire commissioner to alert him. I'm sure he'll be there by now."

"Okay, Captain. This had better be pretty damned important. Or else your boss in Washington's going to hear about it."

"It's important, Newfeld. Just hurry."

Turning back to the intercom he called Sally.

"Yes, Captain."

"Get Jennings. And tell the helicopter crew to have *Rescue One* ready for take-off."

"Yes, sir."

He leaned back in his chair, rubbing his temples with the palms of both hands. Damn migraine was back. He wanted to take one of the pink pills in his desk drawer but knew that he would need all of his faculties this afternoon. That's the way it always was. Resting his elbows on the desk, he closed his eyes. The pain lessened.

Opening his eyes, he saw the blue-and-white schematics of the *Prometheus,* dominated by five circles, lined up one after the other. But that wasn't what they would look like now, he thought, picking up the drawings. One of those circles isn't round anymore.

He wondered what it was like on the tanker now. Poor bastards.

2:55 P.M. *On Board the* PROMETHEUS

"Captain!"

"Mr. Pakins. Miss Yale. Good to see you survived. I was worried about you." The captain sat in his padded chair overlooking the deck. He had a pipe clenched tightly between his teeth. Cybil noticed immediately that it was unlit. His uniform was as spotless as ever, although stained around the arms where the perspiration had soaked through. Obviously the air conditioning on the bridge was off, although, in their suits, neither Cybil nor Val noticed.

"But, Captain!" Val began "where is everybody and why . . ."

"Well, actually, Val, the answer is quite simple. After the tank in the engine room burst————"

"Engine room?" Cybil interrupted. "Don't you mean in the hold?"

"No. That was the second one. The first one was in the secondary gas storage tank. The pressure surge was passed onto the small storage tank before the computer could shut down the link. The smaller tank couldn't take the pressure as well as the main tank and it ruptured. Then the computer—by the way Val, you would have been proud to see how beautifully Valenkia operated. Her programs were perfect. Every electrical system and sparking piece of equipment was closed down before the gas could be ignited. The only thing we didn't realize was that she'd totally disable the tanker while doing it. But I guess that's really not so important after all. It gave the crew enough time to get away safely.

"At least I think they're safe. With this blasted cloud covering everything there's no way to tell whether the boats got away or not."

"You mean you ordered the crew to abandon ship?" Cybil asked. "Why didn't you go with them?"

The captain took a drag on the empty pipe and studied it before answering. "Well, Miss Yale. I wish I could say it was out of a sense of loyalty or tradition. The captain going down with his ship and all that. But I fully intended to join the last boat, after turning the log over to the second mate and, of course, seeing that as many of the crew as possible got safely away. I am enough of a traditionalist to want to be the last to leave.

"By the way, weren't there two others in your party? Chief Dunn and . . . that strong Portuguese seaman; where are they?"

"I'm afraid that they won't be coming, Captain," Val reported. "They never made it out of the hold. Last time we saw them they had fallen back into the tank chamber just before the tank burst."

"I'm sorry to hear that. Good men. I hate to lose good men. The chief was really extraordinary in his ability . . . but then I'm just reminiscing. More important things to do. I suggest that you two take one of the boats. I'm sure there are a couple left. Your best bet is on the starboard side. The port boats will have been taken by the crew. You'd better hurry. She might go any minute. You never know when that cloud"—he gestured out the window to the rolling fog that covered the deck—"might find a spark."

"But, Captain, we can't leave you," Cybil protested.

"You have no choice, Miss Yale. I don't have a cryogenic suit like yours. The only way off this ship is through that cloud. It'd be suicide to try it. And if I must die, I'd prefer to do it on my own bridge."

"But, Captain. There are other suits below. I can get one and be back here . . ."

"No, Mr. Paknis. Thank you, but no. There isn't enough time. Soon, any minute now, that tank is going to go. Some spark, some overheated wire, something will set it off. And then it'll be too late. And two more people will die, uselessly. No, Mr. Paknis, you and Miss Yale here . . . Paknis, where are you going? Paknis, come back here, that's an———" The slamming of the bridge door cut off the captain's last words.

The captain sat mutely in his chair, obviously angry that Paknis had gone for one of the remaining suits.

"Don't be angry at him," Cybil pleaded. "He couldn't have left you behind. I couldn't either. I couldn't live with myself knowing that we had left you here to die."

"But that's my duty, Miss Yale. You can't understand, but it's the duty of a captain to protect his crew, his passengers, and his ship. I've lost my ship and now stand in danger of killing off the last of my crew and passengers. And for what? For another few years of living as the captain of the *Prometheus*. The captain of the ship that was the worst disaster in maritime history. It'd be like being the captain of the *Titanic;* a living death for any seaman. No, Miss Yale. It'd be a kinder death to stay right here."

"But, Captain, you're not responsible. Nobody could fault you . . ."

"Not responsible? I'm responsible for everything that happens on board this ship. That's what being in command is all about. It's my ship and my responsibility. Mr. Paknis would understand; maybe one day he'll have his own ship, Miss Yale."

"Why don't you call me Cybil?" She reached down to open her helmet. "Since we're stuck here until Val gets back."

"Don't do that!" he shouted, knocking her hand away from the air line. "There's no telling whether this place is contaminated or not."

She dropped her hand. "But you're without a suit."

"And wouldn't be if I had any other choice in the matter, young lady. I'm still captain on this ship and while you're on board you'll obey my orders." His voice ended in a chuckle. "Unless of course, you want to threaten to bring the Coast Guard on to take her over at gunpoint again. You know, for a second there I thought you would really do it if I hadn't let you go into the hold."

"I would have," she answered softly.

"Ah." He chomped back down on his pipe. "That's what I thought. That's why I let you go. I'm not often outbluffed. I'm glad I wasn't this time. I'd hate to play poker with you. You have a good poker face. And a pretty one to boot."

Cybil checked her watch-thermometer. Three minutes since Val had gone.

Reading her mind the captain said, "It takes quite a

while to make it from here to the suit storage room. He's not gone long enough to go there and get back. Don't worry, Val's a good officer. He'll be back as soon as he can."

"I'm not worried about him as much as I am about the cloud. It was still climbing the stairway when we came up before. It should be getting close." She looked around the bridge. "Is there any place higher that we can go, Captain? The gas is heavier than air, at least as long as it remains at the temperatures we saw in the stairwell, so if we could get you up, just a few more feet . . ."

"I'm sorry that this isn't one of the old sailing ships I used to sail on when I was a boy. The mainmast stood one hundred and thirty feet above the deck. And we'd have to climb into the rigging in the middle of a gale to take in or make sail. But then, even if we had one, I don't suppose I'd be in any shape to monkey up those ropes the way I was as a lad."

"You look in pretty good shape to me, Captain."

"Well, thank you. Coming from a beautiful woman like you I take that as a real compliment. But I'd think that Mr. Paknis would be more in line for your attentions. As a matter of fact, I think I detected a gleam of interest in your eye. Am I right?"

She blushed, the color rising to her cheeks visible even through the helmet.

The captain laughed. "I thought so. I didn't think I had gotten that old or been out to sea so long that I had forgotten what a woman's interest looked like. Well, I will say one thing. Val's a damn fine man. One of the best officers I ever had serve under me. Never disobeyed an order, not until today, that is. I'll have to write that up in his report as a black mark. But I'd say he's met his match in you. You're as stubborn as he is. Good pair." The captain suddenly shivered violently. His breath became a frosty cloud that lingered in front of his face.

Cybil whirled. At the doorway a thin carpet of white slowly crept underneath the wooden door. "Captain!"

"Yes, I see it, Miss Yale." He stood up and backed away from the cloud.

"Captain, isn't there anyplace higher than the bridge? Is there some way to get on top of the bridge?"

"Yes. I'd forgotten about it, but there is an inspection

ladder leading to the radio antennae and the radar unit right over our heads."

"Where's the ladder?"

"There." The captain indicated a metal ladder fastened to the wall by the door. The first white wisps of cloud had already curled around the base of the ladder. "I'm afraid that it won't be much use."

"Isn't there some other way? On the outside perhaps?"

"I'm afraid not. That's the only way to get to the roof from the bridge. The other way is through the radio room and that's back down the corridor."

"Then it'll have to be the ladder." Cybil looked around the bridge. "Do you have anything you can wrap around your hands? Some gloves would be best, but anything heavy would do. A shirt, a piece of cloth. Anything."

"How about a flag? There are some signal flags in that cabinet over there."

"Perfect." She walked through the cloud and opened the cabinet, searching for the flags. The captain waited, wrapping his arms around his chest to keep himself warm. The temperature was ten degrees below zero and dropping fast.

Cybil grabbed two flags and handed them to the captain. "Wrap these around your hands. Don't touch the metal with your bare skin. You'll freeze to it and there will be no way of getting you free, short of cutting you off." She indicated the ladder whose once green paint had turned miraculously white. "Frost. Wherever you see white that means frost. Don't touch it."

He wrapped the flags around his hands. "That still doesn't explain how I'm going to get there from here. I can't walk there the way you can."

"No, but I can carry you." He sputtered in indignation. "I suggest you hold your breath, Captain. The air is likely to be highly contaminated by now." She leaned over, pulling one of the captain's arms around her shoulder. He stood stiff, unyielding.

"This will be a lot easier if you cooperate, Captain. I haven't practiced my fireman's carry since I took lifesaving in college, so if you will . . ."

Reluctantly, he bent over, putting his weight on Cybil's shoulder. She straightened her legs and lifted him from the deck. In three steps she was alongside the ladder. The captain grabbed hold, reaching up as high as he could from the precarious position he was in. She gave him a boost to make sure his legs wouldn't dangle into the cloud.

"Hurry, Captain. Don't take a breath if you can help it."

With a speed that showed that the young lad who used to "monkey" up the riggings was not dead, the captain scampered to the top. In less than two seconds he opened the hatch and in another second, his legs disappeared through it.

"Are you all right, Captain?" she called.

"Fine," he replied. "Except for my pride, and even that will heal."

Cybil smiled. Before joining the captain she paused to write Val a note, telling him where they were. Scribbling her message on the back of a chart she jabbed it onto one of the spokes on the wheel, where Val was sure to see it. Then she climbed the ladder and closed the hatch behind her to slow the rise of any gas onto the roof.

Five minutes later the hatch opened and Val's head appeared. "Sorry I took so long, but all the suits in the stern locker had . . ."

Cybil sat quietly, stroking the captain's head, which rested in her lap. The captain was quite still. His face had a definite blue tint. Methane poisoning.

"He died in my arms, Val." Cybil cried quietly, stroking the head resting on her lap. "There was nothing I could do, Val. Nothing. The gas was getting to him and he knew it. He asked if he could lie down and put his head in my lap, the way he used to do with his wife." She cried even harder. "There was nothing I could do." Cybil gently lowered the captain's head to the deck.

The two silver-suited figures clasped one another.

The white cloud silently crept over the edge of the roof and slithered toward the still figure of the captain, wrapping him in a frozen shroud.

3:00 P.M. *Weather Forecast for New York City and Vicinity*

TEMPERATURE:	98° F.	36° C.
HUMIDITY:	90 percent	
WIND:	South 0–3 knots	
PRECIPITATION:	10 percent probability	

SPECIAL CONDITIONS: The air inversion that has been covering the Metropolitan area for the past fourteen days remains intact. Unless the low developing along the North Carolina coast or the storm which has remained stationary in Rahway, New Jersey, begins to move, the stagnant air condition will continue in the Metropolitan area. Severe Pollution Advisory in effect. Special warnings for elderly, infants, and anyone with respiratory or heart conditions. Dangerous levels of sulfur dioxide, nitrous oxide, and carbon monoxide have been recorded in Manhattan, Brooklyn, Queens, Connecticut and Long Island. Driving is to be avoided, wherever possible.

NATIONAL WEATHER SERVICE
NATIONAL CLIMATIC CENTER, ASHEVILLE, NORTH CAROLINA

3:00 P.M.   *On Board the* PROMETHEUS

"Take hold of the aft line and lower as evenly as you can," Val instructed. "This is the line you pull on." He tugged to make sure she saw which one he meant. The aluminum lifeboat lowered a few inches, tilting its stern toward the deck. "Understand?"

"Understood." Cybil stepped into the lifeboat and grabbed the line in one gloved hand. She was ready.

"Steady now," Val said. "I'm going to swing the boat out over the water. She might sway a little, but you steady her. All right?"

"All right." Cybil complied, grabbing onto the solid arm of the metal davit as it extended out from the deck of the tanker. The davit, like everything else on the ship, was covered with white frost. Seconds later, Val climbed into the front of the boat, swinging over on a line dangling there just for that purpose. Cybil stopped the boat from swaying. They hung suspended in the cloud, unable to see the water below, or the tanker a few feet away. They could barely see each other, the cloud was so dense.

"Together now. Try to keep pace with me." Following Val's reassuring commands, they lowered the aluminum boat toward the warm waters eighty feet below.

Cybil watched Val and imitated his every move. It was

surprisingly easy to lower the boat with the multiple pulleys linked to give maximum leverage. But they paid for that ease in time. Val took it slowly, and two minutes later, he stopped them about two feet above the water.

"When we get in the water, I want you to do exactly as I say. Have you ever rowed a boat before?"

"Once on a lake when I was a kid. It was a canoe. You know, like the Indians used."

"I know. This isn't anything like a canoe. There one person can paddle, not row, by the way, simply by crossing the paddle from one side to the other. Here, the oars"—he indicated a cluster of them lying on the bottom of the boat—"are fastened in the oar locks. Don't worry about that, I'll do the rowing. All you'll have to do is keep the boat steady. When we touch the water, it will be a little rocky. The current is making a lot of waves against the side of the *Prometheus*. Just stay calm and in your seat. I want you to sit down now. Whatever you do, don't stand up," Val ordered.

She sat, still holding onto the line.

"Good. Now, when I say go, begin to lower the boat just the way we were doing. Only stay seated. Don't, under any circumstances," he emphasized, "stand up. These boats are pretty difficult to capsize, but with all your equipment on, we might just be able to do it."

She nodded.

"Ready?"

She nodded again.

"Go." Together they paid out the lines, lowering themselves the last two feet to the water of the bay. They touched the tops of the waves with a resounding smack. A sound like a pistol shot rang out, seemingly from Cybil's feet. She jumped and sprang to her feet, still holding the line. Pulling on the line released the hook of the pulley from the ring on the boat. They drifted free.

Then the water poured in.

"Val!" Cybil cried. The terror was plain in her voice. "Val, what's happening?"

The water was up to their shins and rushing in faster all the time. "I don't know. Stay calm. Don't move, you might rip your suit." He grabbed the sides of the boat.

Cybil fought the panic she felt growing in the pit of her stomach. She was a good swimmer but the suit was heavy.

Like most swimmers, her first reaction to being thrown in water was to rid herself of excess weight. But she couldn't remove the suit without exposing herself to the cloud. She froze, hands gripping the aluminum bracing of the boat, while her two conflicting instincts battled.

As the waves reached her waist, her paralysis ended and, despite Val's cries to remain still, she struggled to escape. Her struggles succeeded only in speeding the disintegration of the lifeboat as she struck out with both hands and feet. Val made things worse by trying to come to her end of the boat to stop her. He took one step and disappeared through the bottom of the now-nonexistent boat. It seemed as if he had been swallowed up by the cloud. As though he had never existed.

Cybil had seen too many people die that day. Suddenly she was alone. Everyone else, the captain, the crew chief, Miguel, and now Val, her rock of security was gone. She threw herself overboard frantically pushing pieces of the boat out of her way until she was in clear water, and struck out into the cloud.

The ship tried to hold onto her, wrapping her in coils of frozen rope. As she fought, the rope splintered and drifted away, a powder in the white wind.

The next few minutes were a nightmare; images tied together with white strings of terror. The gasping of breath as her air grew cold, then warm. A faraway voice, the voice of a dead man, calling her name. Total disorientation. No sign of the boat that sank beneath the waves or the ship that loomed somewhere above her head. The whiteness of the cloud blending with the thin layer of ice that drifted gently on the surface of the water. Only the movement of her arms broke the uniformly white world. Then her arms, burning with a white pain, gave out, floating gently at her sides.

Gradually the white turned to gray and then to black. The cloud, the water, even her arms were gone. Only darkness was left. The darkness of death.

She was certain then that she was going to die. That the death that had followed her through the ship had finally come to claim her as its next victim. The far-off voice was the call of death. Of sleep. She could rest now.

Closing her eyes, she felt her heartbeat slow. Perhaps she thought dully, there was a leak in the suit. Maybe she was dreaming the dreams of one on the brink of oxygen starvation. But even on the brink of collapse, Cybil's scientific training fought back. It wasn't oxygen starvation, it was panic. It was the panic of blindness and repeated shocks.

She floated passively, gently rocked by the swells, no longer even caring whether it was panic or impending death. Suddenly she was grabbed from behind. An arm reached around her and shook her. She fought, terrified that the ship or her dead crew had returned to claim her. She tried to pull the offending arm off her helmet. With the arm, sight returned. Also sound. The voice she had been hearing suddenly was very close.

"Cybil! Stop it!" the voice called. It was familiar. It sounded like Val.

But he was dead. She struggled again.

"Stop it! Cybil! It's me, Val." He shook her.

"Val?" She stopped struggling. "I thought you were dead."

"So did I for a few seconds. When I went through the bottom of the boat I thought for sure that I had had it this time. But somehow my suit didn't get punctured and I came back up to the surface. I saw you swimming away, right into the cloud. You didn't seem to hear me when I called. You just kept on swimming . . ."

"Oh, Val." She sobbed, turning around so she could look at him. "Oh, Val, it's you. It's really you. I thought you were dead." She cried heavily, pressing her faceplate close to his.

"Well, I'm not. So don't cry." He patted her shoulder with one clumsy hand. Patches of ice fell off their suits as they clung together, two silver people in a world of white. Only their heads showed above water; below, they were wrapped in each other's arms.

"Don't let go of me," Cybil pleaded. "Don't ever let go of me, Val. I was all alone. It was terrible . . . Just terrible. I just kept hearing these horrible voices arguing about how I was going to die. And I couldn't see anything. And I couldn't move." She grabbed him and pulled him close. "Oh, Val, you don't know how awful it was. You don't know."

He just hugged her. He had shared her terror while he beat the empty water for her. When she hadn't answered his calls, he imagined her drifting unfound, just a few feet away. He had cried for joy when he spotted her suit floating nearby. The joy turned to dread when she didn't answer his calls. It would take only a tiny hole to turn her suit into a floating coffin, her body frozen or poisoned. With an unnameable fear in his heart, he had reached around her to turn her toward him. Her response had startled him as much as his arm had scared her.

"That's all right. It's over now. It's all over." He reassured her. "I won't let you go again." Only when he said it did he realize that he meant it. He wondered whether she understood what he was saying.

"I won't let you let me go, Val." She looked up, the water running off her plastic mask, freezing in small blobs of gray-colored ice that soon disintegrated and fell into the water. "I won't ever let you go." The tears stopped. On both of them. Soon they were ready to swim, side by side.

They puzzled for a second, wondering which direction to take, finally realizing that any would do. If they went far enough on any one course, they were bound to come out of the cloud eventually.

"The operative word is eventually," Cybil responded. "If we are going downwind, that could be miles by now."

They chose a direction and, side by side, struck out into the impenetrable wall of whiteness.

Chapter 7

3:15 P.M. *On Board the* FIRELADY

The *Firelady* was the command boat for the New York City Fire Department's small fleet of fireboats. Nobody knew better than Deputy Chief Henry J. Rush how small that fleet was. Only six years before, twice as many boats had been on call. Now only five could be mustered. The fiscal crisis that had cut every city service to the bone had fallen particularly hard on the marine division of the fire department.

Rush was a career firefighter, having spent more than twenty-five years in the department. At the age of twenty, he had been fighting fires in Brooklyn tenements. Twenty-two years and two heart attacks later, he was in command of the marine division. Like all career men in the department he was in excellent physical shape. Only his gray hair showed his age. His gray hair and his eyes. The eyes, also gray, were perpetually crinkled, as though he had seen too much and wanted to shut out the world.

Rush had ordered his fleet to lash their boats together so he could meet with the commanding officers in person before going into action. There was no room for misunderstandings that could occur from a radio instruction. And Rush wasn't taking any chances. He had worked with these men for over two decades. They were his friends as well as his subordinates.

He waited patiently as they assembled on the deck of the *Firelady*, and began his instructions.

"Line up on the *Lady*. Don't get any closer than I do. Remember, have your crews stay in their masks at all times. There's likely to be gas in front of the cloud that we can't see, so don't let the cloud lull you into forgetting that the gas is odorless and colorless." Rush looked at the four firefighters, the "captains" of the department's tiny fleet, huddled in their black canvas coats, the sweat running down their faces. "The only safe indicator is, of course, one of the gas detectors. Keep one on the bow and manned at all times. If you get any reading"—he looked around the group—"and I mean, any, pull back. Remember, it's more dangerous at lower concentrations than at higher.

"Next to your gas detector, the best bet is your sense of feel. It may be odorless and colorless, but it'll still be pretty damn cold. And God knows, in this heat it won't be difficult to feel a drop of a couple of hundred degrees. Wearing these things"—he pulled at the collar of the trench coat he wore—"I can tell you it might almost be welcome."

The men smiled at the joke. They couldn't bring themselves to force a laugh. He hurried on.

"Okay. You know the drill. Spray on 'fog' settings

only. Use all of the fixed nozzles, no portables. Stay in line. I'll be on the east corner and Gale will be in the *Star* on the west. If you get into trouble, pull back. And, God forbid, you find yourself drifting into the cloud, or vice versa, give a call on your horn." He paused. "And if you see you're going into the cloud, kill your engines. Don't hesitate. One second delay and the cloud might be ignited. The engines are our greatest danger this close to the cloud."

"How far back are we going to fall, Henry?" Gale Karr asked. He was Captain of the *Firestar, Firelady's* sister ship.

"Don't worry, Gale. I'll tell you when to pull out. Just keep the *Star* in place. You're one anchor. You've got the toughest job. There won't be anyone on your starboard. If you get out of line, everyone's in danger, so keep a sharp lookout. Any questions?" He looked at his four captains. No one spoke.

"Good. Good luck and the drinks are on me when we get in." He clapped Gale on the shoulder.

"Gale, stay for a second, I want to go over placement of the *Star*."

"Sure." Gale unsnapped the heavy clasps that sealed the canvas coat.

Rush followed the other three officers to the rail and shook their hands before they crossed to their own boats. Then he returned to Gale. Karr was not only second-in-command of the division but also Rush's best and oldest friend in the department. They had saved each other's lives so often they had stopped counting years before.

"Gale, please be careful," Rush warned. "The cloud's likely to come creeping around on your starboard. Keep an extra man on the starboard side to watch for the cloud. It'll be pretty difficult to see it from the wheelhouse because of the fog being thrown out by the front nozzles. Keep a sharp watch. Put your best on it, okay?"

"I will."

"The whole line's dependent on you, so be careful."

"If I were careful, I'd have turned the *Star* around as soon as I got your call. We'd be halfway to Montauk by now."

"I almost wish you were. Then I'd have a reason to pull back. As it is . . . Anyway, Gale, listen for my signal;

two blasts on the horn and we run for it. Until then we'll be pulling back slowly in front of the cloud as it advances. Keep the other boats on line. If you see one drifting off, give one blast on the horn."

The two men shook hands at the railing. "Good luck. Keep your starboard side covered."

"Thanks, I will. You keep an eye on your port."

The boats separated, racing to their positions on opposite ends of the five-boat line. Each boat was about one hundred yards from its neighbor, forming a line four hundred yards long. On Rush's signal, the boats began spraying. The water towered above the boats by a hundred feet. Slowly the boats approached the cloud.

3:25 P.M. *Mayor's Office; City Hall*

"Damnit, Bassil, this better be important," Newfeld growled behind his cigar as he settled into the chair near one end of the conference table that dominated the mayor's office.

"It is," Bassil answered curtly. "Where's LaSalle?"

"It damn well better be," Newfeld repeated, ignoring the captain's question.

Four men sat at the conference table, awaiting the arrival of Vincent LaSalle, Mayor of New York. Newfeld, the press secretary, chomped angrily on his unlit cigar, thrusting it back and forth from one corner of his mouth to the other as though it were an uncomfortable sword. The police and fire commissioners sat silently side by side, with somber faces.

The captain sat at the foot of the table, still seething at the press secretary's comments. On the yellow pad in front of him, he idly scribbled an unending series of spiraling circles. Underneath the spirals the faint silhouette of a ship was obvious. The circles grew in ever-blackening waves until they filled the page. Bassil continued his scribbling after the page was filled.

Only the intermittent hum of the air conditioner's compressor disturbed the peace of the room.

"Sorry I kept you waiting, Captain." The mayor walked into the room, his hand extended toward the Coast Guard officer. "But since I was back, there were a few things that just couldn't wait." They shook hands warmly. The mayor's was the firm, cool handshake of a professional. Even his palm exuded confidence.

"Now then, Captain, what seems to be the problem?" He took his accustomed place at the head of the table and gave Bassil his full attention. Like most politicians, LaSalle had the ability to focus total concentration on any given problem. He appeared completely relaxed, resting his elbows on the arms of his chair, forming a pyramid with his fingers. Inwardly, he was steaming. He was in the middle of one of the most bitter campaigns in the state's history, and he resented having to leave a crucial campaign finance meeting that might decide the difference between winning and losing.

Although running the city came first, LaSalle's heart wasn't in it. It was resting in Albany. In the governor's mansion.

They were in the last hot weeks of a pressure-cooker campaign for the Democratic nomination for governor. It was the culmination of ten months of the kind of bitter infighting that only an intraparty election can inspire. Democratic governor against Democratic mayor.

The two most powerful office holders in the state were at war. Normal state business ground to a halt as political considerations overrode governmental ones. Governor and mayor hadn't spoken to one another for over a year.

The state suffered. Normal programs became footballs to be kicked from Buffalo to Long Island. Essential bills lingered in committee as partisans wrangled over sponsorship, trying to corner the credit for their respective candidate.

Ultimately, as almost all primaries do, it became an issue of personalities. With no substantive differences between the two men, the campaign boiled down to name-calling and buying television ad time. The outcome of the election could turn on who had "All in the Family" or "Laverne and Shirley" on their side.

The battle of the air waves started on the Fourth of July and continued, unabated, until the last week of August. Television costs. Campaign coffers once measured in millions were now recorded in red ink. As money grew short, tempers grew shorter.

In the past two weeks, LaSalle had twice fired and twice rehired no fewer than four commissioners.

Governor Lowe's staff faired no better.

The latest poll results fueled both tempers. For all the months of political maneuvering, all the millions of dollars in advertising, and all the early-morning handshaking by the mayor and the governor, twelve days before the election they were in a dead heat.

Anything could tip the election to one man or the other. Losing would mean political death for either LaSalle or Lowe. In politics there is no second place.

Only through the sternest discipline could LaSalle force himself to pay attention to anything that did not relate directly to the election.

He stared at Bassil, recalling their last meeting. It had been at a port development conference. New plans were proposed that would mean a renewed life for the harbor. The port captain had opposed them and LaSalle had a lasting impression of salt and steel.

Bassil met LaSalle's gaze unflinchingly. "Mr. Mayor, there's been an accident in the harbor. A serious accident . . . a very serious accident. At fourteen hundred twenty hours the *Prometheus,* an LNGC, was involved in a . . . a collision with what appears to be some submerged object. According to the commander of the escort vessel . . ."

"Excuse me, Captain." Newfeld held up his cigar. "I'm not up on your military jargon. What's an LNGC?"

"Liquefied natural gas carrier," Bassil answered as though surprised that it wasn't common knowledge. "It's not military, it's Merchant Marine. Anyway, the important thing is that the commander of the escort ship reported that . . ."

"Excuse me again, Captain, but you said escort ship. Is it normal for the Coast Guard to escort ships into the harbor?"

"For LNGC's yes. Perfectly normal. S.O.P. Standard operating procedure, as a matter of fact."

"For Christ's sake, Abe, let the man finish a sentence, will you," LaSalle snapped. He was rarely short with Newfeld in public. The pressures of the campaign were beginning to show.

Newfeld sank deeper into his chair.

"Go ahead, Captain," LaSalle instructed.

"Thank you." Bassil continued, unruffled by the exchange. "At first, we thought the damage was only minor. An inspection crew was sent below to check on the damage. You have to remember that there are several sets of overlapping safety systems on board these tankers, so we thought everything was, or at least soon would be, under control.

"Something went wrong. I don't know what, and I doubt we'll ever have the full story as to what caused the accident. What we do know is that there was some type of explosion on board the *Prometheus.* The reports were a little muddled, but there appears to have been one in the engine room and another in one of the holds. It wasn't a normal type of explosion, otherwise the gas would have been ignited and, up until now, it hasn't been.

"The next word we had from the *Prometheus* was that the captain had ordered his crew to abandon ship. Most of the crew has been picked up by the *Apple Tree,* the escort ship, and I've sent for some of the survivors to meet us here. They may have some information that we can use.

"So, the *Prometheus* is now a derelict, her engines inoperable and crewless, just north of Sandy Hook. The tugs towing her dropped their lines and high-tailed it for port. We have no way of towing her out of the channel. Her cargo is leaking, creating a hazard to shipping in the area. I've therefore declared a Code One emergency. That's," he looked at the press secretary, "a military way of saying a major maritime disaster. It closes the port to all traffic; until it's lifted, nothing can go out or come into the harbor."

An uncomfortably long silence descended over the table. When LaSalle finally spoke, his voice was calm and deliberate.

"Is that all, Captain?"

"All? Isn't it enough? A major disaster in New York harbor?"

"A major *maritime* disaster, Captain." LaSalle emphasized the added word. "Maritime, not city. It may well be a disaster, but it's yours not mine."

The Coast Guard officer bristled. He grew visibly erect as he sat glaring at the mayor.

"I don't believe you quite understand . . ."

"Understand?" LaSalle snapped. "Understand? Damn right I don't understand. I don't understand why the hell you're bothering me with this. I don't understand why you think I should be worried about your damned maritime disaster. That's the Coast Guard's problem, not mine, Captain. You let the tanker into the harbor. As the federal government often reminds us, the City of New York has nothing to do with running the harbor."

Bassil remained seated, his face turning beer red. "Damnit, LaSalle, I suggest you sit down and stop shooting your mouth off before you know the facts. Yes, ships are my jurisdiction, but something's happening in the harbor that goes beyond the shoreline, or soon will. My authority stops at the shore. Yours begins there. This has to be a cooperative effort. It's bigger than just the *Prometheus*."

"The Coast Guard has nothing to do with letting the tankers into the harbor; we had no choice. Once you city people granted the license for the storage tanks to be built on Staten Island, the Coast Guard couldn't refuse to allow them entry. All we could do was set rules and regulations to see that the ships were safe."

"It doesn't appear that your rules were adequate, does it, Captain?" Newfeld interposed, his voice pitched deathly low.

The captain hesitated for a moment. "That remains to be seen. But I can't stress how serious this situation is."

The fire commissioner broke his silence. "I agree, sir. LNG is the most dangerous substance we have in the harbor. I agree with the captain. I think you ought to listen."

LaSalle glared at the commissioner. A traitor in the ranks. But underneath his irrational anger, LaSalle knew the commissioner was a professional. He wouldn't say something he didn't believe was true.

Newfeld assumed the role of the peacemaker, separating the two fighters with a wave of his cigar. "Gentlemen, gentlemen." His voice was conciliatory. "It's hot enough outside. I don't think there's any need to raise the temperature in here as well." The joke fell flat. "At least we should be able to discuss this in a civilized fashion. We need the facts, Captain, not a dispute about who's responsible for what. I'm certain that the issue of ultimate responsibility will be settled in some court somewhere ten years from now, long after the incident is forgotten by everyone. An insignificant footnote in *The New York Times*."

Newfeld paused, allowing both men time to cool off. In the stillness, the distant thrumming of an approaching helicopter grew insistently louder. The whipping sound of rotors meant that the copter was landing nearby. The City Hall parking lot.

Bassil looked up from the table. "Your facts are arriving now. The survivors of the *Prometheus*."

Cybil and Val were ushered in.

3:30 P.M. *Mayor's Office; City Hall*

The introductions were curt. Names and titles only. Cybil began talking immediately.

"We have to act fast," she said, automatically taking command of the discussion. "There isn't a moment to lose." Her breath came in short gasps as though she had been running.

"Just a moment, Miss Yale." Newfeld continued in his role of moderator, holding up his hand to stop the woman. He had seen her type before. Government was filled with them. Ballbusters, he called them. Always pushing men to the wall. Always thinking they were right. Always certain that there was no room for anyone else's comments. Newfeld yearned for the good old days when women would do the work they were assigned without bitching that they wanted a say in policy.

"We still haven't established exactly who's going to do what. We haven't even decided whether the city should do anything."

Cybil looked incredulous. She turned to Bassil. "Captain, haven't you told them?"

Bassil nodded. "I've tried, but so far the mayor's been too pigheaded to listen."

"Now hold on there, Captain." Newfeld quickly stepped in before LaSalle exploded. "There's no need for name-calling." He swiveled his head to stare at Cybil. "As I was saying, we've yet to decide whether the city should get involved at all. As far as we can see, this is a Coast Guard matter. I don't . . ."

"Get involved?" She shook her head. "You don't

understand. You don't have any choice! You are involved. The entire city is involved. You just can't sit back and ignore it."

LaSalle spoke up. "Miss Yale, I'm sure you mean well, but . . ."

"Damn right I mean well," Cybil spat. "But we don't have time for anything but action. We certainly don't have time for this useless bickering. Mayor LaSalle"—her voice became reasonable—"listen to me. I know what I'm talking about. You've got to listen." She was almost pleading.

LaSalle leaned back in his chair, giving her an opportunity to speak.

"I'm a scientist," she began, her voice retaining that air of calm certainty that came from absolute knowledge of her subject. It was the tone she used when lecturing a class at M.I.T. "I deal in facts. And, factually, I can tell you that we, all of us at this table, all of us in this city are in the midst of the most dangerous situation that any American city has ever faced.

"The tanker *Prometheus* was carrying a cargo of thirty-three million gallons of liquefied natural gas when one of its five tanks burst. I chose the word 'burst' carefully, because it was not an explosion. If it had been, I would not be here, nor would a very considerable part of the harbor. The gas has escaped and has formed a lethal cloud that is heading for shore."

"Cloud?" Newfeld mumbled from behind his cigar. "I thought you said that this stuff was liquid."

"I did," Cybil responded. "It was when it came into the harbor, but it isn't any longer. Some basic facts about LNG." She held up her hand and ticked off the points with her fingers.

"First, LNG is condensed methane. It's commonly used every day in a thousand ways—cooking gas, heating fuel. It's one of the cheapest and most useful fuels in the world. Environmentally, it's one of the best to use since there is virtually no pollution.

"Second, chemically, methane is the lightest of the hydrocarbons. CH^4. In nature, it always occurs as a gas, except in the deepest wells.

"Third, it is odorless, colorless, tasteless, and lethal.

It kills by excluding oxygen, rather than by actually poisoning the victim.

"Fourth, in order to liquefy methane, you can either submit it to extreme pressure, about six hundred atmospheres, or you can cool it to its condensation point, about two hundred sixty degrees below zero. For reasons of safety and economy, liquefaction is done by cooling.

"Fifth, LNG cannot exist in contact with ambient temperatures. In particular, LNG cannot exist in contact with water. It instantly vaporizes, forming a white cloud, the color coming from the tiny ice crystals suspended in the vapor. So any leak from an LNG tanker does not exist as liquid, but as a gas."

Cybil's hand slowly closed into a fist and dropped silently to the table. "Sixth, that cloud is now heading directly for Brooklyn and a lot of people are going to die unless we do something about it. And soon."

LaSalle remained motionless, staring at the pyramid his fingers had formed. He wasted a full minute before speaking, and when he did, he addressed the fire commissioner. "Commissioner, is she right? Do you agree with her statement about this cloud?"

"I can vouch for her reputation, Mr. Mayor." The fire commissioner fingered a worn file in front of him. "And what she has to say seems right. We in the fire department have been worried about this sort of accident. Hell, any sort of accident dealing with LNG. This cloud's only part of the problem . . ."

LaSalle waved him in silence. "Enough!" He looked toward the Coast Guard officer. "Captain?"

"She's the expert, Mr. Mayor, not me. That's why she's here."

LaSalle's eyes flicked to Cybil's. She met his gaze steadily. "You're certain there isn't any mistake."

"No mistake." Unflinching.

Newfeld's chair creaked as he leaned forward. "But what's the problem here? Won't the damn thing just blow away in the wind? I'm no scientist, I just read the newspapers, and from what I know, this stuff rises, doesn't it? Won't it just go floating away?"

"Normally you're right," Cybil answered, treating his question with more seriousness than he expected. "Methane is lighter than air. But that only applies when the gases are at the same temperature. Just as cold air is heavier than hot, cold methane is heavier than warm methane. This cloud is so cold that it will hug the ground. It's actually much heavier than the air around it."

"So don't we just have to wait until it warms up and then . . ."

"I'm afraid that will take some time, Mr. Newfeld. Theoretically, at least, the gas will not reach equilibrium with the surrounding air until it warms up to about one hundred sixty degrees below zero. With the ice crystals acting as insulators and more gas entering the cloud directly from the ruptured tank, I think we can estimate that it will be some hours before the cloud begins to rise."

"Isn't there any way to protect against the poison until the cloud begins to rise, Miss Yale?" LaSalle asked, his eyes still fastened on his digital pyramid.

"But the problem of its being poisonous is relatively minor."

"Minor?" the mayor asked, looking up.

"Yes, sir. Minor, at least compared to its temperature. I'd say that the chances of anyone living in the cloud long enough to die from suffocation are so small as to be almost nonexistent. By far the main danger is cold."

"Cold?" echoed Newfeld.

"Unbelievable cold. Two hundred and sixty degrees below zero. Colder than the worst arctic night. Cold enough to instantly freeze living tissue into rock-hard solidity. Cold that makes steel as brittle as ice, and ice steel strong. Colder than anything nature ever produced on the face of this planet. Cryogenic temperatures have only been created under laboratory conditions, carefully supervised to ensure that the normal environment doesn't, in any way, come into contact with the ultra-cold. No one really knows what will happen when so much cryogenic gas touches a normal environment.

"Death would happen in one of two ways, although there may be others we haven't anticipated. Most commonly, an explosion of the lung tissue would occur, caused by internal pressures created by freezing. One breath would flood the lungs with gas at minus two hundred sixty degrees, which would immediately freeze the alveoli of the lungs. The largest store of blood in the body

—about one fifth of the total body's supply—is on the other side of the thin membrane. Because the membrane is extremely thin, necessary for oxygen-carbon dioxide transfer, temperature would also be easily exchanged. As the cells freeze, the water content expands. The cell walls don't. They rupture. Since the process is virtually instantaneous, it appears to be an explosion. The clinical cause of death is asphyxiation, because the lungs have filled with ice formed by frozen blood. This is the most common type of death, because the first reaction on breathing in the cold gas is to gasp. It's a reflex, almost impossible to control when exposed to a temperature extreme. The second type of death is very similar except that the heart, being proximate to the lungs, is also frozen, as the heat is drained out of the body tissues by the cold.

"Because death is caused by cold rather than by poisoning, standard gas masks are useless. Even cryogenic suits like ours must have the air hoses specially insulated, and, for prolonged exposures, they have to be heated; otherwise the wearer gets something akin to Black Lung disease, as the tissues of the lung are frozen into uselessness.

"Even partial exposure would probably prove fatal. Assuming, somehow, that only a part of your body was exposed to the effects of the cloud. For example, by stepping into a 'pool' waist deep. The body, other than the lungs, does contain some insulation. Fat. The thicker the fat, the heavier the insulation. This protects from the effects of normal cold. But not from cryogenic cold.

"The danger is basically the same as in inhalation. The water content freezes and expands, rupturing the cells. It doesn't really matter whether it's fat or muscle cells, they're both the same. The cells on the edge of the 'freeze' area will pour the poisons of the dying cells into the bloodstream. That is approximately the same thing as gangrene. The person dies from the wastes of their own cells. It's not a pretty way to die. Amputation is the only alternative and, considering the conditions we'll be facing, I'd say almost impossible to perform in any significant numbers. Most of the partial cases will die.

"Death for those facing major, noninhaled exposure will be more humane. If a significant portion of the circulatory system is frozen; if, for example both legs are frozen as someone tries to run through the cloud, the heart will suffer a massive hemorrhage as the blood pressure surges to double, maybe triple normal levels. That would be an almost instantaneous death.

"I think we can assume that anyone who comes into contact with the cloud will die."

The silence around the table was complete.

The fire commissioner broke the stillness. "There's one other thing we haven't discussed." All eyes turned to him. "Fire."

"I was just getting to that, Commissioner." Cybil nodded in agreement. "Thank you. Ultimately our greatest danger is the possibility of fire. Once the cloud becomes ignited . . ." She shrugged.

"Can you ignite anything that cold?" Newfeld asked.

"Good point." Cybil again nodded. "Initially, when the gas is concentrated, it's virtually impossible to ignite. Only at the very fringes of the cloud is there any chance of ignition. As the cloud warms, it mixes with air, with oxygen. Methane forms a combustible mixture in concentrations of between eight and fifteen percent. It burns at a temperature of fifteen hundred to two thousand degrees.

"Below five percent concentrations there is no chance of any ignition, and, between five and eight percent an instantaneous combustion—an explosion—will occur.

"First, let's consider a nonexplosive ignition. The size of the fire would be purely a function of the size of the cloud. The larger the cloud, the larger and more dangerous the fire. It's like burning a can of gasoline. If you ignite the can by dropping a match on it, you'd get a tall column of flame, expending most of its energy upward. It would burn at fifteen hundred degrees but the damage would be rather limited.

"On the other hand, if you took that same can of gasoline and spread it around the floor, the flame would be the same temperature and, physically speaking, would release the same amount of energy, but the effects would be much greater. Spread the same can of gas around a building and then ignite it, and you have the worst situation. The gasoline acts as a fuse, ready to go at the first spark. It then creates the high temperatures necessary to ignite secondary fires; first, the more readily flammable materials such as wood and paper, then, materials like brick, and ultimately, living tissue.

"Computer studies have indicated a potential, but only a potential, for the creation of a vacuum effect at the center of an LNG-originated fire. If such a vacuum effect occurred, it would become self-perpetuating as long as a fuel source remained. A firestorm. And, as I said before, the fuel source could be almost anything. Temperatures in such a condition could reach ten thousand degrees. I think it would be accurate to say that nothing could survive such an environment. Some deep earth vaults might be able to retain their integrity, but in the area we are discussing, there are relatively few of them.

"Now, the explosion. Assuming that the cloud becomes large enough to sustain a simultaneous explosion of its entire volume, it would be of atomic proportions. Conservative estimates put the theoretical yield of such an explosion in the twenty megaton range, roughly twice the size of a Hiroshima-type bomb. But that would probably be much greater than the actual explosion, due to the near impossibility of a simultaneous explosion of the entire volume of the cloud. It's much more likely that there would be a series of explosions rather than a single one.

"Most probably, the initial explosion would spread the gas cloud without igniting the remainder. The gas, now dispersed over a wider area, would probably reach combustible concentrations before explosive ones. These would tend to burn, creating the firestorm condition I described before. Of course, since we're dealing with a high temperature burn, the secondary and tertiary ignitions would also contribute to the overall damage.

"We can be relatively certain that because of its size it is a practical impossibility for the cloud to experience simultaneous ignition of its entire volume. Accidental ignition is a certainty, even assuming that all electrical power and natural gas services were immediately cut off. But for all practical purposes, I think we can safely rule out all possibilities of an explosion on this scale.

"On the other hand, some explosions are almost inevitable. Particularly as the cloud grows and ancillary tentacles spread off, away from the main body of the cloud. These arms would dilute more rapidly because of greater surface area, and therefore ignition and explosive concentrations would be reached more quickly. Due to the nature of the cloud, its tendency to stick together in particular, the ignition of any arm will mean ignition of the whole.

"Such ignition means that the fire would retrace the path of the cloud to the source of the gas: the *Prometheus*. Given the nature of the insulation surrounding the tanks on the ship, there would be a lull period after the fire reaches the tanker, not an immediate explosion. During this period, there would be a rapid expansion of the gas in the remaining tanks. These would rupture in a few minutes, at most. They also include large pockets of air in the holds adjacent to the tanks. You could expect an explosion or series of explosions as the air and gas combined.

"This explosion would not consume the entire contents of the tanks, however. Probably less than one percent of the gas volume would explode. The rest would be thrown away from the center of the explosion, perhaps even swamping the ignited cloud. Regardless of whether the cloud is flaming or frozen, it would expand by a factor of six hundred. Gas would be produced faster than the fire could consume it. The cloud would then continue downwind until the fire exhausted the supply of available fuel. I would estimate that the gas would last about ten to twenty minutes before it was used up.

"That's about it, gentlemen." She looked around the table. "Any questions?"

"Just one," LaSalle said. "How big will it be?"

"The cloud or the fire?"

"Both. Either."

"No one can give you an exact answer on that, Mr. Mayor. It's all a function of time, wind velocity, temperature . . ."

"Just guess, Miss Yale, your best guess."

Cybil hesitated for the first time since she had entered the office. Grabbing a pencil and a yellow pad from the stack in front of her, she scribbled a column of numbers. The column grew. All LaSalle could see were the growing series of zeros that were added at the end of every column.

Cybil held up the pad, her eyes flickering across the numbers, searching for any mistakes. There were none.

"Well," LaSalle asked.

"It's a rough guess, but . . . I'd say that, assuming the entire contents of the tank vaporize, and assuming that the other tanks remain intact, the cloud will be about half a mile wide and five miles long."

"My God," Newfeld whispered.

LaSalle ignored him. "Captain, how far did you say this ship was from Brooklyn?"

"About two and a half miles due south of Coney Island."

"Coney Island," the police commissioner whispered. "There must be a million people on Coney Island beach. A million people."

LaSalle once again lapsed into silence, staring vacantly at his hands. His eyes drooped, almost closing. Cybil had to strain to hear his next question.

"One last thing, Miss Yale."

"Yes?"

"How do we stop it?"

"Stop it?" Cybil answered. "I thought you understood. You can't stop it. Nothing can stop it."

Chapter 8

3:30 P.M. *Mayor's Office; City Hall*

"I can't believe this," Newfeld shouted. "I can't believe you walk in here trying to sell this horror story. Freezing clouds. Poisonous gas. Hell, if it were that dangerous you should never have let it in here in the first place."

Cybil looked uncomfortable. "Well, actually you're right. Maybe the shipment is too dangerous, but before today the record of LNG transportation was virtually without parallel in safety. More people die in nuclear accidents. Every possible safety device known to science was used in the design of the *Prometheus* and the other LNG tankers. We had no way of knowing————"

"Hell," Newfeld interrupted. "It was your job to know. Don't give me that 'we didn't know' shit."

"You're right, Mr. Newfeld. Of course," Cybil answered. "But that doesn't change the facts, and I suggest that we face them rather than yelling about who's to blame. We're all to blame, in our own way. The city is to blame for letting the tanks be built within city limits in the first place. The scientific community is to blame for saying that the tanks and the tankers were safe when we knew, as a matter of pure science, that an accident like this or possibly even larger was inevitable. The federal government is to blame for allowing the ships to come into our harbors.

"I'm sure that we'll all be blamed when it's time for a final accounting, and that, I'm sure, won't be done here today. There will be more than enough blame to go around, I can assure you. Let's worry about the problem at hand. Let's worry about Brooklyn."

"You sound as though you have a plan, Miss Yale. Do you?" the mayor asked, his voice a quiet contrast to the others at the table. "I thought you said there was no way to stop the cloud."

"I did and there is no way to stop it."

"Excuse me, Miss Yale, but that's not exactly accurate. There are still the fireboats." The fire commissioner was almost apologetic in his contradiction.

"Fireboats? What fireboats?" the mayor asked.

"Well, Mr. Mayor, when I was called by the captain, I immediately implemented the pre-disaster plan for an LNG tanker incident in the harbor by dispatching the fireboats to the scene of the accident. They should have arrived on the scene by now and there is a chance that they could control the situation."

"I don't understand. The tanker isn't on fire, is it? I don't see how the boats can do anything . . ."

"So far it's only theory, but it has controlled small experimental spills. The boats can put out a fog spray, normally used to control chemical fires and to wet down dry areas adjacent to a blaze. Several million gallons of water per minute per boat can be produced. In theory at least, the water forms a barrier that the gas can't penetrate because the water warms the gas above its critical temperature and it begins to rise. Once the gas rises, it quickly mixes with air and falls below flammable concentrations."

"But that's only in theory," Cybil protested. "And it's only been tested in small-scale experiments involving a few hundred gallons at most, on a calm lake. Here we're dealing with eight million gallons on a choppy harbor. I don't know about you, Commissioner, but I was out there and I can tell you it isn't the same."

"It's the only chance we have to stop the cloud. And the boats are already there. We should hear from them any minute."

"But . ." Cybil began.

The mayor cut her off. "I agree with the commissioner. We wait."

3:30 P.M. *On Board the* FIRELADY

"Back another twenty yards and hold," Rush ordered as he edged the fireboat closer to the Coney Island shore.

For the past ten minutes they had been slowly retreating before the steadily advancing cloud. At first it seemed as though they were having some effect as the water cut into the leading tip of the cloud, but then as the cloud continued to advance, it began to slip around them, on either side, just as Rush had feared. If it got behind them they would be cut off, unable to escape. An explosion would be inevitable.

Every time Rush lost sight of the land on either side of the thin line of boats, he ordered them to pull back. This was the fifth order to retreat before the advancing cloud. He looked across his line of boats. They were straight as humanly possible. He lined up on a church spire in the Rockaways, almost indiscernible in the smog. Even as he marked it, he could see the first white fingers creep between him and the spire. The cloud was moving again. It wasn't even giving them a chance to take a stand.

"Signal back another hundred yards," he ordered.

"Yes, sir," the helmsman answered, relaying the instructions to the other boats. "At this rate we'll be basking on the Coney Island beach in another hour."

"I know. But . . ."

The wail of a foghorn pierced the air.

"Shit!" He checked the other four boats. They seemed to be in line. Then, as he watched, the far boat was covered with a gentle veil of white that gradually thickened before his eyes. In seconds she was lost. Only the wail of her horn sounded in the white darkness. Then that too stopped.

"It's the *Star*," Rush shouted into the mike. "That means that the whole line is off. Pull back. All boats pull back." The engines of the *Lady* raced as the helmsman obeyed the command. Gale must have killed her engines, Rush realized, as the seconds dragged by and no explosion came. "Good old Gale," he muttered.

The radio crackled. "*Rescue One to Firelady*. What's happening down there? You all seem to be splitting up. Something wrong?"

"We've lost one of our boats. *Firestar*. She was on the west end of the line. Do you still have her in sight?"

"The west end? One second, *Firelady*. I saw her just a little while ago. Ah . . . there she is. I can still see her. But it looks like the cloud's cut her off from the rest of you."

"Is the water pressure still on? Are the fog sprays still working?"

"Affirmative, *Firelady*. She's in a small clearing. I can't tell whether she's still moving. It doesn't look like it. Maybe something's wrong with the engines. Want me to drop down for a closer look?"

"Negative, *Rescue One*. Negative. Your propwash would be murder that close to the cloud. How far from the edge of the cloud is she?"

"About ten yards, looks like. It's difficult to tell exactly where the cloud starts and your sprays end."

"We'll shut them off, *Rescue One*. Then give us a fix on the *Star*." He signaled the helmsman to pass the word along to the other boats. The fog covering that had encircled the fireboats dwindled and disappeared, collapsing on the tiny boats. "Now can you see well enough?"

"Affirmative, *Firelady*. Your boat is about fifteen yards deep into the cloud. She's completely covered by fog. I can't tell how much of that is fog and how much is cloud. They both look so much alike from up here."

"Any sign of life? People moving around on deck? The crew will all be wearing black trench coats, so they should be easy to spot."

"Negative, *Firelady*. I can barely make out the outline

of your boat, let alone tell whether there's anyone moving there."

"Okay. Stand by, *Rescue One*." Rush signaled the other boats to pull alongside. In less than a minute, they were lined up.

"I'll make this quick," Rush explained to the assembled skippers. "The *Star* is stuck in the cloud. There's still a chance the crew is alive. I'm going to take the *Lady* in there to try to pull her out, but I'm going to need you to help. I'm not ordering this since it violates the standing orders on dealing with LNG, so I'm asking for volunteers. I need one, maybe two other boats to back me up. The rest of you can stand by. Who's with me?"

All four boats were. He explained his plan and they hastily passed towlines back and forth across the deck linking the *Lady* to the other boats, forming a chain. In seconds, all was ready.

"*Firelady* to *Rescue*, can you still see the *Star*?" Rush radioed to the circling helicopter.

"Affirmative. The fog's getting thicker. She's lost water pressure. I've lost sight of her a couple of times already. You're not thinking of going in there, are you?"

"We are, *Rescue*. We are. I need your help. I want you to direct the *Firelady* so we're as close to the Star as we can get without touching the cloud. We're going to go full speed ahead for about ten seconds and then kill our engines and drift into the cloud. So it's up to you to get us headed in the right direction. We'll be out of radio contact as soon as we hit that cloud, so there won't be any chance for corrections. Understood, *Rescue One*?"

"Affirmative, *Firelady*. It sounds crazy to me, but it's your funeral."

Finally they were in place. The cloud rose serenely in front of them; about twenty yards of open water separated them from the wall of gas. Rush stood on the bow of the *Lady*, a tow rope coiled in his hands. The shadow of *Rescue One* flitted briefly across the deck as the pilot made one last survey. Rush signaled the helmsman, and as the engines gave a gentle shove, the bow turned in response.

Rush had explained his plan to his crew. After all, they were risking their lives, so they had a right to know. The danger of sparks from the engines or even from the radios was too great to allow power of any sort to be used once they entered the cloud. He had ordered the helmsman to turn everything off after the initial burst of speed. The radios, the engines, the pumps would all stop when they entered the cloud. If they were lucky, there would be enough time for one last course correction before the cloud closed over them. If they were lucky, they would reach the *Star* before they lost too much speed. If they were lucky, they would be on course. If they were lucky, they'd be alive when they found the *Star*. If they were lucky, they'd get out again. If they were lucky . . .

The engines raced just before he felt the acceleration. Rush grabbed onto the railing, wrapping one gloved hand against the steel cable that served as his line against falling overboard. They began to move slowly, more vertically than horizontally, as the opposing forces of acceleration and inertia battled for control of the *Firelady*. Rush concentrated on holding on as the bumps got greater and greater, threatening to throw him overboard.

As suddenly as they began, the bumps ended. It felt as though the bow finally decided to seek the bottom as she tilted forward. All engine power had been cut. An instant later the engines died and there was silence. And the approaching white wall.

Rush had time to wonder whether the pilot of *Rescue One* had gotten any last-minute course corrections through before they hit the wall. It approached so silently and smoothly that it was almost impossible to tell whether the cloud or the boat was moving. The silence was total.

All firefighters have a deep gut fear of cold. After years of fighting fires the heat becomes somehow comforting. No matter how hot the fire, the warmth is still a friend. But cold . . .

It swept over him like an arctic night. At first it touched his face, where the mask left a few square inches of skin below his chin exposed. It felt like fire. He tucked his head down to protect the tissue and could almost hear the skin crack as it creased. He could feel it pressing like leather against the bottom of his mask. The pain soon disappeared, leaving only a vague discomfort.

Nowhere else on his body was his bare skin exposed to the cruel cold. He and every other man on board had donned every inch of protective clothing in the *Lady*'s lockers. Still the cold cut through. His coat was of heavy canvas specially treated with chemicals to withstand the full fury of an industrial fire without passing the heat on to its wearer. His helmet could withstand not only heat but physical abuse from falling debris. His hip-high boots enabled him to walk over flaming embers without so much as scorching the feet within. The pants were designed to protect against the ravages of man's oldest enemy, fire.

But they could not deal with the cold that sucked the heat from his body.

Silently he passed through the visible wall that separated the natural environment from an alien one. In two seconds the temperature dropped more than three hundred degrees; more than the difference between ice and boiling water. In two seconds the air changed from hot to supercold. In two seconds, Deputy Chief Rush found himself fighting not only for the lives of his friends and fellow firefighters but for his own life as well.

The mask froze against his face. Every movement brought tender skin against brittle rubber. His skin tore, flooding the edges of the mask with blood. It quickly coagulated and formed a stiff seal against the cold. The air from the backpack chilled but stayed above cryogenic limitations, barely. Rush could hear the dry rasping of his breath in the narrow confines of his mask. He tasted the iron saltiness of his own blood.

But he never stopped looking for the *Star*. She must be out there somewhere. Just in front of him. He strained against the impenetrable whiteness, looking for some sign of his sister ship. All that he saw was white.

One gloved hand wiped the outside of his mask as he tried to remove the mist that blocked his view. Suddenly the mask cleared. The temperature in the mask had dropped to less than one hundred degrees below zero, the temperature at which ice begins to lose its ability to cling. Rush concentrated on taking shallow breaths, knowing that he would do less damage to his lungs that way. His chest burned with each frosty breath. Every breath eroded part of the soft, delicate lung tissue. Shallow breaths. Take in as little air as possible. Kill as little lung as possible.

Ignoring the searing pain, he searched for the dark hulking form of the *Star*. She should be directly ahead. It seemed as though the *Lady* had stopped moving; only the gentle and constant sloshing of the water against the bow reassured him that they were still coasting ahead into the depths of the cloud. The time dragged.

Cold seeped through every weakness in his clothing. He felt it first through his boots where the maximum contact with the frozen deck penetrated his armor. He lifted each foot and stamped it hard against the deck, grateful for the reassuring agony of pain. On the third series of stomps the agony evaporated, leaving only the now familiar dull ache. His hands, covered by only one layer of canvas, were next to go. The tips of his fingers began to burn. He could see his fingers flex against the coiled hemp of the tow rope but he could no longer feel them.

They couldn't go much farther. He had ordered the other boats to pull them back after one hundred feet of line passed into the cloud. That, he calculated, should allow them to remain in the cloud less than a minute. Two at the most. If the pilot of *Rescue One* was correct, that should be enough. Hell, it should be plenty. If they were on course, and if the pilot had actually seen the *Firestar*.

Rush forced himself to think of something other than the cold. He knew that what he was feeling was nothing compared to what the men on the *Star* were feeling right now. He refused to think of the possibility that they weren't feeling anything.

A shadow. Off to his right. Yes. Well, maybe. No. It was gone again. He couldn't tell whether he had actually seen anything or it had just been his imagination as he struggled to find the other boat. Nothing. It should be directly in front anyway. Only if *Rescue One* was correct. Just a few feet off and they would never find the missing *Star*. Rush stared ahead. Nothing.

Then suddenly something. Something undeniably solid loomed directly in front of him. Not far away. Only a few feet and drawing closer with every passing second. He recognized the rounded curve so similar to his own boat. The boat was completely covered with ice, a craggy mountainside in winter partially frozen and partially clear. The outline was enough.

The *Firestar*.

Rush fought the impulse to jump, knowing their momentum would bring them together. He bided his time, taking short breaths as he waited for the two boats to pull alongside. The shape grew and grew as the two boats drifted toward one another, pulled by the invisible forces of momentum and the sea. The stern was about two feet lower than the bow and Rush hopped down seconds before the gentle collision.

The pain of landing was excruciating. It shot up his legs and pounded in his chest. Rush fell to the deck, unable to move because of the fire that paralyzed his legs. His first thought was that they were broken. Dimly, he felt the reassuring pressure of the rope against his body.

He pushed himself to his knees, using all the leverage his arms could provide. His legs were next to useless. In the distance he heard the revving of powerful engines and the shouts of men. It was strangely quiet otherwise. The sound meant that the *Lady* had literally reached the end of her rope and that the other boats were readying to pull her out of the cloud. Each had a towline secured to the stern of the *Firelady*. They would tow her, and the *Star,* into the clear air, if only he could fasten the rope to the cleat in time.

The deck of the *Star* was a sheet of ice. Rush felt it through his knees as he slid toward the edge. In a moment of panic he feared he might slide overboard, but he reached out and caught the steel cable that rimmed the deck. The heavy gauge steel crumbled like ice between his fingers. His knees banged dully against the wooden bulwark, stopping him short of the edge.

He knew the cleat was nearby. It should be at the stern of the boat. It wasn't. There was only a snowdrift. Actually a sleet drift, Rush realized, as he pawed through the grainy ice crystals, each one no bigger than the head of a pin. It had the consistency of dry sand. Each handful was quickly replaced as neighboring supplies slid into the cavity he created with his digging. Using his body to block the shifting ice, he threw the excavated ice overboard and finally found the gray cleat at the bottom of the pile. With relief, he wrapped the line around it, only seconds before it strained and held. They were being towed out of the cloud.

Rush allowed himself a few deep breaths as reward, feeling the searing pain in his chest only peripherally as he listened to the growing sounds of the water against the hull of the *Star*. They were saved.

Surprisingly enough, the cold had almost entirely disappeared. He could feel a few twinges of the now-familiar burning pain against his chest and the small of his back. He knew that the insulation was heaviest there and frostbite hadn't yet set in.

He decided to check the boat for survivors. Wearily, he pulled himself to his feet, using the rope as his balance. He tried to remember to take small breaths. It was easy to forget. It felt as though he was never getting enough air. He fought the impulse to breathe more deeply. Sometimes he lost.

The deck was covered with the same kind of ice crystals that had obscured the stern cleat. It was like walking on tiny ball bearings. Twice he stumbled and caught himself rolling toward the edge. Each time he brought himself up short against the lip of the deck. It wasn't far from the stern to the first of the seven stationary nozzles, but it felt like miles.

He didn't recognize the first station when he saw it. Everything on the *Star* had changed so much that he ignored the mound of ice. Only his familiarity with his own ship drew him back. Something was here. Something important. He pulled against the frozen inner rail that lined the side of the wheelhouse. The starboard stationary nozzle should be here, he realized. One of the crewmen should have been on duty, manning the fog spray to fend off the oncoming cloud. There should have been life. Instead, there was only ice.

The ice was even heavier here. The water from the stationary nozzles would have drifted back on the men operating them as the cloud rolled in. Almost against his will, Rush envisioned what must have happened.

The cloud had crept alongside the *Star,* unseen by her skipper as he directed his attention forward, intent on keeping the boat in line. He wouldn't have seen the first small fingers of white at water level as they crept to the side of the boat. The men wouldn't have seen it either; they were looking for signs of the cloud from the front.

Then Gale must have noticed the silent approach of the cloud. He must have hit the foghorn and the controls simultaneously. They never had a chance to put the engines in reverse. It probably wouldn't have worked anyway. Gale's quick thinking saved the other four boats and probably half of Brooklyn from an incandescent death. All it cost was the *Firestar*.

Residual pressure in her pumps would have been maintained for a little while as the gas cloud, sensing a powerless victim, closed in. The reserve pressure tank would have allowed the nozzles to function for at most a minute, long enough for the pilot of *Rescue One* to get a fix on her. Long enough for the cloud to completely cut her off. Gale Karr would have realized that his only hope was to conserve pressure and try to create a free space around the boat while waiting to be rescued. He would have ordered the fog nozzles turned upright, making the *Star* the center of a large ball of warm water.

It was a good plan, and, given the same conditions, Rush might have done the same. But there was a glaring hole in the logic of the idea. Water does not create air. It only warmed the gas so it would rise. The gas would mix with air at the fringes of the cloud and overhead. But if the warming point was in the center of the crowd, the water would only warm the gas and create a bubble of warm gas.

On deck it must have been a frozen hell. The fog, incapable of remaining suspended in the air, would cascade back to the deck of the boat. It would concentrate most on the points of origin, the nozzles. At first it would fall like a gentle snow, easily brushed aside by the men as they desperately struggled to stay alive until help came. Then, as the pressure dropped on the pumps, the fog would become less and less dispersed. It would climb shorter and shorter distances into the air before falling back to the *Star* again.

Soon it would cease to be a nuisance. It would become a hazard. The water would barely make it out of the nozzles, lazily spraying the men nearby. As the water pressure fell, so would the temperature. The fog was the only protection against the cold. Finally the fog would be little more than a gentle shower. The cold would close in.

Water would spray onto the uniformed men as they stood at their stations. It would freeze instantly on contact with the cold canvas of their coats. A man, particularly one of the stronger men, might be able to shake off the coat of ice that threatened to cover him. But eventually the cold and the ice would be too much. There would be no fear of suffocation. The air packs that each man wore prevented that. And even the effect of cryogenic gases would be minimized because of the layer of ice acting as an insulator. The men would be able to breathe until the last.

The ice would build up, concentrating first on the head and shoulders of the man stationed at the nozzle. The deck would mean certain death as the ice piled up around his boots. With that thought, the crewman might have tried to move his feet only to find that they were frozen to the deck, unable to move. The layers of ice would have continued to pile up, burying the man under layer after layer of ice. A frozen tomb.

Terrified at what he might find beneath it, Rush leaned against the great gray stalagmite that covered the starboard nozzle. He scraped the surface, hearing the frozen material of his gloves rasp against the ice. The powdery surface cleared under his ministrations. He enlarged his area of concentration, energy coming unbidden from untapped reserves. The motions became frantic as he cleared a portal into the column of ice.

He stared in. There, only inches away, was the face of a man caught in the middle of a scream. Somehow, his mask had been torn away and Rush could see the bloodless cheeks distended in a final yell of agony or release. There was a puddle of blood frozen as it had escaped from his mouth. The eyes were colorless; only an impenetrable white gaze met Rush's stare.

With a suddenness that startled Rush, the boat emerged into the light. The *Firestar* was out of the cloud.

As four fire boats poured streams of water on the frozen *Star*, Rush fell to his knees, tore off his mask and retched. The water washed the bloodstained vomit away almost before it could form a puddle at his knees.

3:45 P.M.   *Mayor's Office; City Hall*

The fire commissioner read the note aloud. "*Stony Brook* to Commissioner. *Firestar* lost with all hands. Boat recovered but inoperable. *Firelady* heavily damaged in rescue attempt. Entire crew in need of medical attention. Deputy Chief Rush suffering from severe frostbite, en route to Bellevue Hospital Burn Unit via U.S.C.G. *Rescue*

One. With two boats out of action no alternative but to withdraw. Commander W. Friel." The commissioner slowly folded the note.

"Well, it seems Miss Yale was right." The commissioner creased the paper with one fingernail, making the edge razor-sharp. "There isn't any way to stop it." He paused for a second. "There were ten men on board the *Firestar.* Ten men."

"I'm sorry, Chief. I know how close you are to your men." The mayor looked around the table. "But we have an even more critical situation to deal with. Miss Yale, you're the expert. What do you suggest we do?"

"Well, Mr. Mayor, there hasn't been anything like this before and, to be perfectly honest, I've never even heard of any plans for such a situation." She hesitated. "You see, there's a branch of the National Security Agency that studies . . ."

"Miss Yale!" Captain Bassil exclaimed. "You know those studies are secret."

"Yes, Captain, but if the mayor doesn't have a right to know I don't know who does," she snapped back. "You see, the N.S.A. has run a series of projections for civil disasters created by either internal or foreign agents. One of the highest potentials has been the shipment of LNG into highly populated areas, like New York City, Los Angeles, and New Orleans. Those studies have shown that the probability for civilian deaths once the gas is released is almost a certainty. The controlling force is the wind."

"Couldn't we set up those fans that movie studios use?" Newfeld suggested. "Wouldn't they keep the gas from coming into Coney Island?"

"I'm afraid not. Even if you could find them and get them there in time, their effects would be purely local, blowing the cloud back on itself, and by the way, mixing it with a great deal of air, only making it more dangerous as far as fire or explosion is concerned. Besides, it would only come ashore somewhere else, somewhere beyond the edge of the fans. Totally out of the question," she concluded.

"Unfortunately, the computer studies have never considered the precise situation we have here. It was always assumed that either the force of the explosion or the collision, the two most probable ways for the gas to be released, would ignite the cloud. And it was also assumed that the wind velocity would be such that the cloud would reach land in a few minutes, not nearly an hour. Given that time frame, nothing could be done. Nothing except to stand by and pick up the pieces and bury the dead."

"You mean you expected this to happen?" Newfeld jabbed at her with the end of his unlit cigar.

"No, not exactly."

"Not exactly, Miss Yale?" The mayor echoed quietly. "Could you explain that?"

"We had no way of foreseeing that there would be an accident like today's. But there is a computer complex in the N.S.A. that continually monitors domestic industry for potential areas of sabotage. The most successful type of sabotage is nothing more than precipitating an industrial accident, using the potential for destruction that is already there. For example, the derailing of a train is a possible accident that could be created by the throwing of a switch at a crucial moment. If it's done inadvertently through human error, then you have an industrial accident. If the same switch is thrown on purpose, then you have sabotage.

"According to the computers, certain industrial sites are highly prone to the second type of accident. Nuclear generating stations, large refineries, large chemical plants, and LNG shipments are among the most probable type of targets that such sabotage might focus on, due to the inherent stores of energy that would be released by such an accident. Good sabotage always leaves as few clues behind as possible. If people think it was an accident, then there won't be any attempt to track down the real culprits. In a major explosion it's almost impossible to tell a real from a staged accident.

"So, there's a lot of attention given to potential accident sites. And, as you probably could have guessed, since most of them deal with energy sources, the Department of Energy is, of course, deeply concerned with these potentials. And, incidentally, since we're working to reduce the possible opportunities for sabotage, we are also reducing the chances of a natural accident.

"And LNG is one of the more serious potentials. It has all of the necessary elements to make a perfect target. It would provide its own destructive power, needing only a small triggering force to release it. A stick of dynamite equals an atomic bomb, if placed properly. The destruction would reach far beyond the point of the initial act of sabotage, obliterating evidence of foreign intervention. Property damage and loss of human life would be maximized. LNG shipments are particularly prone to such attacks because of the instability of the material. For political reasons, it would also force us to switch to more traditional, easily controllable types of fuels."

"Are you trying to tell us this was some sort of—" Newfeld stuck his cigar back into his mouth—"act of war or something?"

"No," Cybil answered immediately. "Not at all. All I was trying to say is that all the elements of a good industrial accident are here. The unstable chemical. New, untested technology. Highly complicated and overlapping control systems, any of which could have easily caused this type of accident. I think this is a genuine accident. An act of sabotage would probably not have given us the one advantage that we do have."

"Advantage?" questioned the mayor. "What advantage?"

"Time, Mr. Mayor. We have time. Sabotage would have exploded that tank in a twenty-mile-an-hour wind, not in a near dead calm. Before we even knew anything had happened it would have been over. It would have come rushing into Brooklyn, possibly into Manhattan itself before we had a chance to react. As it is, we have a chance. Not much of one, I'll grant you, but it's better than nothing.

"We don't have much but we have to try to stretch it. Time is our enemy as well as our ally. Every minute, even as we sit here, the cloud is creeping closer to Coney Island and closer to certain ignition. Once it is ignited, gentlemen, I can assure you that there is nothing we can do. The cloud will ignite, not only its entire length, but the ship as well.

"So, we must use the time we have to create more time. More time before the cloud warms enough to be ignited and finds its first spark or flame."

"Time for what, Miss Yale?" the mayor asked. "You keep talking about time, yet you've said there isn't anything we can do to stop the cloud, so what's the use?"

"To save lives, Mr. Mayor. Millions of lives. It's true there isn't anything we can do to control the gas that's already been released, but that doesn't mean that we can't move the LNG that's still on board the *Prometheus*. It's more than four times as much gas as in the cloud. If it gets released, the damage will be four times as great, maybe more. So we have to try to tow the tanker out of the harbor. Out to sea where the gas can't do any damage."

"How do you propose to do that, Miss Yale," Bassil asked. "The tanker's totally surrounded by the cloud. It would be suicide for any ship to venture in there. The engine would freeze if it didn't ignite the cloud first."

"Not if it were a rowboat, Captain. Not if the crew was wearing cryogenic suits. I suggest that we have a chance to tow the tanker out of the harbor before she explodes. All we need is a chance to tie a new tow rope on the tanker and then she can be pulled by tugs outside the cloud."

"Is that possible, Captain?" LaSalle leaned forward. "Can it be done?"

"Technically, I would say that it's possible. But practical? I'm not certain. The route out of Sandy Hook would take some time to navigate."

"About half an hour, Captain," Val said, speaking up for the first time. "It took us about half an hour to round Sandy Hook coming in. And that was at low speed, only five knots. With two tugs at full speed we should be able to go twice as fast. Of course, there'll be inertia since we're starting from a dead stop, so it'll take some time before we get up to full speed. Once we pass Sandy Hook we ought to be able to make ten knots. I'd say an extra half hour before she's five miles out to sea. That ought to be far enough."

"Barely," Cybil said. "Barely enough. Ten would be safer. The cloud that's approaching Brooklyn is already two miles long and will probably be twice that before it's ignited."

"All right," said the mayor. "How much time?"

"I'll let Captain Bassil answer that." Cybil deferred to the port captain.

"Well," Bassil examined the ceiling as he calculated the times and distances involved. "About half an hour to row in, fasten the line, and get back out again. Another half hour, no, say forty minutes, to pass Sandy Hook, and another half hour to get her out to sea. All told, about an hour and forty minutes."

"That settles that," the press secretary answered. "It'll reach Coney Island, long before that."

"Yes, and that's where the second part of the plan comes in. People are the most dangerous source of ignition. In a crowd of ten, four are likely to be smokers and almost certainly one of them will be smoking. All it takes is one cigarette, once the cloud reaches the proper concentrations, and then the entire cloud goes. People have to be moved out for at least the forty-five minutes or so that we need after the cloud touches Coney Island. You'll have to cut off all electricity and natural gas, of course. And ban the use of cars, trucks, or anything else that might create a spark. Even two-way radios could be dangerous. But we have to buy time. The longer the better, but we must have that forty-five minutes." She turned to look the mayor directly in the eye.

"Mr. Mayor, you have to order an immediate evacuation of the area."

"Impossible!" the police commissioner exploded. He had been so quiet that his presence had almost been forgotten. "I'm sorry, Mr. Mayor, but I can't allow this to go on. Any plan that calls for the evacuation of Coney Island is not only foolhardy but murder. You may know physics, Miss Yale, but you sure as hell don't know people. And you sure don't know New York. I do. That's my job, and I've been at it for over twenty years.

"You may be able to tell the captain here how to run his port, but you can't tell me how to run the streets of the city. If you try to evacuate Coney Island, thousands will die. There's over a million people packed shoulder to shoulder on that beach. If just one person starts running you'll have a riot on your hands in no time. Have you ever seen a panic? People smashed against fire doors, trampled to death because no one had the sense to push the handle. I've seen it happen. And I'm warning you that more people will die rushing the subways and stopping traffic than if you just let them stay there. Maybe we can move out those sections we can handle, the hospitals, summer schools, day care centers. Other large groups that are controllable. We should start that right away. But leave the crowds and the general public alone. Otherwise, mark my words, you'll have a massacre on your hands.

"And I want to remind you that this cloud may never make it to Coney Island. As you said, it's all a matter of wind direction. God knows that can change any second. We're just about due for a break in the weather. I say wait it out."

"Mr. Mayor, you can't." Cybil pleaded. "You can't wait. There isn't enough time. I need that forty-five minutes or else millions more will die. And as for panic, you have no idea how many people will die if that cloud reaches the beaches and there are still people there. That'll be panic. As soon as the cloud touches the first person, the entire beach will panic. You can't let it happen, Mr. Mayor!"

"Commissioner," the mayor's voice was, as always, calm. "Is there any chance you could control the panic? Any chance at all?"

"None. I'm not even certain I could get my men to go there, considering that they might not get back out again. I'm not sure I blame them either."

"If the people were told the truth about the cloud, they'd listen," Cybil persisted. "They'd follow instructions. Just tell the truth. There isn't any need for panic."

"Ha," the commissioner snorted. "I'm sorry, Miss Yale. You simply don't know what you're talking about. You look like a bright girl, but this isn't something you can think out. People aren't logical. If you yell 'fire' in a crowded theater the people will be too busy killing one another to get out to hear you explain that there's plenty of room at the exits. No, I'm afraid that you could never evacuate Coney Island in an hour. Not with the beaches packed as they are today. Never."

"I'm afraid you didn't understand me, Commissioner. I didn't mean Coney Island."

"Oh?"

"No, I meant all of Brooklyn. The path of the cloud continues into Brooklyn."

The commissioner sputtered. "Impossible." He slammed his fist on the table. "Absolutely impossible! This is utter insanity."

"I know it sounds crazy, but it must be done. You don't have to evacuate everything at once, only the area directly in front of the approaching cloud. And there wouldn't be that much of a need for transportation. The cloud is only coming in at about three miles an hour. It will slow down once it reaches land and the ocean breezes die down. Most people will be able to walk out unaided. Only the sick, the elderly, and the very young will need help. It can be done," she pleaded. "It must be done if we're to have a chance to tow the tanker out of the harbor."

The mayor was thoughtful for a moment.

"How about Coney Island? That seems to be the crux of the problem. If we could clear the beaches fast enough there might be a chance. Commissioner, what do you think?"

The police commissioner answered with one word, "Impossible."

"Chief?" He turned to the fire commissioner.

"Well, there are the subway lines at Coney Island. Most of the major lines terminate there. We could route extra trains there to take off some of the bathers. And, since we would have to shut off power and gas to Coney Island as soon as the cloud hit, that would limit the use of the subways through the rest of Brooklyn. I'd have to say, try it." He shrugged. "What can we lose?"

"Captain?" LaSalle asked.

"We might be able to tow the tanker out, if, as Miss Yale points out, we have time. We have extra cryogenic suits. I've already ordered them flown to the *Apple Tree.* I say, go ahead."

"Abe?"

Newfeld pushed back his chair and, sticking the cigar firmly in his mouth, stood up. He paced the room, his feet scraping deeply into the plush red carpet. He finally stopped behind the mayor's desk, staring out the window. LaSalle rose to join him.

"Abe, you know I trust your advice," LaSalle spoke quietly to his closest advisor. "I really need you on this one. I don't know, the police commissioner might be right. The wind could shift and the whole thing could blow out to sea. If it does and there's a panic, I'll be blamed for it. On the other hand, what if it comes in and I do nothing?"

Newfeld looked out the window. There was so much

green in the heart of Manhattan. The view of the Brooklyn Bridge was blocked by the aged arms of an elm tree. Dimly, he could hear the noise of the traffic as it fought to get off the bridge and onto the FDR Drive.

He spoke without turning away from the view. "Let's be honest with ourselves, Vince. This is a political question. How will the people, the voters, think you did in a tough situation? Let's face it. The campaign is on the verge of falling apart. We don't have any money and the governor does. Unless something happens, it'll all be over in three weeks. This could be a godsend." He pulled the cigar out of his mouth and rolled it in his fingers. "Or, it could be the end of your career."

Newfeld watched as a squirrel appeared on the casing of the air conditioner and calmly began to crack open a nut. He pointed to the squirrel. "First sign of fall."

"Abe."

"I know, Vince. I know. You want an answer. You don't have any choice. One thing everyone forgets to mention is that it's rush hour in another forty-five minutes. More than a million commuters are soon going to be shoving their way onto subways and fighting for lanes on the BQE. Unless you stop them. The people, God bless them, might, just might, be able to forgive you for letting those who are already in Coney Island die. But would they forgive you for letting those millions commute to their deaths? Never. No, Vince. In this case you don't have any choice. The way I see it, you've got to stop rush hour. And the only way to do that is to order the evacuation."

The squirrel finished his meal and stood on his hind legs staring at the two men behind the window. In a second, the tiny animal scampered away.

"You're right, Abe. As always."

3:50 P.M. *City Hall Rotunda*

"Come on, Abe, give us the word," one of the reporters shouted at Newfeld as he stepped out of the confines of the mayor's inner sanctum. Two burly policemen, backed by a waist-high iron fence, blocked the crowd of newsmen who strained to get close to the press secretary. He approached the barrier. Microphones were thrust at him, ready to record his every word. "No comment."

The groan was universal. Only the two policemen remained silent.

"Abe, you can't do that," one reporter shouted.

"What about that Coast Guard helicopter, Abe? What has that got to do with it?" another shouted. Abe didn't recognize the reporter. Must be from the *Post,* he thought, they change staff every two weeks.

"No comment. I said it and I meant it. There will be a press conference in a few minutes. All your questions will be answered then."

"Has it got anything to do with that ship that's on fire in the harbor," the latter reporter continued. "Is that why the Coast Guard was here?"

"Just wait for the press conference, boys. Until then," he looked at the persistent one, "no speculation. You'll only make yourself look stupid. Now excuse me." He turned to go to his office. "I have work to do." He disappeared down the marble-floored corridor and ducked into the back hallway that led to his office. He brushed past his secretary, signaling her to follow him in.

Ever efficient, she produced a list of phone calls and proceeded to read them as he walked in. "Commissioner Goldstein called. He wanted to know about finding those extra jobs for the Labor Day weekend. Commissioner . . ."

"Forget the calls. Drop everything. First get all the deputy mayors and tell them to be in the Blue Room right away. The mayor wants 'em all, fast. Get one of the other girls to help you make the calls. Then get me the manager of WNYC, whoever's in charge. I want him on the phone now. Then see if you can find out the number for the Civil Defense or whatever they call that thing where all the TV stations are taken over in case of emergency. I want him on the phone. After that get the heads of the stations, you know the list. Start with CBS and work your way through. I want only the managers. Use the private lines.

"Then get me the Brooklyn borough president, the chairman of the M.T.A., Con Edison, and Brooklyn Union Gas, for starters. Get extra help if you need it, but don't let those reporters hear any of the calls. And no incoming calls until I'm done."

"Yes, sir."

In a second he was alone. His phone began to light up as calls were made. This was the quiet before the storm, he thought, as he reached for the bottle of Excedrin he kept for emergencies. He snapped open the bottle and popped the pills into his mouth as if they were candy. Later he would need to do the same with an equal number of Tums, but he'd wait until his ulcer started acting up before reaching for them.

The phone buzzed. He snapped it up. "Yes."

"WNYC on fourteen, sir."

He pressed down the appropriate button. "This is Abe Newfeld, who's this?" he demanded.

"Robert Cronin, WNYC general manager. What can I do . . ."

"Plenty." The image of a thin, weasel-faced man flashed into Newfeld's mind. "Cronin, we met at Gracie Mansion the other week, didn't we?"

"Yes. It was to celebrate the start of a new series of radio shows I'm producing." The pleasure at being remembered was obvious in his voice. The station manager would now do anything Newfeld asked.

"Right. Listen, Cronin. I can't explain now, but I want you to get a camera and a crew over here right away. Say, is that live camera still on the second floor?"

"Yes, we were planning to shoot some background tomorrow for . . ."

"Never mind that now, Cronin. Just get that crew over here right away. The mayor's going to appear live on the emergency network in about five minutes. Less if you can get your crew over here sooner. Be ready to take whatever you have on the air off as soon as I give you the word."

"But . . ."

"No buts, Cronin. Just get that crew over here fast." The phone buzzed. Newfeld switched to the intercom, cutting off the confused Cronin in mid-protest.

"Yes?"

"The manager of the Emergency Broadcast System on fifteen."

Newfeld switched lines again. "Abe Newfeld here, who's this?"

"Gerald Miller."

"Gerry, listen, I don't think we've met, but I've got a favor to ask. I need your system. The mayor's about to make an important announcement and it must be on all the networks at the same time. Only you have the hardware to do that."

"I'm sorry, but that's out of the question. The EBS is only to be used in case of a state of emergency."

"That's what it is, Gerry. I just left the mayor not two minutes ago and we've got one hell of an emergency."

"You sure that this isn't some kind of a publicity stunt?" Miller's voice was tainted with disbelief. "I know that LaSalle's running for governor and . . ."

"Damnit, I wish it was. No, this is a real emergency."

"Can you get that to me in writing?"

"Gerry," Newfeld said very slowly, "if there was time to give it to you in writing I wouldn't need to use your system."

"No, that's true," Miller admitted. "Well, I guess it'll be all right if you confirm it in writing. But I don't see how I can help. We're only set to take signals from Washington, not from City Hall."

"WNYC has a live camera here and will be doing the shooting. Can you take their signal?"

"I guess so," Miller stammered. "It's never been done before, but I don't see why not. All we have to do is hook up the . . ."

"Listen, Gerry, call Bob Cronin over at WNYC and work out the details. Okay?"

"All right. You'll have that confirmation over to me . . ."

"Sure, first thing in the morning. Thanks, Gerry." Newfeld switched lines, catching his secretary on the intercom before she could buzz him. "Yes?"

"CBS on twelve."

"Good. Keep them coming. It shouldn't take more than a minute for each."

"Yes, sir. There's a cameraman from WNYC at the security desk. He says you called and told him to come over. The guard wants your okay to let him in. I said it was all right."

"Good girl. You did just fine. I owe you a steak dinner when this is over." He switched to twelve. "Sid? This is Abe. I gotta big one to ask . . ."

3:55 P.M.   *Mayor's Office; City Hall*

This was his time to think. To decide what to say. La-Salle, like most veteran politicians, spoke best without a prepared speech. Someone else's words, no matter how skillfully written, could never convey the spontaneousness or the sincerity of an off-the-cuff speech. Vince LaSalle was one of the best, having talked his way through four years of the City Council and six years in Congress.

But never before had he had such a speech to make. He had talked about strikes, about budgets, about education and civil rights. Now he was talking about life and death. He nervously rubbed his palms together. They had left stains on the trouser legs of his suit. He couldn't remember ever being this scared before.

LaSalle forced himself to relax, closing his eyes and leaning back in his chair. To an outside observer, he appeared almost asleep.

The door opened a crack. Even though the movement of the door was almost totally noiseless, LaSalle's eyes instantly flew open. "Yes, Abe. Come in."

Newfeld closed the door behind him. "Everything's set. I've already talked to the deputy mayors. Camera's all ready to go in the board chambers. I've got it fixed so that you'll go out live to all the stations, radio and TV."

"Good. I knew you'd take care of everything. Abe, have a seat, let's talk for a second." He looked at his watch. "We have time, don't we?"

"Sure, Vince. The station won't be ready to carry you until three thirty sharp. So we got a minute before we have to go. You wanna talk about what you're goin' to say? You know better than me that you don't need a speech writer. You're the best . . ."

"No," LaSalle dismissed that with a wave of his hand. "No. Once the lights go on, I'll be fine. It's just a nagging feeling I have that the police commissioner might be right. You know I hate that old bastard, but he usually is right. I hate to go against him."

"Vince." Newfeld pulled out a fresh cigar and slowly unwrapped the cellophane. The rich aroma of tobacco filled the room. "Like I said, you don't have a choice."

"I know politically I don't have one, but for once, just

once, I really wonder whether there is something other than politics that we should consider."

"Like what, for instance? Like what's best for the people? For Christ's sake, Vince, that's politics. Like what's going to make you look good in tomorrow's papers? That's politics. Like what's going to save the most number of lives? Hell, that's politics. It's all politics, Vince. That's what the whole thing's about.

"Let me tell you something." Newfeld pulled his chair closer to LaSalle. "Politics is more than life to me. I've spent my entire life being a politician. Even during the dark days when Vietnam and Watergate made politics a dirty word, I was still proud to be a politician. Why? Because it meant that I was one of the ones who was willing to do something. Maybe I didn't always make the right decisions, and if I had it to do all over again, I probably would have made a few different decisions. But I still would have done something. I wouldn't have sat around on my ass crying into my beer in some bar that it was those dumb politicians' fault.

"And that's the difference between people like us and people like everybody else. We're ultimately ready to do something. Not to let everything just happen. Now take this poison cloud. We could sit back and hope it drifts out to sea. That's the safe thing, maybe, if you don't think like a politician. But you and me, we got to try. We've got to do something, even if it's wrong, at least it's something.

"In politics, inaction is death. And in this case, I think it's right. What else could you do? Let the cloud come in and kill a million unsuspecting kids and their mothers without giving them a chance? What would you tell their families—'At least they didn't die in a panic'? No, like I said, everything is political. You don't have any choice."

There was a discreet knock on the door. Phyllis stuck her head in. "Mr. Newfeld, you told me to interrupt at fifty-eight after."

"Thank you, Phyllis." She gave them a smile as she closed the door.

LaSalle rose from his chair. "Thanks, Abe."

Newfeld just grunted, sticking the cigar back in his mouth. "Your suit's all wrinkled. Wish we had enough time to get you a clean shirt, but it'll have to do." He straightened LaSalle's tie, stepped back to inspect his handiwork and then returned to nudge it an imperceptible fraction of an inch in the other direction. That seemed to satisfy him. "There. It'll do."

LaSalle led the way up the back stairs to the Board of Estimate chambers. The police guards respectfully opened the series of gates and doors before the mayor reached them. A technician pinned a mike to his tie, carefully concealing the wire under the mayor's coat.

He sat in his regular seat, in the center of the horse-shoe table that dominated the room. The chamber itself was reassuring. It was the scene of his greatest political victories. The smell of oak and leather was comforting. He was at home.

The garish green light of the television camera came on, momentarily blinding him. LaSalle spread his hands out on the smooth surface of the desk, steadying himself while his eyes adjusted. Dimly over the glare of the light he could see the cameraman focusing on him. The sound-man, his face partially hidden behind the earphones, adjusted the volume meters.

The calm professional voice of an unseen director called out to the mayor. "Ten seconds. Nine. Eight . . ."

LaSalle cleared his throat. His hands were totally dry.

"Two seconds. One. You're on."

LaSalle looked directly into the lens of the camera. "My fellow New Yorkers. Today is a day of crisis and courage. The crisis affects all of us. And each of us must find that courage within ourselves that will allow us to deal with this crisis. Today at about two-forty, a ship carrying . . ."

In all, the announcement took slightly over five minutes. Within seconds of his opening remarks, national news directors for the networks cut regular programs to cover LaSalle live. By 4:05 P.M. Vincent LaSalle was talking to the entire nation.

His speech would later be praised as one of the turning points in the crisis. He would be held singly responsible for preventing panic on the beaches and highways of New York. The speech would be compared to Churchill's "Finest Hour" speech of World War II. LaSalle would remember none of it.

Abruptly the light clicked off and LaSalle's face was bathed in darkness. He was momentarily blinded as his eyes fought to adjust. His hands, his entire body, was soaked with perspiration. His knees wobbled as he stood up, removing the mike with numb fingers.

The applause was scattered at first, then rose in volume until the entire room was filled with it. He looked out, seeing for the first time the City Hall staff filling the spectator seats. Even the camera crew joined in.

LaSalle smiled and shouted to his assembled staff. "Well, come on. We've got a lot of work to do. Don't just sit there. Get to work."

They did.

Chapter 9

4:00 P.M.   On the Boardwalk; Coney Island

"Rebecca?"

"Yes, Sadie. I was listening. So tell me, how is your daughter?" Rebecca's voice was barely a whisper.

Sadie looked at her friend, worry wrinkles creasing her forehead. Rebecca had been dozing uneasily for the past hour, resting heavily on her neighbor's shoulder. Sadie had tried to rouse her several times, but she had merely stirred in her uneasy sleep. Sadie had thought of calling for an ambulance, thinking that her friend had had a heart attack, but each time Rebecca's labored but steady breathing had stopped her.

"She's fine, Rebecca. Just fine." Sadie patted her hand, the dry leathery skin warm under her fingers. She had stopped talking about her daughter almost an hour before.

"Good." Rebecca leaned against her friend. "It's good to have family. You know, Sadie, you're the only family I got."

Sadie looked out at the crowd helplessly. She couldn't leave her friend, but she was certain that she needed help. If only she could find a policeman.

But the beach was packed with oiled, half-naked

bodies. There was a group of teen-agers, their Budweiser towel spread right in front of her bench, but they were too engrossed in a card game to notice her plight. Even if she shouted they probably wouldn't hear her over the blare of the radio.

Everywhere there was sound, music, and activity. No one had a passing glance for the two old women sitting together on a bench on the boardwalk.

Then it happened.

The music stopped. All at once the drums, guitars, and bass voices of announcers ceased. The cacophony of different radio stations, each playing its own brand of music, blended into one voice repeated thousands of times on the radios dotting the beach. Records, even commercials, were cut off in midsentence. There was little or no preamble to the transition.

"Ladies and gentlemen. Mayor Vincent LaSalle."

All activity ground to a halt. Everyone listened.

The mayor's voice with its distinctive nasal **Brooklyn** accent boomed out over the beach, carried by a thousand radios. It came from everywhere, seemingly having no source. It was like the voice of God.

When the mayor finished, the stations returned one by one. None of the announcers could match the intensity of the mayor. Few tried. Most reacted like the average listener. Shock. Years of training were forgotten as they repeated the mayor's call for calm. Surprisingly, the people obeyed.

There was no panic, only haste, as the throngs wrapped up their towels and gathered in their picnic baskets, abandoning bulky umbrellas and other weighty objects they couldn't carry. Even the children obeyed docilely. The beach mobilized itself like a well-trained army, ready to move in minutes.

The evacuation had a momentum of its own. As one family moved toward the exits, three others started. As one umbrella was left standing in the sand, mothers stopped struggling with theirs. Soon a trickle of families became a downpour. Then a deluge. Finally a flood. The crowd moved as one organism with a single goal, the subway entrances only a block away.

Sadie watched the crowd flow toward her like an incoming tide. They swarmed up the stairs that raised the boardwalk a few feet above the sand and poured down the other side, taking the shortest routes for the subway. She tried to stop some of the passing crowd, asking them to help her friend, but her old hands were quickly shrugged off as the people hurried toward safety.

Her cries for help were swallowed by the noise of the crowd. It was a medley of sound: a rich mixture of Spanish, English, and other foreign languages assailed her senses; isolated her from the real world. She was the observer; the actors flowed past. A river of ants, not to be turned aside by any obstacle, human or otherwise.

Down the boardwalk, she could see that the famous Cyclone had stopped. The racket of the cars racing along the tiny track at breakneck speeds to the accompanying screams of terrified girls was silenced. The park was strangely quiet.

In the distance there were occasional sounds of sirens and horns as cars fought for entrances to the narrow roadways of Coney Island. The rumble of the subways and the high-pitched squeal of wheels as they rounded a turn came faintly to the boardwalk.

The faces of the people reflected fear, Sadie thought, as she tried vainly to attract someone to her plight. Adults gripped their children in visibly painful grasps, afraid to let them squirm away in the crowd.

Only the two old women were motionless. Sadie tried to awaken Rebecca, but her eyes refused to do more than flutter. There was no choice but to leave her, or stay, hoping someone would come along.

The raging river thinned to a stream and then to a trickle. A last teen-ager, his arms encumbered with various trophies scavenged from the abandoned blankets, rushed past, and then they were alone. Only the waves moved, crashing gently into the sand, sliding away to reform and crash again.

Sadie had no way of telling how much later Rebecca had the heart attack. One moment all was calm, the next Rebecca began to gasp. Her fingers dug painfully into Sadie's thin arm. Rebecca's eyes stared wide as the pain swept through her, curving through her arm and exploding in her chest. She uttered a small cry from between clenched teeth and tears ran from her eyes as she threw her body across the bench in an effort to escape the unendurable pain.

As suddenly as it began, it was over. The pressure eased as the tight band of pain surrounding her heart loosened. She sucked in a ragged gasp of air. Breathing was torture. She stayed doubled over, her head cradled in Sadie's lap as she fought for air. She could only manage small gasps, each a little deeper than the last. She clutched her friend for support, trying to drag herself erect. Each breath was a sob.

"Rebecca! Rebecca, are you all right?" Sadie shouted. Rebecca didn't answer. All her strength was focused on fighting for the next breath.

"Don't try to talk, Rebecca. Don't worry. I'll get help." Sadie tried to pry her arm loose from the clutching fingers, but they were too strong.

Rebecca shook her head. "No!" she finally managed to gasp, her voice barely a whisper. "Don't leave me! Don't go." She clutched her friend with the strength born of fear and desperation. Purplish bruises began to form under her fingers. "Stay!" It was a prayer.

"All right, Rebecca. I'll stay." She stroked the gray hair, wiping it away from her face where the perspiration had plastered it to the wrinkled brow. "I'll stay."

The pressure in the fingers immediately eased. Rebecca's breathing became easier and she relaxed, laying her head in her friend's lap. She closed her eyes, her body craving rest.

"I'll stay," Sadie crooned, gently stroking the old woman's hair.

Out at sea, Sadie could see the gray wall of pollution hanging over the harbor. Everything looked the same as it had every other day they had shared that bench, Sadie thought. Except for the people. "I'll stay, Rebecca," Sadie whispered. "I'll stay."

Rebecca was already asleep.

4:15 P.M.   *Jay Street; IND Station*

With a squeal of brakes and a rattle of loose fittings the aging train rounded the hairpin curve leading into Borough Hall station. The train bucked as Elliot Faust brought it to a screeching halt in front of the platform.

Empty trains were always louder than full ones. A drum effect, he thought, as he edged up to the white marker with a number 10 mostly obscured by years of accumulated dirt and grime. He eased the pressure off the brake and heard the train give a grateful sigh.

Diaz, the conductor, dressed in his regulation blue uniform, sat on the two-seat bench next to the driver's compartment. He was small, only about five foot three, needing a shave and reeking subtly of last night's wine. He smoked an acrid cigar, calmly blowing the smoke toward the center of the car. He tried unsuccessfully to make smoke rings.

"You know, *amigo*," Diaz puffed his cigar, "you're crazy if you do it. Me, I look out for number one. Besides, I got a wife and three kids. If you want my advice . . ."

"I didn't say I was going, Diaz," Faust replied. "I just said you can get off here if you want to. I've just not decided yet." Faust couldn't stand the conductor. They had been doing runs together, off and on, for the past two years and he couldn't remember once when the smaller man wasn't bitching about something. He rubbed Faust the wrong way.

Faust towered over the conductor, his six-foot-three frame looking even larger as he loomed in the small doorway of the driver's booth. The deep blackness of his skin and his massive girth made him look like a Kodiak bear emerging from his cave. Even his voice sounded like a growl. He wrapped one of his huge hands around the doorjamb, bracing himself against the metal door.

"Well, *amigo*. Good luck. You wanna kill yourself, don't let me stop you." The Hispanic took a large key off his belt, inserted it in a slot next to the door and turned it. The door slid open with a gentle hiss. "Far as I'm concerned, the mayor can go stuff it. I'm not dying for nobody. I'd have thought you'd have gotten your belly full of that over in Nam. Me, I quit." He tossed his cap onto the seat. "If you're smart, you'll do the same." With that he scampered out the door and headed for the exit.

Faust watched him go, filled with conflicting reactions. Part of him agreed with the departing conductor. Another part of him, a part he had thought dead ever since his return from Vietnam, despised the man as a coward.

"Faust? Faust, why have you stopped?" The speaker blared into life, echoing in the tiny trainman's compartment. "You heard the order, Faust. No stops. Express to Coney Island."

Faust hit the speak button. "You gotta be crazy. Or think I am. I can't make it in twenty minutes. It's a suicide run." With Diaz gone he let his true feelings out.

"You can do it, Faust. The boys at Central have run it through the computer and say that you can make it with time to spare. The track's all cleared. No delays. It'll be green all the way." Faust could hear the doubt in the dispatcher's voice. He didn't think Faust could make it either.

"If the boys over at Central think they can make it to Coney Island in twenty minutes, let them drive it. I'm not." Just fifteen minutes ago Faust had been pulling a full train into Broadway Lafayette, the last stop in Manhattan, when the order came in to drop all his passengers and pull the train out of service. He was instructed to head for Brooklyn. The track in front of him was clear. Green all the way. That in itself was strange. It was almost rush hour. Trains were always backed up by this time, yet he hadn't run into one yellow light all the way to Brooklyn.

Of course, all became clear when they heard the radio announcement as they crossed the tunnel. It was the first time that Faust had ever appreciated Diaz's habit of bringing his radio with him on the job. They listened and realized together that they were being sent to Coney Island. Where the mayor had said the cloud was coming. Diaz immediately had said, "Let me off at the first station. I'll walk home."

In front of the train, Faust could see the first three of a series of green lights that meant a clear track ahead. Maybe he could make it. On the other hand . . .

"You the last train?"

Faust looked around. A young transit cop stood in the open door. In his uniform he looked older, but Faust had spent enough years in the service to be able to tell. He was less than twenty-five.

"Nah," Faust answered, casually spreading his legs before him in the aisle. What could the cop do to him?

Threaten to shoot him if he didn't take the train? Besides, it would be good to have a tangible opponent for once.

"You mean there's another one behind you. Funny, they told me you were the last train."

"Well, they were wrong. The last train left some time ago. This one ain't goin' nowhere. Not," he added, "not with me at the controls, that is."

The kid in the uniform was obviously confused. "But I thought they said that you could make it to Coney Island before the gas does. That's what they said. I'm sure. And there's people down there that's waiting for this train. Maybe they'll die if it doesn't come." The young cop sounded as though he put civilian lives before his own. Faust decided that he could not have been on the job very long and reassessed his age downward accordingly.

"Look, kid." Faust moved out of his lair. "You got a lot to learn. So what if there's people waiting? They'll either make it on their own or they won't. What's it to me? You have to look out for yourself in this world, you know." Somehow that had a familiar ring to it. Faust's mouth went dry.

"Faust?" The loudspeaker in the driver's booth squawked. "Faust, you still there?"

Faust pulled out a pack of cigarettes and took one. He extended the pack to the cop. He shook his head. "Aren't you going to answer that? Isn't that for you?"

"Nah. It's for some guy that left. They thought he was going to take the train to Coney Island. Musta been crazy to think that."

"Faust, I know you can hear me," the radio continued. "You've got only another two minutes. Then it'll be too late. You'll have used up the margin. Faust, answer me, goddamnit. Answer me."

Faust took another drag on his cigarette.

"Okay" the loudspeaker continued. "If you won't answer, at least listen. They think they can give you some extra time. Don't ask me how, it's something about a staged shut-off. About turning the power off sequentially, rather than all at once. They say that they might be able to squeeze out another ten, maybe fifteen minutes. Maybe more, depending on the exact speed of the cloud. Faust! Are you listening? For Christ's sake, Faust, answer me."

The black man extended one arm and covered the

speak button. "Okay, okay. Don't bust a gut. Like I said before. I ain't buying it. You want this train to run, you come here and do it yourself. Me, I'm walking."

"Thank God, you're still there, Faust." The relief was evident in the dispatcher's voice. "I was afraid you might have gone."

"I'm on my way. Diaz already split and I'm not going to be far behind."

"That the guy I saw running up the stairs?" the T.A. cop asked.

"Yeah. I guess that was Diaz. He was my conductor. So it doesn't matter much anyway. I couldn't go if I wanted to. Can't run the train and the doors too, you know. Not on this run."

"I could do it," the cop volunteered, his voice sounding younger all the time. Maybe twenty-one, Faust estimated. "If you told me what to do."

"Who asked ya?" Faust snapped. "I don't need you. Or a conductor. Or a train. 'Cause I'm not going. I'll tell you where I'm going. Home. That's where. Home to watch this on the six o'clock news. With a cold can of beer in my hand."

Faust paused, listening to the mental echo of his last words. Christ, he sounded like Diaz. Or like some of the chicken-shit lieutenants he had met over in Nam. He looked at the young face of the T.A. cop. He looked about as old as Faust was when he shipped out at nineteen.

"But you can't . . . you just can't walk away and leave those people to die. You can't."

The worst part was that he was right, Faust realized. He couldn't blame anybody for running to save his own life, but living with yourself afterward was a different matter. Faust had never deserted one of his men in the field or in a brawl. He couldn't live out his life thinking he was no better than Diaz.

"All right, hero." Faust stepped over and twisted the key left behind by Diaz. The door almost slid smoothly shut.

The cop jumped as the door almost closed on him. He paled noticeably as Faust accelerated. They screeched around the exit turn and immediately began picking up speed. The wind blew through the car from the open driver's window, making normal speech impossible seconds after they started.

"Faust," shouted the radio. "Faust. Is that you?"

"Who the fuck did you think it was? Santa Claus? Course it's me. It's my train, isn't it? Now, shut up and listen. I'll keep going south as long as I keep seeing green in front of me. Got that? Green. All the way. First yellow and I'm throwing her into reverse and I'll back all the way to Manhattan."

"Sure, Faust. I got it. Green all the way to Coney Island. Track's all cleared for you." The dispatcher's voice was relieved

"Good." Faust looked ahead. The dark of the tunnel was empty except for the reassuring pattern of green that stretched out straight ahead. He applied a little more throttle. The train rumbled louder in response.

He turned to the young cop. "Okay, hero, watch me. 'Cause I'm going to give you a short course in driving as well as door tending. You're going to do both. So watch close. You won't have time to make mistakes on this run."

Ahead a seemingly endless string of the green lights led them through the underground heart of Brooklyn.

The train rattled and shook as she raced at full speed toward Coney Island.

4:15 P.M. In a Car; En Route to Coney Island

The tires screamed their protest as the car swerved onto Ocean Parkway. Melba York fought the wheel, trying to control the skid. She overcompensated and the car fishtailed, almost side-swiping a parked van. The flashing red light of a police car appeared momentarily in her rearview mirror, then turned north, dwindling into the distance. Melba accelerated into the empty street.

She was getting into familiar territory now. There was the park she and Judith would walk to on warm summer evenings. There, the music store where she bought Judith her first violin. "God," Melba whispered over and over again. "Let her be all right. Please, God, just let her be all right." She slammed on the brakes, locking the already overheated wheels as a mother led her three small children across the street directly in front of the speeding car. The terrified mother barely gave Melba a glance as she hurried her children toward the subway entrance on the other sidewalk.

Melba rested her head against the steering wheel and sobbed. If it hadn't been for the official city seal emblazoned on the car's doors, she would never have made it this far. She had bluffed her way through one roadblock, and two patrol cars that had pulled after her had backed off when she pointed to the seal and shouted, "Official business." With a wave and a nod they let her pass. There was surprisingly little formal challenge as the car sped southward. Who in his right mind would want to head south?

Twenty minutes ago Melba York had been sitting at her desk in the Brooklyn borough president's office. As the president's private secretary, she was, as always, swamped with phone calls from community leaders and lobbyists seeking favors. In three years at the office, Melba had learned to distrust them all. She had heard enough private promises refuted in the following day's papers to become the world's greatest cynic. Today there had been a sit-in from the South Brooklyn Community Association, protesting that they hadn't been given their fair share of federal grants. Three of the demonstrators were under indictment for tax evasion. They were noisier than most, but all in all, it had been a normal day in the borough president's office.

Until the call came from Newfeld.

Melba had committed the cardinal sin of eavesdropping. Her boss had taken the call at Melba's desk. She tried not to listen but the few muttered exclamations drew her attention. Then the borough president said, "Coney Island! My God!"

That made it personal. Melba lived in the heart of Coney Island and her fifteen-year-old daughter, Judith, was at home. Alone. She froze in the act of pouring herself another cup of coffee. The entire conversation lasted less than a minute, but Melba heard enough to know that she had to go home. She had to find Judith.

Judith couldn't take care of herself. She was blind.

Without saying a word to anyone, Melba grabbed her purse and took the extra set of keys for the borough president's car out of the file cabinet.

She would get fired for this, she knew. But she didn't

care. Judith was worth more to her than her job, more than life itself. She was her whole world. Judith was the last remnant of her husband, the only man she had ever loved. He had been killed seven years before, while covering a story on student riots in Africa. He was the "best black reporter" *The Times* had, according to the obituary, "with a bright future cut off by an act of criminal terrorism."

Judith was in the car when Melba ran it off the road as she raced to Kennedy Airport to catch the last plane to Johannesburg. Melba walked away from the flaming wreck with a few scratches. Judith was blinded for life. The fact that her husband had died instantaneously hadn't made Judith's injury any easier to accept.

Melba had dedicated her life to her blind daughter, trying in every way to make up for her loss of sight. For her part, Judith adjusted to her darkened life with few of the traumas that an adult would have. She loved music and could often be found sitting on their balcony playing her violin.

Melba raised her head from the steering wheel and pushed the accelerator to the floor. No response. The car had died.

Grabbing her purse, she abandoned the car in the center of the street. She could pick it up later.

On the next block she ran into the first wave of the beach crowd. They were carrying their towels, portable radios, and, occasionally, children. Most of them were young, too impatient to wait for the trains, too proud to run, walking defiantly up the center of Ocean Avenue. Melba would have been stopped by them anyway, she realized, as she pushed through the beginnings of the crowd, the only one heading toward the beach.

The people, even the normally cocky teen-agers, were friendly. It was a party to them. It reminded her of the first blackout when everyone had helped their neighbors. Then she remembered the second blackout. She hurried onward, pushing when people were slow to move out of her way.

Sirens filled the air as police cars came to direct the crowd. Melba fought her way to the edge of the mob and broke free of the restraining hands and bodies that blocked her path. In the distance she could hear the police cars' P.A. systems warning people to leave their homes. As the evacuation became more organized, she was the only one heading south.

Finally she reached her apartment building. Anxiously, she shaded her eyes and scanned the side of the building, automatically seeking out her balcony. She found it. The potted palm that she and Judith had grown from a coconut hung limply in the humid air. Nothing else moved on the balcony. No Judith.

She hurried toward the front door of the building, fighting her way past the familiar yet unknown faces of her neighbors. She passed the reassuring sign, WELCOME TO CONEY ISLAND VILLAGE, that had less cordial remarks scribbled on it in red spray paint.

The security door had been left ajar by the departing tenants, a gross violation of the normal safety procedures of the village. The open door disturbed Melba. It was as though the tenants weren't expecting to return. She closed the door, listening to the reassuring click as the lock snapped home.

She ran to the elevator and paced nervously, unable to contain her impatience as it ascended slowly to the twelfth floor. Finally, the doors opened and Melba raced down the corridor toward her apartment.

Sobbing, she unlocked the double locks on her door. "Judith! It's Mommy. Honey, I'm home!" She threw open the door.

The living room was empty. "Judith!" Melba called again, rushing to her daughter's bedroom. "Honey, we have to go. There's not much time. Judith?" The bedroom was empty. The violin case was gone.

"Judith?" Frantically Melba ran from room to room, throwing the doors open, looking for the familiar figure of her daughter. She had to be there somewhere. She never left the apartment without her mother. She had to be there.

Melba found herself alone on the tiny balcony, looking out across the teeming crowd as they streamed north. There were so many people. And Judith was so helpless. In desperation, Melba found herself crying her daughter's name across the courtyard to the crowd. A few faces looked up, but no one answered.

"Judith!"

4:25 P.M. *In a Rowboat; Lower Bay*

The regular creak, splash, creak of the oars was hypnotic. The sun glinted off the water, casting a shadowless white glare over everything it touched. The waves lapped gently against the bow of the small skiff. It was an idyllic scene, fit for a calm Sunday afternoon in Central Park.

Cybil sat in the bow, her back to the two men as they rowed. She cared little for the beauty of the moment. She was only faintly aware of the sounds of the boat; the constant hiss from her air regulator blended mesmerically into the surroundings. It would have been easy to fall asleep, Cybil realized, as her body automatically responded to the elemental motions of the sea. Only her nerves kept her alert as she scanned the surface of the water for some sign of the floating tow ropes. So far, nothing.

Cybil could see only a few hundred feet before her vision was abruptly cut off by the white veil perched on the water. Some invisible force of nature seemed to hold the cloud together, preventing it from mingling with the clear air. The *Prometheus* was totally obscured.

"See anything?" Commander Wade asked as he pulled an oar through the water.

"Not yet," Cybil called over her shoulder.

"You sure that this skiff won't come apart the way that lifeboat did?" Val asked.

"I don't think so," Cybil responded. "That life boat was aluminum and it contracted immediately upon exposure to the cryogenic temperatures of the cloud. The aluminum struts and braces, although thicker, also contracted. In fact, because the aluminum skin was pulled so tightly against the braces, the boat was even stronger than it would normally have been at ambient temperatures."

"Then why did it disintegrate?" Wade asked.

"The strengthened condition lasted only as long as the boat remained at the same temperature as the cloud, minus two hundred sixty degrees. As soon as the aluminum skin touched water, it warmed to the temperature of the bay, about sixty degrees above zero, and it expanded. The braces, however, were still in contact with the cryogenic atmosphere of the cloud. The rivets, which fastened

147

the skin to the braces, were caught in the middle of a three-hundred-degree temperature differential. They couldn't take the strain and simply popped out of their holes, and the boat fell apart immediately.

"However," Cybil continued, "this skiff shouldn't give us any problems because it's held together by pressure from swelling wood, not aluminum bolts. Seasoned wood doesn't contract when exposed to cold. Besides, we won't be staying in the cloud that long. Ten to fifteen minutes at the most. We don't have air for much longer than that.

"The cloud should only be a few hundred feet thick on this upwind side, judging from the view from the helicopter. We should be able to reach the *Prometheus* a few minutes after we enter the cloud. If you two row hard, that is."

"You ever try rowing in one of these suits?" Val asked.

"Nope," she answered with a lightheartedness she didn't feel. "And I intend to keep it that way. I'm the brains of this team, remember. You're the brawn."

"Yes, ma'am." Val grunted as he pulled against his oar. "Anything you say, ma'am."

"I don't think this is exactly the right time for jokes, you two," Wade snapped.

They lapsed into silence. Only the regular splash of the oars broke the stillness. Cybil became increasingly apprehensive as they neared the cloud. Each stroke forced the skiff closer. She felt a cold lump rise in her stomach, threatening to choke her. She wasn't afraid of the cloud, but of what lay within. She hadn't told anyone, not even Val, about her fears. As a scientist she had to be certain before sounding the alarm.

She remembered the shape of the cloud as the helicopter flew them to the *Apple Tree* earlier. It was thin. Too thin for its length. Somewhere on the *Prometheus* something was happening. Something unexpected. Something dangerous.

The cloud wasn't large enough. Width was determined by volume of gas released; length, by wind velocity. The shape of the cloud showed that not all of the LNG was vaporizing. That meant that something was keeping the LNG cold. Since the refrigerators were shut off, there could only be one other answer. One she refused to think about.

There is one unbreakable rule of thermodynamics: energy is never destroyed. Temperature is one form of energy. It can be transmuted into other forms, kinetic or chemical, for example, but it must be conserved. The total of all the energy must remain constant. On the *Prometheus*, however, this apparently was not so. That meant that the millions of calories of heat were being absorbed.

She didn't know why or how, but she knew where. Hold number two held the answer and she was determined to get it.

"Hold it," Cybil called. "I think I see something."

They rested their oars and turned around to look.

"There." She pointed. "To the right."

Rising out of the fog like the sheer side of a mountain, it was a cliff that disappeared into the mist above. A dark brooding presence in the pristine white cloud.

They paddled to the side of the tanker. It proved to be only a few strokes away.

"Commander," Val instructed, "use your oar to keep us from hitting the hull. I don't know how much strain this skiff can take at these temperatures. I don't want to have another one fall apart under me."

"That goes double for me," Cybil said from the bow.

The skiff lurched suddenly. Cybil was thrown from her seat, regaining her balance as she leaned precariously over the bow. Her hand splashed into the water.

"What is it?" Paknis called, concern in his voice. "Are you all right?"

"We hit something," Cybil muttered, as she pulled herself back to her seat. She cautiously inspected the forearms of her suit. Even the slightest tear could mean death in this atmosphere, either from cold or asphyxiation. "I . . . I'm okay."

Once she was satisfied that her suit had no visible damage, her scientific curiosity took over. Dangling over the edge she searched the waters with one gloved hand. "I wonder what we hit?" she murmured as she fished a frozen block of ice out of the water. "Whatever it is, it's pretty big." Her hands slid across the slick surface.

"Professor, I don't think we have time . . ." Wade began.

"Of course, Commander. Of course. This will only take

a second." She pulled the object into the boat. "Help me with this, will you Val?"

At first glance, it looked like a massive snake encased in ice. It was about five feet long and as thick as a man's waist. It landed in the bottom of the skiff with a heavy plop.

"What is it?" Wade asked, slightly repulsed by the alien object.

"The towline," Cybil answered. She began chipping the ice away and the familiar outline of the four-inch hawser emerged. She leaned closer to examine the exposed hemp.

"What is it, Cybil?" Paknis asked.

"There's something . . ." A section of the hemp suddenly broke off in her fingers. As the two men watched in amazement, the hemp disintegrated between her fingers.

"But that line was in perfect condition," Paknis protested. "I inspected it myself."

"I'm sure it was, Val," Cybil agreed, "when you inspected it. But since then it's been floating in this cryogenic cloud."

"I thought that hemp was supposed to be pretty immune to the cold," Wade said.

"It is, Commander," Cybil agreed. "But that's under laboratory conditions. Who know's what the action of the sea and the cold can do to any material." She held up another piece of the hemp and watched it disintegrate as the first one had done. "I'd say that it might be due to the oil and other impurities that were absorbed into the fibers. When exposed to the cold, the impurities froze and the fibers were caught next to the hard crystals. They probably rubbed against the fibers until there was nothing left."

They watched the last yellow strands of hemp fall gently to the bottom of the skiff.

"What about our line?" Paknis asked, pointing to the thin lead line that trailed the boat. It led to the *Apple Tree,* where a four-inch hemp hawser waited to be drawn to the *Prometheus.* "Will the same thing happen to that?"

"I wish I could answer that. I honestly don't know. It will be exposed to the cold for a much shorter period of time than this line was. And it is a new line, isn't it, Commander?"

He nodded.

"Perhaps it will hold. All we can do is hope."

Silently, they secured the skiff and proceeded to the Jacob's ladder. Val and Wade started up the ladder carrying the lead line. Cybil followed them onto the deck of the *Prometheus*.

It was just as she remembered it. The frosty white. The stillness. The white silence. Death lingering on top of the bridge. Her eyes stung as she remembered the gentle captain laying his head in her lap.

Val saw a completely different vision of the ship than he ever had before. The years he had sailed on her, walking this same deck in the calm of an evening or in the fierce pummeling of an Atlantic storm, he had always been part of the crew. Now he was her captain. She was his ship. He was responsible for her. In that instant he knew he would do everything he could to save her. But, if she had to die, it would be by his hand, no other.

"Come on, Paknis!" Wade urged. "Let's get this line to the stern and get the tow rope on board. The sooner we're done, the sooner we'll be off."

Val shook himself free of the moment. This was the time for action, not reflection. "Right." Then he noticed Cybil on deck for the first time. "Cybil, I thought I told you to wait with the skiff."

"I've never been good at taking orders," she replied. "Besides, I've got work to do."

"Work? What work? Wade and I can handle the rope alone and there isn't anything else . . ."

"Oh, yes there is. Maybe more important than the rope, in the long run. Don't worry about me. You two just pull in the line. I'll be back before you're done." She disappeared into the fog.

"Wait a minute," Val called after the departing figure. "Where do you think you're going?"

Cybil had reached one of the entrances in the bridge superstructure that led to the crews' quarters and, ultimately, to the tanks. She turned around to call back. "Hold number two." Then she disappeared through the hatch.

"Damn fool," Val cursed. "Commander, can you pull in the line alone? She doesn't know her way around down there and will probably get lost before she goes ten paces. It's a maze down there."

"Sure. Just don't take too long. We've only got another fifteen minutes of air," Wade cautioned.

"Don't worry." Paknis handed the line to Wade and disappeared into the fog at a trot.

Wade lost sight of him before he reached the side of the bridge. The dull clang of the closing hatch resounded hollowly. He glumly put the line across his shoulder and began to weave his way to the stern.

Behind him the shattered dome of hold number two loomed. Its shell was twisted and turned from the force of the expanding gases seeking and finally finding release. Shards of steel, jagged daggers that could easily cut through his suit, lay scattered across the deck. He carefully picked his way along the rail, one eye on the rope, the other on the deck.

4:30 P.M.   *In a Train; En Route to Coney Island*

The doors of the speeding train opened and a hurricane entered. Old newspapers and abandoned bottles danced in the aisle until they were drawn out the opened doors by the vacuum created by the train's passage.

The train raced through the dark tunnel. Faust's huge black fist curled around the drive control, holding it firmly against it's forward stop. It was like being the driver of a roller coaster, with the added danger that the train could jump the track at any moment. He had driven these trains for seven years and had never before gone this fast, nor even heard of anyone trying it. The wheels protested the unaccustomed pressures and the track seemed to loosen as the train rumbled through. He could feel every rivet, every length of track through the throttle and through the soles of his shoes. His body was in harmony with the whole train. The train seemed to disintegrate around him as the vibrations grew with each passing mile.

But he kept the throttle open wide. It had been this way ever since leaving Borough Hall. Green lights led the way to Coney Island and he had driven the train furiously to get there in time. Only when sharp curves blocked the path had he pulled back on the throttle. Even the curves were taken at dangerously high speeds, with a scream from the wheels and the track itself as he rammed the train down the tunnel.

Faust's world had narrowed to two senses: vision and sound. He saw nothing but the flashing green lights as they sped by his window, only four inches from where he stood. His body tensed as he searched for, and never found, a yellow light that would mark the end of his journey.

The sound was overwhelming, louder than the worst jet revving its engines for take off. It filled the train, giving it a voice as well as a body. Any change in the sound was a warning. It told Faust when he was traveling over bad track, loose track, and even when he was approaching a turn. It was loudest at the intersections, where the wheels rattled and skipped from one track to another.

Lights appeared on the right side as a station whizzed past. Avenue U, the black-and-white sign said. Faust didn't need the sign to tell him where he was. He knew instinctively. Two stops from Coney Island. Two long stops. He chanced a quick glance at his watch, its face visible in the eerie green light of the traffic signals. Three fifty-eight. He cursed the men who said he could make it. He was running his train to pieces and was still behind their predicted time. Hell, he should have been there already. He pressed the throttle more firmly against the forward stop. It didn't budge.

Faust hit the P.A. switch. It was the only way he could talk to the T.A. cop who, by now, should be standing in the driver's booth at the rear of the train. "Hey, hero. You there?" His voice rumbled through the length of the train.

"I'm here," a voice rumbled back.

"You got the doors open at least."

"Glad you noticed. How close are we?"

"Two more stations. About three minutes."

"Is it safe to go this fast? Feels like the train's shaking itself apart back here."

"Let's put it this way, it's not safe to go any slower. We're behind schedule. Just remember what I told you. When we stop, I'll turn control over to your end, so pull out of there as fast as you can. I'll give you a call as soon as we're loaded. Don't wait for anything. And for Christ's sake, don't slow down. You never know how soon those boys back at Central will pull the plug and we'll be sitting in the middle of a very dark tunnel. You remember how

153

to turn on the power and run this thing until I get there?"

"I think so."

"You'd better. I don't have time to give you a refresher course. Here's the next station. I've got work to do, hero, so hang tight. It's going to be a pretty rough stop."

"Pretty rough" was an understatement. There wasn't time for the normal procedure of slowing down as they approached the station and cruising to a gentle stop before the concrete-and-steel barrier that blocked the end of the track at Coney Island. It was the end of the line, and the only thing beyond the station was the Atlantic Ocean.

Faust planned to maintain his speed for as long as he could, then slam the brakes on full emergency stop, locking the wheels instantly. The ten-car train would slide to a halt, hopefully before ramming the front car, and Faust, into the terminal barrier. Every second counted. That was why he had the cop open the doors before they got to the station. That was why he would leave with the doors open. Faust would close them as he made his way to the rear of the train.

A red signal glowed ahead. Coney Island. He could see the tiny figures standing on the platform, looking down the track for the train. The lights of the station grew larger. Faust's hand began to twitch at the throttle. He held it at full speed.

He jerked back suddenly, slamming it against the rear stop. He slammed down on the brake control, leaning on it with his full two hundred pounds. It fought back as the train buckled and complained.

He was thrown forward, bashing his head against the window. He heard it crack. Still he leaned on the brake. Sparks flew up in front of the window as the metal wheels locked and rasped against metal tracks. The stench of ozone filled the air, soon replaced by the acrid smell of burning grease. Still he leaned on the brake.

The white lights of the station flashed past his window. Too fast, he thought. Too fast as they blurred by. He saw the terrified faces of the would-be passengers as they scattered before the rushing train.

The yellow-and-red striped barrier grew closer. It came directly at him. The red-and-white sign marked DANGER appeared at eye level. The sparks were worse now, shooting out in front of the sliding train. He couldn't see anything but the bright yellow glare of the sparks as they glinted off the cracked glass. Faust leaned all his weight on the brake, using both feet, one on top of the other.

They were going to hit! He covered his face with his arms, ready for the impact.

Then, silence.

Slowly he uncovered his face, not believing they had made it. He stared out at the sign, DANGER, two feet from his window.

He heard the sound of shouting as the passengers ran toward the open doors, rocking the train with their onslaught. The train creaked and groaned as it settled on its shock absorbers. Faust wearily reached over and cut power, allowing the cop to transfer control to the other end of the train. The lights disappeared from his control panel. The train was no longer his.

The shouting became louder. No one wanted to be left behind by what they knew was the last train leaving Brooklyn. Weary, but knowing that his job wasn't over, Faust emerged from his booth. He quickly saw that there wasn't any need for fighting. There was plenty of room on the train for everybody.

He returned to the control room and called the dispatcher on the radio. "This is Faust. We're loading now. You bastards have the track changed for our return?" His voice sounded as tired as he felt. He couldn't even curse with enthusiasm.

"Already done, Faust. You better get moving. Reports are that the cloud's moving faster than they thought."

"Don't pull that fuckin' plug on me, you hear. You do and I swear I'll come back and ram this train down the mayor's throat. Personally." He added as an afterthought, "All ten cars."

"Just hurry it up, Faust. We won't cut the power. Just hurry, that's all."

Faust checked the platform. Almost empty. He watched the last passengers fight their way into the middle cars. He shook his head. There was plenty of room in the rear and probably in the front cars as well. Won't people ever learn?

He reached the P.A. system. "All right, hero. Let's go."

He felt the train lurch in response. He smiled, then returned to the P.A.

"Attention, all passengers. Attention, all passengers. This train will be going nonstop to Brooklyn Bridge, Manhattan."

A cheer reverberated through the cars. He waited for it to die down. "For reasons of speed, the doors will temporarily remain open until the conductor can reach the middle car. There are seats in the rear of the train and probably the front as well. Please proceed to those cars if your car is overcrowded."

The train was beginning to pick up speed. Not as fast as Faust would have liked, but at least it was moving. He began to run forward, trying to reassure those he passed that everything was all right.

The crowds became denser as he neared the center cars, and he had to fight to get through.

Chapter 10

4:30 P.M. In a Building; Coney Island

Kevin Griffin lay on his rumpled bed drinking his fourth, or maybe his fifth, beer of the day. He had promised his father, who was picking up the tab for the apartment, the beer and everything else in Kevin's life, that he would spend a day looking for work. But it was just too hot today. Of course when the rain came, as the weatherman had been forecasting for the past week, it would be too wet to look for work.

Then, of course, there was always the problem of waiting for the Sunday *Times* Want Ads. And by Monday all the choice jobs would be gone, leaving the underpaid ones for people like Kevin.

Life was hard, Kevin Griffin mused, as he finished his beer. It had taken him six years to get his B.A. at CCNY, as compared to the normal four. It wasn't that he had flunked; on the contrary, his grades were all A's and B's.

He just couldn't make up his mind what he wanted to study. He had finally chosen music, more or less by default, when the administration office notified him that he had enough credits to qualify for a degree. He had been depressed when the news came, although his father was elated.

This was his last summer of freedom. His father, a successful insurance salesman, had promised to cut off his monthly five-hundred-dollar allowance if he didn't get a job by Labor Day. Well, that was still three weeks away. He had plenty of time. Might as well make the best of it by lying around listening to good music and getting high. Too bad he couldn't afford some grass, but money was short and he couldn't hit his old man for an advance since there wouldn't be a check next month.

He had tried to finagle money for a graduate school, but for once his father was firm. "Six years of supporting a good-for-nothing student is enough," he had said. So for the past three months Kevin had lain on his bed, drinking beer, reading science fiction, listening to his tapes and trying hard to forget that he had to go to work soon.

Kevin wasn't lazy; he worked hard at things he liked. He was an excellent diver, a sport well suited to his five-foot-six and one-hundred-twenty-pound stature. He would have been killed in any of the regular contact sports where height and weight meant advantage. He might have even made the national intercollegiate diving championship if he had only worked at it. But as soon as it became work, he dropped it.

Time to get another beer he decided, stripping the earphones from his head. He was proud of his stereo and his collection of tapes. They had been patiently put together after years of borrowing friends' records and taping them while they were new. He was very picky about what he listened to and, consequently, never listened to the radio. His television lay idle for weeks at a time.

Grabbing another beer, Kevin wandered through the apartment, wondering vaguely how he was going to pay for it next month. Twelfth-floor apartments were expensive, particularly when they came with a view of the harbor. In his four-year tenancy, Kevin had become a skilled harbor watcher, able to identify most ships by sight. He checked *The Times* Arrivals and Departures column, so each ship became very familiar to him. He would hate to lose that.

He opened the venetian blinds and looked out at the harbor. Not much action, he thought. The heat must have gotten to the ships, too. A bad omen for jobs, he decided.

About to return to the bedroom, he was suddenly distracted by a sound at the door. It sounded like a dog scratching.

Shifting the beer nervously from one hand to the other, he leaned his ear against the door. There it was again. A faint scratching.

"Who is it?" he called through the closed door.

"Judith?" came the weak reply.

"Judith?" Kevin repeated. "I don't know any Judith."

"Judith?" A note of hope was evident even through the door.

"Judith, are you in there? Judith! It's me, honey. It's Mommy. Let me in, Judith."

Kevin decided to take a chance and open the door. It was against all of his city-trained instincts but there was something in her voice that made him think that this was legitimate. Besides, it was a woman's voice and he was twenty-three years old, an athlete, and in pretty good shape. He should be able to handle anything that came up. He quietly unlocked the Yale lock and, blocking the door with his foot, opened it a crack. Just enough to see out.

A woman's form was huddled at his doorstep. She looked vaguely familiar. He checked the hall for any signs of a lurking accomplice and, seeing none, opened the door wide.

"Are you all right?" he asked, leaning over the woman. He recognized her now. He had seen her going to the trash room to dump her garbage and occasionally in the elevator as they traveled to the twelfth floor together. They probably hadn't said more than "Good morning" or discussed the weather in four years. She lived at the other end of the hall. They were neighbors.

"You're from down the hall, aren't you?" he asked, a half-remembered picture of a young girl clinging to her arm forming in his mind. "The blind girl. Is that Judith?"

"Judith! Is she here? Tell me. She's not in our apartment and I've been so worried. So worried. There's not a lot of time and I have to find her."

"Listen, lady. I don't know anything about your daughter." Images of statutory rape charges leaped into his head. "I haven't seen her today. Christ. I don't think I've seen her in weeks. And then only in the elevator. I haven't seen anybody today. I've been inside all day. Honest." In an unusual moment of observation, Kevin saw the look of terror? grief? flash across the woman's face.

"You've got to help me. She's here someplace. I know it. We've got to find her before the cloud comes. I don't want her to die. You've got to help me. The building is too big for me to search it all alone. We don't have much time. The cloud! The cloud will be here soon."

"What cloud?" Kevin asked, trying unsuccessfully to extricate his arm from the woman's unbreakable grasp.

"The cloud. The poison one. You know. You must have heard the announcements. The mayor. Just a little while ago. That's why they evacuated everyone. You know."

That blows it, Kevin thought. I knew I should never have let her in. A crazy: She's gone off the deep end. "The poison one?" he asked, his disbelief obvious despite his attempt to control it.

"Yes, damnit," she said, her voice losing the edge of insanity. "The poison one. It was on all the radio and TV stations. Where were you? Don't you know what's happening?"

"Of course. That cloud. The poison cloud," he reassured her, finally disengaging his arm from her clutches. "Why don't you just sit right here and I'll call the police. I'm sure they'll be able to find your daughter before the cloud gets her. I'll tell you what. We'll even go looking for her ourselves before they get here. How's that?" Kevin edged toward the door. He didn't want to be left alone with a madwoman.

"Oh, stop it. I'm not crazy! You don't have to humor me. It's true. Really, it is. Anyway, the police will be busy with the evacuation. I passed enough of their patrol cars on the way down here to know. They're on the streets with sound cars doing a house-to-house search in the flats," she said, referring to the section of single-family homes at the other end of Coney Island. "There's millions of people on the streets, heading from the beach to the Brooklyn Bridge. Didn't you hear the radio announcement?"

Kevin stopped edging away. She sounded rational. If only she would stop talking about that cloud. "No," he admitted slowly.

"Well no wonder." She was clearly exasperated. "Where's your radio?" She spied the radio cum tape recorder in its place of honor near the window. She reached out for the controls.

"Hey!" Kevin protested. "Don't touch that!" It was his pride and joy.

She twisted the right knob and, after the barest hesitation, punched the correct button, and the announcer's voice filled the living room. ". . . the latest estimates on the cloud's progress indicate that it will reach Coney Island at five o'clock. Repeating the description of the cloud: it is white, like a dense fog. It can be clearly distinguished from a normal cloud since it hugs the ground; and from haze, because of its distinctively pure white color. So far it is moving slowly and is still over water. There will be ample warning before it touches land somewhere near Coney Island. There is no cause for panic. The police department has issued the following statement. . . ."

Melba looked at Kevin sympathetically. "Listen. I know it's hard to take all at once but it's really happening. It is. All over the streets you can see people just leaving their cars, their belongings, their homes. Everything. I need help. There's no one else I can turn to. Everyone else has gone.

"I know Judith's in the building somewhere. She has never left the building without me before. I even take her to school myself, every day." The tears began to glisten at the corners of her eyes. "I'm a good mother to her. I try to be, at least. It's so hard trying to be a mother and a father, especially when your child's . . . handicapped." The tears flowed freely down her cheeks. She made no move to wipe them away. She didn't seem to notice they were there.

"Please," she begged. "Please help me find her. I know she's here somewhere. Lost. Scared to death. You have no idea what it's like to be blind. No idea. She's only fifteen. She needs you. I need you." She finally broke down, sobbing, not quite hysterically, but with a desperation that Kevin had never heard before. It awoke something in him he had never felt before. Responsibility.

"All right," he agreed. "Where do we start?"

4:30 P.M. *Coney Island Boardwalk*

"Oh, please God," Sadie prayed, "don't let Rebecca die." The tears rolled freely down her cheeks leaving thin wet streams. She cradled her friend's head gently in her lap. "Don't let her die."

Rebecca stirred only occasionally in the heat, gasping when the waves of pain once again surged through her body. Fortunately they were small ripples of pain, not the overwhelming crests of a heart attack. Biological aftershocks. The delayed protests of a damaged heart.

As she looked toward the shore, Sadie saw the perpetual haze of pollution change color and shape. The gray of various carbon and sulfur compounds gave way to the absolute white of methane and ice. Death stalked the beach of Coney Island.

She could still leave, Sadie realized. Without Rebecca, she could save herself. Rebecca would never know.

The fog solidified into a wall of unnatural white. It rose straight up into the sky, blending silently with the gray sky. It took her breath away. She continued to stroke Rebecca's head, giving her comfort by her presence. Never once did Sadie move to shift the head from her lap to the bench. They would face this together.

The cloud silently advanced.

4:35 P.M. *Mayor's Office; City Hall*

Vincent LaSalle rested his head in his hands, leaning on the conference table. He was alone. More alone than anyone should ever be. The last of the plans had been made; the last of the orders had been given. Now all he could do was wait.

Abe Newfeld stuck his head in the door. "Vince?" he called "Got a minute?"

"A minute?" LaSalle laughed. "How about a lifetime?"

He waved his friend in. "Come in, come in, Abe. I could use someone to talk to."

"Good," Newfeld replied, closing the door behind him. "I'm looking for some place to find some peace and quiet. Those reporters are chewing my ear off." Newfeld lowered himself into his accustomed chair. "Seems like your office is the only place they haven't snuck into. I can't even go to the john without having a microphone jabbed at me. Wouldn't be surprised to hear a WCBS newscast with the sound of my piss hitting the urinal."

"How's it look?" LaSalle asked, ignoring Newfeld's attempt at humor.

Newfeld shrugged, pulling a fresh cigar out of his pocket. "The press is eating it up. Biggest story of the year. You're the man of the hour. Maybe of the century, if we get out of this thing alive."

"Not the press." LaSalle responded, his voice unnaturally flat. "The evacuation. The cloud."

"Oh," Newfeld hesitated. "Well, no real news on that. The Coast Guard has put a ban on all over-water flights. Too dangerous, they say. Too great a chance of an accident near the gas. The TV boys are pissed as hell. They want some live action shots, but the captain's a real stickler." Newfeld chuckled. "He threatened to shoot down one NBC helicopter when it went over Coney Island beach. Son of a bitch probably would have done it, too."

"The cloud, Abe. How about the cloud?"

"Still moving in." Newfeld's voice grew serious. "They estimate it will reach Coney Island at about five o'clock. Right on time. It's still hanging together the way that energy broad said it would. The whole harbor's shut down, so there's no chance that it might catch on fire before it reaches Coney Island. We've got half an hour before that anyway."

"How's the evacuation?"

"Good," Newfeld answered a little too quickly. LaSalle looked up at him, reading the lie on his face.

"Abe?"

"Well, as good as can be expected." He unwrapped the cigar and stuck it in his mouth, chewing deeply into the Virginia tobacco. "Fire department has their men in the field to pick up as many stragglers as possible. The police are concentrating on alerting the people in the fringe neighborhoods. What with the radio and the TV boys doing their bit and all that sound equipment on the streets we ought to do real good. Get most of the people out of their homes before the cloud comes. Brooklyn Union has already cut off gas and Con Ed's ready to cut everything off as soon as we give the word. Figured they'd give everybody the most time to get out before they cut the entire borough off."

"Abe?" LaSalle repeated. This time his tone left no room for equivocation.

Newfeld surrendered. "Best estimates are that eighty percent will get out. Some say seventy. I think eighty's closer." He hurried on. "But that's really almost a miracle, given the time they've had to get everybody out. And a lot of it's due to your speech. That almost totally prevented a panic. They're only scattered reports of any . . ."

"Eighty percent," LaSalle repeated, not listening. "Eighty percent. There were over a million people on Coney Island alone. That means that two hundred thousand . . . two hundred thousand," he shook his head, repeating it over and over again. "Two hundred thousand people will die when the cloud comes in."

"No," Newfeld corrected. "There we're pretty lucky. With everybody in the open the news got to virtually everybody right away. The evacuation of the beach is termed a one hundred percent success. Everybody who can walk is gone. The subways were working perfectly for once, thank God, and they got every last train they could to Coney Island. The place is deserted. The trouble areas are the high-rises. The sound cars are only so effective in getting to high-rise apartments. And the police, of course, can't spare the time to knock on every door. Hell, even if they did, half the tenants wouldn't believe they were cops anyway. So that's where the biggest losses are going to be. Nobody really knows how many people there are in some of those older buildings."

"Abe," LaSalle sighed, leaning back in his chair, staring at the ceiling. "Do you have any idea how many people live in Brooklyn? Two and a half million. Add another million or so for the beaches and you get three and a half million. Twenty percent of that's seven hundred thousand. If the evacuation is an overwhelming success," he waved his hand in emphasis, "we might be very lucky and

163

only lose half a million, not three quarters of a million. Hell, maybe even a million, if the wind blows the wrong way."

LaSalle pounded his fist on the table. "Damn. Damn. damn. How the hell could this happen? How the hell could it happen? Why here? Why New York? Always New York. Why not Boston? Or New Orleans? Why does New York get the blackouts? The financial disasters? Why? Is it a cursed city? It's just so unfair."

Newfeld sat silently, waiting for the mayor to finish. He had to get this out of his system. It was what most New Yorkers were feeling. What most newscasters were saying. LaSalle was a human being too, entitled to his feelings.

Only he didn't have the luxury of letting them interfere with his job.

Newfeld rolled his cigar between two fingers. He dreaded having to ask the next question. "Vince?" He hesitated.

"What, Abe? You've been sitting there like a cat with a canary stuck in its throat ever since you came in. What now? What the hell else could be wrong?"

"Vince, I think you ought to call Lowe."

"That son of a bitch? Why?" The mayor got up and began to pace the room nervously. "He's as likely to tell me to go to hell as he is to help. Knowing him he's more likely to offer to set the damn thing on fire than to offer help. Especially since it's my strong area. The last polls showed me beating him in Brooklyn two to one. He's probably celebrating his victory now."

Abe just kept rolling his cigar. "He's still governor, Vince. It's his state and, if things are as bad as that scientist said, we're going to need all the help we can get before this thing's over."

"Help, yes; hindrance, no. Besides," LaSalle dropped back into his chair, re-erecting his finger pyramid. "I just can't do it. It would be like crawling to him to do my own job. Like admitting defeat. And damnit, I just can't do that. He knows what's going on. Everybody in the whole country does. If he really wanted to help he'd have called me."

"That's not true, Vince. He's got his own problems; his own ego to worry about. Maybe all he's waiting for is a call. Just the opening crack of a discussion so he can offer his help. Maybe he's worried that you'll tell him to go to hell. Ever think of that?"

"Abe, have you called Lowe?" That dark suspicion filled his mind.

Newfeld shook his head. "No, Vince. That's not up to me. It's up to you to do that. I wouldn't go behind your back on something like this. Not even today. But I thought you ought to at least consider it." The press secretary heaved his bulk out of the chair.

"Well, I've got to get back to the wolves. You know how the press is when you don't feed them regularly. They begin to eat each other. I'd better give them some dramatic rescue stories. They're beginning to come in now." He stretched, his bones audibly cracking in the quiet of the office. "By the way, you might try turning on the television. All the stations are carrying the story live. Channel Four has a helicopter over Brooklyn taking live shots of the evacuation. You might be interested."

Newfeld turned just as he was leaving. "And you might think about what I said. About Lowe. We may need him." He closed the door.

LaSalle slowly left his place at the head of the conference table and turned on the television. A recognizable shot of the Manhattan skyline as seen from high over Brooklyn flickered, then steadied.

The camera slowly panned downward until it focused on Coney Island Avenue. It was packed with people. Shoulder to shoulder. The faint sounds of the crowd roared through the television's tiny speaker.

4:35 P.M. *On Board the* PROMETHEUS

Val found Cybil on C deck, just below water level. She was lost. He grabbed her by the arm and spun her around. "Where the hell do you think you're going?" he demanded. "You're going to get yourself killed."

She tried to pull her arm free. He held it firm. "Let me go." She ceased struggling, knowing that it was futile. "I've got to get to the tanks." She struggled again. He increased the pressure, holding her even more firmly. "I've got to."

"Why?"

"I . . . I can't say," she stammered. "At least, I mean I don't know. Not exactly. It's just a suspicion. A theory." Her enthusiasm grew. "But it's important. Very important. Maybe more so than anything else we can do here. Particularly if . . . if the line fails the way the other one did."

He grabbed her with his other arm and pulled her close, looking deep into her eyes, partially hidden by her helmet. "What do you mean? Are you hiding something from me? Tell me. She's my ship. I have to know. Tell me!" he shouted.

She broke away. "No. At least not yet. I don't know enough. I have to see the tanks for myself before I can say anything more. Maybe it's nothing. Maybe it's important. I just don't know." Her frustration was obvious "That's why I have to get to the tanks."

Val relented, his voice and manner softening. "Cybil," he said almost apologetically, "that's out of the question. You can't make it down there and back in time. We're running out of air even now." He took her arm gently this time. "Come on. Whatever it was, I'm sure it won't matter. There isn't anything that anyone can do to save the *Prometheus*."

"That's not true. At least there might be a chance. I won't know until I get into the holds and see what's happening. You don't understand," she protested as she saw the impatience in his expression. "The cloud is wrong. It's the wrong shape. Something is holding the gas back. I don't know what, but I know something is. And that may mean that there is a way to save the *Prometheus*. Oh, you must let me go, Val; it's the only chance we'll have to check."

Val felt a faint flicker of hope. He tried to suppress it, but it grew of its own accord, feeding on the fuel of desire. He looked at Cybil. "Are you sure? Is there really a chance that the *Prometheus* might be saved?"

"A chance," she acknowledged. "I'm not certain, but there is a chance. It might be something else . . ."

"What else?" Val's voice was that of a captain fighting for the life of his ship. "Tell me!" he ordered.

"It might mean that it's worse than we thought. That she might never withstand the strain of being towed out of the harbor. She might be . . ." Cybil shook her head.

"No! No more. Not until I get to see the tanks. Now will you let me go?"

"No," he answered. "You'll get lost and there isn't time to go looking for you. We'll go together."

The deep white of the cloud thinned as they descended to the lowest level of the gas. Pockets of air kept the gas at bay. They walked knee deep in the white fog as they approached the corridor that led to the hold.

Val spun the wheel, opening the door. The room was as they had left it. The lockers were overturned, benches thrown against the wall, shattered against the metal. Loose clothing lay in a heap against the floor, tiny fingers of the white cloud weaving their way in and out of the frozen material. Val ignored the scene while he waited for Cybil to enter and seal the door behind her.

Only then did he begin to open the inner hatch. The stainless-steel fittings operated smoothly. He held the door open for Cybil and they entered hold number two for the second time.

Everything looked as it had the last time they entered the hold. Angry red ice crystals danced in front of Cybil's helmet, welcoming her back and warning her away at the same time. The floor was littered with the ever-present crystals, making walking a conscious effort. Far above, hidden by the curvature of the tank, sunlight entered through the shattered dome of hold number two.

Cybil reached for Val's hand and encountered his halfway. They grasped each other firmly and hurried across the catwalk, heading for the center of the tank where the inspection stairs led to the depths of the hold. Val hesitated at the stairwell.

"Are you certain you want to go on with this?"

Remembering another, more pleasant time, Cybil replied, "Lead on, my captain."

The hurt in Val's eyes immediately made Cybil regret her words. She wished she could reach out and touch him, reassure him that the captaincy she referred to was not of the ship but of herself. The suits and her own self-respect stopped her.

Without a word, Val turned and led her down the stairs.

He did not know what she expected to find. As a seaman, he had pictured the water rushing the tanks, filling the hold. He had thought that the hold would be flooded; the tanker listing, inviting more water to occupy her innards, her tanks spilling their cargo onto the waters, raising the level by its contents.

Instead, he found everything quiet and calm. The tank gaped open; at least half its contents had escaped. Cybil focused her light on the crack. The beam glinted off a gray liquid sloshing gently in the tank. The ice crystals gave the light a blue tinge. She tapped his shoulder, motioning him to proceed.

Deeper and deeper they went into the hold. Still no water. Cybil detached the light from her suit, shining it around the cavern looking for . . . something. Val, not knowing what to look for, followed suit. Their footsteps crunched as they echoed off the distant wall of the cavern. That was the only sound. Gone was the reassuring chugging of the compressors as they chilled and recirculated the LNG to the tanks. Gone was the sound of the bilge pumps as they sucked at the intruding water. And gone was the sound of the water itself as it bubbled through the rupture in the hull.

"What's happened?" Val asked as they reached the bottom deck. "I'd have thought the water . . ." The sentence trailed off. Cybil wasn't listening. She was leaning against the edge of the tattered remains of the spray shield, peering into the drip pan.

"Give me your light," she said, sticking her hand out behind her. He complied. Using the safety cord that attached it to his suit, Cybil lowered the light into the dark of the drip pan. She leaned way out, almost losing her balance. Val grabbed her from behind.

"Thanks. See if you can brace yourself against something. I have to get a better look."

Val wedged one boot against a half-torn brace that once supported the shield. It wasn't secure, but it would have to do. He looked around for something for his other foot and finally settled on a two-inch crack in the steel deck. He had read about the effects of LNG on steel, rupturing even the hardest carbon steel on contact, but this was the first time he had ever seen it. Carefully, aware that even the slightest rip in his suit would mean death, he found a secure position where he could hold onto Cybil with both hands and onto the deck with both feet.

"Okay," he grunted. "But not too far. I don't know how long I can hold this."

Without answering, Cybil squirmed farther out, leaning over the drip pan. Her helmet almost reached the side of the tank four feet from the edge. Val's arms strained against her weight. She lowered the light, swinging it like a pendulum. Finally, it glinted off a liquid filling the bottom of the pan. Cybil emitted an interested "Ahhhh" and lowered it until it reached the liquid. The light entered with a faint splash. She leaned over even farther to watch.

Val's arms were beginning to cramp as he held Cybil against the forces of gravity. He blinked away the perspiration that ran down his brow and threatened to enter his eyes. Between blinks, the light glinting out of the drip pan disappeared. He wondered what that meant.

"Okay," Cybil called. "Pull me back."

His arms trembling from the strain, he gave one tug and Cybil came flying back, landing in his lap. Together they lay there for a second while Val caught his breath. Carefully, always aware of the dangers of ripping their suits, they disentangled themselves.

"Find what you wanted?" Val asked.

"I'm not sure. I have one more place to check."

"One more? We don't have time." He checked his watch. "We barely can make it back to the rowboat and out of the cloud as it is. We can't afford——"

"We can't afford not to." Cybil cut him off. "I'm almost certain. But almost isn't good enough." She stood up, pulling Val's light out of the drip pan, wrapping the cord around her crooked arm. "Come on. Only one more. The faster we get started the sooner we'll be done." She handed him back his light. It had returned to life. "Keep that out. I'll need it again."

They headed forward. Cybil used her light to lead the way, tracing what appeared to be patterns in the ice on the deck. "Where are you going?" Val finally asked as they weaved their way back and forth across the deck.

"I'm following the LNG," she said as she sifted the crystals in her fingers.

"What? That's impossible. There's nothing under there but solid steel . . ."

"I know." Her answer was cryptic. Suddenly she shone the light off toward the bow. "There. That way."

Something glinted in the darkness. "What's that?" Val asked, putting a restraining hand on Cybil's arm. He pointed. "Over there."

She focused her light in the indicated direction. All there was to see was ice. A lot of ice. The light suddenly picked up something different. It glinted metallically against the white crystals. A hand.

Dreading what they would find, they approached the sprawled figure together. He motioned her to stop. "You wait here," he suggested.

She shook her head. "No. I have to see. There may be . . . something important."

Val turned the body over. The suit sloshed. A face floated to the top of the helmet. It was distorted from the pressure of the exploding blood vessels. The eyes had swollen, extending the white orbs out of their sockets. The eyelids had visible cracks where the thin tissue tried to stretch and couldn't. The skin was eggshell white. The lips were blue.

Cybil peered at the face. "It's Lopez. Isn't it?"

Val averted his eyes, looking at the identification numbers on the suit's cuff. "Yes. Although I've never seen . . . I never thought it would look like this."

"Direct exposure to cryogenic liquids. I've read about it but never seen it before. He must have been alive when the wave caught him." Val tried to pick him up. She placed her hand on his elbow. "Don't. That's LNG in there." She pointed to the liquid in the suit. "These suits weren't designed to withstand contact with the liquid form, only the gas. You never know when a seal would give."

Cybil straightened. "That way," she indicated, her light picking out some signs invisible to Val. He followed.

Her light found the open hatch, disappearing into the dark of the adjacent hold. The airtight door was ajar, wedged open by the body of the crew chief. Dunn lay like a rag doll. Val didn't move to examine the body. Neither did Cybil.

They pushed open the hatch, dragging the body with the heavy steel door. They only opened it as far as was necessary for them to pass by the dead crew chief without stepping over his still form.

Cybil shined her light over the side of the tank. It appeared to be intact. The air was a reassuring shade of blue, but on the edges of the hold, the first faint traces of yellow were beginning to make their appearance. At first there was only silence. Then as they became accustomed to the stillness they heard the faint trickle of running . . . water?

"Where's the inspection hatch?" Cybil asked. "Like the one Lopez used."

"Over here." Val indicated a rectangular area on the floor.

"Open it," she ordered. It took both of them to lift the heavy steel plate. When they slid the plate to one side, she knelt down next to the opening.

As she lowered his light into the inspection hatch it showed the gentle wavy surface of a liquid.

"What!" Val exclaimed. "There shouldn't be any water here. The leak was in the next compartment. And that's separated by a solid bulkhead."

Cybil didn't answer as she concentrated on lowering the light evenly until it dangled above the surface. She held it steady until it stopped swaying. Carefully she dropped it the few remaining inches until it entered the liquid with a splash. She counted to ten slowly as the yellow light continued to glow beneath the surface of the gray liquid. She reached ten. It stayed lit.

"Okay." She heaved a sigh. "Now for the big one." She continued to lower the light, sliding the line through her fingers. It descended another two or three inches before it stopped, bouncing off some unseen barrier. Cybil bit her lower lip.

She raised the light, pulling the line like a skilled fisherman and dropping it back again. It stopped. There was only a thin layer of liquid. The rest was solid. She pulled the line up, handing the light to Val. It was covered with ice.

"I've seen enough. Let's get back to the boat."

"What is it?" Val asked.

"Not now. Later. When we get back to the boat."

Val looked at his watch. "Come on, then. We'll have to hurry. We only have a few minutes of air left." He grabbed her hand and pulled her forward, leading her toward the exit hatch from hold number three. "This way. It's closer."

Cybil never clearly remembered that race to the deck.

It was an endless succession of identical stairs followed by identical corridors. She didn't even try to figure out where she was or where she was going. She was content to follow Val. It was enough to know that he knew. She followed along blindly, trustingly. Her world was reduced to the burning pain in her legs. The agony of running up too many stairs with too much weight. The suit was like a heavy field pack. She ignored the pain, but in the end her legs refused to carry her. She felt Val's strong arm surround her waist and heard his reassuring voice call to her. She tried to follow but couldn't.

Her world turned upside down and her breathing became difficult as he tossed her over his shoulder and carried her the rest of the way. The world suddenly flashed white as they crossed the deck and headed for the Jacob's ladder. Dimly, she wondered whether the commander had waited for them. No matter, Val would take care of her.

She felt herself slipping into the darkness of unconsciousness. There was no longer any pain, any anxiety. She accepted it almost gratefully, without a struggle.

4:40 P.M. *In a Train; En Route from Coney Island*

"Out of the way," Faust shouted as he shoved his way forward. The crowd had become almost impassable now. The roar of the wind tearing through the open doors of the train drowned out the screams of the terrified passengers. "Sit down!" He elbowed his way deeper into the center car, using every pound of fat and muscle for leverage.

People fought back. They were afraid to relinquish their grips on the metal straps and the poles that blocked the aisle. The more tenuous the grip, the harder they fought to maintain it. The ever-present noise only added to the terror as the train clattered down the track.

It wasn't a smooth ride because Faust had damaged the train on the trip south. He didn't regret the rattling or the shaking as the metal wheels skittered against the old track; he only prayed they would make it before the power was cut. He didn't trust those bastards for one second. If they got the order to pull the plug on his train they'd do it without a second's hesitation.

The train lurched into a turn. He fought to hold on to a metal railing, feeling his fingers, slippery with sweat, slide across the smooth metal. He slammed into a passenger in front of him.

In a kind of human domino effect, the person was thrown off his precarious perch into the two people in front of him. They, in turn, sprawled against their neighbors, and suddenly dozens of people were shaken free of their insanely guarded grips. The train slammed into the turn, wheels squealing their protest as the shocks fought to keep the train upright and on track. They were going too fast. Faust, as a trainman, knew that. The passengers instinctively sensed it as well.

Panic began as someone wailed, "Oh, my God, we're going to crash!"

Pandemonium broke out as people fought to escape. There was no place to go, but they all wanted to be anywhere other than where they were. The greatest shoving took place next to the gaping doors. The people stranded there wanted to reach the security of the interior of the car. Those in the interior fought back; they wanted the security of a human wall separating them from the roaring doorways.

Faust never actually saw the man who fell.

A scream suddenly cut through the other sounds in the car. Not because of its volume but because of the sheer terror it conveyed. It chilled Faust's blood. Everyone in the car froze as though it was their life that was in danger. In slow motion Faust sought for and located the source of the scream. The middle door. He moved toward it. Everyone else moved away. He was suddenly in a clearing. He saw the hand, no more than four painfully white fingers, clenched against the edge of the door frame. The knuckles were flamed red, the fingernails were ghastly white as the pressure increased.

Faust leaped for the hand; an irrational action to pull the owner back into the car. Back to safety. Steel beams spaced four feet apart raced by, each adding its own whizzing note to the drone of sound in the speeding train, each creating a small vacuum that sucked at the side of the train and the trailing body that lay pressed against it.

It might have been one of the beams. It might have

been the person's strength, either physical or moral, that failed. One second the white fingers were there. The next they were gone.

Faust's fingers closed around empty air. Off balance, he stood erect for a second, arms still extended. He knew immediately, instinctively, what would happen beneath the speeding train.

The body would hang suspended against the I-beams lining the track for a split second. Then it would fall beneath the speeding wheels, dragged under as the loose clothing was caught. It would be thrown to the center of the track, directly beneath the center of the cars, reaching the relative security of the open space between the tracks.

A red lever, riding just one foot above the track, would speed toward the now unfeeling object and strike it. The body would be thrown forward; the lever backward. The lever was connected to an electrical relay. One the conductor could not override. It was connected to the master brake circuit for all the cars. When the contact was closed, every brake on every car would lock. Faster than when Faust had applied the brakes at Coney Island. The fastest stop that the train could withstand. It had to be. This was the dead body circuit. A person's life was at stake.

The brakes slammed on. Mechanical screeching filled the air. Human screams were drowned out. People were thrown forward as the irrefutable laws of physics came into control. An object in motion tends to remain in motion. The people were moving at nearly sixty miles an hour. The train underneath them slowed. They did not.

Bodies became battering rams, flying forward, picked off their feet and tossed as though they were weightless. When they crashed against other objects, their weight returned with a painful and sometimes fatal suddenness. Those in the most heavily crowded cars were cushioned by the resilient flesh of their neighbors. Only those against the unyielding metallic walls suffered injury.

Faust found himself flying through the air. His feet trailed somewhere behind his head. He struck out, trying to grab one of the metal straps that dangled just inches away. He missed. Looking forward, he saw the line of silver flying at him. A central pole. He put up his hands to fend it off. He felt it sting against his palms and then he felt . . . nothing.

Chapter 11

"Ahead dead slow, helmsman," Commander Wade ordered. He was in his element now, calm and confident as he commanded his ship. He turned to the radioman. "Signal the *Sea Maid* to keep pace with us. She's not to get ahead of us under any circumstances."

"Yes, sir."

Val watched the Coast Guard officer with a sense of professional satisfaction mixed with remorse. It was always good to see a skilled officer handle his ship. But it only served to remind him that his ship, the *Prometheus,* lay at the other end of the tow rope that trailed off the stern of the *Apple Tree.* He put his arm around Cybil as she stared out the window at the fog bank that hid his ship. The silhouette of the tug was sharply etched against the white background of the cloud.

Cybil moved closer to Val, reaching up and grabbing his hand as it clasped her shoulder. She watched the tug begin to move. The deck throbbed under their feet as the engines responded to the commander's orders.

She turned to Val, her eyes seeking and quickly finding his. "Let's go outside. I want to watch from there."

"Of course," Val said. He turned to the commander and pointed to the door, motioning that they were going out. He nodded. Val opened the door, ushering Cybil outside. The confident voice trailed after them, "Helmsman, keep her dead slow. Take up the slack as slow as—" Val shut the door, cutting off the voice altogether. Only the sound of the engine remained.

Cybil walked to the stern and leaned over the railing. They were directly over the deck where two seamen stood watch over the tow rope. It sank out of sight like a large sea snake a few yards from the stern of the cutter. As the

175

ship pulled forward, more of the snake rose, dripping from its water habitat. It rose slowly, almost reluctantly.

Parallel to them, the *Sea Maid* did the same. Behind her, a second snake rose from the depths.

Cybil had been strangely quiet ever since their return from the tanker. She had recovered consciousness moments after they emerged from the cloud. The combination of exertion and tension had caused her to use her air faster than either of the two men, she explained as they rowed the final few yards to the *Apple Tree*. Neither man disagreed with her, at least not openly.

But when Val tried to question her about what she had seen in the hold, she had been silent. She refused to discuss it, claiming that it wouldn't matter anyway until they knew whether the tow ropes would hold. They hadn't had a chance to discuss it in private since they had reboarded the cutter. Now that they were alone, he tried to broach the subject again.

Once more she parried his question, changing the topic. "How did the commander get the second tow rope to the *Prometheus*? I thought we carried only one line with us."

"We did. But one of the trailing lines had another line tied to it. When that came on board, all he had to do was untie it and pull them in one at a time. Now about what you saw . . ."

"But why two? For speed? I would think that it wouldn't really matter how many lines you had."

"True. The speed is determined by the mass of the ship being towed in relation to the force that the tugs can apply. It's for maneuverability more than anything else. We have to make some sharp turns as we pass through the mouth of Sandy Hook Channel and it's a lot easier to control a ship with two separate lines than with only one. But you know all of this. What are you trying to avoid telling me?"

"I told you I didn't want to talk about it." She moved farther down the railing to watch the towing operation.

He followed. "You have to talk about it," he insisted. "If it concerns the fate of the *Prometheus,* I have to know. What were you saying about there being some chance that you might be able to save her?"

Cybil stared out to sea, ignoring the question. The lines were now almost totally out of the water; the angle was becoming more and more shallow as they pulled farther away. Mentally, Cybil traced the line to the heart of the cloud where it rose to the deck of the *Prometheus*. There it would be subjected to the unearthly cold they had so recently left.

Like a child's string, the four-inch hawser rose with startling swiftness as the last dozen yards leaped into view. It disappeared into the side of the cloud about ten feet off the water. It looked as though it were suspended in mid-air. It hung there, silently dripping for a second, and then began to rise as more tension was put on the line. One of the seamen spoke into his radio. The engines dropped into a deeper beat as the information was translated into action by the commander.

"Do you think the tows will hold?" Val asked. He joined Cybil by the railing, putting his arm around her again. This time she did not move away.

"I hope so, Val," she answered intently. "I hope so."

The twin hawsers began to climb an invisible ladder into the cloud, rising higher with every throb of the engines. Cybil wrapped her fingers around Val's wrist, squeezing with unconscious strength as she watched the line climb. It was almost level with the stern of the *Apple Tree* now.

"Come on," she whispered between clenched teeth. "Come on." Her fingers closed more firmly around Val's wrist. Circulation stopped as her fingers cut in deeply. One fingernail drew blood. Val didn't notice. His eyes were focused on the rising hawsers.

"Come on. Hold, damn you. Hold," Cybil chanted quietly.

Suddenly the line that connected the *Sea Maid* to the cloud came hurling back out of the cloud. It looked as though someone had taken it and thrown it back at the tug. Two seconds later, the pistol-like shot reached the *Apple Tree*. The hawser dangled in the air for an instant and splashed down into the water between the tug and the cloud.

"Damn," Cybil muttered. Another fingernail drew blood.

The *Apple Tree*'s line continued to hold. Val found himself holding his breath as though he were afraid that any movement might bring that line flying back at them. It continued to climb into the cloud, reaching higher and higher. Just as he thought it was going to hold, it happened.

Almost in slow motion the end of the line rose suddenly, flipped upward by the release of tension. It went straight up and then coiled back, flinging itself toward the *Apple Tree*. A shot rang out—the dying gasp of the line as its tortured fibers, stressed from within and without, burst asunder. It drifted gently in the calm, quiet waters of the bay, only momentarily disturbing the placid surface.

Cybil slowly released Val's wrist. Her fingers were wet with his blood. She looked at them numbly, rubbing the scarlet liquid with her thumb as it slowly coagulated.

Val let out his breath with a sigh. "Well, I guess that's it." He put both hands on the railing and leaned against the wooden support. "That's the end of the *Prometheus*." He stared silently onto the deck, watching the seamen reel in the broken hawser without seeing them, his vision blinded by his loss.

There was nothing Cybil could do or say. She placed a hand against his back, just to let him know she was there. A red fingerprint glinted off the back of his rumpled white uniform. "Val?"

He straightened. "I guess we'd better get back to the bridge."

She blocked his path. "Val. There wasn't a chance. Even if we got her out of the harbor, she was doomed. In fact, she probably would never have made it out of the harbor, even if the lines had held. Come on." She took his arm. "I think it would be easier if I told everyone at the same time."

Wade looked up as they entered the bridge. "You were right, Professor." He turned and paced away. "They didn't hold. They burst just like the other one." He turned and came toward them.

The radio crackled to life. The voice of the captain of the port filled the tiny bridge. "Report, Commander."

Wade ceased his pacing, snapping almost to attention as he spoke into the microphone. "Mission was a failure, sir." He cleared his throat. "The towlines parted when pressure was applied. According to Professor Yale"—he looked at her for corroboration and she nodded—"it was probably due to freezing of the towlines when they were exposed to the cryogenic temperatures of the cloud."

"Thank you, Commander." The captain sounded tired. "Do you or Miss Yale have any further suggestions? I'd be grateful for anything just now."

"No, sir. I suggest that we evacuate the area. I don't think that there's much chance of getting another line on her before the cloud reaches land and——"

"I have a suggestion, Commander." Cybil interrupted him. "Could I?" She held out her hand for the microphone.

"Captain, this is Secretary Yale. I do have a suggestion, but I want to make it while you and Mayor LaSalle are on the line. Could you arrange that?"

"Certainly, Miss Yale. Just hold on. I'll have a conference call set up immediately. Keep this line open. I'll be only a moment." The steady hum of a carrier wave filled the bridge.

"What's this all about?" asked the commander. Cybil steadfastly ignored his question. He repeated it to Val.

Val shrugged. "I don't know any more than you do. She's been like this ever since we got back from . . ."

"Professor Yale?" A woman's voice crackled over the loudspeaker. "Are you on the line?" It was Phyllis from the mayor's office.

"This is Professor Yale," Cybil answered.

"The mayor will be right with you."

The port captain came back on the line. "Miss Yale, is the mayor on the line yet?"

LaSalle answered the question for himself. "Right here, Captain." The Brooklyn accent filled the speaker. "Miss Yale, I understand you have some bad news for us."

"I'm afraid so, Mr. Mayor. I suggest, no, I urge you to order the immediate destruction of the *Prometheus*." She heard a gasp from the other side of the bridge. She didn't have to look up to tell it was Val. "I suggest the use of high explosives, either a bomb dropped from a military plane or possibly artillery fire from the *Apple Tree*. In either event, I believe that this action should be taken before the cloud reaches land."

"But isn't that what we were trying to prevent?" La-Salle asked. "I thought we were trying to keep it from exploding."

"We were, Mr. Mayor," Cybil answered, "but only as long as there was a chance of towing the *Prometheus* out to sea before the other four tanks ruptured. If their unignited gas is added to the cloud, it will quadruple in size. It's safer to get rid of it now, before it has a chance to spread possibly as far as Manhattan itself."

She looked directly at Val. "In short, Mr. Mayor. I believe you have to order the *Apple Tree* to open fire on the *Prometheus* immediately."

5:00 P.M. *Weather Forecast for New York City and Vicinity*

TEMPERATURE:	97° F. 36° C.
HUMIDITY:	100 percent
WIND:	South 0–3 knots
PRECIPITATION:	15 percent probability within the next four hours; 30 percent before morning.

SPECIAL CONDITIONS: The air inversion covering the Metropolitan area for the past two weeks appears to be breaking up, allowing the storm stationary over Rahway to begin to move eastward. Pollution Advisory still in effect and warnings for elderly, infants, and people suffering from respiratory conditions should still be heeded. Dangerous levels of sulfur dioxide, nitrous oxide, and carbon monoxide have been recorded throughout the Metropolitan area. Driving should be avoided wherever possible.

NATIONAL WEATHER SERVICE
NATIONAL CLIMATIC CENTER, ASHEVILLE, NORTH CAROLINA

5:00 P.M. *On the Boardwalk; Coney Island*

It was peaceful on the boardwalk. The cries of the children were long-forgotten memories. The raucous screeching of the blaring radios was silenced. The shrill screams of the seagulls fighting over the remains of the afternoon lunches were absent. Even the sound of the surf as it attacked the white sandy shore was somehow muted.

The peace was visual as well. Gone was the litter that marked the presence of humanity. The empty beer cans. The crumpled cigarette packages, their internal foil catching the brilliance of the sun in tiny bursts of silvery radiance. The brown plastic tubes and bottles of suntan lotion, advertising the shade that would be the most popular that summer. Gone. Or at least covered.

The white blanket lay evenly across the beach. As though hesitant to step onto land, the cloud lingered at the shoreline. Then slowly it climbed forward. Silently it covered the debris of humanity.

Sadie was dying. Not like Rebecca whose enemy was internal. Not dying because her body had failed. She was dying because she was living her last moment.

Rebecca was sleeping quietly. She tossed in her sleep but was always comforted by the dry, warm hand of her friend, who gently stroked her brow. Rebecca would probably have survived this heart attack, Sadie realized. But now neither of them would.

The cloud crept closer to the elevated boardwalk. It was like a living thing. It moved in ways that seemed to be intelligent, or at least self-willed. It advanced and then, for no apparent reason withdrew, to renew its strength and advance again. Like the incoming tide, each advance brought it a little closer.

Sadie worried about her family. Would they worry about her? Would they think she had suffered? Would they even notice? Bittersweet sadness engulfed her. She would never again talk to her son David. All he ever talked about was how he hated his job and how much private school cost for the kids. Not that they appreciated the work he did for them. A private smile crossed Sadie's lips. He would learn. He would know how it felt to sacrifice everything for your children and have them do nothing but take, take, take. He would see.

And Barbara, her ungrateful daughter. She had married a doctor and never wrote to her mother; didn't even send a card on Mother's Day. Sure, there was always a call on her birthday but there was nothing, absolutely nothing they could talk about, what with her tennis friends and her parties. But Sadie fought to control the bitterness in her heart. It's not good to die with such feelings, she thought. I must forgive Barbara her years of selfishness, snobbishness, and, most of all, her years of disrespect. I must forgive . . . no, Sadie resolved, I *do* forgive Barbara her faults.

And who would take care of her plants? She had a green thumb. Everyone said so. She could get anything to grow. Her apartment was an urban greenhouse. All except the bedroom. The plants steal the air at night, so Sadie slept alone. It wasn't fair that her plants had to die just because she did. They were healthy and, with a little love and a little water every few days, they could live forever.

The cloud crept silently closer. She had to keep her eye on it or it would sneak past her. Every time her mind wandered the cloud advanced.

"It's coming closer, Rebecca," she muttered, using the same tone she had for the past ten years as the two women shared their lunches, their bench, and their loneliness. It comforted both the speaker and the listener. Rebecca stopped her turning and sank deeper into sleep.

"But it won't get here. No, it won't get up this high," she intoned. "We're higher than the cloud can reach. It won't get us. Someone will save us, Rebecca. Someone will."

The boardwalk was about five feet above the level of the sand. Six steps linked the walk to the beach, marking the depth of the cloud. Each step meant that the cloud was ten inches closer. The first step disappeared, covered by the white veil.

A faint chill filled the air. Sadie pulled her shawl closer around her. Then, aware of the exposed skin on Rebecca's arms, she leaned forward, pulled the shawl off her shoulders and draped it over Rebecca. "There you are, Rebecca. Isn't that better. Must be something in the air. A sudden chill." She tucked the black material under her friend's shoulders. "Maybe the weather's finally changing. Won't that be nice? Then the air will get all clean and we'll be able to breathe again. Won't that be nice, Rebecca? Won't that be nice?"

The cloud swallowed its third step and greedily lapped at the fourth. As it grew, it changed. The cloud, once a thin wedge, now became wavelike. It undulated. There was a definite roundness to the top, Sadie noticed, that was not evident before. It was like the tide. Always moving. Ever changing.

A fifth step disappeared.

Sadie pulled her friend closer, trying to protect her with her body. Rebecca turned in her sleep. Gently, Sadie relinquished her hold, letting the gray hair fall once more across her lap. The hair was matted with sweat. She mopped her brow.

"Don't be afraid, Rebecca," she murmured. "Don't be afraid."

Sadie watched as the sixth step was covered with white. The cloud slowly billowed upward. It climbed the wooden supports to the boardwalk above. Sadie watched through the spaces between the slats. More wood disappeared behind its white veil.

A sudden shiver shook her body. She felt Rebecca's skin. Cold. She pulled her close, lending the warmth of her body. She could see her breath in front of her. It was like a cold February day.

The white fog crept through the spaces between the boards, undulating in a long, slow wave that silently washed across the boardwalk, rising as it came. When it struck, it seemed to explode across Sadie's legs, covering her lap in whiteness.

For an instant there was no pain, no feeling at all. There was no weight, no sensation. She almost laughed. Then, suddenly, her legs were on fire. They burned as though immersed in scalding water. The temperature around her dropped more than three hundred degrees in less than a second.

Sadie screamed. She tried to jerk her legs back, pulling the unresisting body on her lap with her. The legs didn't respond. The shock to her system was great. She was on the verge of her own heart attack when the sensations seemed to disappear with the same suddenness that they appeared.

Rebecca, lying as she was with her head in Sadie's lap, was exposed to the full effects of the cloud. She didn't even have a chance to scream out before her already damaged heart stopped beating.

The cloud receded. It pulled back, waiting for the strength to attack again. Sadie's legs slowly reappeared.

There was no feeling in them, but at least she could see them.

"There now," Sadie patted the still hand of her friend. "We got through that one all right, didn't we." Her breath came in short gasps. "I'm sorry I yelled like that. I don't know what got into me. I hope I didn't scare you. It was just so painful, but it must have been my imagination. You didn't even wake up. You didn't feel a thing."

The cloud had fully receded, exposing Sadie's legs to the light once more. They began to throb. Sadie leaned over and examined her legs as though they belonged to someone else.

Her stockings and her dress sparkled with a million tiny jewels, each facet sending off a rainbow of colors. She leaned over and ran a finger across the sparkling surface. She heard rather than felt her finger rasp down her leg.

She never saw the second wave approach. It began far down the boardwalk, picking up momentum as it came. It towered over the women, hiding not only the benches but the full height of the handrails as well.

If Sadie had a chance to scream, there was no one left to hear.

5:05 P.M.   *Mayor's Office; City Hall*

"I'm sorry, Miss Yale, I'm not certain I understand." LaSalle sat at his desk, covered with dozens of pages of one-paragraph reports on the progress of the evacuation. "You said you needed time. That was the purpose of the evacuation, wasn't it? I mean besides rescuing everyone at the beaches. I must say I owe you a great deal of thanks for your advice. But I'm totally confused by this one-hundred-and-eighty-degree turnabout in your position."

LaSalle punched the button that put Cybil's reply on the speakerphone, motioning for Newfeld to listen. "I know it seems strange, but I can assure you that it's absolutely necessary. When I suggested at the meeting that we try to tow the *Prometheus* out of the harbor, I was assuming that the greatest danger lay in the cloud becoming ignited, acting as a fuse leading back to the *Prometheus*. I expected that the resulting explosion would cause the four remaining tanks to rupture, adding their gas to the fireball. That way all of the gas released by the four tanks would be almost immediately consumed by the flames. There would be virtually no chance for the gas to spread. But that isn't going to happen."

"Oh?" LaSalle pursed his lips. "What is going to happen?"

"I believe the *Prometheus* is on the verge of tearing itself apart. If that happens, the contents of the remaining four tanks will almost certainly be released unignited. That means they will have a chance to spread, adding their volume to that already heading toward Brooklyn. The cloud will be at least four times as large. The damage will probably be even worse than that."

The captain interrupted her. "But, Miss Yale, I don't understand. The *Prometheus* is sitting in the middle of the harbor. There are no heavy seas, and the report that I've seen indicates that the extent of the physical damage was relatively minor, except, of course, for the nature of the cargo. The *Prometheus* is a well-built ship. She could withstand the damage she has sustained indefinitely. If it weren't for the potential of fire and explosion, I'd say that she'd be a perfect candidate for salvage."

"But, Captain, you are forgetting the nature of the cargo. That's the whole point. That's what everybody is always forgetting. Liquefied natural gas is not something that disappears the second the tank is opened. It's not immediately turned into a gas. It takes energy to do that. Energy is heat. And in this case, that energy is being provided by the hull of the tanker and by the water that was trapped in it."

There was a moment of silence as the mayor and the captain absorbed this. "Do you understand what I'm getting at? The LNG is absorbing the heat from the entire structure of the tanker. When we were on board the tanker, Mr. Paknis and I inspected hold number two. We found cracks in the steel decking and, worst of all, when we inspected hold number one, there was evidence of ice."

"Ice?"

"Yes, Mr. Mayor, ice. That's what's tearing the tanker apart. Ice. The water in the bilges, even the water that flooded hold number two, has either been consumed by the LNG as ice crystals, or, where direct contact was not made between the water and the LNG, the water was turned to ice. And when water freezes . . ."

"It expands," LaSalle finished the sentence for her.

"Precisely. And that's tearing the *Prometheus* apart. Her hull is filled with water. Water is used as ballast. As more LNG escapes into the hold, more ice is formed. The steel hull was not designed to take that type of stress. It was not intended to protect from pressures applied from within. That's why you have to order the *Prometheus* destroyed."

Captain Bassil commanded the line. "Miss Yale, is the first mate from the *Prometheus* there? You said he was with you when you inspected the hold. Does he concur with your findings?"

Val answered for himself. "No, sir. I do not. I don't believe that the pressures Miss Yale is talking about are great enough to cause you to order the destruction of my ship."

The mayor shouted. "Listen, I don't give a goddamn about your ship or anything else, except saving my city." He calmed down slightly, regaining his normal political control. "What I mean is, I don't care if we have to blow up your ship or sink it or anything else as long as that will save the lives of the people of this city. There is no competing consideration, is that clear?"

Bassil's voice cut through the resulting babble of voices from the *Apple Tree*. "Mr. Mayor, Mr. Mayor, please." The babble ceased. "My instructions are clear. I am to cooperate with you to the fullest extent of my authority. No decisions will be made that would put the value of the *Prometheus* ahead of human life. But we are not talking about striking such a balance right now. I believe that we are discussing the need for ordering the destruction of the *Prometheus* as a way to save lives, not property. Is that correct, Mr. Paknis?"

"Yes, Captain." The hesitancy in Val's voice was thinly disguised.

"Good. Now about destroying the *Prometheus,* do you think that Miss Yale is correct in her appraisal of the pressures involved? Did you see any signs of the cracking and the ice that she reported?"

"The cracking, yes. There were a lot of cracks in the base of the hold. Hold number two, that is. I don't remember seeing any in hold number one. Nor do I remember seeing any evidence of the ice that she seems to think is important."

An angry voice interrupted Val. LaSalle strained to pick up her comments. All he caught, was some reference to a light.

"I am reminded by Miss Yale that there was evidence of ice in hold number one. I didn't recognize it as such at the time. But even so, I don't believe that it could possibly be so much of a problem that the ship's structural integrity would be jeopardized. I haven't heard of anything like that in my career as a seaman. Not since the Roman days, that is."

"Romans?" asked Newfeld. "What have they to do with this?"

"In ancient times, Roman galleys used to disappear at sea for no apparent reason. They were grain ships, hardly worth any pirate's time. Finally, they discovered that the ships that disappeared were all carrying rice. When rice gets wet, it expands. The ships just burst from the swelling of their cargo," Val explained. "But I don't see how that could apply here. The Roman galleys were wooden ships. The *Prometheus* is steel. I hardly think that rice could destroy a ship her size."

Cybil's voice replaced Val's. "The force of ice expanding is one of the strongest forces in nature. It was used to crack boulders by the American Indians and has been responsible for such things as the New Jersey Palisades. It's a force to be reckoned with and could easily tear the *Prometheus* apart."

"I'm afraid Miss Yale is a little beyond her field of expertise here," Val said. "This is a question of maritime engineering."

"It's a question of physics," Cybil cut in. "Pure physics."

"Engineering."

"Physics."

"All right," LaSalle shouted, trying to restore order to the discussion. "Enough. You've both made your points. Now, let's assume that we accept Miss Yale's analysis." He heard the beginning of Val's protest and cut it off quickly. "I said, 'assume.' So let's just assume that happens. How does that change what we're doing? And what should we do that we aren't presently? I think that about sums up our position. Miss Yale, this is your field. What do you think?"

Regaining her professional demeanor, Cybil took the microphone. "First, I believe that we should destroy the *Prometheus* by artillery fire. The smaller the initial explosion the better. That would allow the hull of the tanker to remain intact, acting as a container for the escaping gas, forcing more of the energy to be released upward. This is, of course, preferable to vertical displacement that would push the new gas toward Brooklyn."

"You mean sort of like keeping the gasoline contained in the can and then igniting it?" asked the mayor.

"Exactly. As I said in our meeting, pouring the gas on the floor would maximize the damage. This would minimize it. Since it's inevitable, we may as well try to minimize the damage. We can't change the volume of the spill."

"All right, that makes sense," LaSalle agreed. "Anything else?"

"Yes, you'll have to speed up the evacuation. Get as many people as possible out of Brooklyn, and do it as quickly as possible. Those who can't go must take cover in basements as soon as they can."

"Take cover?" LaSalle asked. "Why?"

"Because shelling the ship will ignite the cloud. The fuse runs both ways. The cloud approaching Brooklyn will be ignited as well."

"Let me see if I understand this, Miss Yale. You're asking me to order what could be the worst fire in the city's history, because you think that the tanker might, just might, burst from internal pressure caused by water freezing into ice. Is that correct?"

"Yes, sir. And that's why I suggested you do it right away so the cloud will not be over land when you ignite it."

"I'm afraid I'll have to think on this for a moment, Miss Yale. I can't make a decision like this without time to think."

"Mayor LaSalle, I also have a problem with Miss Yale's plan."

"Oh? And what's that, Captain?"

"I'm afraid that I can't order one of my ships to open fire on a foreign vessel. Not on my own authority."

"Whose authority would you have to get?"

"The President's. It's technically an act of war."

Chapter 12

5:07 P.M.   Mayor's Office; City Hall

LaSalle punched off the speakerphone, plunging the office into silence.

"Well, what do you think of the broad's story?" Newfeld asked, leaning back in his chair. "Think she's got a point?"

"Hell, Abe, I don't know. I'd like to dismiss it. But, damnit, she's been right so far. Right on the fireboats. Right on the cloud coming in; right on the towlines. If only she were wrong, then I could just say that it was an error in judgment."

"Look at it this way, Vince. You might be the first mayor ever to declare war on a foreign country." Newfeld twirled his cigar. "That's something even old Fiorello"—he pointed to the portrait on the wall—"never did. You'd go down in history."

LaSalle couldn't help smiling. "Come on, Abe, be serious."

"Just trying to throw a little levity into the situation. And also put this in perspective. Sure it's an impossible situation, but this is no time to lose your head. All right, I agree the broad's been pretty good up till now, but that doesn't make her right about this. Besides, the odds are against her."

"What do you mean?"

"Just what I said. The odds are that she'll be wrong sometime. The more she's right, the greater the chance of her being wrong the next time." He waved away the mayor's objection. "I know. I know. Faulty logic. But still you know I'm right. She's not perfect and this time she's gone out of her field. Didn't that guy, that Greek, say she was wrong. And who should know better? It's his goddamn ship, isn't it? If he says that she'll hold together, it's my bet that it'll hold."

"Are you saying I should ignore her advice?" LaSalle's tone became official; he was asking for the record, as the mayor, not the friend.

"Did I say that?" Newfeld studied the end of his cigar, taking a piece of well-chewed tobacco off his tongue at the same time. "No, I never said ignore it. Just the opposite, I think you ought to follow it. I think you ought to blow the hell outta that damn ship. Blow the mother right outta the harbor."

LaSalle looked at his long-time advisor as though he had just lost his mind.

Newfeld waved his hand. "Sit down, Vince, and listen. Hear me out. I said I think you ought to do it. But, and here's the all-important qualification, you can't. Only the President can order the *Prometheus* blown up. You heard the man. An act of war. You can't do anything. Perfect. You're doing everything you can. You've declared martial law, you've ordered the evacuation of Brooklyn, and maybe a million people owe you their lives. You've done all anyone could ask of a mayor. That's it. And now there's something that only the President can do. So the buck passes."

"But, Abe, you don't understand. What if she's wrong? All those people . . ."

"What if? What if? What if? Hell," Newfeld retorted disdainfully. "If the queen had balls . . . who cares? You can't live all the possibilities. You can only take the ones that come your way. You're the mayor, not God. You can't be all-seeing, all-knowing. All you can do is your job. You've done that. Now's the time for the President to do his. Now's the time to pass the proverbial buck. So pass it. What are you waiting for?"

LaSalle sat quietly digesting Newfeld's lecture. "I guess you're right," he admitted finally. "I guess I should call—" The buzzer interrupted. "Yes, Phyllis."

"The governor on line three."

"Lowe?" LaSalle answered in surprise.

"Yes, sir." Phyllis responded. "Personally. No secretary. He's holding."

Newfeld clapped his hands together. "Good. Good. This gets better with every passing second. Tell Phyllis to have him hold on."

LaSalle mechanically complied with Newfeld's suggestion and hung up the phone.

"Let the bastard wait," Newfeld said. "He won't hang up. I knew he would come to us. I knew it."

"Abe, I don't think you have the right perspective on this. This goes beyond politics. This isn't just about winning an election, it's about saving a city."

Newfeld's eyes glowed with outrage. "Nothing, nothing goes beyond politics. Wars were started over politics. People starve every day because of politics. Nothing is more important than politics. Besides, we've got the winning hand. There's nothing the governor can do to help. There's nothing he can do except ride on your coattails. All you have to do is listen to him and then tell him that you need to shell the *Prometheus* in order to save the city. Then see what he says."

"Okay, Abe. I've always taken your advice, but this time I don't know." He picked up the telephone and put it on the speaker. "Governor, Mayor LaSalle here. What can I do for you?"

"Vince." The Irish brogue of the governor filled the room. He had never spent more than a week in Ireland, but it was a definite advantage in certain areas of the state, so he carefully cultivated the lilting meter of the Irish. "I hear you're having a tough time of it." He paused, waiting for LaSalle to answer. LaSalle waited. Lowe hurried on. "Sorry I couldn't get to you earlier, but I was detained on other state business."

Probably in some bar, Newfeld thought.

"That's all right, Governor. I appreciate your interest." LaSalle spoke with the confidence of a man who was in total control of the situation.

"I . . . I was wondering whether there was anything I could do to help. Call out the National Guard. Declare a state of emergency. You know, anything at all." The desperation was evident in Lowe's voice.

Suddenly LaSalle felt sorry for him. He buried that emotion under the need of the moment. "That would be nice, Governor. We could use the National Guard to help us keep order. We've set up Central Park as a temporary shelter for the Brooklyn refugees and could use all the help we could get. The Army Corps and the Red Cross are already there with shelters and the like. How soon do you think the National Guard could be there?"

"Not before morning, I'm afraid. As soon as I heard, I called them into a state of readiness, just in case you'd need them."

"Thanks, but I don't think they'll be much good at anything but helping us pick up the pieces. I'm afraid that the show won't last much longer. It'll be over in the next couple of hours. Certainly before morning. And about declaring a state of emergency, I'm afraid it's a little late for that. I declared a state of emergency myself just before the broadcast, over an hour ago. If you'd like to add yours to that . . ."

"Oh. I didn't know." Lowe's voice toughened with resolve. "I guess that means you have everything well in hand and don't need any further assistance. I'm glad to hear it. Well, if there's nothing I can do . . ."

"No, Governor. I didn't say that there was nothing to do. As a matter of fact I was just getting ready to call you."

"Yes?" Lowe became cautious. A politician's wariness of a trap.

"Yes. Something just came up that reaches beyond the city limits, where my *present* jurisdiction ends. As mayor, I don't believe I have the legal authority to make any decisions that would cross city limits."

The speakerphone registered a series of whispered comments. The governor had his staff with him and they were listening in, as was Newfeld, to give advice. From the urgency of the whispers there was obviously a disagreement. That meant at least two were lawyers. LaSalle sat back and waited.

"Quite right, Vince. Quite right. If it crosses city limits it's clearly a state issue. Umm, pending further clarification of the issues, of course." Lowe was also a lawyer, LaSalle remembered.

"Good. That's what I thought as well. You see, according to the Deputy Secretary of Energy on board the *Apple Tree*—that's the Coast Guard escort ship that normally leads LNG tankers into the harbor—there's an imminent danger that the tanker will break up from internal pressure. She thinks that the ice freezing inside the tanker will cause it to burst, the way the old Roman grain ships did, you know, and if that happens, the remaining four tanks will rupture, adding their gas to the cloud. She estimates that the cloud will be four times larger. According to my estimates, that would take it somewhere out to Westchester. Maybe farther, depending on the wind velocity."

"Ice????"

"That's what she said, ice. Now I can't swear that she's correct, but so far she's been right on the button about this thing and I don't think her advice ought to be dismissed out of hand, do you?"

"No . . . no, not at all. Not at all. If she's an expert I say listen to her. But ice?"

"That's what she said. Assuming she's right, and the captain, or acting captain rather, disagrees with her by the way, she recommends that the *Prometheus* be blown up in the harbor as soon as possible. Right away, preferably. Since this involves a decision that crosses city limits, I thought you ought to have the final word. Do we blow it or don't we?"

Pandemonium broke out on the other end of the connection. Half a dozen voices at least added their loud and contradicting positions to the argument. Finally one of them realized that they were yelling at each other over an open telephone circuit and cut the connection, putting them on hold.

Newfeld laughed. "Right pretty, Vince. Right pretty. I couldn't have understood a thing you said if I didn't know what you were talking about. I doubt that any of Lowe's people could either. I'll bet they pass it right to the President. They don't have the smarts to do anything else. Except maybe pass it back to you. I'd stay away from that, though. Either do it on your own or don't do it at all."

"Abe, I can't say I didn't enjoy making that bastard squirm, but I still don't know. I still think that—"

The speaker blared, suddenly. "Vince, you still there?"

"Right here, Governor."

"Sorry, we seem to be having trouble with the connection."

Like hell, LaSalle thought. "Happens all the time, Governor. I can hear you perfectly now. How am I coming through?"

"Fine. Just fine."

"Good. Now about that decision . . ."

"Yes, I was thinking, Vince. This seems to be purely within the city limits. I mean that so far, at least, it hasn't gotten beyond the confines of New York City. And any action that you want to take would be purely local as well. If you decide to blow up the tanker, well, I don't see how I could be of any use to you. That's something that I don't have any control over. And, besides, you've been doing such a damn good job so far I don't see that there's anything to be gained by my sticking my nose where it isn't necessary."

"I understand, Governor."

"I'll have the National Guard ready to come in in the morning. Just give me a call and I'll have them wherever you want them. And if I can give any other help just let me know."

"Certainly, Governor. Thanks for calling." La Salle broke the connection. "Spineless bastard. Doesn't deserve to be governor."

"Can't say that I'm surprised," Newfeld grunted. "Now I suggest you call the President. I don't know that he'll do more but I know that he'll be a sight better informed. Maybe he'll be able to give some real help, not just good wishes, like our Albany friend."

LaSalle buzzed Phyllis and told her to call the President. In less than a minute, the call was placed and he was on the phone. His southern accent sounded almost foreign in the mayor's office. After cordial greetings were passed back and forth, LaSalle got to the heart of the call.

"Mr. President, I'm calling about the *Prometheus* . . ."

"I figured that, Vince. Naturally I heard about it and called in Director Dillon of the National Security Agency. He's been studying this problem . . ."

"Yes, I heard about some of those studies."

"You did?" He paused, "Ah, yes. That's right. That Yale woman from Energy. That's right, I did hear about that. She's quite a woman. A little impetuous at times. I'll have to talk to her about that when she gets back to Washington. But that's not what you called about.

"Dillon here tells me that he's run some computer projections on the problem and he might be able to help you some. If you want help, that is?"

"To be perfectly honest, Mr. President, that's exactly why I called. I have a problem here that I don't believe I'm authorized to handle."

"Oh?" The accent couldn't hide the same tone of caution Lowe had used just minutes before.

"According to Miss Yale, the tanker is breaking up. Her recommendation is to have the Coast Guard ship that was escorting the *Prometheus* into the harbor open fire on the tanker. She says that's the only way to prevent the cloud from growing to four times its present size. She thinks that fire could be contained to the ship area itself. Except, of course, for the cloud that has already reached Brooklyn. That would be ignited no matter what happened. According to Captain Bassil, the captain of the port, he could not authorize one of his ships to do that since, as he put it, it would be an act of war. Only you could give such an order."

"Could you hold on for a moment, Vince? I have to check with my staff on this. I hadn't thought of this precise question. Hold on." There was the muffled sound of conversation as a hand was held over the mike.

LaSalle drummed his fingers on the desk top, feeling the eeriness of déjà vu as he waited for the President's response. He gave up trying to translate the noises into intelligible remarks as the Washington debate dragged on. He began thinking about Brooklyn, wondering how far the cloud had gotten since he had been on the phone.

"Abe," LaSalle whispered, "find out how far the cloud has gotten, will you? I think this is going to take a little while."

The press secretary rose from his chair. "Right away." He paused at the doorway. "How much you want to bet that he gives you the same answer as Lowe?"

"Nothing. I never bet against myself. You know that."

"Right." Newfeld closed the door behind him. LaSalle was left alone with his thoughts and the gnarled noises of a distant conversation.

"Vince, sorry to keep you waiting so long but there seems to be a disagreement here about the best course of action to take. I'll tell you what we've agreed on, so far. First, it would be a technical act of war to fire on a foreign vessel. However, since our relations with Greece are pretty good, at the moment anyway, and since the ship has been declared a navigational hazard, I feel pretty confident that we don't have to worry about the legal questions of firing on the *Prometheus*.

"On the other hand, Director Dillon, who tells me he has studied this question in detail, says that he can see no reason why the tanker should be breaking up. Since Miss Yale isn't available right now, you might tell us exactly why she thinks it's going to happen."

"Certainly, Mr. President. Ice. Miss Yale thinks that the formation of ice in the hold of the *Prometheus* will cause the hull to burst from internal pressure as the ice expands. She says that the cold from the tanks of LNG is coming into contact with the water in the hold's ballast and that will cause the tanker to burst, as she put it."

"One minute." The hand clamped down again. This time not quite so thoroughly as before. LaSalle could hear the muffled "Ice? Is she crazy? Ice?" before the conversation became unintelligible.

LaSalle waited, wishing there were something he could do that was more effective than simply sitting in his office with his hands folded calmly on his desk. But there was no one else who could make this call, no matter how much time it wasted. There were thousands of others who could manage the evacuation; get people out of their buildings, into cars, trains, and buses, and, most importantly, get them to safety. Only one person could sit here and listen to the garble of sounds that was the President of the United States and his chief advisors debating whether ice could tear a ship apart or not. Sometimes leadership was hardest because it was least effective.

"Vince, I have to say that there is disagreement again on my staff. The director thinks the ice theory is just so much hogwash. But the Secretary of Energy has a lot of faith in Miss Yale. So does the director, I might add. But the director can't get his computers to agree with her. Or disagree, either. So we're down to personal beliefs, Vince. You and me. It's going to be up to us to come up with a solution, or, at least a choice. One of two equally unacceptable evils. Has Miss Yale given you an estimate of the death toll if you shell the *Prometheus?*"

"No, Mr. President. Only that it will be large. I estimate about twenty percent of Brooklyn would be destroyed. About two to three hundred thousand."

"Oh. The director tells me it's more in the neighborhood of half a million, assuming that the weather conditions remain the same. And, unless there is a total turnabout in the wind, the computers say about half a million."

"Half a million?"

"To a million. They say. Of course, that's a worst case estimate, so the actual will probably be lower. Say a quarter of a million to four hundred thousand."

"Mr. President. With all due respect, I can't accept those estimates."

"What do you mean 'you can't accept'?" The calculating tone reentered the President's voice.

"Simply that I can't accept that; I can't think of decimation in my city in terms of acceptable losses. As far as I'm concerned, there are no acceptable losses."

"I understand," the President agreed. "I totally understand. But you must understand that certain losses . . ."

"Mr. President. I don't have to understand anything." LaSalle was on the edge of losing his temper. "Half a million of my constituents are going to die in the next few hours. I don't have to understand anything other than that."

"Of course, Vince. Of course."

"Well, what the hell are you going to do about it?"

The President had never been put on the spot like that before. He answered as any politician would. "Whatever I can, of course."

"What's that?" LaSalle shot back.

Like the skilled politician he was, the President counterattacked.

"What do you suggest, Vince? You're the man on the scene. You've been on this from the beginning. What do you want me to do?"

"I . . . I don't really know, Mr. President. I don't know what we should do," LaSalle admitted. He was stopped cold. "You've got all the experts, the computers, the secret technologies that I've never heard about. Surely there's something that could help. Something . . ."

"I only wish there was, Vince. I know how you feel. But there simply isn't anything anyone can do."

"But . . . what about Yale's suggestion?"

"What about it, Vince?"

"I can't order the Coast Guard to open fire on that tanker. That's an act of war. I can't do that. You've got the authority. I don't."

"Vince, I've already told you not to worry about that. I've notified the captain that you have my full authority and he's to obey your orders as if they were mine. My advisors here tell me that I'll have to declare a state of emergency and make you my deputy or something, but don't worry about that now. Anything you need, you got. Medical supplies, troops to keep order, doctors, anything. You just call my director and he'll get them for you. And if he or his computers come up with anything, he'll let you know right away.

"This is not something that can be handled by remote control, Vince. You're right there. There are too many splitsecond decisions that have to be made. I heard your speech. It was good. Mighty good. I couldn't have done any better myself. You're handling the situation very well and I don't want to interfere. So, just remember. You call the director for anything you want. Anything. Just ask."

"Thank you, Mr. President."

The line went dead.

A moment later the door opened and Newfeld entered, carrying a sheet of paper torn from the A.P. wire.

"What'd he say?"

LaSalle looked up. "What you thought he'd say. Said he'd give me anything I wanted. Had his full support. Made me a deputy or something. Would do anything but take responsibility."

"Bastard." Newfeld sat in his chair. "What else?"

"It's up to me."

"The whole thing? Shelling and all?"

"The whole thing. You'll be glad to know we have his prayers."

"Shit," Newfeld exclaimed. "He said that? The gutless bastard."

"So it's up to me, Abe. The whole thing's up to me." He leaned back, closing his eyes. The room was filled with his sigh. "And I haven't the faintest idea what to do."

"Well, this might help." Newfeld pushed the yellow scrap of paper across the desk. "It's not good news, but at least it'll help you make up your mind."

LaSalle looked at the scrap. He pushed it back. "You read it. I don't have the heart. I've had enough bad news."

"The cloud," Newfeld said, without bothering to look at the paper. "It's reached Brooklyn." He paused, waiting for some reaction. There was none. LaSalle's eyes remained closed. "You hear me, Vince? The cloud's reached the shore. It's too late. You don't have to worry about that broad's idea. She said it had to be done before the cloud reached land."

Still no response.

"Vince." Genuine concern tinged the press secretary's voice. "Are you all right?" LaSalle opened his eyes and laughed hollowly. "All right? Sure. I'm just fine." He stared at his desk top for a long second. "It's just that it's not too late, Abe. It's not too late to order the *Prometheus* blown up. It's more costly, as the President would say, meaning that more people would die. But it's not too late."

"I don't understand, Vince. I thought she said that it had to be done before the cloud reached shore. Isn't that what she said?"

"Sure, Abe. That's what she said, but what she meant was that I had to do it before someone on land set the damn thing on fire. That was only a nice way of telling me I had an out. That I didn't have to order anyone killed immediately. I only had to wait and let the wind do it."

"You don't mean you're going through with it!" A sudden thought occurred to Newfeld. "Did the President tell you anything? That his experts . . ."

The mayor waved him into silence. "No. No, nothing like that. I only wish he had. He said it was up to me. A human judgment, he said. But Yale has been right all along. She's called this one from beginning to end. You don't think it was just by coincidence that she happened to be in New York when this happened, do you? No, she knows too much. Even the President said to pay attention to her advice. Even the Director of N.S.A. said that she was to be trusted. I think they were trying to tell me something. I don't think I can afford to go against her advice. Especially when it coincides with yours."

"Mine?"

"Yes. Weren't you the one who told me that inaction was death? Well, I've decided to act. I'm going to order the *Prometheus* destroyed."

5:10 P.M. *In a Train*

Pain. All-encompassing pain. A red haze that colored every sensation, every movement. There was nothing but the pain.

With a patience learned from years in Vietnam, he waited for the feeling to pass, neither pressing for full consciousness nor fighting against it. Without lessening in intensity, the pain slowly made room for other sensations. The first was smell. An acrid odor, bringing to mind stale bars and back alleys. Vomit. Mixed with blood. That was it, he realized, strangely proud of being able to recognize and identify the odors. The smell of someone who has just lost a back-alley fight.

Faust began to differentiate different sources of pain. They became more localized. He didn't try to hurry the process, using the time to piece together the circumstances that surrounded the fight, which, he decided clinically, he undoubtedly had lost. Only the loser wakes up amid the blood and vomit. The victor gets to go home and throw up.

Funny, he couldn't even remember the vaguest outlines of the fight. Usually he could at least remember the first few blows. Unless he had been caught from behind. But that wasn't possible. Combat reflexes would have given him a chance to get in at least one blow. He couldn't be getting that old.

Old? How old was he? Memories of Vietnam and combat seemed no more than dim recollections separated from reality by years, not hours. The image of a train raced through his mind. A subway. Hell, he hadn't been on a subway since he left the States. The recollections of never-ending trails of green lights nagged at him.

Discharged. That was it, he groaned aloud, welcoming the sound with a new wave of pain, he had been discharged. He was a trainman. The war was long over. And he was out of it. Safe and alive. But then why did he hurt so much. He groaned again, as much from the injustice as from the agony that had now become centered at the top of his head.

Some damn mugger, he thought, as he tried to gather the energy to pull himself upright and survey the damage. After all those years in combat without a scratch, he had to get busted by some damned hyped-up kid on a subway. Sometimes it's safer to be a marine.

Faust struggled to open his eyes. They fluttered and opened. He took one look and closed them again. Bright yellow balls of pain erupted inside his head. They slowly faded as the darkness once more closed in. His stomach churned with the vertigo that followed. He rested.

Gradually the nausea receded but stayed close, a constant warning against sudden movement. Faust once again opened his eyes, fighting to focus. Only one responded. The other one was sealed shut, glued tight with a layer of blood.

The eye showed Faust a twisted and tilted world as the images resolved themselves from an abstract pattern into reality. The gray blob that dominated one corner of his field of sight turned into the base of a subway seat. The white blob became a newspaper. And the brown one became a shoe.

His eye followed the line of the shoe, seeking and finding the leg that was still attached to it. The leg was twisted in the unnatural stillness of death. Faust didn't have to check the body to know the person was no longer breathing. He had seen death before; he didn't need to see any more to know.

Dread clutched at his stomach, driving away the remaining fingers of nausea. Something terrible had happened. He wished he could remember, but he knew that it had to be something terrible. And that could only be an accident. Collision.

It flashed through his mind like an old alarm. Collision. That had to be it. Why else would he be lying on the floor of a train, next to the body of a dead man? Why else would he be knocked unconscious? Only one thing could do that. Collision.

That meant it was his fault. It was his train. He was certain of that. His train. And he was lying here on the floor doing nothing. Christ. He groaned again; this time the pain was internal.

He brought his hand to the source of the pain and his fingers felt liquid. Blood. And lots of it. He grabbed the pole for leverage and tried to pull himself erect. His fingers slid down the cool metal, leaving a trail of red behind. He reached up again and pulled. This time the blood aided him and his face came off the floor with an audible sucking sound. One more heave and he propped himself against the pole, resting one shoulder against the silent support.

The world spun around him. Concussion, he analyzed. Possibly a fractured skull, but otherwise, nothing immediately fatal. He closed his eyes and waited for the world to slow down. He ran his tongue across his teeth, wishing for a drink of water and knowing that it would probably only make him sick again. The spinning stopped.

He opened his eyes. The body of the dead man lay directly in front of him. The neck was clearly broken. The eyes were vacant and staring. No more life there than in his shoe. The car was filled with the scattered remains of personal belongings; they lay clustered around the body, as though drawn to him by some magnetic force. Faust noted that they were only on one side. The collision must have been on the other, he concluded.

He surveyed the rest of the car. The doors were open. The regular lights were off and the emergency battery-powered ones gleamed feebly in the dark. They had been on for some time. No other bodies, but the train must have been packed, judging from the amount of junk left behind. He counted more than a dozen women's purses. Something must have caused them to panic after the accident, driving them out of the car, abandoning everything.

Fire? He sniffed the air. No, there wasn't even the faintest hint of smoke. But some memory was stirred as he breathed deeply, as though he should be smelling for something, something dangerous. In a sudden flash he recalled the mayor's speech, the orders from Central to go to Coney Island, the flashing lights, and finally the ride back. The hand clinging to the door. Disappearing. The scream of the brakes. Everything.

He slipped back to his knees, horrified by the memories. He remained there, holding onto the pole for support and comfort. He remembered the cloud.

Faust rose to his feet, his hands finding and momentarily marveling at the dent his head had left in the pole. That was quickly forgotten as he stumbled forward, slamming into the wall as he lost his balance. The car was canted at a steep angle. It must have jumped the track when the emergency brake cut in. Lucky there wasn't greater damage. A train skidding along one of the subway tunnels could knock down any number of supporting beams, bringing the whole tunnel down on the train, burying it beneath a mountain of concrete.

He pushed himself off the wall and onto the platform separating the two cars. He slid back the door. It jammed partway open. Faust automatically looked for the obstruction and saw a battered pile of rags caught in the door. Thank God, it wasn't a body.

The next car was free of bodies, Faust noted with relief, hoping he wouldn't find others. The car was even more severely tilted, forcing him to grab the metal straps and swing from one to the other like some overgrown subterranean ape. He moved quickly, the action clearing his senses. He felt the blood begin to drip down his forehead as the wound was freshly opened by the exertion.

The next car had been the lead car. It was skewed at a forty-five-degree angle from the second car. A supporting beam had ripped through the tissue-thin wall of the car when the train derailed. It lay across the center of the car at about chest height. Faust knew that anybody standing in its way when that beam came down would be dead. The lights in the car flickered.

The floor was littered with debris. Those passengers who had managed to carry their belongings this far had dropped them as soon as they saw the obstruction. He kicked his way into the car.

His foot struck something solid, yet yielding. Another body, Faust thought, as he cleared the litter off the fallen form. The face came into view. A woman. Young. Maybe twenty-five. No more than thirty. In life she might have been pretty. In death she was merely plain. Huddled around her outstretched and unfeeling arms were two small children, each staring at Faust with terrified eyes, as big as half dollars. One of them, the older one, Faust surmised, spoke for both. "Are you a doctor?"

"No, honey," Faust replied. "I'm not. Is this your mother?" He pointed to the uncovered body.

The girl nodded. The boy only huddled closer to the silent form. Faust guessed the girl couldn't have been more than seven years old. The boy looked a year or two younger.

"She's sick," the girl said, holding her mother's hand. "She won't wake up. I tried but she won't wake up." She was close to tears. "Can you get my mommy a doctor?"

"Sure, honey. You stay here while I see whether there's anyone else on the train." He looked at the girl, her face momentarily illuminated by the pulsing light. The dirt on her face was smeared by the passage of unnoticed tears. "And keep an eye on your brother," Faust advised.

He swung underneath the beam, carefully giving the two children a wide berth. The car was a shambles. The force of the impact had been greatest here. He could see another body propped up against one of the seats. A boy, no, a teen-ager. From the blood spattered on the floor, most of the less seriously injured had managed to make their way out of the wreckage. Thank God there were as few dead as this.

"Ahhhghhh."

Faust tensed, swinging toward the sound. The light dimmed to nothingness. He waited in the darkness. He could do more damage to anyone still alive by blundering around than by waiting another few seconds. The lights rose in intensity once more.

It was a teen-ager. He had opened his eyes. They were glazed with shock.

"Oh, God." The boy's lips barely moved.

Faust picked his way through the litter to the boy's side. He examined him visually, afraid to complicate any injury he might already have. What he could see was enough. The boy's right arm lay twisted on his lap, a shard of white sticking out like a truce flag. One end was covered with the familiar reddish brown stain of dried blood. Compound fracture. Puffiness and swollen tissues around the neck, probably internal bleeding. Glassy eyes. Shock. Maybe a concussion as well. One eye suddenly focused on Faust. "Thank God! I was afraid you'd never get here. I'd almost given up hope and made a try for it myself."

The blank look on Faust's face showed he didn't understand a word the boy had said.

"You know," the boy insisted. "You're with the rescue party, aren't you? I knew they'd have to send someone as soon as they found out about the accident."

"There isn't going to be a rescue party," Faust said, quietly, partly to keep the boy calm and partly to keep the nearby children from overhearing. "They aren't going to send anyone. I'm, or at least I was, the trainman on this thing." His gesture encompassed the entire train. "Before this happened. You just rest, now. I have to check to see whether there is anyone else alive."

"I heard a couple of kids crying a while ago," the boy said, grimacing as he tried to sit up. "I think they were over there somewhere." He pointed to the rear of the car.

"I've already seen them. Mother's dead." He shook his head. "I don't look forward to taking them away from the body. Anybody else?"

"Not that I've seen. Oh, there were a lot at the beginning but they were in too much of a hurry to stop. Haven't seen anybody for . . . oh, maybe fifteen minutes."

"Okay. I just have to check. It's still my train. So you just take care."

"Sure," the boy replied. "What else can I do?" He smiled back at the trainman.

Faust rose to leave. The boy reached out and grabbed his arm. "You're comin' back, aren't you?"

"Don't worry. I'll only be a minute." He disengaged the boy's hand and continued his prowl. The car was only seventy-five feet long; there can't be any more bodies, he thought.

In the flickering light he made his way to the front. He was relieved to find only small piles of trash, none of which could accommodate a human body. He reached the front door. It was slid back, held open by its restraining lever. Outside was only blackness, the eternal darkness of the subway tunnels. The yellow light cast a faint pool of illumination on the track directly in front of the train. It only made the darkness of the rest of the tunnel more total. The glow faded.

He leaned against the jamb, feeling suddenly a little queasy. He closed his eyes, waiting for the spinning to stop. He wondered how he could take the two children and the boy with the broken arm. He allowed himself only a second of self-doubt before banishing the thoughts.

He couldn't afford that now. That cloud was out there somewhere. The mayor had said that it would sink, so the tunnels would be dangerous. He had to get out soon. He had to get them all out before it came down the tunnel to surround them.

He peered into the darkness. It could be out there. Just beyond the feeble pool of yellow light. Out there in the darkness, waiting for them. Waiting for him to step out of the train. Out of the safety of the train. Maybe they should just wait here. Like the boy said, they're bound to send someone to investigate. Someone to help him with the injured boy.

He pulled away from the door. His pocket caught on a protrusion, ripping the material. He reached for the offending object. Something jangled familiarly in his hands. His keys. The ones he had given to the T.A. cop. The hero, Faust smiled to himself, somehow pleased to know that the hero had made it out safely.

He turned to go back to the boy when he caught sight of the driving compartment's door. It was slightly ajar. He had driven the train from there hundreds of times. It was a second home to him, but now he didn't want to open the door. He looked at it as though it were an alien object. Reluctantly, he reached for the knob, his fingers automatically sliding into the familiar groove. One twist and the door was open.

The light flickered and died, leaving Faust in darkness once again. The after-image still burned in his mind. The front window was shattered, a network of glass roadway leading to one central point. In that point the glass had been broken through. Only darkness filled the center. Darkness and the corpse of the cop. The blood had colored the glass below, where the throat had met and rasped against glass.

With a crackle and a buzz from the circuit breakers behind the rear wall of the trainman's cabin, the relays once again powered the emergency lights from the failing power of the car's internal batteries. The body hung there, silent and efficient in its neatly pressed uniform. Faust looked away.

He thought he might be sick for a second. The other bodies, even the woman's, had been just bodies. They never had been real. The cop had. Serves him right, Faust thought as he gently closed the doors. I told him not to play hero.

Faust started back to the boy and the two children, trying not to think of what lay ahead, and what might possibly be lurking just outside the black windows of the train.

From the back of the train, faint at first and then growing louder, a sound crept toward them. A clicking, faintly metallic sound repeated at irregular intervals. It grew closer.

5:10 P.M.   *In a Building; Coney Island*

The door was like its thousand neighbors. The red paint had faded and a small mirrored peep hole glistened vacantly in the gloom of the hall. Kevin stopped in front, his hand frozen in the act of pounding.

The door was ajar and the faint strains of Beethoven's Fifth drifted into the corridor.

Kevin gave the door a gentle push and it swung open silently.

The room was a disaster area. The first impression, an overwhelming one, was of ashes and smoke. The air was filled with stale smoke and fine particles of ash rising from the overflowing ashtrays that littered the room. A trail of cigarette burns stained the edges of each horizontal surface with telltale black-and-brown marks. Kevin almost gagged.

He stepped into the room.

Books and magazines dog-eared and heavily used, were piled in disarray on the bookshelves that lined the walls. A series of spotlights lined the ceiling and peeked out of unlikely crannies. When working they must have given the room the illumination of an operating theater, but now they added only a sinister feeling of drabness to the dark surroundings.

In the center of the room was a drafting table tilted away from the front door. A series of ashtrays, cigarettes still smoldering faintly, surrounded the rear of the table in a semicircle. The gray haze hovered overhead.

"Well, just don't stand there gaping," a deep bass voice snapped. "Either come in or get out. And shut the door behind you. You're letting all the fresh air in."

Startled, Kevin hesitated. He looked for the source of the voice, but except for the table, the room was bare. "Uhhh, I'm sorry, I didn't mean to disturb you. The door was open . . ."

"So. Does that give you the right to come barging in? What did you think it was, an open invitation?"

Kevin slowly stepped farther into the room, angling off to one side of the table. "No, I . . . I was looking for a girl." He reached a point where he could look over the tilted wooden edge. There, sitting on a high stool, was the owner of the bass voice.

"Does this look like a singles' bar?" The man took a heavy drag on a cigarette and balanced it on the end of a thin wooden ledge that bore the scars of similar heavy usage in the past.

"No . . . I . . ." Kevin stuttered.

The man was as strange as his environment. He was small, almost a dwarf. His balding head was covered with a few stray wisps of brown hair standing away from his temples in chaos. Behind each ear was a colored marking pen, red on his right, blue on his left. A mat knife dangled in his mouth like a cigarette.

His hands were most startling. They were huge. They flew across the graph paper tacked onto the table with a sureness and a steadiness that was hypnotic. The chaos of the man and the room ended at the corners of that paper. The lines he inscribed on the graph were absolutely neat and clean, incredibly precise.

It was the schematic of a ship, Kevin realized as he watched the hands at work. He recognized the sweeping lines of the keel and bow. The circles in the center of the ship were totally alien to him, but the man seemed to know what he was doing.

The hands stopped. The man looked up. His eyes were piercing as they stared into Kevin's. Hazel eyes, showing a softness that was nowhere else reflected in the man, with perhaps the exception of his work.

"Well . . ." the man said, "see for yourself. She's not here. What do you think I would be doing with a girl, anyway." He smiled. A series of upturned wrinkles. "I'm not the dating type."

"It's not that," Kevin hastened to explain. "She's a girl.

A young girl, and she's blind. She's lost and her mother asked me to help her look . . ."

"As I said," the eyes were lowered to the paper, "she's not here. Now if I were you, I'd get moving. There isn't much time." He took a drag on the cigarette, obviously enjoying the taste.

"You'd better get out of here before the cloud gets here," he continued checking his watch. It was a fancy underwater one, with dozens of dials and hands, marking the time, phases of the moon, dates, and other nonessential information. It somehow looked right on the man's wrist. "Not much time at all."

"Say, how come you're still here? I mean with the cloud coming and all," Kevin asked.

"Oh, I don't know." The man picked up his cigarette and took a deep drag. "I just couldn't see myself running away." Another drag on the cigarette. "Or walking away, for that matter."

Kevin looked down at the man's legs. They were misshapen, bent, like the rest of his body. Two oversized shoes stuck out at odd angles from the pant legs. A steely glint of metal told him that the material hid braces.

"No, they're good enough in regular times, but in that crowd?" He shook his head. "It wouldn't be worth it. I decided to stay here and wait." Another drag. The tip of the filter flared briefly as the last of the tobacco burned away. He looked at it for a moment before stubbing it out in one of the overcrowded ashtrays. "Ah, well," he sighed. "That's the last of them, I'm afraid. It's getting too close."

The slapping of feet in the hallway interrrupted them.

"Kevin," she called. "Kevin!" A note of hysteria touched her voice.

"In here, Mrs. York," Kevin called back.

The man gave him a quizzical look. "Another one? Or is she the one you were looking for?"

Kevin shook his head. "The mother. We're looking for her daughter."

"Oh." He reached down and lifted one leg across the other in a parody of casualness. "I haven't had this much company in years."

Melba York banged into the room, thrusting the door

unnecessarily hard against its stop. "Kevin!" She gasped. "Have you found her? She's all right, isn't she? Judith, honey, are you . . ." Then she saw Kevin and his host. Her hand flew to her mouth as she gasped.

"Sorry, no." He smiled at her, hazel eyes glinting in the reflected light from the room's only window. "I really wish I could help you but . . ." He shrugged. "I haven't been in a position to see your daughter."

Melba broke down in tears. Sobbing, she explained Judith's disappearance, her own fears. "She's got to be here." Melba repeated. "She couldn't leave without me. She couldn't."

The man took her by the shoulders, his hands both strong and gentle, and shook her. Once. Twice. "Now stop it." His deep voice was commanding. The voice of a leader. "Stop that nonsense right now. You're just making things worse, not better."

"But she might be lying somewhere, needing me and . . ." Another series of hysterical sobs. Another series of shakes.

"I said stop it," he commanded. The tears stopped. "Get a hold of yourself."

She wiped the tears away.

"That's better. Now listen to me. I don't have time to repeat this. Your daughter's blind. She's not crippled. She's capable of taking care of herself."

Melba shook her head. "No . . ."

"I know what I'm talking about. So listen to me. It sounds to me like you just don't want to believe she can take care of herself."

"No," Melba protested. "She's blind. You don't understand . . ."

"But I do. I understand perfectly. There are millions of people who are blind who lead perfectly normal lives. They have jobs, go to work, have families. Everything. So why should your daughter be different?"

Melba hesitated. "But her violin . . ."

"Oh," the man brightened. "Is *she* your daughter?" He smiled. "Well then, you don't have anything to worry about."

"I don't?"

"No." He pushed his chair back to the drawing board. "I saw her this morning. In the park. She was playing for the old people on the benches. She's a regular part of the daily routine around here."

"She is . . . I never knew that."

"And I bet there are a lot of other things you don't know about her as well. She's a lot stronger than you think. Don't worry. She's probably already on her way to Manhattan by now."

He picked up his stylus from a ledge on the drawing board and began sketching in some details on the almost completed ship.

With a final stroke he finished and leaned back to admire his work.

Kevin leaned forward. His eyes were drawn to the logo at the top of the paper. HAL LEE INVESTMENTS AND INVENTIONS, it read.

"What is it?" he asked.

"Death;" Hal Lee answered.

Just below the bow the black ink slowly dried on the last letter of the word PROMETHEUS.

5:15 P.M.   *On Board the* APPLE TREE

Wade listened to the last transmission from the Coast Guard captain, "Please repeat, sir," he requested.

"You heard me, Commander. I told you to execute Miss Yale's plan to destroy the *Prometheus*. You are to open fire on the tanker and ignite the remaining supplies of LNG while they are still confined to the area of the ship. Is that clear enough, Commander?"

"Yes, sir," he answered. "Do . . . do I have permission to withdraw the *Apple Tree* to a safe distance before opening fire?"

"How far is that, Commander?" Bassil snapped. He was plainly unhappy with the order. "Ten miles? I don't think your guns have that range. Use your discretion. No," he immediately corrected himself. "Check with Miss Yale. It's her plan. Ask her how far you can pull back. If at all. Just let me know before you open fire. But as of now, you are to commence firing as soon as you are in position. Work it out with her."

"Understood, Captain." He hesitated for a moment before asking the next question. "Sir, if you don't mind my asking, who authorized this action? Does the President know . . ."

"Damnit, Wade, I do mind your asking. And yes, the President does know. He's put LaSalle in charge of the whole thing and he's ordered it. The White House is backing him up, so you can take it from there. Just do what Miss Yale tells you, Commander." The captain sounded very tired. "Just listen to the civilians. We're only the military. That's our job. Listen to the civilians and follow orders. You have your orders and I have mine. Good luck, Commander. Good luck."

"Thank you, sir." Wade was strangely touched by the old man's parting. It was the first time he had ever expressed anything other than strict military orders. It was the first time that he had seen a human side to the captain.

He turned to Cybil and Paknis who stood at opposite sides of the bridge, pointedly ignoring one another. Paknis had not said one word to Cybil since she radioed her recommendation to LaSalle. Her attempts at communication rebuffed, she retreated into her shell of scientific detachment. They hadn't spoken or even looked at one another for almost half an hour.

"I assume you heard," Wade said, addressing both. He felt as though he were stepping into the middle of a lovers' quarrel and a political war at the same time. He took the Swiss role. Total neutrality. "They," he emphasized the word heavily. To him it meant all civilians. ". . . have decided to go forward with your plan." He nodded at Cybil.

"Execution"—the double meaning of the word did not escape anyone on the bridge—"will commence as soon as we are in position. If it would not interfere too much with your plan, I would like to have the *Apple Tree* withdraw to a safe distance before we open fire. Is that agreeable?"

"What's the maximum range of your guns?" Cybil asked.

"Maximum effective range, two point five miles."

"I've been trying to calculate the effect of an explosion on the deck of the *Prometheus*. The force of the explosion must be focused downward as much as possible. That means the highest trajectory you can get. The shell must come directly down when it strikes the tanker. As close to perfectly vertical as possible. That will maximize the damage to the tanks. A shot against the side of the hull could be worse than useless. It could set the cloud on fire without breaking open the remaining tanks." She looked directly at the commander. "That's what's important. It has to destroy the structural integrity of the tanks before igniting the cloud. Think you can do that?"

"High trajectory. Armor-piercing shells. At a range of one and a half miles we should do it."

"Position this ship wherever you can guarantee the destruction of the tanks with a vertical shot. You must blow them open before the cloud catches fire. You must." Cybil was adamant.

"I understand." Wade addressed the helmsman. "Pull back to a range of one point five miles. The gunnery crew will signal when we are in position. Take her to her position at full speed and then hold her steady. I want the gun crew to have the best possible conditions for their shot."

"Yes, sir." The helmsman rang the orders on the engine room telegraph. The twin engines surged in response, filling the ship with the deep throb of power.

Wade turned back to Cybil. "I assume that you have no objection to my heading to the most upwind position for our firing location?"

"No objection whatsoever, Commander. Not that it'll do much good, I'm afraid. Captain Bassil is right. It won't really matter too much. As long as you're in range of the *Prometheus*, her tanks are in range of the *Apple Tree*. If the explosion doesn't get us," she shrugged, "I'm afraid the fireball will."

"Thank you for the warning. I will advise my crew accordingly. I have a launch standing by to take you ashore. Thank you for your help." He extended his hand. "It's been a pleasure working with you, Professor. I wish we were parting under different circumstances . . ."

"I'm not leaving, Commander, so you can save your farewells." Her voice carried conviction. She was not to be denied. "I'm in this to stay. I will remain on the *Apple Tree* until . . ." She faltered. "Until the shot is fired. You never can tell what might happen and I intend to be available if anything happens at the last moment. Is that clear, Commander?"

"Perfectly clear, Professor. Perfectly clear. You have your responsibilities and I have mine. Mine is the safety

of the ship and her crew. Yours is the successful comple-
tion of this action. I'm sure you could get even the
President's permission to commit suicide. And I, for one,
wouldn't think of standing in your way." He saluted. "If
you'll excuse me, I have to check with the gun crew and
make preparations." He stormed out of the bridge, slamming the door behind him.

Paknis remained on his side of the bridge, watching the
cloud diminish in size as they headed away from the
Prometheus, his first, and now his last, ship. He clasped
his hands behind his back, staring intently at the receding
cloud, longing for one last look at her before they blew
her out of the water. Only the formless white cloud was
visible. It covered the water, snaking one tentacle toward
the distant Brooklyn shore. There was no sign of the
ship.

Val was unapproachably cold. As cold as the cloud,
Cybil thought as she watched him staring out the window.

On the deck below, Wade supervised the gun crew in
loading the forward gun. She watched silently as the end
of the muzzle slowly elevated, pointing to the gray sky.
Radar guided it, pointing to the white cloud and the ship
that lay behind.

"How long before we reach the firing position?" she
asked the young helmsman.

"About two minutes, ma'am."

Over the din of the engines, Cybil imagined she could
hear the heavy metallic click of the shell being rammed
home in the forward gun and the breech being forcefully
locked in place.

5:17 P.M.   *Mayor's Office; City Hall*

"The *Apple Tree,* sir, on line three." Phyllis's cool, professional voice filled the office.

LaSalle motioned Newfeld to take the call.

The press secretary punched the connection through the
speakerphone. The whisper of static that signaled a radiophone call crackled into existence. "Go ahead, *Apple
Tree,*" Newfeld said from behind his cigar.

"Commander Wade, here. We will be in position in
another two minutes. Per my orders from Captain Bassil,

I am requesting final confirmation of your instructions to destroy the *Prometheus.*"

Newfeld looked at the back of his mayor. LaSalle didn't move. The seconds ticked silently by. Newfeld covered the speaker with his hand.

"Vince? It's up to you. What do you want me to tell them?"

The only response was a slight hunching of his shoulders.

"Vince, you have to say something."

As though to emphasize the press secretary's point, the muffled sound of Wade's voice vibrated against Newfeld's hand. "Mr. Mayor? I need confirmation of my orders to open fire."

"One second, Commander." Newfeld took his hand off the speaker and then recovered it. "Vince, you have to say something, for God's sake. Do you want them to go through with it or not?"

Slowly, as though pained by every tiny movement, LaSalle nodded.

"Go through with it?" Newfeld asked.

Again the slow nod.

"Commander." Newfeld uncovered the speaker. "Go ahead. As soon as you're ready."

"We'll commence firing at seventeen twenty hours. That will give us time to get into position and stabilize the ship. I hope to be able to get two, perhaps three, shots off before the explosion. I hope to God you know what you're doing," he added.

"So do we, Commander. So do we," Newfeld answered, breaking the connection. Silence descended over the room. Even the perpetual hum of the air conditioners seemed muted.

"Abe, what do you think? Am I doing the right thing?"

Newfeld hesitated. "Right? Only history will tell. You had to make some decision and you did. That's the most anyone could ask. Even the goddamn President couldn't say what's right on this one. You can't blame yourself for being uncertain. You did your job."

"How many people did they say would die?"

This was the third time LaSalle had asked that question in the past fifteen minutes. Newfeld knew the number by heart. So did LaSalle.

"Seven hundred thousand, plus or minus two hundred thousand. But, Vince, think about the people you already saved. More than a million people were on the Coney Island beach only an hour ago. They'd be dead right now if it weren't for you. Over a million people. Vince . . . that's more than anyone would have thought possible. You have to think about the ones you saved, not the ones you couldn't."

"Couldn't? That's the real question, isn't it, Abe? Could I have saved them? If I only knew for sure, then at least I'd be certain that I'd done everything in my power. Power!" He laughed bitterly. "What power? Even the President shouldn't have power of life or death. What the hell good is it to have power if you can't save people who are depending on you?"

Newfeld joined him at the window. Through the trees, the landmark of the Brooklyn Bridge rose in graceful splendor. The queen of the East River, elegantly spanning the turgid waters below. Now it was the center of the nation's largest evacuation ever.

Its four lanes were packed with throngs of people, shoulder to shoulder. It was a silent and orderly crowd; a solemn procession. Police lined the edge of the bridge directing traffic, keeping the people moving.

At the base of the bridge, an interminable line of blue-and-silver buses waited, their doors open to receive and welcome the arriving crowd and take them to the safety of Central Park.

Below ground the faint rumble of racing trains, the rattle of metal on metal, indicated that the subways were carrying their share to Central Park. A system that carried four million passengers every day was taxed to its limit in handling the flow from across the river. It was a tribute to the system that they coped.

Together, the mayor and his press secretary watched the scene silently.

"They're the ones you have to think about, Vince," Newfeld said quietly. "The ones you saved. They're the ones that'll need you now. They're the ones that'll love you or curse you for what you did today."

LaSalle sighed heavily. "I know, Abe. I know. But I can't help thinking about all those thousands who will never cross that bridge. All those who will die today because of what I decided to do. God, how I wish I could only think about the living."

He fell silent again as he watched the crowd flow across the bridge. It seemed as though it were a still picture, always moving but somehow remaining the same. No matter how many buses pulled away, more remained to be filled. No matter how many people disappeared into the darkness of the subway entrances, more waited to enter. Ever changing, but static.

"What time is it?" LaSalle asked.

"Two minutes to go," Newfeld answered, checking his watch.

"I suppose we'll hear it from here."

"I suppose," Newfeld agreed.

The intercom buzzed. Newfeld went to answer it. "Yes, Phyllis?"

"Director Dillon on line one. Says it's urgent."

In two paces, LaSalle reached his phone. He picked up the receiver, not bothering with the speaker. "Yes, Dillon? You have something . . ."

The color drained from LaSalle's face as he listened to the N.S.A. director. He slammed down the receiver without another word. He hit the intercom. "Phyllis, get me Commander Wade on the *Apple Tree*. Immediately!"

"Yes, sir."

"What is it?" Newfeld asked.

"They have a new computer projection. I was wrong. More than two million dead if we blow the tanker." He paced the room.

"My God," Newfeld whispered.

He slammed his hands together. "Damn, I knew it . . . I knew something like this would come up. I just knew it." He hit the switch on the intercom. "Phyllis, where's the *Apple Tree*?"

"One second, sir. I have to go through the Coast Guard operator and . . ."

"Damn it, Phyllis. Just get them. It's a matter of life and death."

"Yes, sir." She broke the connection.

"A matter of life and death . . ." LaSalle muttered as he checked his watch. The second hand inexorably swung on its predetermined course.

Chapter 13

Rene Maresco was worried. He was so distraught he actually yelled at the wine steward. As maître d' of one of the finest, at least in his own opinion, and most expensive restaurants in the country, such conduct was unheard of. Absolutely unheard of.

Ever since the mayor's announcement, his restaurant had been packed. At first it was only a few officials from the Port Authority, and since they were his employers he opened the restaurant early. They were soon followed by various officials from the state government who exercised similar prerogatives. Then the people from the news media arrived with their cameras and their lights. And finally the public ascended in hordes. It was standing room only. Unheard of.

But Rene was doing a land-office business. He had doubled and then redoubled his prices, trying to stem the consumption of his highly valued wine cellar, only to see the carefully selected wines flow out even faster. It had taken him almost one year to complete his cellar to his satisfaction, and to see it depleted in one afternoon was . . . unheard of. That was the only word for it.

"Rene, we're out of Burgundy," Leopold, the wine steward, reported.

"All my beautiful Burgundies," Rene wailed. He was particularly proud of them. He had personally gone to France to tour the wineries and visit the vineyards before making his selection.

He cursed the view. It was the view's fault. Windows on the World, located on the one hundred and tenth floor of the city's largest building, was a front-row seat for viewing the disaster. The south-side tables provided an excellent view of the cloud as it crept toward Coney Island, disappearing into the depths of the streets.

And, of course, along with the excellent view was the equally excellent air conditioning. And the wine.

Where else could you watch a live disaster unfolding while sipping some excellent Bordeaux or, his favorite, a mature Burgundy. Where else was a disaster so comfortably viewable?

"All right, Leopold," Rene said, controlling himself. He couldn't let the situation get out of hand. "Double the prices again. That might get us through the evening. Maybe we'll have to get some more wine delivered. Call the distributor . . ."

"I already tried, Rene. He asked if I was crazy, with the disaster and all . . ."

"Disaster?" Rene wailed. "Disaster? He doesn't know what a disaster we're having right here. All right, Leopold. I'll just have to take care of this myself. I'll call him personally." He turned and disappeared into the kitchen.

"My Burgundies," Rene lamented. "All my beautiful Burgundies."

5:20 P.M. *In a Train; Somewhere in Brooklyn*

Darkness and death surrounded the small subway car. Only the faint and failing lights of the shorted battery provided the survivors with a semblance of hope. Light meant life.

The distant tapping grew louder. Faust mentally followed its progress as something clanged hollowly against one of the supporting columns in the next car. He strained against the gloom. Nothing.

With a crackle and a strong odor of ozone, the lights faded and dimmed into nothingness. One of the children sobbed. The other echoed the first.

When the lights returned, weaker than before, Faust discovered the source of the noise. A young girl stood at the rear of the car, one hand outstretched as though to ward off some unseen menace. In her other hand, the tattered remains of a beach umbrella was held in front of her. A cane. The tapping resumed as she stepped toward them. She was blind.

"Who's there?" she called. "Someone's there, I can hear you breathing."

The young boy, frightened by the sudden appearance

of the girl, began to cry. His sister shushed him into a sobbing silence.

"Right here," Faust said. "Just ahead of you."

The girl lurched forward. "Where?" She almost ran into the beam that cut through the car before Faust could stop her.

"No! Stop!" he called. "Stay where you are. I'll come and get you. There's a lot of debris on the floor"—he looked at the silent body between the two children—"and you might get hurt."

He made his way to the girl and put his hand on her arm to guide her. "This way."

Tears filled her unseeing eyes. "I . . . I was so afraid that I'd miss you." She gripped his arm with her other hand. "I . . . heard you moving a few minutes ago. But you kept going away. I couldn't find anything to use—" she lifted her umbrella shaft—"as a cane so I had to go on my hands and knees . . . I think I touched some dead . . ." She shuddered, leaving the sentence unfinished. "And then finally I found this and could walk. I was so afraid you'd leave. So afraid that you'd leave like all the others."

"Don't worry. Nobody's going to leave you. A few of us got left behind. We'll have to take care of each other." He peered at her face in the flickering dim light. Her skin was the color of freshly ground coffee. Her features were more Roman than Negroid. Her nose too clipped, too narrow. Her lips too thin. Her brow too long. She had the unlined skin of the prepubescent yet the stature of a near adult. Only her unmoving eyes showed her disability. That and a slight tendency to turn her head from side to side when she listened.

"Come," Faust urged. He guided her around the children and underneath the beam, finally sitting her next to the boy. He was conscious again and looked at the girl.

"Another one, huh?" he said thickly.

"Yes, our party's growing." Faust checked the boy's arm. It was bleeding again. "I'll have to set this before we can go anywhere. You might cut an artery if I don't. And once we're out there," he nodded toward the darkness, "you'd die before we could set it again. It's going to hurt. Think you can stand the pain?"

"Sure," he said, his teen-age bravado showing as he

eyed the silent girl sitting next to him. "I don't have much choice, do I?"

"No, you don't." Faust smiled at the youth. "Wait here while I look for something I can use as a splint."

While Faust prowled the car, picking up and discarding article after article, he learned that the boy's name was Emanuel and the girl's was Judith. He was sixteen. She was fifteen. They exchanged school names and other equally irrelevant trivialities until Faust returned.

"Okay," he explained to both youths. "Emanuel has a compound fracture. That means that the bone is sticking out through the skin."

"Uuugh!" Judith exclaimed. "That must hurt something awful."

"Nah," Emanuel answered. "It's not too bad. It was pretty bad at first, but now it's okay."

"All right," Faust continued. "I'm going to need both of you to help me." He handed Judith the piece of wood, wrapping her hands around it to make sure she wouldn't drop it. "This is the splint, Judith." Then he tore a piece of what had once been a beach towel into strips. When he had four he handed them to Judith as well. "And this is what we'll use to tie the splint to Emanuel's arm. But first I have to set it; that is, put the bone back where it's supposed to be. Understand?"

Emanuel nodded. Judith whispered a quiet yes.

"Okay. Now I want you to sit up straight, Emanuel. Brace yourself against the back of the seat and push against it as hard as you can with your feet." The boy did as instructed. His face flushed as he moved into position. A small cry of pain escaped.

"Don't I even get a bullet to bite on?" he quipped behind clenched teeth.

"We stopped using bullets a long time ago," Faust replied. "They used to go off." Faust grabbed the arm in both hands and gently lifted it off the boy's lap. The cry was louder. Faust raised it until the arm was at shoulder level.

Emanuel sat there gasping for breath. "Wait. Wait. Just one second."

"This is going to hurt, now," Faust warned.

"You mean it hasn't already?" Emanuel grunted. He

took a deep breath, looked at Faust's face, and nodded. "Go ahead."

Faust pulled. The scream filled the car and echoed down the tunnel. It stopped abruptly as the boy fainted. The faint smell of urine rose from the limp body. Faust continued to pull. Evenly and firmly. The jagged edge of white disappeared through the break in the boy's skin.

Faust braced himself against the boy's shoulder, glad he had fainted. This was the worst part. He shifted his grip so one hand was on the biceps just above the elbow and the other encircled the wrist. He took a deep breath.

"Is . . . is it over?" Judith whispered.

"Not yet. Almost." He pulled, keeping the pressure as smooth and as even as he could. This was the dangerous part. One slip and he could easily cut an artery. The boy would be dead if that happened.

The bone twisted in his grasp as he fumbled blindly to mate the two ends. The grinding of bone against bone set his teeth on edge. Judith gasped in sympathetic pain. The bones refused to match up. He twisted again, seeking the proper alignment. It should fit together like two pieces of a puzzle. Perfectly. Unless there was a splinter of the bone floating unseen in the wound. Or an artery.

More to the right. He pulled the bones and allowed them to slowly settle back together. It was right. This time it was right; he could feel the bone seating itself. Perfect. No splinters. No arteries.

He heaved a sigh of relief, retaining his hold only on the two sides of the arm; the rest of his body relaxed. "Okay. Now Judith, feel you way down my arms until you reach my hands." She did as ordered and they completed the slow process of tying the splint in place. Her hands had the surprising agility of the blind and she tied the knots skillfully.

With the splint secured, Faust and Judith sat side by side, resting from the exertion and the tension. Only the sounds of their breathing and the whimpering of the two small children could be heard. The cries brought Faust back to their problem.

Judith also heard the cries. "What's wrong with them?" she whispered.

"Mother's dead," he answered flatly.

"Oh. Are they all right otherwise? No more broken bones . . ."

"They look all right, from what I could see. But maybe you ought to take a look, uh." He stumbled over the word, remembering her blindness. "I mean, they wouldn't let me get too close to them and maybe since you're a girl they might let you come closer . . ."

"Sure," she replied, her voice taking on a light note. The sound of youth. "I've always had a way with kids." She stood up, resting her hand on his shoulder for orientation. "Kids and old people. That's my specialty."

Sliding her feet along the debris-littered floor, she made her way toward the sound of crying. Faust watched her kneel next to the two children and begin to talk to them, amazed at the ease with which she communicated with them. They immediately seemed to trust her.

Emanuel would be coming around soon.

Then they could get started through the tunnel to the nearest emergency exit.

Faust walked to the front of the car and peered into the darkness, wondering how far the nearest exit was. And how close the cloud was.

5:20 P.M. *In a Building; Coney Island*

Kevin, Hal and Melba stood on Hal's balcony, staring bleakly at the street below. It was silent and deserted, but already a death trap. Seconds before, Kevin had noticed a puff of white clinging to the sidewalk near the southern corner of the building. Thicker than fog, it obscured everything behind it. A disembodied cloud.

"We're trapped," Melba whispered, as the impact of what she was seeing hit her. "We're completely cut off."

As she spoke, the wisps of white swept across the green lawn. It was preceded by a carpet of death. Two feet before the cloud, the grass turned from summer green to winter brown. The color of life wilted and disappeared in an instant.

The cloud reached the street. Blacktop turned to white. The whole street was covered.

Across the street an elm, one of the remaining three in the entire complex which had survived various on-

223

slaughts of Dutch elm disease and rampaging teen-agers, was dying.

Like all living creatures the tree was mostly water. Its cells were more fibrous than animal cells but contained nearly as much water. The sap, lifeblood of the tree, rose through miles of veins extending from the deepest roots to the topmost leaf. Even the bark itself was dependent on an abundant supply of water. When the cloud touched the tree, heat was drawn out through the bark and the outer layers of the wood. The water froze, bursting the cell walls. The cells became brittle immediately. The foundation of the ancient tree turned to glass. Like glass it shattered. Explosively.

With the majesty of age, the tree toppled, its leaves turning brown as it fell into the street. In slow motion it settled into the cloud, dispersing a blanket of white that surrounded and covered it. In a series of recurring shudders, the once graceful limbs crumbled into the cloud and, in less than a minute, the tree was gone. Nothing but the memory and the fading echo remained.

"What is that stuff?" Kevin whispered. "Nerve gas? I've never heard of anything like that. Never."

"Cold," Hal answered. "Cryogenic cold."

"Cold?" Kevin sputtered. "I thought the cloud was poisonous. It's merely cold?"

"Listen, Kevin," Hal said patiently, "that cold isn't 'merely' anything. It's cold, yes. And it's poisonous, too. If one doesn't get you, the other will. That cold's as deadly as anything you'll ever face. Don't forget what happened to that tree. That was 'merely' the cold."

Hal returned to the apartment and began opening cabinets.

"What are you doing?" Kevin asked as he watched Hal search through the myriad of concealed drawers.

"Oh, just getting a few things together." He looked around the room and spotted a canvas knapsack in a corner. "Here, get that for me, will you?"

Kevin pushed himself off the couch and retrieved the designated object. He held it open while Hal filled it with his accumulated possessions. It became quite heavy.

"Do you know some way out of here?" Kevin asked hopefully. "Is there a secret tunnel? A sewer perhaps?"

"Don't be an ass," Hal chastised. "Tunnels are out.

Physics will tell you that. The cloud is cold. It's heavier than air. It sinks. Tunnels would be death traps. The first place the gas would go. No, use your brain."

"What?"

"I said use your brain for a change. Don't let someone else do your thinking for you. You are a relatively intelligent, although clearly uninformed, adult. Think for yourself. If the cloud goes down, where do you go?"

"Up." Like a Jungian word association test, the answer popped out unbidden.

"Good. A little slow, but finally you got the right answer." He turned to Melba, who was still panting on the couch. "Think you can take some more work? There's a lot to be done before we leave."

"Up?" Kevin repeated. "What's up? We're trapped. We can't set a foot outside the building without getting it frozen off, so what good does going up do? And where are we going?"

"In reverse order," Hal answered. "The roof. And, possible salvation." He watched the statement slowly sink in. "But, of course, if you'd rather wait here until the cloud . . ." He let the sentence hang.

Kevin hefted the sack. "No. No, I'm with you. Just tell me where to go and I'm with you."

"Melba." Hal looked at the woman on the couch. She didn't look up. "Mrs. York!" The tone of command forced her to look at him.

"We're leaving. You have to come with us. Now. There's no time to waste. No time at all."

"But . . . where are we going?"

"The roof."

"I have to find my daughter. She's lost out there somewhere, and she needs me."

Hal grabbed her shoulders, the same grip he had used before. "Wrong, Mrs. York. We need you. We need you here and now. You can't do your daughter any good by dying. And what you're doing to yourself is the same as dying. Wake up, Mrs. York. Open your eyes and see the world." He shook her gently. "Open your eyes, Mrs. York."

"Open your eyes," Hal commanded. "Open your eyes and live."

5:20 P.M. *On Board the* APPLE TREE

Paknis had to admire the efficiency of Wade and his crew as they prepared to open fire. He hated them for it, although he knew they were not to blame. He tried to blame Cybil. Her recommendation was, after all, responsible for the actions of the gun crew below as they carefully loaded the forward gun with its armor-piercing shell.

But he couldn't hate her either. It wasn't her fault. The *Prometheus* had turned killer. Like a mad dog it had to be destroyed. No matter how painful it was, he knew it was the right thing. As long as there was no way to neutralize the poison that spilled from her, she had to be stopped. He only wished it was he, not Wade, who stood by the gun and gave the order to fire. It was his right as her captain, no matter how illusory his command. The law of the sea.

Not that it really mattered, he realized as he watched Wade stand back and check his watch. Ever punctual, Wade would fire precisely at five twenty. Just as he had promised. He positioned the loader, cradling a second shell in his arms. A third shell lay to their left. There wouldn't be any need for a fourth. Nor would there be a chance to fire it.

Cybil had made that clear. In her cold, professional tone she explained that the force of the explosion would spread the gas outward in a self-expanding cloud of frozen fire. At its heart, the cloud would be two hundred and sixty degrees below zero. Only the fringes would burn at the white heat of eleven hundred degrees. The gas would vaporize faster than the fire could consume it, expanding to six hundred times its liquid volume. The force of the initial explosion would provide only the initial impetus for the cloud. It would be driven by the internal forces until all the gas vaporized and burned.

It would assume the shape of a large mushroom, she said. Like an atomic explosion. Only the mushroom would be yellow as the sides were bathed in the bright heat of burning gases. It would soar two to ten miles in the sky. It would be seen as far away as England as the methane flared, changing into its component parts, leaving only carbon dioxide and water as a residue.

The Deadly Frost

It was the funeral pyre of the *Prometheus*.

And somewhere in the heart of that flaming mushroom would be a tiny speck of metal, adding a few kilograms of fuel to the fire, an unnoticeably small amount of energy compared to the tons of burning gas surrounding them. The small speck would be the *Apple Tree*. Cybil had calmly and patiently explained that the cloud might cover them before the fire reached them. That way they'd be in the frozen stem of the mushroom. They'd die the quick death of cold.

Not that it mattered much. If the stem didn't reach them, they'd be caught in the resulting firestorm at its base. They'd share the flaming death of the *Prometheus*. Either way they would all die before the third shell reached the deck of the tanker. So, of course, there was little need for a fourth shell.

Wade ordered only three brought out on deck. Never a wasted motion. Never a wasted piece of equipment.

Wade raised his arm, peering at his watch. Paknis could almost hear the drawn out "Reaaaady" as he waited for the second hand to reach the twelve.

Paknis felt Cybil press against him. He looked down into her deep brown eyes. Was there a hint of a tear there? No, he couldn't hate her. Not the woman he loved. He reached out and put his arm around her shoulder. He pulled her close. Together they watched the commander's arm descend in a rapid, choppy motion.

"Fire!" They could read the word on his lips.

As the roar of the erupting shell momentarily deafened them the radio crackled into life. Paknis, nearest to it, was the only one who heard the desperate cry from LaSalle. "*Apple Tree,* do not fire! *Apple Tree,* this is LaSalle; I repeat, do not fire on the *Prometheus*. Answer me, goddamnit, answer me. Don't fire on the . . ."

Paknis was out on deck before the scream of the shell cleared the deck. He leaned over the rail and shouted, "Don't!" He waved his arms trying to get Wade's attention. The commander was intent on reloading the gun, readying her for the next shot. He didn't hear Paknis.

Cupping his hands, he yelled again. This time one of the crewmen heard and, tapping the commander on the arm, pointed to the waving officer. It was too far to be heard, but Paknis made himself understood. Shaking his head and waving his hands, he told them not to fire. Wade had the crew stand down after completing the loading. He pointed to the microphone on his helmet, indicating that Paknis should call him on that.

Inside the bridge, Cybil was on the radio with the mayor. "It's too late, Mr. Mayor. We've already fired the first shell. Val stopped them from firing the second, but there's no way we can stop the first."

"Any chance it might miss?" LaSalle asked desperately.

"I'm afraid not. They aimed by radar. Near perfect probability."

"Oh," was all LaSalle could say.

"What is it, Cybil?" Val asked.

"Nothing, Val," she answered. "Nothing that matters, anyway. How soon will the shell hit?"

Val looked at the clock. Only thirty seconds had passed. "Ten seconds." It was on a high trajectory, more like a lob than a regular artillery shot. It would arch high in the air and then fall back to earth. A slow, wasteful shot militarily. It took too much time. Each second meant an extra second of life for the *Apple Tree* and her crew.

Val took Cybil under his arm and they stepped back onto the walkway where they could watch the final moments of their lives.

The scream of the returning shell was a shrill whine as it tore through the blanket of haze that covered the harbor. It grew in volume, changing from a scream to a roar. Val unconsciously tightened his hold on Cybil, trying to pull her closer to him. Trying to protect her with his body.

The roar filled the air. It sounded almost as though the shell was coming down on top of the *Apple Tree*. And then, silence.

A second later the diminished sound of a splash came faintly to the *Apple Tree*.

No explosion. No fireball. Nothing. A clear miss.

Val slowly released his grip on Cybil. "It missed," he whispered. "It missed!" This time it was a shout.

Cybil turned to him. "It missed!" She shouted back at him. They were laughing and hugging one another, crying out "Missed" over and over again.

Wade found them in hysterics. "What the hell's going

on?" he demanded. "What's happening? Won't someone tell me what's going on?"

Cybil gasped out an answer. "It missed."

"Damnit, I can tell that much," Wade snapped back, angry at what he thought was an overt crack at his marksmanship. "So what's so funny. We'll just have to do it again. Must have been a defective shell. The next one will be right on the . . ."

"There won't be a next one," Cybil said, finally gaining control of herself.

"Won't be a next one? What do you mean?"

"LaSalle called. The shot's called off. Don't you understand? That means the *Apple Tree*'s saved too. And all because it missed."

As the impact of the news hit the commander, a grin slowly spread over his face. "It missed," he said.

"Yes, isn't it wonderful? You missed!"

In seconds all three were in hysterics, laughing uncontrollably. The laughter spread over the ship like a contagious disease. The men didn't know why they were laughing. They only knew they were alive. It was enough.

Cybil stopped short. "Oh my God, the mayor." She raced back into the bridge and grabbed the dangling microphone as it gently swayed against the radio.

"Mayor LaSalle, are you there? This is the *Apple Tree*. Mayor LaSalle?"

"*Apple Tree?* Is that really you? Professor? I thought . . . what happened? I thought you couldn't stop it. I thought it was too late. I kept waiting . . ."

"We missed!" Cybil shouted into the microphone. She wiped a tear out of her eye. "The shot missed! The *Prometheus* is intact!"

"You missed?" The mayor was incredulous. "You really missed?"

"Yes," Cybil shouted joyously.

She heard a cheer go up from the mayor's office. She could almost hear the cigar hitting the floor as Newfeld joined in.

Minutes later the *Apple Tree* regained a semblance of sanity. At least the crew had ceased spontaneously hugging one another, and the laughter was reduced to broad grins. They had been given a new lease on life and every one of them appreciated the future that had suddenly been given back.

Cybil and Val were most affected. They couldn't let go of one another. They had been separated by the near death of the *Prometheus*. Her resurrection brought them back together again. Like new lovers they hovered over the chart table, hands surreptitiously clasped underneath the cover of wood as they reviewed their position with the commander.

"We have no choice," Cybil stated, her voice taking on a lilting tone of enthusiasm, a tone that had been absent ever since their return from the tanker. It was a timbre that Wade had never before heard in her voice. More feminine. Warmer than she had ever been before in his presence. He was startled and, seeing the hands disappearing below the plane of the chart table, he smiled to himself. She was human after all.

"We have to find some way to get the *Prometheus* out of the bay." She jabbed her pencil at the chart, spearing the "X" that was the tanker with a compass point. "Since we can't ignite the gas, we have to get it out of the harbor. That means only one thing. Towing. We've got to tow her out of the bay, past Sandy Hook and out to sea before her tanks burst, or, worse yet, her hull cracks open, exposing the tanks to the warm bay. You two are the sailors. Any suggestions?"

"How about trying to get a line to the *Prometheus* without touching the water? Maybe then it wouldn't give under the tension," Val suggested.

"Impossible," Wade answered immediately. "Too long a run. Must be three hundred yards between the ship and the edge of the cloud. You'd never get a line to make that distance without hitting the water. Especially," he added, "since you have to take it in from a rowboat that's almost at water level itself."

"How about dropping someone with a line from a helicopter?" Cybil asked.

Wade and Val were silent as they considered the plan. Val finally vetoed it. "Negative. First, you'd never be able to pinpoint the tanker in that cloud, so it'd be a matter of guesswork whether the person would land on the ship or in the bay. Second, even assuming you could get the man and the line on the ship, the line would still drop into the water before you could draw it taut."

"That reminds me," Wade interjected. "I meant to ask before. How did we miss? Not," he added hastily, "that I'm complaining, of course. It's just that we calculated that shot as carefully as any I've ever ordered. We had the *Prometheus* dead in the radar sights. I can't believe we missed her."

"I wonder about that myself," Cybil answered. "And I can only come up with one theory. Thermal layers. The ice crystals probably gave the radar a false image of the tanker, somewhere between the tanker and the edge of the cloud. You weren't aiming at the tanker, only her reflection." She pointed to a spot midway in the circle that surrounded the "X." "And, I'll bet that you were right on target. Fortunately that target wasn't real."

"Oh." Wade digested her analysis, trying to put it into his frame of reference. "Like sonar hitting a layer of cold water, showing a false bottom, or a submarine showing a false reading when it passes through a cold current."

"Exactly," Cybil agreed "Just like a submarine, only here the cold is on the surface, not below the waterline."

As though she had dropped a bomb on the table all three of them froze for an instant. No one wanted to be the first to speak, fearing that someone would point out the fallacy in his logic. They looked at each other in silent conference.

"Do you think . . ." Val began.

"It could work," Wade agreed.

"You wouldn't have to worry about the cold at all," Cybil added her confirmation.

"But how . . ." Val began.

"There's a special submarine rescue unit based nearby. I'll bet they could be flown in within half an hour," Wade replied.

They fell silent again, each mentally checking the unverbalized plan for defects. As the silence grew, so did their optimism.

Val glanced at the chronometer over the table. He checked it against his watch. "Within half an hour?" he asked. "That's cutting it awful close."

"Why?" Cybil was confused. "If the cloud ignites, that's it, no matter what time it is."

"It's not the cloud I'm worrying about," Val explained. "It's the tide. It's turned. In another hour the channel will be too shallow for the *Prometheus* to navigate. She'll be aground."

He pointed to the shallow waters just off the sides of Sandy Hook Channel. They showed only twelve feet of water. The *Prometheus* took twice that. "And once she's run aground, she'll be stuck there until next high tide."

"About twelve hours," Wade supplied, staring at the chart.

Suddenly, the bay seemed awfully shallow.

Chapter 14

5:25 P.M. *Mayor's Office; City Hall*

"Want a drink?" Newfeld held up a bottle of Scotch taken from the liquor cabinet disguised as a filing cabinet behind the mayor's desk.

LaSalle waved off the offer. "We're still a long way from home, Abe," he warned as he watched the press secretary pour a generous helping into the crystal glass with the city seal embossed on its side. A gift from the Dutch UN ambassador, LaSalle remembered, on the day he had won the election. Probably would have gone to his opponent if he had won. Probably, hell! Positively would have. Politics was like that. If you were a winner, everybody was your friend. If you lost, you were nothing.

"I know, but that news deserves a drink."

"Okay," LaSalle agreed, holding out his hand for the proffered glass. "But keep it light. We've got to have clear heads for this."

"Don't worry." Newfeld poured his own, the amber liquid covering about an inch of the bottom of the tumbler. "It's my experience in situations like these that it's virtually impossible to get drunk. Adrenaline burns the alcohol away too fast." He eased himself into his chair, cradling the glass between both hands like a fine wine. He savored the aroma.

They sat together quietly sipping the twenty-year-old Scotch, enjoying the peace and quiet. A mere interlude they both knew, but the human organism could operate only so long under constant tension. A moment's rest was to be treasured. Neither spoke, knowing that the moment couldn't last. It didn't.

The intercom buzzed insistently.

5:30 P.M.   *In a Train; Somewhere in Brooklyn*

Faust knelt next to Emanuel. "How are you feeling?"

"Next time, I'll take a bullet," he replied weakly, smiling.

Faust grinned back. "If you can joke, you can walk." He checked the splint. It was holding. It wasn't perfect and it might have to be reset once they got to Manhattan, but at least the bleeding had stopped. The boy's eyes were clearer. That meant he was in less pain.

"Sure." His bravado showed again. "Anything you say." His face clouded. "I made kinda a fool of myself, didn't I? What with screaming like that and . . . peeing in my pants and all." His voice dropped to a whisper.

"Don't worry about it," Faust reassured him. "Happens to the best of them."

"Do you think she . . ." he nodded toward Judith who sat on the dirty floor of the car, talking seriously with the two children. "She didn't notice, did she?"

Faust couldn't suppress a smile. "No, I'm sure she didn't," he lied.

"Good," he relaxed. "I just wouldn't want a girl to see me like that."

Faust put his arm around the boy's waist. "Think you can stand?" He pulled him to his feet before he had a chance to answer.

He swayed for a second as the blood rushing to his feet made him lightheaded. "Sure." He clung to Faust's arm for support. "See, I told you I'd be okay."

"Judith," Faust called. "Are you ready?"

She rose steadily to her feet and nodded. "Yes, and Mary and Timmy are ready too, aren't you?" She addressed the two small children as though they were adults.

"Yes, Judith." Mary answered for both of them.

"Take my hands." Judith extended her arms, hands spread wide, waiting for the two to grab hold. They did; Mary first, then Timmy, more hesitantly, took her other hand. "And don't let go. Remember, I told you that you're my eyes and I'll get lost if you let go. So hold tight."

"We will," Mary said. "Don't worry, Judith. We won't let you get lost." Timmy just shook his head.

The threesome walked slowly toward Faust and Emanuel, stopping a few paces away. "We're ready," Judith said. "I see that you're up, Manny."

"Huh?" Emanuel said. "But . . ."

"I could hear you breathing. There were two of you, so it had to be both you and . . . I don't even know your name." She looked directly at Faust.

"Faust. Elliot Faust. My friends call me El."

"I think I'll call you Elliot. It's stronger. It fits you better than El." She wrinkled her nose in distaste. "Elliot, I'd like you to meet Mary and Timmy. They've decided to come with us." The two children tried to hide behind her legs but she pulled them forward. They looked at the floor instead.

"Mary, Timmy, I'd like you to meet Manny and Elliot. Mary," she pushed the girl gently forward. A tiny hand was extended. Elliot solemnly shook it. It disappeared into his paw like a doll's hand. She shook Manny's next.

"You smell funny," Mary said after she let go of his hand. "Did you have an accident? Timmy sometimes has accidents at night."

"I do not," Timmy protested, aiming a kick at his sister. She easily skipped away.

"Do too," she taunted.

"Do not."

"Now, Mary," Judith reprimanded the older child.

"But it's true," she wailed back. "He does. Just last week . . ."

Timmy began to cry.

"Now see what you've done," Judith scolded without anger. "You and Timmy have to help one another too, you know, not just me."

"Okay." Mary apologized. Timmy's tears disappeared with the swipe of a grimy hand.

The introductions over, Faust took them to the front door of the train. Outside there was only a small pool of dim yellow light glinting faintly off the smooth steel rails. Lining up his four charges he outlined his plan. He told them that they had to stay together and he assigned partners. Each child was to hold the hand of an adult, either Judith or Manny, both of whom he found himself considering as adults, at least in the way they acted, if not in years.

"It shouldn't take long," Faust explained as he lowered Judith to the track four feet below the floor level of the car. "There's an emergency exit between every two stations." Next, he reached for Mary. He lowered her as he spoke. "So we might not be in the tunnel for more than a few minutes, depending where we derailed." The tiny girl giggled as she swung through the air and landed gently on the rocky roadbed below. "It's all a matter of luck." Timmy swung down next. He, too, was light as a feather to the burly ex-marine.

Manny was last. His broken arm made the transfer difficult. And painful, Faust realized as he lowered the youth. He heard the suppressed grunt of agony as the weight shifted from the good arm to the bad. But he didn't cry out. He kept as quiet as he could. The boy was a real trouper, Faust thought.

Faust reached behind the control room door and cut the circuit to the emergency power. He felt as well as saw the lights die. Outside, Timmy, Mary and even Manny shifted nervously in the sudden darkness. Only Judith was calm. She had long ago conquered her fear of the dark. Her strength met their fear and calmed them. In seconds, they were ready to proceed.

With a minimum of confusion they linked up in their prearranged order. Faust took the lead. They were all in line as he fumbled his way along the wall. The exit could not be far away, he realized, as his eyes tried to pierce the black veil.

Ahead, darkness blocked the way.

5:50 P.M. USN Helicopter; En Route to New York Harbor

"*Angel Three* to *Apple Tree*, do you read me?"

"*Apple Tree* to *Angel Three*, loud and clear. What's your E.T.A.?"

The pilot checked his watch as the giant jet-assist Sikorsky roared toward the harbor. "E.T.A. five minutes your location, *Apple Tree*. Where do you want your fish delivered?"

"We'll direct you when you get here, *Angel Three*. Approach the harbor from the south. Repeat. From the south, *Angel Three*."

"Roger, *Apple Tree*, approaching the harbor from the south." The giant rotors roared as they slightly changed their pitch. They were going at their maximum speed. Emergency full. The copter vibrated only slightly as the pilot pushed it to its limit. The President himself had told him to "get there as fast as that bird can fly." The pilot pushed his "bird" for every revolution it could take.

"And, *Angel Three*, stay clear of the cloud. The white cloud. It looks like smoke from the air, but isn't. Don't even let your propwash hit it."

"Roger, *Apple Tree*. Avoid the cloud." He checked his watch. "E.T.A. three minutes. I should be in sight any time now."

The pilot looked at his co-pilot. "Check the fish, Charlie. See that they're all ready. We'll be on target in another three minutes. Let them know that we'll be dropping them from pretty high, so buckle up tight."

The co-pilot gave him the okay sign, unbuckled his harness, disconnected his headphones, and slid out of his seat into the cramped passage that led to the giant cargo space. It was larger than the average trailer truck.

Along one side, dwarfed by the immensity of the space, stood three men. One was dressed in a drab regulation flight suit. The other two wore brightly colored wetsuits, one yellow, the other orange. Each had a black stripe on the left sleeve, stark against the fluorescent colors of the rest of the suit. Over the breast was an emblem of a whale with a hook in its mouth. The insignia of the elite submarine rescue squad. The stripe meant that both men were lieutenants.

With professional thoroughness they checked their gear as the co-pilot relayed the message. The one in orange didn't even look up from examining his air regulator. They relied on the fliers to get them here. Then their work started.

On the floor lay two nylon duffle bags, color-coded to match the suits. They were carefully weighted to have neutral buoyancy once immersed in water, so they could be towed with minimum resistance.

The co-pilot waited for some response from the men. Finally the one in yellow just nodded. As he returned to his seat, the co-pilot thought, for what must have been the hundredth time since he had started ferrying the submarine rescue squad, that they were undoubtedly the strangest men he had ever known in the service. Before a job they never spoke or joked around the way the rest of the men did. Not even among themselves. Must be swimming in the water all the time, he mused as he wiggled into his seat. It must do something to their brains.

"Fish are ready," the co-pilot reported.

The pilot nodded, opening the line to the *Apple Tree*. "*Apple Tree,* this is *Angel Three*. Have you in sight. Am approaching from the south as instructed. Please inform as to drop point."

"Roger, *Angel Three*. Come in at minimum height and drop your divers at one hundred yards short of the cloud. That's about midway between the *Apple Tree* and the base of the cloud."

"Acknowledged. One hundred yards short of the cloud. Minimum height." He reduced speed, throttling the engines down to slow. They were a little hot, he noted. He would have to take it easy on the way back.

He buzzed directly across the *Apple Tree*'s deck, only fifty yards above the radio antenna. It trailed after him in the wind.

"*Angel Three*. Is there any way to cut your wash down?"

"Affirmative, *Apple Tree*." He made a few adjustments on his controls, setting the Sikorsky's props for minimum pitch. That would focus most of the force of the thrust straight down. It slowed them to a crawl as they neared the imaginary point he had selected as the drop point. He rotated the copter so he could check the position of the *Apple Tree*. Perfect. Right on the nose.

"Pilot to fish," he called into his intercom. "Time to get your feet wet."

The copter barely bounced as the two men jumped. Only the most skilled pilot would have noticed it. This pilot did. Looking out the window he saw the two brilliantly colored heads bob to the surface and wave. Two more tiny jolts as the packs were thrown overboard. Tiny threads followed them into the water. Nylon leader, attached to two rolls in the cargo hatch, the pilot knew.

Slowly he edged toward the nearby *Apple Tree*. He would drop the spools on their deck, linking them to the two divers.

"*Apple Tree*, the fish are in the water." The pilot looked out his window. The divers had disappeared. Already on their way underneath the cloud.

5:50 P.M.   *In a Tunnel; Somewhere in Brooklyn*

The first hint they had was from Judith. She said she heard something. Maybe her hearing was more acute than the others but, in the absolute darkness of the tunnel, they were all equally blind. Faust told her not to worry, they'd be out of the tunnel soon. There had to be an emergency exit nearby. There had to be.

They had been walking in the dark for what seemed an eternity. Faust realized that the first exit couldn't be too far as he groped along the wall, running his hands against the filthy concrete, feeling his way north. They had one between just about every station. Some, he remembered, had been sealed up because of new construction and others had fallen into general disuse, although the Authority would never admit it. He knew for a fact that there were exits that you couldn't open without using a crowbar. He silently prayed that he wouldn't find one of them.

Ahead a warm yellow patch of light showed through the grating. Dust motes danced in the air. A ventilation shaft. It opened onto a sidewalk. No way they could open that. It was sealed in concrete and steel. Only the air could come in. And the gas.

Then, almost without recognizing it, he reached an exit. Its emergency light, powered by normal current, was extinguished. His hands passed into thin air, showing him that the exit was there. He let out a shout. The others crowded around him. He carefully disengaged the hands that linked him to the others and reconnected them to each other. No sense in getting lost now that they were on the brink of safety.

He crawled up the emergency ladder. Bright light cascaded over his body. It was as refreshing as taking a bath. He laughed aloud as he climbed to the street. The catch was just above his head. He tripped it and it sprang free with a well-greased snap. This wasn't one of the defective ones, he thought as he shoved against the metal cage. It didn't budge.

He looked at it as though it were a personal enemy and tried again. Nothing. He put the full force of his back into it. The veins in his forearms bulged as he strained against the trapdoor. He couldn't budge it an inch.

His exhaustion exploded out in one breath. He released his hold on the trapdoor. Something must be blocking it, he realized. Peering through the grillwork he surveyed the top of the exit. Moving his head to get a better angle he looked for some type of catch that he had forgotten about. There was nothing. Nothing but a shadow on one corner of the trap.

Shadow? He strained against the grill, pressing his face painfully into the greasy steel. The shadow resolved into a solid form. Black. With lines that showed tiny bits of sunlight through the edges. A tire.

Tires were normally attached to cars, Faust reasoned. Cars were too heavy to lift.

Resignedly, he crawled back down the ladder to rejoin the group. In a curt sentence he told them that the exit was blocked. He broke and then reformed the human chain. They had to go forward.

"There it is again," Judith warned, stopping the group. "That sound."

"What?" Faust asked, straining his ears in the darkness. "I don't hear anything." Then suddenly he did. The sharp clicking sound of something against metal. The high chittering squeal uttered by inhuman throats.

239

Rats.

Far behind, the cloud slipped silently into the dark tunnel. Its mere touch meant death to any warm-blooded creature. It preferred depths, always sinking to the deepest holes and crevices, following any number of twists and turns until it reached the bottom. Rats built their nests in small pockets carefully excavated from beneath the tracks, tunneling into the stones and gravel where the digging was easy. The cloud followed them into their nests. When it touched them they died.

Protected by centuries of evolution, the rats were already on edge. They lived in a world filled with rushing trains and the ever-present stench of ozone. They thrived on it. Suddenly the tracks ceased to sing the warning song of the approaching train. The air slowly cleared of the metallic taint of ozone. Even the emergency lights that provided a minimum of background illumination faded into darkness. All was silent and dark in the tunnels.

That was strange.

Strangeness meant danger. It meant death. The males stood close to the entrances of their nests. Females and young waited within. Waited for the signal to flee. Or, if necessary, to fight.

But their keen senses were not able to detect the drifting methane as it slunk through the darkness. There was no odor to smell. There was only the almost instantaneous death of the methane cloud.

Almost instantaneous.

The rat community was on the alert. Anything could set them off. The cloud silently touched a male rat poised over his nest. The rat died, thrashing once in agony before its muscles froze solid.

The thrashing was enough. The nearest rat ran. Death was in the air. Running, the rat tumbled through the community of nests, knocking into other males and near-adults in its panic. They too began to flee the unseen menace.

In a biological chain reaction, the rats careened down the tunnel, jumping and skipping ahead of the cloud. Not knowing what they were fleeing, only knowing that the other rats were running. Danger and death followed close behind.

Penned in by the concrete-and-granite walls of the tunnel, they had no place to go but forward, following the track. It was survival of the fittest. Infants were deserted by their nursing mothers who chased after the long-departed fathers. Sick and injured were left behind. The old rats, whose weight had increased with age, lagged behind, soon swallowed by the cloud as it swept forward in the darkness.

Like a tidal wave they grew, picking up new colonies of rats as they fled.

And as they ran, their nails clicked against the rails. They screamed in their panic as death pursued them in the darkness.

Faust had only an instant to realize what was happening as the black wave neared them. "Rats!" he cried into darkness. He reached out to grab the nearest body he could find and pulled it close, trying to protect it with the bulk of his body, as he pressed against the wall. "Against the wall!" he shouted.

Judith felt a heavy mass thump against her legs, just below the knees. She was knocked to the ground, losing her grip on Faust's belt. Sharp stones cut deeply into her shins. She cried out in startled agony. Another mass struck her. It was alive. She reached out to push it away. It was gone before she could touch it. Then another and another struck her.

Her scream was more animal than human.

Manny heard Faust's cry just as he felt the first rat brush past him. He reached out for the tiny figure of Mary, but she was swept from his grasp by a superior force. With only one arm, he was off balance. In the darkness he was blind. He couldn't withstand the onslaught of the rats as they crashed into him. He fell head-first.

He struck out with his good arm, but it wasn't enough to break his fall. He crashed into the wall. Blackness closed in, washing away the darkness of the tunnel. He crumpled to the ground, unconscious.

The waves of terrified bodies seemed unending, like the sea itself. Finally the wave crested and broke. A few slower ones scampered across the fallen bodies, leaving behind the still, the dead, and the dying.

6:00 P.M. On Board the APPLE TREE

Commander Wade adjusted the headset dropped by *Angle Three* along with the spools of bright yellow nylon line leading to the two divers. He looked forward and waited for the okay signal from his communications chief, who lowered the transponder into the calm gray waters of the bay.

He heard the splash through the sensitive earphones of the underwater communication equipment and then the rush of bubbles as it was lowered to operational depth, just deep enough to prevent the wave action from interfering. The radioman gave Wade the signal and tied off the coaxil cable on a forward cleat.

"Communications check." Wade spoke into the microphone, pulling it closer to his mouth so it would be more comfortable. "Do you read me?"

"Affirmative," came the immediate reply. "Loud and clear." The voice was slightly distorted, sounding as though the speaker were in an echo chamber. That was the effect of speaking into a mask underwater.

"Report progress," Wade ordered.

"Who can tell?" one of the divers answered. "It's so damn mucky down here that it's impossible to see more than a foot in front of your face." The divers were renowned for being insubordinate while underwater. There was something primal about the sea that made it almost impossible to maintain civility and military order underwater. But as long as they did their job, Wade didn't care. "We're heading due north and I'd estimate that we've gone about two hundred yards. The tide's against us and the equipment's dragging against us as well. I don't suppose you want me to go up for a look?"

"Absolutely not!" Wade was horrified. Hadn't they briefed these men at all before dropping them?

"I didn't think so, but I just wanted to make sure. Those stories true about the cloud?"

"I don't know what stories you're talking about," Wade replied, disturbed about the lack of discipline. "But if you try going to the surface, you won't be coming back down again."

"That's what I heard."

The Deadly Frost

It was like swimming in a garbage pail, Charles Etkin thought as he maintained a regular, measured kick. He swam with the ease of a practiced swimmer, his arms dangling at his sides, head down, letting his legs do all the work. Below and slightly behind him the supply bag trailed, jerking him back with its mass as it was tugged by the tide. Wish they had dropped us on the other side so we'd have the tide with us, he thought as he checked on his partner swimming next to him. It was the automatic action of a practiced driver, checking his rearview mirror, done without thought. It could save his life. It had before.

Etkin and Harper had been teammates on dozens of missions, most more dangerous than today's. They were regularly rotated to different stations around the world, probably following the submarine fleet, although no one would admit it.

"See anything?" Etkin asked.

Harper looked up. "Who can see in this shit?" He checked his wrist compass. They were still on course. "Should be coming up on it soon. Want to spread out a little, just in case we miss it?"

"Nah. Did you see the specs on that mother? She must be a thousand feet long. Can't miss her. Not in this puddle."

As they spoke, a dark shadow grew in the murky gray-green water. It was solid against the shifting shades of the water. It could only be one thing. A ship.

"*Apple Tree*," Harper reported. "Have visual sighting on the target. Am approaching now."

"Acknowledged." Wade's voice was mechanical.

They swam along the side of the tanker, kicking easily as her bulk protected them from the tug of the tide. Etkin whistled into his mask. "Would you look at that? Ever see a bigger one in your life?"

Harper didn't bother to answer. It was huge. They were used to working with subs that were one tenth the size of the *Prometheus*. Even the largest nuclear sub could be cradled easily in the hold of the mammoth tanker.

Wade cut off their conversation. "Where are you in relation to the tanker?"

"I'd guess somewhere amidships, but I'll be damned if I can tell which way's forward and which way's aft. I can't see any curvature so we're probably just about center."

There was a sound of whispering over the phones as the two divers floated alongside the tanker. By mutual unspoken consent they waited to decide which way they should go.

"She was headed just about due west when she was abandoned. That means her stern would be east."

Harper checked his compass. "She must have turned in the tide, 'cause she's headed north-south now."

Again a whispered conference. "I have her mate here," Wade explained. "He suggests you head north."

"North it is," Harper replied. They kicked off and swam alongside the ship. Her keel disappeared into the murky darkness below. It was like swimming alongside a steep cliff, so straight was the drop-off. There was almost no curvature to the side of the hull as in a normal ship. There was no graceful sleek tapering ro reduce friction. It was boxlike. Ungainly.

Finally the hull began to curve. Like everything else on the *Prometheus* it was unexpected. The curve was abrupt, almost a right angle, veering off sharply.

"You're right," Harper informed the *Apple Tree*. "Her bow's pointed south. We're heading for the placement points."

Etkin and Harper swam around the stern. The rudder weighed eighty tons. It towered over them like a six-story building. It seemed impossible that it could ever be moved.

"As for placement, I suggest . . ."

"Sir," Harper spoke into his mask. "I suggest you allow us to decide that. The Navy has spent a lot of money training us how to use these things, and one of the lessons they were particularly thorough on was placement."

"Certainly," Wade replied, stung by the diver's comment.

With practiced efficiency, Harper ran a gloved hand along the hull, brushing aside the voyage's harvest of sea life. Etkin pulled his knife out of its sheath and scraped it against the dark red steel. A streak of silver appeared behind the silver blade, almost as though the knife were leaving some of its substance behind. He nodded his orange head in approval. "Good," he muttered.

They swam closer to the rudder, kicking a few sharp beats and then coasting. Etkin floated about five feet above Harper as they slid their hands along the hull. They stopped as if by magic at the same point. Their trained hands found what they were seeking.

"Right here," said one.

"Right," the other agreed. An orange-gloved hand scraped a silver "X" on the hull between the two men.

They pulled the bags to them and unzipped the nylon fastening. Twin bubbles of trapped air rose out of the bags and streaked to the surface twenty feet above, shimmering in the indirect sunlight.

"Yours or mine?" one asked.

"Yours," the other answered. "I'll hold the light."

A yellow hand produced a powerful underwater flashlight from the satchel. An orange hand produced a square box about an inch thick. When released, it floated gently in the water, its buoyancy carefully calculated to be neutral. Harper ran his hands over the metallic surface, a final check. He had carefully examined it before taking it on the helicopter. Had he seen even the slightest defect in its seals he would have discarded it.

In theory the operation was simplicity itself, deliberately so, since the Navy had designed the apparatus for emergency situations. All they had to do was position the casing against the hull, stencil-side out, tighten a clamp that would magnetically seal it to the hull, and pull a dangling tab that would ignite the two-stage fuse.

In theory, the first stage would purge the space between the metal plate that rested inside the casing and the hull. Barnacles and paint would be reduced to ashes and washed away with the boiling water. The reaction would continue until all the water was boiled away, leaving the space between the plate and the hull free of any chemicals that might poison the second stage.

The second stage would ignite. A magnesium wire, winding along the surface of the plate, would then burst into flame, melting the gel that separated a layer of powdered aluminum from a layer of powdered iron oxide. Aluminum is a powerful reducing agent. Mixed with iron oxide, a violent exothermic reaction occurs, creating a temperature of five thousand degrees Fahrenheit. The iron oxide is reduced to iron and melts under the high temperature.

The reaction is so hot that even the surface of the plate and the hull melt and mingle in the chemical fury. When the aluminum is transformed to aluminum oxide, the reaction stops, and the plate begins to cool.

When cooled, the plate is no longer a separate entity. It becomes part of the hull. Not welded to it. That would only entail the melting of the plate around its edges. Here the entire surface of the plate would be welded to the hull.

In theory it was simple.

In practice, it wasn't so easy. The combining of iron oxide and aluminum, a thermite reaction, had been known for centuries and was used on the railroads to join track and make spot repairs. It was simple and relatively safe. But it had only recently been introduced underwater. The reaction could be "poisoned" by the presence of any number of chemical impurities. One that prevented the reaction altogether was water, particularly seawater. It was critical that all the water be purged in the first step. Even a drop could spoil the entire reaction.

The determining factor on a successful purge was the condition of the hull. If it was too curved, too pitted, too dirty, the seal wouldn't be enough to keep all the water out. The second stage would never occur.

Etkin and Harper had had more than one of these plates fail.

Harper waited while his partner scraped the surface of the hull with his knife, knocking off little tufts of sea creatures with his sweeping blade. He ran his hand across the hull, feeling for unseen irregularities. He carefully worked himself back and forth on a section of the hull, marking a four-foot square. Finally he was satisfied and backed off, shining his light on the spot.

Etkin swam in, pushing the plate before him. He centered it on the spot marked and gently floated it against the hull. It struck the shiny steel with a hollow metallic clang that reverberated in the water. Harper helped him straighten it before they tightened the magnetic clamp. They were satisfied and Etkin gave the clamp a tug. It slammed into the hull. Now the combined strength of the two divers couldn't budge the plate. They backed away, surveying their handiwork, both satisfied. This one felt right.

Etkin trailed a thin wire from one corner of the casing. It was the fuse. They swam ten feet away from the hull and looked back at the casing. Harper spoke into his mask. "Ready with plate number one."

"Acknowledged," Wade replied instantly.

The two men looked at each other and nodded. Harper pulled the wire.

Instantly a small explosion of bubbles erupted from the casing as stage one began.

The two men hung there, using only occasional lazy motions from their flippers to keep them even with the plate.

Chapter 15

6:00 P.M. In a Building; Coney Island

The roof was an inferno. Black tar below and white sun above combined to make the temperature well above one hundred and twenty degrees in the shade. Only there was no shade. Not even a decent shadow on the harsh surface. The heat was tangible; visually evident by the waves of heated air that shimmered as they rose.

One block long and one block wide, the rooftop was larger then most collegiate football fields. It was surrounded by a chest-high wall, enclosing the area with a dull red border. The monotony was broken by three structures. In the center there was a small red brick structure—the elevator motor room. It also housed the emergency stairwells.

The water tower, an unpainted brown wooden tub wrapped by steel cables, rose an extra thirty feet above the surface. Metal struts, supporting the tower, were streaked with tar from vain attempts to seal myriad leaks in the tub.

Otherwise, the roof was bare. Hundreds of silvery pipes poked through the uniformly black roof. Guy wires and miscellaneous television antennas clung to the sides of the building, fastened by rusting metal plates to the brick walls.

It was a desert. An urban desert. Never visited unless necessary. Shunned by all. Austere.

And unbearably hot.

Kevin burst from the cool darkness of the stairwell into the white heat of the roof. Momentarily blinded he stood rubbing his eyes as multicolored dots danced across his field of vision.

It hurt to breathe. The dry heat sucked the moisture from his body. Throat and sinuses dried out almost immediately, allowing the blazing air to scorch sensitive tissue. He took short breaths, gasping rather than inhaling.

The door behind him opened. Melba stepped out. She stumbled at the first impact of the heat. Her hands covered her eyes. It was physically painful to keep them open.

Kevin reached out and steadied her as she began to sway. "You'll get used to it in a moment." He squinted at her. A headache was already beginning.

"Just wait until we've been up here an hour," Hal commented, as he used one of his crutches to open the door. He wedged it open and pushed his way through onto the landing. Reaching into his breast pocket he extracted a pair of sunglasses. They were the same type used by the Air Force. Sun-sensitized, they cut out the maximum amount of glare while leaving most colors unchanged. "Then things will really start to get bad."

"Must you always be so negative?" Kevin complained as he put his arm around Melba.

"I'm not negative," Hal replied. Kevin bent down, giving Hal access to the knapsack. "Just practical." He rooted through one of the sets of pockets that circled the pack and extracted two cases. "Ah, here they are." He handed one to Kevin and the other to Melba. "For a second I was afraid that I had left them in my apartment."

Kevin opened his and found another pair of sunglasses like Hal's. Just putting them on made it feel ten degrees cooler.

Kevin scanned the roof looking for a hint of shade where he could rest. That climb had been rougher than he would have guessed. He was getting out of shape. Too many beers. But a rest was not possible now.

Hal pulled out a series of packets and lined them up against the wall.

"Kevin, Melba." Hal called them over. "Take these." He opened one, breaking the seal with a hiss. "And use it to seal up the cracks around the doors and the vents." He demonstrated by rolling the green-colored clay into a ball. "Just stuff one of these into one of the vents and there's a perfect plug."

Kevin rolled the contents of one of the containers into his hand He hefted the green ball. "What is this stuff?"

"Play-dough," Hal replied, straight-faced. "One of the most profitable inventions of the last decade. One scientist's mistake is another man's profit. It made a fortune for those fortunate enough to get in on the ground floor." He tossed the youth his handful of the compound. "It's enough for you to know that it might just save your life. Go on." He pointed toward the tar desert. "Get to work."

Hal wasn't just lucky that he had these materials on hand; his life was a conglomeration of accidents and he had learned from each one. He had succeeded through tragedy.

He had had a normal birth more than forty years ago. Then, three days past his seventh birthday, tragedy struck. Polio.

Years later, Jonas Salk would discover the vaccine that would forever end the crippling disease, but then it was incurable. He would live, the doctors told his anguished parents, but he'd never walk again.

It took him six years, but he finally performed what the doctors called a "miracle." He learned to walk on crutches. He never did get to run, but he was finally freed from the prison of a hospital bed.

During the period in the hospital and throughout the years afterward, Hal had learned that the only way to free himself from the limitations of his body was through his mind. Although only a marginal reader and student when the disease struck, he began to excel intellectually. With a crippled body, his mind flourished.

Hal tried going away to college, but the strain of being "different" was too great. After one year of getting straight A's, he dropped out and went into business for himself.

He had always had a scientific bent and mathematics was his favorite subject. Choosing a career was no problem. There was only one option. The stock market. He started with a few hundred dollars left after his father's death, and studied the market for weeks, reading everything available.

The broker at Merrill Lynch had first refused to take the account. It was too small. But when he met Hal the broker relented and agreed to invest for him. Then Hal showed him the list of stocks he wanted him to buy. The broker argued against it, advising him that he should buy GM or ITT. Something secure. But Hal insisted. Two months later, Hal told him to sell. Again, the broker argued against it. It was the hottest stock on the market and had an unlimited future. Hal said sell. He gave him another list of stocks to buy. The broker's eyes bulged when he saw the list. He followed Hal's orders.

By the end of the year, Hal was the broker's main source for inside tips. It seemed as though he was never wrong. He found the new industries just before the market became aware of them and left the old just before new discoveries made them obsolete.

Hal's portfolio was a composite of every new and growing industry in the United States. One of his major holdings was a small company called Transgasco. It had one asset. The *Prometheus*.

Like all of his investments, he studied LNG carefully before pouring money into the stock. There was a fortune to be made there. The risk was small, for the investor at least. The international oil lobby had convinced Washington to guarantee the $150 million price of each of the LNG carriers, making it safer than putting money in a bank. Even if the ship went down at sea, the investors were protected by the federal government. If the bottom fell out of the LNG market, the investors would again turn to Uncle Sam to pick up the tab. An investor's dream. No risk and almost unlimited profits.

But it was not just the financial end of the industry he studied; Hal devoted equal energy to the technical end. He was fascinated. It was truly an infant industry, the type he had always sought. So he became enmeshed in the technical problems of LNG and even came up with a number of suggestions that he sent to Transgasco, later learning they had patented some. So Hal was a self-made safety expert in LNG.

Under his insistent urging, Kevin and Melba attacked the points of entry on the roof. First the motor room. It led directly to the basement, Hal explained. Then the doors. They carefully sealed all the cracks on the bottom and around the edges of the doors. He was particularly careful about these preparations. Then, finally, every standpipe and vent that stuck its metal head onto the roof. There must have been a hundred of them, Kevin thought, but there was always enough of the play-dough to go around. His and Melba's hands were tainted green with the stuff by the time they finished the job. And still, Hal was not satisfied. He checked each spot personally, carrying a blob of the stuff and sticking it around the corners where he thought they hadn't done a thorough enough job.

Finally, Kevin came to a halt. Every orifice was plugged. Every crack was sealed. Not even a gnat could attack their impenetrable fortress. Neither could they escape.

"We're done!" Kevin said as he slipped down against the side of the motor room, the only source of shade on the roof. "And I'll be damned if I know what we did. But whatever it was, we're done."

Hal, who had already assumed a reclining position against the eastern wall of the building, accepted the report. "Good," he said. Both Melba and Kevin sank gratefully to the tar-and-stone encrusted surface, their backs against the heated brick. It was enough. They were safe.

They panted their relief.

"So," Kevin ventured, regaining his breath and his audacity simultaneously. "How come you know so much about this stuff?"

"How come?" Hal mused thoughtfully, sucking on half an orange that he passed around. The juice was sweet, cutting into their thirst better than any soft drink or water could. "That's a long story, but," he looked around the deserted rooftop, "I guess there's nothing else to do. I guess we have the time."

Kevin squinted into the glare of the sun. "I don't think I'm going anywhere. For the time being, at least."

A dull boom rolled up the stairwell, silencing them.

"What's that?" Melba asked, her voice a whisper.

"Shhh," Hal motioned for silence. One ear was cocked

against the distant sound. The unnatural stillness of the bay closed in on them. Kevin fidgeted. Hal stilled him with an angry motion.

A second rumble sounded from below.

Kevin grabbed Hal's arm. "What is it?"

"The cloud," Hal answered, his voice calm, methodical. "It's broken out of the basement. Those are the water pipes bursting as they freeze," he said without emotion. "It's in the stairwell. It's coming up."

6:00 P.M.   *In a Tunnel; Somewhere in Brooklyn*

The high-pitched squealing of the rodents faded slowly into the darkness, leaving only the vacuum of silence and the smell of terror behind.

"Everyone all right?" Faust whispered into the darkness. Only the insistent sobbing of the tiny figure he held in his arms broke the silence. He felt the child's head. Long hair. A memory of yellow hair and large eyes. The girl. Mary.

"Don't cry, honey," he said in what he hoped was a soothing tone. "Don't cry."

Faust called into the darkness. "Judith? Manny? Are you all right?"

A groan. Manny's. "I'm okay."

"Judith? Is she with you?"

"No," Manny answered, struggling to stand. "I thought she was with you."

"Judith!" Faust called. The darkness swallowed his call. "Judith!"

A soft wailing cry was his response. A whimper of agony. Of utter fear. But it was Judith. Of that he was certain.

"Judith?" he called. "Judith?"

The whimper stopped. He froze, trying to locate it. Mary's continued sobbing was reduced to mere background noise. The whimper came again. There. Off to his right.

He found her crouched against the far wall of the tunnel. She was crying softly in a singsong of a child's nursery rhyme. He reached out for her. She recoiled when he touched her.

"Judith, it's me, Elliot. Remember? Elliot Faust. From

the train." He edged closer, reaching out his free hand. "Everything's going to be all right now. They've gone. They've all gone." He touched her face gently with his fingertips.

She let out a scream that was terrifying in its intensity and suddenness. Faust fell back, startled. He grabbed her and shook her, bringing her back to reality. One second she was straining against his strength, the next she lay sobbing in his arms. He cradled her tenderly against his body. "Judith. Judith," he whispered over and over. "Everything's all right. Everything will be all right," he crooned.

"It was awful," she sobbed.

"Don't think about it, Judith. Don't think about it," he whispered. "Everything will be all right. Manny's here. Mary is okay."

"Where's Timmy?" Judith asked.

The name hit them like a blow. Faust had totally forgotten the boy.

"Timmy!" Faust shouted. "Timmy, where are you?"

"Timmy!" Judith echoed Faust's call. "It's Judith, Timmy. Answer me!"

One after another they called. Mary called. Faust called. Judith called. But there was no answer. After ten minutes of calling and groping in vain in the darkness, Faust said, "I'm sorry. We have to go on."

Manny and Judith protested.

He refused to listen. "Now listen to me," Faust shouted them down. "Those rats were running from the cloud, remember? That means it isn't too far behind us. We have to move before it catches us. All of us, that includes Mary as well."

"But we just can't leave him," Judith protested. "You and Manny take Mary and I'll stay down here and see if I can find him. I can function better in the dark than any of you can," she reasoned. "If anybody has a chance to find him I do."

"No," Faust said. "And that's final. We can't waste time arguing. You're coming with us." He laid a gentle hand on her shoulder. She was crying. "It wasn't your fault. You can't blame yourself for what happened. He just wandered away and got lost."

"It's my fault," she cried. "I should have never let go of him."

There was no way he could dissuade her. "Let's go." His voice and his hand were gentle yet insistent as he urged her forward. Faust carried Mary. It was faster that way. Her silken hair drifted in the gentle breeze created by their pace and tickled his nose. Her sobs were muffled in the thickness of his shoulder.

They walked quietly in the darkness, the crunching of gravel the only sound. Every so often, Judith would call out Timmy's name. They would all stand silently, waiting for some response.

"Hey," Manny said suddenly. "We're going downhill."

Faust stopped. "You're right. Now I know where we are. The track dips just before making the turn to enter the station. It's not too far ahead."

They started off, faster now than before. The slope became more noticeable with each step.

Judith stopped to call, "Timmy!" They paused to listen. Faust heard nothing.

"Come on . . ."

"Shhh," Judith quieted him. "I hear something."

He fell silent again. At first there was nothing. Then he heard it. From behind them. A faint metallic sound.

"Rats?" Manny asked, his whisper trembling ever so faintly.

"No," Judith answered slowly. "Not rats. They sounded—" she hunted for the right word "—thinner. Smaller than this. This is more substantial somehow. It fills the entire tunnel. I don't know how to describe it. It's just bigger somehow."

"But it's not Timmy. You're sure?"

She sighed. "No, I'm positive it's not him. His noise would be smaller than this."

It became more distinct, filling the entire tunnel. It sounded like the stones were being raked by some unseen force. Then the rail began to sing; an eerie high-pitched whine, almost electrical. A hum of awareness. The sound of the rail contracting as it cooled. A metal coupling joining two sections of the third rail next to Faust's foot popped with a sharp ping.

"The cloud," Faust whispered. "Run!" It changed into a shout.

But running was impossible in total darkness. They were reduced to a fast shuffle. He grabbed Manny's good hand with his left and Judith's in his right. He let Judith lead.

The air grew cold as the track sucked heat from it. The sweat that saturated Faust's shirt dried with chilling suddenness, causing goose bumps to rise over his exposed skin. The hairs on his forearms rose and his teeth began to chatter. Manny's and Judith's hands grew cold in his. He held onto them with painfully tight grips.

"Hurry." His voice broke as he spoke, his teeth chattered so violently. "It's getting closer. Run as f . . . fast as you can."

They picked up speed for a few seconds, but they stumbled so often that they were soon forced back to a shuffle. If only they had some light, he thought. Judith veered sharply to the left, catching Faust off guard. The curve just before the station. He stumbled, thrown off balance by Mary who chose just that moment to shift her weight forward. His ankle turned under him.

He fell to one knee. Mary almost tumbled off his shoulders. Judith and Manny stopped beside him, helping him to his feet. "I'm okay," he grunted as he lurched to his feet. "Keep going. I'll keep up." He put their hands together in the darkness. "Don't let yourselves get separated. Go." He lurched forward.

Manny and Judith hung back. "Go," he bellowed. It echoed off the walls of the tunnel, dwindling in the distance. They scooted forward. He heard their steps shuffle through the stones.

Gingerly he put weight on his ankle. It hurt like hell, but it would carry him. Mary's weight didn't help, but he didn't dare put her down. She would never keep up, not even when he was half crippled. He hobbled into the darkness.

He shivered violently. Mary began to cry from the cold. He had never felt anything like this. Not in the worst day of winter had he felt the cold cut so deeply into his body. He lost feeling in his fingers and toes. His nose burned with every breath and his lungs rasped as the moisture was ripped from their soft tissues.

But the cold was an anesthetic to his damaged ankle. He could put more pressure on it now with the pain gone.

As all feeling disappeared, he broke into a trot, leaning heavily on his good leg with each step. There was nothing but the cold and the running. His world was reduced to the heavy pounding of his feet against the stones and the beating of his heart against his chest.

Ahead, a yellow spot grew in the darkness. The station. The yellow sunlight streamed into the tunnel like a ray of life urging him on. He saw Manny boost Judith onto the platform and then hoist himself to safety.

He pounded on. Now that he could see, he could run faster. He tried to pick up speed, but his breath burned too much. It was all he could do to maintain his pace. The twin tracks gleamed with an unearthly brightness; wisps of frost clung to the steel track.

He dimly heard the far-off voices of the two teen-agers, urging him to hurry. They could see behind him; he couldn't. Maybe they could see the white cloud following him, reaching for his feet as they pounded into the road-bed. Maybe they could see that it was only inches away. He wished he could turn around, but knew if he ever stopped running, he could never start again. The cloud wouldn't let him.

All he wanted to do was reach the edge of the station. He might not even have a chance to make it up the platform once he stopped. He didn't have enough breath to jump. He could at least save Mary by dumping her onto the concrete station before he succumbed to the cold.

Suddenly he was bathed in light. A ventilation grill opened to the sky above him. It added no warmth to his numb body. The sweat from running dried immediately, chafing his skin and chilling him to the bone.

Then he was there. Hands reached for him and pulled against his weight, trying to drag him onto the platform. He fought them off, unseating the little girl who clung to his neck first. He set her down on the station landing. Her skin was blue. She shivered violently, her whole body trembling with cold. She looked like death. He looked worse.

Manny and Judith tore at his arms, lifting against his two-hundred-and-five-pounds. They'd never do it, he thought, as the hands slipped off his shoulders. They don't have the strength. And he didn't have the strength to help them. All he wanted to do was sleep. Only a few minutes.

Only until he got his breath back. And then he could go on.

His body began to relax and he started to slide onto the track. Only Manny's strength held him back.

A sharp red pain cut through the darkness. His right foot was caught in a circle of fire. The feeling of cold disappeared. The deadly lethargy went with it.

He looked at his foot. There was no fire. Only a faint wisp of white that curled gently around his foot, covering it, hiding it from view. The finger of white grew, as though it were feeding off his flesh, bulging as it ate.

Like a wounded bear, Faust rose out of the tunnel in one leap, knocking Manny over as he cleared the edge of the platform. He rolled once, twice, before coming to a stop. Faust lay on his knees, crouching in the pool of yellow light, his eyes dilated with fear. That had been close. Too close to death.

He panted, gulping in the relatively warm air that rushed down from the exits. He dragged himself away from the edge of the landing, pulling his right leg behind him. He stopped against a steel fence, propping himself up.

His legs stuck out before him like sticks. He couldn't feel anything in either of them. At least he could move his left foot a little; his right was totally immobile. It was covered with a thin layer of white. As he watched, the color disappeared, revealing the heavy black of his uniform shoe. Ice, he realized, as the white melted and formed a small puddle under his foot.

6:00 P.M. *Weather Forecast for New York City and Vicinity*

TEMPERATURE:	95° F. 35° C.
HUMIDITY:	80 percent
WIND:	South 0–3 knots; variable.
PRECIPITATION:	90 percent within next hour; 100 percent before morning

SPECIAL CONDITIONS: Due to a local temperature anomaly in New York bay, the air inversion that has been dominating the region's weather for the past days is breaking up. Unusual and fluctuating weather conditions can be expected as the inversion continues to disintegrate. The storm once centered over Rahway, New Jersey, is now moving toward New York City. Jersey City reports severe thundershowers.

Due to the lifting of the inversion, the Pollution Advisory is canceled. Air quality unhealthy.

NATIONAL WEATHER SERVICE
NATIONAL CLIMATIC CENTER, ASHEVILLE, NORTH CAROLINA

6:10 P.M.   *Mayor's Office; City Hall*

They watched the disaster on television. The somber voice of the announcer described the floating death in dispassionate terms as the camera panned the length of the cloud. So many billion cubic feet of gaseous destruction.

Newfeld cradled a fresh glass of Scotch in his hands as he sat in front of the set. With a professional eye he appreciated the camerawork that made the cloud seem so close that you could almost feel the chill. The helicopter rose, now panning toward the New York skyline seen faintly in the distance. Zooming in, the lens caught the geometric shape of the World Trade Center. From that angle, it appeared as though the cloud were reaching out for Manhattan.

Newfeld whispered, "Son of a bitch!" He snarled at the screen. "Look at that. That bastard'll start a panic if he keeps that up. People'll think that the damn cloud's coming into Manhattan." Someone at the station must have agreed because the announcer hastened to clarify that the cloud was almost five miles due south of Manhattan.

The camera returned to Coney Island, panning over the tops of buildings that stood above the cloud. The impression that the insubstantial vapor was a substantial snowdrift was universal. "It really looks like snow, Walter," the announcer went on. "It's hard to think of it as a gas. Only on the leading edges can you see any movement at all." The camera continued to pan across the stillness, flashing from one building to another.

Suddenly the camera stopped. It zoomed in for a close-up. An arm waving a piece of red cloth. The picture enlarged, disturbed only slightly by the vibration from the helicopter's engines. "What's that?" Cronkite asked as the picture cleared. "It looks like——"

The announcer cut him off. "Survivors. I know, Walter. We've seen quite a few of them trapped on various roof-tops for the past half hour or so. It's my guess that they probably stayed in their apartments until the cloud started to rise in the buildings. The roof was the only place to go."

There was a close-up of an arm with a handkerchief. A young man. Next to him stood a young black woman. Their mouths clearly formed the word help over and over again.

"It's good to know that they got out at least," Cronkite said, his voice noticeably strained as he tried to control his emotions.

"I'm afraid it will be only a temporary haven, Walter," the announcer said. The faces filled the screen. "Help!" they silently cried.

"It's only a matter of time until the cloud covers these buildings." The camera focused on the black woman. The tears were clearly visible on her cheeks. "And then, of course, when the fire . . ." He stopped, unable to continue.

The camera pulled back, panning over the face of the building showing the cloud lapping at the bottom floors.

"I guess that there's nothing anyone can do." The announcer continued after a moment. They're too close to the cloud for helicopter aid. They have to be sacrificed in the interests of the others. Those who are still fleeing from the edge of the cloud and, of course, those who would be killed in the explosion of the tanker, if it went off while still in the harbor.

LaSalle looked at Newfeld. The press secretary took a heavy slug of Scotch. The ice cubes tinkled against the side of the empty glass.

"Nothing?" LaSalle snarled. "Nothing we can do?" He slammed his fist against the top of the television. The screen fluttered once and then focused on the shirtsleeved figure of Walter Cronkite sitting in the middle of his newsroom.

"Nothing!" LaSalle growled. "We'll see about that! Phyllis!" It was a bellow that carried through the heavily insulated walls of his office. In a second the door opened and Phyllis stuck her head in, her face ashen. "Yes, Mr. Mayor?"

"Get me the President on the phone! Right away!"

"Yes, sir." Her head withdrew, the door closing firmly behind her.

LaSalle went to his desk and slowly raised his glass to his lips. "We'll see about that!" he vowed as the liquor stung his mouth. "We'll see!"

6:15 P.M. *On Board the* APPLE TREE

"Please repeat." Wade's voice was tense as he spoke into the microphone.

"The second package malfunctioned. The second phase did not operate." A voice echoed back. "We do not have a replacement with us."

Cybil asked for the microphone. Wade reluctantly handed it to her. "Will one hold, if we try to tow her out of the harbor?"

The diver hesitated before answering. "It's chancy. The first one is in real solid. It'd hold almost anything. I'd stake my life on that. But to tow a ship this size into the Atlantic on one cleat? I just don't know."

"Is there any way you could correct the problem with the second 'package' as you called it?"

The answer was immediate. "Negative. It's completely self-contained. There's no way to effect repairs."

"How long would it take to get another 'package' here?"

"Flying time, about ten to fifteen minutes. You'd need another diver as well. Then add swimming time, maybe half an hour."

Cybil turned to the commander and Val. "Any ideas? I don't think we can afford to wait. Val, you know the *Prometheus* better than anyone else; do you think she can be towed out with just one line on her?"

"I'm not sure. Ordinarily I'd say no, but I don't see that we have much choice." He stopped for a second, a distant expression crossing his face. "Where did they say they put that cleat?"

Cybil repeated the question into the microphone. "About ten feet to the right of the rudder, twenty feet below the waterline," was the answer.

"You could try looping the line around the rudder.

That would give it extra strength. It might be enough."
Val shrugged. "But . . ."

"Commander?" Cybil turned to Wade. "What do you think? You have a better idea about the waters around here than I do. Do you think that might be enough?"

"Well," Wade answered hesitantly, "the tide's with us. That'll help. You don't have any rough waters until after you pass Sandy Hook. If it's ever going to hold, now's the time."

"Good. I agree." She handed the microphone back to the commander, acknowledging his authority. "Thank you, Commander, I believe we're all agreed then."

Wade was surprised. This was the first time she had ever acted as though he was anything more than a taxi driver. He accepted the microphone with a nod and a half-smile. "Thank you, Miss Yale."

Cybil left the wheelhouse and wandered out onto the foredeck. There she stood behind the two seamen who manned a large spool of heavy hemp line. It was the final four-inch hemp hawser, she noted as she watched the two men tirelessly feeding the line into the water. It wouldn't be long before it reached the distant *Prometheus*.

Like a sentient eel, the brown hemp line disappeared over the side and struck out for the cloudbank that dominated the horizon. It slunk into the bay with barely a ripple on its glassy-smooth surface. A faint gurgling sound marked its progress. Cybil stared, hypnotized, at the line and the water.

"Cybil."

She wasn't startled. She expected him. "Peaceful, isn't it?" She looked out at the water. The first hints of orange tinted the high clouds, heralding the approach of sunset. "Reminds me of my family's home when I was a kid." She backed into Val's arms. They encircled her easily.

Her brown hair fluttered in the weak breeze. He smelled the subtle aroma of her body. "Where's home?" he murmured.

"Connecticut. Lockport. A small town. Fishermen mostly. Except for the few people from the university, almost everybody in town was a fisherman. Or married to one."

"Me too. Small town. Fishing town. My father was a big man there. He went on the ocean, not just the Mediterranean. That was something to the townspeople. A man of the sea. That's all I ever knew when I was growing up. The sea. Where men are made."

They stood together, secure in each other's presence. There was no need for words. There was no time for words. The line continued to play out, being swallowed by the endless maw of the sea.

Small scraps of colored cloth marked every hundred yards of the hawser. A different color for each section. Yellow marked one hundred yards. Blue marked two hundred. Green for three and red for four. The *Prometheus* was only four hundred yards away.

The yellow marker fluttered in the gentle sea breeze and disappeared into the bay. One of the seamen called out. "One hundred yards." The call was echoed as word was passed to the commander standing in the wheelhouse. The roll of line never stopped its motion, feeding yard after yard of hemp into the water.

"Do you think it'll hold?" Cybil asked, wrapping her arms over his, shivering with a sudden internal chill.

"It has to." They clung to one another more tightly. "How far out before you think it'll be safe?"

"Five miles, minimum." Her voice regained that direct quality that Val had learned to love. "With the New Jersey refineries south of Sandy Hook and Manhattan to the northeast, every mile is critical."

"Every mile is a miracle," Val replied. "If we clear the harbor we'll be luckier than we have a right to expect."

"Oh, Val, why did this have to happen? To meet just before we . . ." She stopped suddenly, the words cut off.

He turned her so she faced him. Cybil stared at the deck. He raised her chin with the palm of his hand. Her eyes glistened with unshed tears. He brushed his lips against them, feeling the silky softness against his mouth. Salt tickled the end of his tongue. He savored the taste.

"We'll be all right, Cybil," he whispered. "We'll live through this."

She sagged against him, letting his strength surround her. "No, we won't, Val." Her voice was quiet. "No, we won't. I know that better than anyone else. There's just no way that we can survive that explosion. We'll be too close." Her tone turned bitter. "It just isn't fair. It isn't fair."

"Two hundred," called the seaman.

"Two hundred," came the echo from the bridge.

The *Apple Tree* rocked gently. The sloshing of the waves as they tapped against the metal hull merged with the hiss of the line as it sank into the murky green waters. Slowly, Cybil pulled herself away from Val and wiped her eyes.

"I'm sorry, Val," she said softly. "I was acting like a woman. And we don't have time for that now."

"You were acting like you. And you are a woman. Don't ever apologize for being you."

She smiled and turned around, pulling his arms around her and hugging them to her chest. "How are they going to tow her?" she asked suddenly. "With the *Apple Tree* or the tug?"

Val laughed. "Always the scientist, aren't you? Have to know everything. Well, we'll use the tug. Its engines are more powerful than the *Apple Tree*'s. She was built for towing. The cutter's built for speed. We'll need the tug's power, particularly when we cross the tip of Sandy Hook and start getting hit by the ocean waves. As long as we're in the bay, Sandy Hook blocks the big waves. We only get the little ones, those reflected as they ripple around the edge of the peninsula." He indicated the beaches of Sandy Hook, lying a few hundred yards off to their left.

Cybil stared at the protruding piece of land. It was mostly untouched. The beach glistened white in the sunlight, untainted by the normal debris that seems to mark humans wherever they go. The sand dunes rose behind the beach, their green-and-rust-colored vegetation rippling in the ocean breeze.

"It looks like a vacation resort in the Caribbean, doesn't it?"

"Yes, it's much more beautiful than the Mediterranean. You have such beautiful beaches here. When I first came to New York, I spent a whole day walking the beaches on Sandy Hook. It's beautiful. There were only a few fishermen and campers. No crowds like your other beaches. It's a national park. They keep it up very well."

"I wonder whether there's anybody still there," she said, suddenly alarmed. "The cloud's going to cover the Hook and they'll . . ."

"Don't worry," Val assured her. Her body relaxed against his. "I'm sure they've warned everybody away. I doubt that there's anyone on the East Coast that doesn't know about the *Prometheus* by now." He sounded suddenly sad.

"Three hundred."

"Three hundred," came the echo.

Val pulled himself erect, reclaiming his arms from Cybil's grasp. "Well, I have to talk with the commander about towing my ship out of the harbor." He gave her a wan smile. "I'm still her captain, you know."

"I'm coming with you," Cybil said simply.

"Of course," Val agreed, allowing her to precede him as they returned to the bridge. The wheelhouse was as calm as the waters of the bay. There were ripples of activity. Crew Chief Spector quietly conversed with the divers through the headset. The loudspeaker had been turned off and Wade leaned over a chart of the harbor, a pencil and parallel ruler beside his elbow as he reviewed the course he had laid out. But beneath the ripples there was a sense of waiting.

"Ah, Val. Miss Yale. I was just going to call you." He motioned them to join him at the chart. "I wanted to go over the route I propose the *Prometheus* follow. The tide's running out and she'll have only a few feet of water to spare in the center of the channel," he explained as Val examined the map. "We have to be particularly careful right here." He jabbed his finger at a blue area just north of Sandy Hook. "Flynn's Knoll. The channel's only four hundred yards wide there and it shoals up sharply on either side. I don't have to tell you that we'd never be able to pull her off if she's grounded. Not with one line on her. We'd have to wait until next high tide. Another twelve hours."

Val traced the route with his finger. It was the obvious one, with the fewest turns and the deepest water all the way out of the harbor and into the Atlantic. "You realize, of course, that the ship will fishtail." He put his hands together and made a wagging motion. "With only one line on her, and that not centered, she'll drag back and forth as we pull her. The faster we go, the worse it'll get. If we stray out of the channel . . ." He let the sentence dangle.

"True, she'll slip like that," Wade countered, "but with the line tied through her rudder, that'll compensate. Not much, I'll grant that, but it'll be better than on any other part of the ship."

"Okay, I can't disagree," Val said slowly. "And on the whole, there's no better course for the *Prometheus*." He reached out and knocked off the corner clips that held the chart in place. It rolled up automatically. "So, it's time I said my farewells and got underway."

He tried to pick up the chart, but Wade's hand stopped him. "What do you mean 'you got underway'? Who said you're going to take that tug?"

Val looked genuinely surprised. "The *Prometheus* is my ship. Who else would take her out?"

"Your ship? She's a derelict. She's a danger to navigation and under the Coast Guard's jurisdiction. She's my responsibility, not yours. Not any longer."

"The hell you say," Val snarled. "The *Prometheus* is still under my command and, as long as I'm alive, nobody's going to take her out to sea but me. Is that clear? Nobody but me!"

"Four hundred," came the report from the bow.

The two officers stared at one another, each willing to fight for what he believed was his responsibility. Neither man was willing to back down.

Cybil physically pushed herself between the two men. "Val, Commander. Now stop this. Both of you. This is something we are all in together. It's not a matter of petty rules and . . ."

"It's not petty," Val snapped. "It's the law of the sea. The oldest law that man knows. Older than the Bible. A captain is law on his ship. And the *Prometheus* is my ship."

"And the *Apple Tree* is mine," Wade retorted. "And you, Mr. Paknis, happen to be on board my vessel not yours. And here, according to the law of the sea, as well as the law of the United States which I've sworn to uphold I'm in command. And I say that the *Prometheus* sails under the U.S. Coast Guard's authority and command. Not the command of some private merchant."

"What difference would it make, Commander . . ." Cybil started to object.

"What difference does it make?" Wade exploded.

"What happens if the *Prometheus* gets out to sea and her captain here decides that he thinks he can save her? Even if it costs a few more lives. U.S. lives. What happens then, Professor? Are we going to open fire on her again? With her captain telling us not to? That's a whole different ball of wax than when there was no chance to save her. Do you think he'll consent to let us sink her then? Ask him. Go ahead, just ask."

One look at Val's face told her the story. There was no need to ask. If Val saw a chance to save the *Prometheus* he'd take that chance. No matter what the risk.

"All right," Val acknowledged, clearly beaten. "You're right. I was thinking of saving her. Who wouldn't? If it were the *Apple Tree,* what would you do?" He looked directly at Wade. "Wouldn't you try to save her?"

Wade returned the stare. "Not if I were ordered to destroy her. Could you do that? Would you do that?"

Val lowered his eyes. "I . . . I don't know. I honestly don't." He looked up; sadness in his expression. "Yes, yes, I do know. I could do it. If the *Prometheus,* if my ship were going to be responsible for people dying, then I could do it. I stood by while she was shelled. While she still had some of her dignity. Her majesty." His tone became reverent. "She was the queen of the seas. The top of her line. There's a certain pride that goes with that. Something that can never be duplicated in any other vessel that's just a little bit less. And to save that majesty, that reputation, I could order her sunk. I could order her to be destroyed. That's the way she would have wanted it, to go out while she was at the top. While she was still the best."

The commander leaned back, not looking Val in the eye. He was torn. On one hand he knew that Val was correct about the laws of the sea. On the other, he knew his duty to the service.

"I'm sorry." It was an apologetic whisper.

Val sank back into his seat, a look of total defeat on his face. "I'm sorry," Wade repeated.

Cybil looked at the grief on Val's face. She couldn't stand it. "Commander, isn't there some way that . . ."

"No, Professor. This is a Coast Guard matter. Not even the Department of Energy has a right to intervene.

There's nothing I can do. It's really out of my hands."
He shrugged.

"But couldn't Val operate under your orders. I mean,
under Coast Guard authority. That way you'd still be in
command and the Coast Guard would have their rules
met."

The commander thought it over. "Well, I'm not sure.
I don't think . . ."

"But don't you use civilian tugs when you have to tow
wrecks out of the channel? So there's precedent for the
Coast Guard to act through non-Coast Guard personnel."

"Well, yes," he admitted, "but . . ."

"So if Val agrees to be subject to your authority . . ."

"He hasn't said that," Wade countered.

Cybil turned to Val. "Val?"

He looked at the chart of the harbor partially rolled
up on the chart table. The dark line of the *Prometheus*'s
route curved around Sandy Hook. "Yes, I'll do it. For
my ship, to be in command of her on her final voyage,
I'd put myself under the devil's authority if I had to."

"It's settled then. Val and I take the tug and tow the
Prometheus out of the harbor."

"Commander." Spector, who had been speaking quietly
into the microphone, interrupted. "The divers have finished. Do you want them to remain in position or come
back to the *Apple Tree?*"

"Tell them to wait," Wade snapped. "Professor, the
tanker's ready to be towed. As soon as the line is secured
to the tug she's going to start towing the *Prometheus* out
of the harbor. Can't you understand this is a shipping
matter? A Coast Guard matter. You've done your job,
Professor. Now let me do mine."

"He's right, Cybil. This is something that we have to
handle alone. It's for sailors, not scientists."

Cybil's face flushed with anger. She looked from Val's
face to the commander's. Both were set and uncompro-
mising.

She bit back her comment and stormed out of the
wheelhouse, slamming the door back against its stops. She
disappeared onto the deck. Her absence made the room
feel twice as large. Twice as empty.

The two officers looked at one another. Wade shrugged.
"She'll get over it. Don't worry. It's only the tension."

"I don't know. She's pretty stubborn. Once she sets her mind on something she doesn't quit."

"Towline is ready on the *Sea Maid*, sir," Spector called out.

Wade acknowledged the information with a nod. He rolled up the chart and handed it to Val. "I'll walk you over." Together they left the wheelhouse, talking over last-minute problems and plans in low voices.

At the side where the *Sea Maid* was moored against the *Apple Tree*, they shook hands. "Remember," Wade said, "as soon as you clear the harbor, set the automatic pilot heading it straight out to sea. We'll be alongside all the way. As soon as the pilot's set, we'll come alongside and take you off. Don't hold her any longer than you absolutely have to. Just set the pilot and go."

"I'll remember." Val lingered on the deck for a second. He looked over the sparkling deck and polished chrome.

Wade followed Val's gaze.

"I guess she's still mad."

"Give her time," Wade counseled. "She hasn't had time enough to cool off."

"I guess you're right."

They shook hands one final time just before Val leaped the short space between the two vessels. The commander waved to the crewmen, their Coast Guard uniforms sodden with perspiration. It had been a long day for everyone. "Prepare to cast off."

"Yes, sir."

The tug slowly crept away from the *Apple Tree*. Veering off to the center of the channel, the towline trailed behind her like a thin tail. Val watched with mixed emotions.

It was a suicide job.

Chapter 16

"*Red Leader* to Red Squadron. Close it up, you're falling
behind back there."

A chorus of affirmatives filled the air. *Red Leader*
checked the formation. It was pretty tight and normally
he wouldn't have been that demanding but today it was
different. Today precision was everything.

Red Squadron consisted of twenty-five transport helicopters. Red was one of the four squadrons in Able Wing.
Able Wing was one of the five wings in the task force.
Code name for the operation was "Skyhook." And it was
the largest air evacuation since the last days of Vietnam.

Red Squadron had just finished a month's refresher
course at Fort Dix. They had been training on movements
of combat teams and on joint amphibious assaults. It
called for close coordination and communications. And
precision flying. Even after a month of constant practice,
Red Leader felt a growing knot in his stomach every
time he thought about the mission.

Five hundred helicopters landing and taking off in a
confined space was dangerous enough. But the added fact
that they were landing and taking off from the tops of
buildings, some of which might not have been properly
cleared, only seemed to invite disaster. His every sense re-
belled. But duty drove him onward. He looked out over
the wing again.

"*Red Leader* to Red Squadron. Where do you think
you're going? On a Sunday picnic? Tighten it up."

The helicopters drifted into formation.

They cruised over Jersey City.

To the north, the first flickering of lightning cut the
darkness of the black storm clouds that lined the horizon.

6:20 p.m.   *On the Roof; A Building in Coney Island*

Like distant thunder slowly growing closer, the sounds of chaos approached the roof. The bright tinkling of shattering glass was combined with the dull thuds of falling masonry. The building was tearing itself apart as the forces of an alien environment rampaged in the halls below.

The three survivors rested against the eastern wall of the motor room, the only few feet of shade available. Even then, it offered the mere illusion of coolness since the reflected glare and radiant heat more than made up for the absence of direct sunlight.

Hal had passed the time by spinning tales of his life. Kevin and Melba listened intently, forgetting their own plight as Hal reminisced. Twice a millionaire and three times a pauper, he had more than his share of stories.

Kevin idly balled up a piece of the artificial clay between his hands. Suddenly, he interrupted a story about a laser beam scalpel that Hal had lost half a million dollars on. "Hal, what are our chances?"

The small man shrugged. He dug the foot of his crutches into gooey tar. "We're pretty safe, for the time being, anyway. There's no way for the gas to get up here, as long as the seals remain tight." He reached over and plucked the ball of playdough from Kevin's hands. "This has a high water content, but it isn't held together by the water the way something like clay is. When this gets cold, even cryogenically cold, it will become hard but not brittle. It'll keep the gas out better than anything else I could think of." He tossed the ball back.

Kevin caught it one-handed. "How come you know so much about this stuff? The cloud and all?" He tossed the ball into the air and caught it. It made a satisfying smack against his palm. "I never heard about it before."

"Nobody's tried to keep it a secret. It's been all over the newspapers and television. LNG has been part of a national debate on energy. Where have you been for the past five years?"

"Ahhh," Kevin admitted. "In college. You know college students. If it isn't part of a course, it doesn't exist."

Hal snorted. "Some education."

Melba roused herself from her troubled thoughts. She had been thinking about Judith, wondering where she was; whether she was safe; whether they would ever see each other again. "I've heard about LNG. Something about Staten Island. We once had a group of crazies in the office, protesting about some tanks over there. We didn't do anything about it. It was out of our borough. It didn't affect us." She shrugged. "At least we didn't think it did." She looked out at the empty sky, not needing to see the whiteness to know it was there. "I guess we were wrong." She lapsed back into silence.

"A lot of people were wrong," Hal agreed. "We thought that modern technology could deal with anything. Scientists could always solve any problem, given time and enough money." He dug the back of one of his boots into the tar; it slid in front of the inoperative leg, forming a black crest against the heel.

"Money," Hal mused aloud. "That's really what this whole thing's about. Money. High profits and the risk be damned. Insure when you have to, go bankrupt if anything goes wrong. That was one of the beauties of LNG." He stared vacantly at the fate of the brick wall just a few yards away. "You couldn't lose. The investors, that is," he amended quickly. "The public, that was a different matter. The cost of this accident will never be borne by the investors. They're immune from financial loss."

"What?" Kevin asked, the outrage tempered by disbelief.

"It's true," Hal continued. "The owners of the *Prometheus* won't lose a cent on this accident. The ship's mortgaged for almost her full value and the insurance will go to pay off the creditors first. That'll wipe out any insurance. The owners themselves only risk the value of their ship. After today, I'd say that that would be reduced to zero."

"But," Kevin protested, "what about all the people who died today? How about all the homes that are being ruined? How about my stuff? My tape recorder? My clothes? Who's going to pay for them?"

Hal smiled. "I wouldn't worry much about that if I were you. I'd be thankful enough just to get off this roof alive." He paused. "And I'll tell you what. If we do get out of this alive, I'll personally buy you a new tape recorder. And as many clothes as you can carry. That'll at least be one owner who pays his debts."

"You mean . . ."

"Right." Hal scraped the tar off the side of his boot with the tip of his crutch. "I'm part owner of the *Prometheus.*"

Kevin sat back, speechless, torn between conflicting emotions. This man had saved his life. Yet . . .

The thought was cut off by a sharp clang, metal on metal, behind them. Tortured steel, rendered brittle by the cryogenic cold, had given way. The steel cable holding the car snapped. It recoiled from the sudden release in tension. The heavy metal broke through the protective casing that sealed the top of the elevator shaft, sending pieces of metal flying through the motor room.

Kevin, the youngest of the three, had the fastest reflexes. He sprang away from the wall like a bullet fired from a gun. He went rolling on the tarry surface.

Melba could only utter a scream as the sound of shattering glass filled the air. Tiny shards battered against her and Hal. She jumped up, beating at her hair to rid herself of the slivers.

The motor room was filled with seething white gas. It bubbled through the space left by the broken pane and, in slow motion, poured down the side of the building directly toward Hal.

"Hal!" Melba screamed, pointing at the finger of white. It grew rapidly in size.

Hal looked up and saw the gas headed directly for him. His skin became chilled as the cold that preceded the gas washed over him. He couldn't rise fast enough to escape. That would take him even closer to the cloud. He rolled to his right, scraping his back against the wall and curling forward at the same time.

The sun glinted off the shiny steel of the braces that held his legs straight. He couldn't bend them, and the angle of his body against the wall forced him tighter against the unyielding brick. He couldn't move, trapped by his own body. The gas rolled down the side of the building, its leading tip growing thinner and thinner as it reached for the pinned man.

The gas was between Kevin and Hal. Kevin couldn't reach him directly. Rolling to his knees, he scuttled away from the wall. He reached for Hal's legs as he moved. He pulled. Feeling the tug, Hal pushed against the ground, lifting himself into the air with his arms. He almost flew with the strength of their combined thrust. He landed in Kevin's lap. They rolled backward in a heap.

The cloud, seemingly cut off from its source, drifted to the ground and lay there in a puddle of white. Before their eyes, the puddle grew noticeably smaller, thinning from pure white to wispy gray to a shadow in seconds. Then it was gone. The heat from the roof warmed it until the crystals disappeared.

"You all right?" Kevin asked as he unwound himself from the pile of arms, legs, and steel.

Hal was totally helpless. His braces pinned him to the ground. "Yes, yes. I'm fine. Or I will be as soon as you get off me."

Kevin moved away and leaned back on his knees. He started to help Hal to his feet, but the man stopped him. "Wait. I have to fix these braces. You just about pulled them off when you yanked so hard." He reached down to unfasten the right brace so it could be moved back up his leg. It dangled below his foot. Kevin moved to do the same with the other leg.

Hal slapped the hand away. "I said I'd do it myself. What do you think I am? A cripple? Do something useful. You and Melba see if you can find some piece of canvas in my bag. If there isn't any, use the bag itself. Stuff it in that hole. Wet it first. The ice will act as a seal."

While Hal rebuckled his braces, Kevin and Melba found the right-sized piece of canvas and doused it with water. They approached the broken window, carrying the canvas stretched between them.

"What are you trying to do? Become martyrs? Get those gloves on. And there are some oxygen tanks in my bag. Don't you know that there's gas floating out of that hole now?" He reached for and grabbed the end of one of his fallen crutches, dragging it toward him. Using it as a support, he levered himself upright. He hobbled over to the front of the window, peering into the darkness of the closed room.

A puff of white rose and fell in the gloom of the small enclosure. It didn't reach the window.

"Hurry," Hal called. "The room's beginning to fill." He leaned heavily on his one crutch. "Hurry."

Wearing the masks and gloves, Melba and Kevin approached the window. Luckily only one pane had cracked. It was no more than three inches square. Kevin took the canvas away from Melba using both his hands. "This'll be easier for one than two," he said, his voice muffled through the mask.

She looked at him, her eyes concerned. He was right. She reluctantly relinquished her hold on the wet canvas and stepped back. "Go ahead," she said. "I'll be right here if you need any help."

Kevin adjusted his grip on the canvas so it rested upright in his hands, as though he were carrying an infant, cradled in his open palms. He felt the warm water sop through the woolen work gloves and run down his arms to drip in tiny streams from his elbows. He stepped forward.

His arms passed through some unseen barrier. Sweat ran down his back and he felt the heat of the weakened sun on his neck, yet his hands were plunged into a river of cold. Goose bumps rose on his muscular forearms. He couldn't stop. He was still four feet from the window. It was more than one hundred degrees below zero on his arms and in the nineties on his body.

Another step and his chest passed through the barrier. He gasped and shook. The oxygen mask felt tight against his face as he sucked in a deep breath. Rich oxygen filled his lungs. He felt a little lightheaded as the oxygen raced to his brain.

Another step and he was bathed in the river of cold. Total immersion. The sweat froze on his back and brow. He felt the tiny tracks of water that ran down his arms contract as they hardened into ice. His eyeballs burned. He closed his eyes and stumbled forward blindly.

His hands felt for and found the broken window. He jammed the canvas into the slot, pushing until it forced its way through. He opened his eyes for a quick look. The pain was excruciating. But he saw a gap near the upper right-hand corner. He shoved more canvas in that direction.

His hands began to burn. The fingers stiffened and throbbed. Then, suddenly, the pain stopped. He ran his hands around the metal framework, seeking any gap in the plug. It seemed solid. He moved to back away. His hands refused to go.

He let out a cry of terror and pulled. His hand stayed, the gloves frozen to the metal.

Kevin was trembling all over. The cold sucked at his strength. He pulled one last time and something gave. One more tug and he was free. He stumbled back, right into Melba's arms. She dragged him to safety.

He lay on the roof, shivering violently, the heat seeping through his back almost imperceptible against the cold of his skin. He tried to open his eyes, but they continued to burn and the bright sun directly overhead hurt too much. He closed them again.

He heard Hal calling for someone to get a blanket and thought it was funny that anyone would need a blanket in this weather. Christ, he thought, it's the middle of August.

As the shivering began to subside, he felt someone pulling his arms away from his chest. For some reason, Kevin resisted, but then Hal's calm voice told him to let them go. He did. Kevin heard a sharp intake of breath as his hands slowly came into view and Hal's sharp, "Don't just stand there gaping, woman. Get me my bag."

Minutes later, Kevin felt a gentle pressure against his palms and tugging against his fingers. He sighed, as he sank into the painless abyss of sleep, faintly wishing he could have another beer. He was awfully thirsty.

6:20 P.M.   *In a Tunnel; Somewhere in Brooklyn*

"Help me to my feet," Faust groaned. Manny and Judith grabbed hold and lifted. It was like trying to move a mountain. Judith's legs buckled under the weight but she held on. He lumbered erect, leaning on a steel grillwork for support.

Pain flashed through his entire body. He hurt in so many places he couldn't begin to isolate the individual points of agony. His legs hurt unbearably. They ached with the dull throbbing of an abscessed tooth. His knees refused to support him and his vision swam. His head felt as though it were being pounded on by a crowd of tiny sledgehammers, and his stomach churned.

All he wanted to do was sleep. If it weren't for the

children he probably would have given up and slid back to the cool concrete floor and allowed the rising river of white that filled the tunnel to claim him. He looked over the edge and saw that it was nearly halfway to the level of the platform. They'd better get going. "Maybe the air will do some good," he thought.

"Okay." He hobbled forward, leaning heavily on Manny and as lightly as he could on Judith. "Let's go."

Judith took Mary's hand and followed Manny's lead. They passed through the bright yellow gates and moved into the sunlight that cascaded down the stairs. Getting Faust to the top of the stairs was a five-minute project. They were forced to stop frequently to rest. The warm breeze of fresh air constantly flowing down the stairs saved them. Once they reached the street, Faust admitted that he did feel a little better. He was too tired to go on right away, so he rested on a nearby bench. His eyes closed as exhaustion and the earliest trembling of shock claimed him.

Manny had never felt so alone or so adult in his life. He looked up and down the street hoping to see someone who could help them. He couldn't do it all himself. Judith was blind. Mary was just a baby and Faust was crippled. Manny was on the verge of crying, but every time he looked at Judith calmly playing a child's game with Mary, he knew he couldn't let them know he was scared. He couldn't let them see him cry.

Manny had never seen the streets so deserted. It was rush hour and there wasn't a soul in sight. The stores on either side of McDonald Avenue were completely deserted. Most of them had their steel gates drawn protectively across their glass exteriors, scant protection against the cloud but proof against the human marauders who had ravaged the streets of the city during the last blackout. Other stores, their owners more concerned with saving their lives than their property, were left wide open.

None of the windows was broken. None of the cash registers had been disturbed. Even the television sets that lined the display cases were ignored. Proof that death was more terrifying than the prospect of continued poverty.

Far to the north, Manny could see the flashing red lights that signaled the edge of the evacuation. He remembered the blare of loudspeakers and the press of the crowds as they fought to get to safety. He remembered following the commands of the policemen. They seemed to know everything. He knew nothing.

He couldn't decide whether to go looking for help and leave Faust and Judith there or try to head to Manhattan as they were. One thing was certain. They couldn't carry Faust. Getting up the stairs had proved that. On the other hand, he couldn't just take Judith and Mary and leave him. He owed the man his life. Faust could have left them in the train the way the others had. He could have saved his life at the expense of the children.

He could have left them there to die. But he didn't.

Nor could Manny.

He wished again for someone, something to take this responsibility off his shoulders. He looked again at the storefronts, hoping he would see some sign of life. There was no one.

Manny sat next to Judith. Faust was resting, eyes closed, breathing deeply.

"Judith," Manny whispered.

"Uh, huh," she replied, stopping her game with Mary.

"We have to talk."

"Okay." She turned to face him, staring at him with sightless eyes. Manny saw for the first time that they were blue. A startling deep blue in her deep brown face. He couldn't believe that they couldn't see.

"I didn't know you had blue eyes."

Her hands went to her face. She laughed. "Oh, I forgot. We're in the light. I got so used to everybody not being able to see that I almost forgot I was blind." Her hand came slowly down to rest in her lap. "Isn't that funny."

Manny couldn't answer that. "Listen, Judith. We have to do something. We can't just sit here."

"When Elliot wakes up . . ." she began.

"We can't wait that long," Manny protested. "The cloud's got to be close behind us. It'll fill the subway tunnel first but then it'll come up on the streets and then we'll be trapped. Faust's asleep and we have to get moving."

Her face hardened. "You're not suggesting that we leave Elliot, are you? How could you think of anything like that? After what he did . . ."

"No, I'm not saying that at all." Manny laid a hand on hers, restraining her tirade physically as well as logically. "No. We have to find something to carry him in. A bicycle, a wagon. Something. Now I can go and try to find something but that would mean that I'd have to leave you and . . ." He stumbled, unable to go on.

"And you're afraid to leave me behind because I'm blind. Is that it?"

"Well . . ."

"That's it, isn't it?" she insisted. "Well, let me tell you something, Emanuel whatever-your-name-is; I can take care of myself. And Mary too. So you just run off and find whatever you have to find and get back here. Because we," she emphasized the *we*, "have to take care of Elliot." She reached out to put her arm protectively around Mary. Her hands struck thin air. They fell to the seat on the bench.

"Mary?" she said. "Mary?" She groped on the bench, seeking the girl. Panic set in as she called out the little girl's name.

Manny hadn't seen her slip away. She had been blocked by Judith's body. "Don't worry," he said. "She was just here a moment ago. She can't have gone far." He checked the street. Empty.

"Do you see her?" Judith asked. "Manny? Do you?"

He didn't answer immediately. He was trying to find places she might have been able to get to without crossing his line of sight. It could only be one of the stores behind them. If she had gone any farther he surely would have seen her.

"Back there," Manny exclaimed. "She has to be there."

"Do you see her?" Judith asked frantically.

"Not yet, but I know where she has to be." He raced into the first store. It was as likely as any of the others.

Judith heard him calling out Mary's name. She could tell from his tone that he still hadn't found her. She fidgeted in her seat, unable to keep still. Manny emerged from the store, his feet slapping hard on the concrete. The slapping of his feet faded as he entered the next store and Judith was left alone in the silence.

Her hearing was keyed to its highest pitch. She could hear the steady breathing of Faust as he slept and the frantic calls from Manny as he rooted through the second store. In the distance, she heard the faint rumble of thunder and the thin wail of sirens. All these sounds she isolated, identified, and ignored. She was listening for something else. Mary.

Little children have a special pattern of sound that accompanies them wherever they go. They never walk, they run, even if it's only a few steps. Their feet never stay on the ground and never stop moving. Sitting in a chair, the child will keep up the pattern by beating on the legs of the chair with his heels. This Judith knew from her afternoons in the park.

She was listening for that sound. That high-frequency pattern of a child. Everything else was filtered out. She became as deaf to Faust's breathing and Manny's calls as she was blind. Then she had it. Off to her left. In a different direction than Manny was searching.

"Mary," she called. No answer. The pattern hesitated but quickly resumed.

It was inside a building. The sound of shoes on linoleum. A heel dragging on polished tile. She rose and followed the sound. Her hands outstretched, she felt a doorjamb. The smell of jasmine and chocolate. A market? A candy store? She couldn't be certain.

But the sound was there. Still distant, but audible. "Mary?" she whispered, holding her breath, waiting for a reply.

"Timmy?" came a little voice. It was Mary. "Are you there, Timmy?"

"Mary, where are you?" she whispered again. "It's Judith. Where are you, Mary?"

"I told you not to play hide-and-seek, Timmy," Mary scolded. "I told you."

Had she really found Timmy? Judith wondered. He might have come out of the station the way they had. He would have been hungry. Maybe he was there? Or was it just the imagination of a small girl who had lost her mother and brother in one day? She listened.

Only one pattern. One child.

Unless the other one's hurt.

"Come out, Timmy," Mary cried. "I don't like this game anymore."

The pattern against wood. Slowed. Long spaces between

sounds. Hollow sounds. A sound that sent chills down Judith's spine. Stairs! She was going into the basement.

"Mary!" she cried. "Mary, don't go down there."

The hollow pattern continued. It ended abruptly. Leather on concrete. She had reached the bottom. She was in the basement.

Judith frantically made her way toward the source of the sound. She raced recklessly toward the sound of Mary's feet, stumbling into display cases, sending one spewing across the floor with a clatter of broken glass. She brushed it aside without a second's thought. Then her hands struck a wall. She ran her hands along the cool plaster, knocking signs taped to the wall flying as she sought the door. Her fingers slammed into the doorjamb.

She stood in the center of the doorway. "Mary," she whispered, not wanting to alarm the girl. "Mary, it's Judith. Won't you come upstairs?"

The faint tapping of her pattern was the only answer.

"Mary?" The pattern continued.

Taking a deep breath, she reached out for the banister. After a few seconds of groping, her hand struck the cool metal. It rang dully in the stillness. Judith's foot sought the first step and she moved downward.

Halfway down she felt the first wisps of cold wrap around her legs.

6:30 P.M. *On Board the* SEA MAID

As first mate on supertankers it was rare that Val ever laid his hands on the wheel. And even when he did, it was like putting his hands on a computer simulation of a ship. But on a tug, even the slightest wiggle of the wheel brought an instant response. It was like being on a small sailboat again, something Val hadn't done in years. Despite the seriousness of the situation, he enjoyed himself as he jockeyed the tug into position directly downstream of the *Prometheus*.

At first, naturally, he overreacted. The *Sea Maid* slewed from side to side as he tried to hold her steady. Then, realizing what was happening, he deliberately stopped thinking about it and let his hands take over. His mind may have forgotten what it was like to be a sailor, but his hands had not. The *Sea Maid* stopped her swerving and cut a clean course to the center of the channel.

Now came the tricky part. Taking up the slack. If he took it too quickly, he would snap the line, tearing it apart as surely as the other lines that failed. If he took it up too slowly, they'd never have enough momentum to start the mammoth tanker moving. If he misjudged, the results would be disastrous.

He leaned out the window and looked back, trying to see the bollard that held the towline. It was blocked by the rear of the superstructure. He couldn't see the line as it disappeared into the water. He couldn't tell how much tension there was on the line.

Val cursed the lack of a crew. He had rejected Wade's offer of assistance as they walked to the tug. The *Prometheus* had already taken enough lives. And the mission was suicidal. Both men knew it. Neither would say it aloud.

No automatic pilot yet devised could steer the *Sea Maid* accurately enough to make certain that her distance from shore was maximized. No machine could account for the difference in mass and maneuverability when you had a ship as large as the *Prometheus* on the end of a four-hundred-yard line. It was like trying to land a thousand-pound shark using fifty-pound test lines. It could be done, but only with skill, playing into the pressure when it became too rough and leaning into it when the time was right. No automatic pilot could do that. It took a skilled seaman.

There was no way he could let go until the tanker could do no more harm. And that was only when she was already on fire. Anything a mere four hundred yards from that flaming inferno wouldn't be alive for long.

Val stuck his head as far out the window as he could, trying to spot the line. He couldn't.

"Having trouble?" Cybil asked.

Val pulled his head in so fast he bumped it on the window. He saw stars.

"What the hell are you doing here?" he demanded.

"Nice way to greet the woman who's to become your wife."

"My wife? But . . ."

"I know. I know. Where you come from the man's supposed to propose, but we don't have the time to waste with formalities." Cybil turned and stared out the window. The view was dominated by the pure white cloud. Bride's colors, she thought. "So are you going to marry me or not?"

"Well . . . of course, but I . . ."

"No time for buts," she said, turning and walking to his side. "We've got other things to worry about." She leaned over and planted a generous kiss on his mouth. After a few moments of shock he participated. It grew longer and longer. Cybil finally broke it off.

"Enough!" she protested. "Before we start something there's no time to finish." She flashed him a smile. "We've got work to do." Her voice turned serious.

"You're right." He straightened up. The *Sea Maid* had been idling in neutral. He nudged her engines once. They were in position. "First thing is to have the *Apple Tree* take you off." He reached for the radiophone. "How did you get past the crew, anyway?"

She moved between him and the radio. "Oh no you don't." She smiled. "First, you two men were so busy that you didn't bother telling the crew that I was barred from coming on board. They were used to my having the run of the ship, so they didn't question me when I asked to board the tug." She smiled again. "One of the benefits of being a civilian. And, as for having the *Apple Tree* pick me up, you don't have time. Every second we waste means just that much less time to tow the *Prometheus* out of the harbor. Furthermore, you need me. You can't run this tug alone. You need someone to watch the towline. To make sure you don't snap it. Am I right?"

Val hesitated, staring into Cybil's deep brown eyes. Finally he nodded. "You're right, damnit. Aren't you ever wrong?"

"Sometimes," she admitted, smiling. "But I try to keep them to a minimum."

"All right. Get on the stern and watch the line. I need to know when we begin to put strain on it. There's a lot of slack between us and the *Prometheus* so that'll come up quickly. Then there will be a period of tension, when we're putting pressure on the line and on the tanker. I'll have to use more power then. If I start increasing power too soon, we'll lose the line."

"I understand. Dead slow until the line goes taut and then more power."

"Right." He reached into a shelf below the wheel and pulled out a small two-way radio. "Here. Take this. And stay clear of the line. If it lets go, it'll have enough force to cut you in two."

She saluted. "Aye, aye, my captain." She scooted out the cabin door and her footsteps were quickly lost under the deep rumble of the powerful twin diesels.

Val shook his head in disbelief. His lips still tingled as he reached for the radiophone to call the *Apple Tree*.

Cybil took only a minute to reach the fantail. Like all tugs, the *Sea Maid* was extremely low to the water and had the lingering odor of fuel oil. Half came from the exhaust vents that released their gases just a few feet above deck level and the other half from the oily waters of the bay.

At the stern, tied securely by experienced seamen, the heavy towline dangled into the bay. Cybil examined the line without touching it. It was as thick as her arm, but compared with the bulk of the tanker it seemed insignificant.

"Val," she spoke into the radio, "I'm here." She looked over the edge of the tug. The dark brown line disappeared almost vertically into the oily water. "Go ahead. There's nothing on the line now."

A revving of the engines was her response. A blue-brown cloud of exhaust fumes drifted over her, making her gasp. The sound of churning water rumbled from the stern.

Giving the towline a wide berth, Cybil leaned over the side. A small trail of bubbles followed the *Sea Maid*. Their wake. They were underway. The line hung straight down, like a limp sock. Slowly, as they pulled farther and farther away, the spot where the line emerged from the water seemed to recede. A few more inches and then feet of line emerged from the water, dripping as it came into the light. The line was slightly bowed.

"Keep going," she radioed. "Still no tension." The *Sea Maid* maintained her speed, her engines a notch above idle as she pulled away from the frozen cloud that marked the presence of the *Prometheus*. Cybil moved to the massive bollard that restrained the towline and gently laid her fingertips on the seasoned hemp. It felt cool and dry to the touch. "Keep going. No tension yet." The angle of the line to the water grew more acute. The bowing disappeared.

"Slowly now," Cybil warned. "We're almost there." She reached out and put a hand on the hemp. She could feel the growing tension, a deep, slow vibration. She could feel the weight of the tanker on the other end.

With a suddenness that was frightening, the line became taut. The hemp creaked as the fibers were pulled tight. The line that had lain loosely around the cleat tightened. The steel bolts that fastened it to the deck groaned as the pressure was applied.

"We're there," Cybil called. The engines slowed a beat as Val adjusted the throttle accordingly. The *Sea Maid* continued to pull against the *Prometheus*.

Four hundred yards away the *Prometheus* lay calmly in the water, her bow nudging the shallows to the west of Sandy Hook. She lay dead in the water, her stern slowly drifting in the receding tide.

As the towline tightened around the cleat on the *Sea Maid*, it tightened on the rudder of the *Prometheus*, sliding slowly against the heavy steel. Finally it tightened against the cleat, newly married to the hull. The tension mounted as the line continued to be drawn more taut by the distant tug. Every part of the ship protested the pressure. Protested, but held.

Pushed by the unseen hand of the tide and pulled by the small but determined *Sea Maid*, the *Prometheus* surrendered to the forces of physics. Her stern swung farther west. Her bow dug deep into the silt, smashing through years of accumulated dirt and sand. But her stern moved.

The line sang a resonant song of protest. Cybil backed away, remembering Val's warning. She had never seen the power of the sea and the ships that sailed it displayed so vividly before. "It's as taut as you can get it," she radioed.

Val answered her for the first time. "Okay, back away. If the line's going to go, it'll be soon. So get out of there."

Cybil backed away, but stopped as soon as she reached

the apparent safety of the bulky cabin. She looked around the corner, staying in sight of the bollard. The creaking sound was everywhere, but she couldn't tear her eyes away from the sight. She had to know what was going on. "All holding," she radioed.

The engines took on a deeper throb. A blue cloud puffed out of the vents and covered the stern to the tug, obscuring her view. The sound of rushing water grew as power was fed to the screw. The creaking was lost between the engines and the water. She couldn't tell whether they were still linked to the *Prometheus* by their fibrous umbilical cord. She almost raced out through the cloud to make sure that the bollard was still there.

The smoke drifted away. The bollard was still there. Cybil released a breath she hadn't realized she had been holding.

The engines throbbed more deeply as Val continued to increase power. From his position he could tell that they were not moving. The restraining hand of the *Prometheus* had given them some room, but then stopped. One hand on the wheel, the other on the throttle, Val could feel the *Prometheus* on the other end of the line. He closed his eyes and envisioned the two vessels struggling for physical supremacy.

The *Sea Maid*'s bow lifted partially out of the water as Val moved the throttle forward a fraction of an inch. Her prop bit deeper into the bay, increasing her power as her angle shifted. The entire boat strained against the line.

At the other end, the *Prometheus* dragged against the silt that held her pinned to the bottom of the channel. It cut a deep groove into the silt. The groove widened into a large V as the tanker slid farther into the channel.

Then she was free. Her hull floated in the channel. The twin forces of tide and tug drew her east.

Val felt the engine quiet as the *Prometheus* pulled free. He smiled. There was no doubt in his mind that the tanker was now afloat and moving. He knew that they were on their way. It was only a matter of time until they were out to sea. For the first time since he and Cybil had left the *Prometheus* he felt they had a chance.

He took a deep breath, flexing the fingers on his hands

to relieve the cramps that had made them suddenly stiff.

They were on their way.

6:35 P.M. *Mayor's Office; City Hall*

"Dillon on line two."

"Thank you, Phyllis." LaSalle punched in the speaker-phone. "Dillon, what the hell's going on?"

The director was nonplussed. "We're not certain, Mr. Mayor. The computers . . ."

"I don't want any more of your computer shit, Dillon. I want to know what's happening." He grabbed a yellow sheet of telex paper and waved it in front of the phone as though Dillon could see. "I want to know about this. About the storm. Why didn't you let me know? I thought you were supposed to be feeding me information. Isn't that what the President said?"

"I think you have the essence of his . . ."

"Essence, hell, Dillon. Tell me what's going on. I get this standard blurb off the wires about this damn storm coming into New York and doing God knows what. And I don't hear a word from Washington. With all your computers you couldn't tell this was going to happen?"

"You must understand, Mr. Mayor," Dillon was silky smooth. He exuded confidence, as though he knew that everything would be all right but just couldn't tell you all about it yet. It was a skill that had come in handy before more than one congressional committee. "There are limitations to computers. We can't keep track of everything. But I assure you we have been following the progress of the storm and my meteorologists are relatively certain that the storm will not materially affect the cloud. The storm is very limited, they tell me, and it's not expected to move into Brooklyn. It probably won't even get much farther than midtown.

"You have to understand that this is, of course, under constant surveillance. We have a weather satellite focused on the storm and it's keeping us apprised of its progress minute by minute. I've ordered the total complement of our computer bank to watch the storm's progress against the cloud's. They're working on that right now. These things take time, Mr. Mayor. You have to be a little patient . . ."

"I don't have time to be patient. This city doesn't have time to be patient. If that cloud starts to move in some direction that we aren't prepared for, do you have any idea how many people could die?"

"Yes, I have." LaSalle knew that was true. Some computer in a secret basement in Maryland had spent several nanoseconds totaling how many people could be killed by the cloud. To the tenth of a percent. That's what his computers were designed to do, predict ways to maximize death. LaSalle didn't want to know the latest estimate.

"Ah," Dillon continued, "patience does pay off. Here's the latest computer print-out." A rustle of papers filled the air. "Just one second, Mr. Mayor, and I should be able to answer your questions."

LaSalle waited impatiently for Dillon to finish reading the report. He nervously rapped his fingers on the table.

"Ummm, Mr. Mayor?"

"I'm here, Dillon."

"Ahhhh." The slickness had totally disappeared. "I'm afraid that these reports aren't as helpful as I had hoped. Do you mind if I call you back? They've started on another run and . . ."

"I do mind, goddamnit," LaSalle snapped. "I need to know any information you can tell me. Where's that cloud going next?"

"I'd really rather wait, Mr. Mayor. It's never advisable to act on partial information. In my experience . . ."

"Your experience be damned, Dillon. Tell me." LaSalle had a queasy feeling in his stomach. When someone refused to give information it usually meant that the news was bad.

"Well, here goes. First, the earlier predictions of the storm stalling in Manhattan seem to be holding up. The computer gives it a ninety-five percent chance of remaining in Manhattan for at least an hour and . . . by then it won't matter too much anyway."

"What does that mean?" LaSalle asked.

"What it means, Mr. Mayor, is that the storm will have some definite effects on the speed and the direction of the cloud. You can't dump what amounts to an arctic cold center in the middle of a near-tropical climate without severe environmental repercussions. Since nothing like this has ever happened before, we, of course, have no experience to go by. These projections are merely logical extensions of known meteorological trends, plugging in the local conditions that are quite bizarre. There's no way of telling the reliability of these projections."

"All right, Dillon, you've told me it's not your ass. Now tell me what it says."

"It seems that the computer's come up with two equally probable scenarios. The first is that the storm could displace the air that is now over Manhattan, forcing it east and south. That would act as a buffer between the storm and the cloud, pushing the cloud before it. In effect, pushing it out to sea."

"That doesn't sound that bad," LaSalle mused. "What's the second one?"

"On the other hand," Dillon continued, "the cloud, the Brooklyn cloud, that is, could break up the ceiling that has kept all the pollution centered over New York City. In that case, the Manhattan air mass would merely rise over the LNG cloud. And then the normal meteorological laws would control."

"Meaning?"

"Thunderstorms are low-pressure areas. New York, and in particular the cloud, are high-pressure areas. Winds tend to flow from high pressure to low. The cloud would be sucked into the low-pressure area."

"Holy . . ." LaSalle whispered.

"Exactly. The cloud would be sucked into Manhattan. And the wind velocity would be ten to fifteen miles an hour. There wouldn't be a hope in hell of evacuating in time."

"How many people?" LaSalle whispered to himself. Dillon overheard.

"About six to eight million. And there's something else I should tell you, since you asked for all the relevant information." His tone indicated that LaSalle had asked for it, and by God he was going to get it all. "The computer also notes that the wind velocity would have the effect of speeding the dispersion of the cloud if it were drawn into the storm center. The gas would reach combustible concentration within minutes. Including explosive concentration." He paused as if for effect. "And, of course, you know that it's a thunderstorm. Thunderstorms mean lightning. There's not one chance in a million that the cloud won't be ignited, probably explosively, if it's drawn into Manhattan."

LaSalle and Newfeld sat mute in their chairs.

"Now if you'll excuse me, Mr. Mayor," Dillon continued smoothly, "I have to call the President." The line went dead.

In the sudden silence, the distant rumble of thunder sounded close.

Newfeld's glass rolled out of his unfeeling hands and dropped to the thick carpeting with a dull thud. It bounced once and then struck the maple leg of LaSalle's desk. The fine crystal shattered, splintering the seal of New York City into a thousand tiny slivers.

Chapter 17

6:40 P.M.   Windows on the World; World Trade Center Tower One

There wasn't a bad seat in the house. On three sides every window was packed with the eager faces of some of the state's most powerful and influential people. Since the action had spread to other sides of the restaurant, the pushing and shoving matches for prime window space had slowed. People now rotated somewhat smoothly from south to east to north. There was something to see on each side.

To the north, the view was dominated by the growing thunderstorm that seemed to be moving with incredible speed toward the Trade Center. It had grown from a mere speck to cover the horizon in the space of fifteen minutes. Flashes of light illuminated the cloud from within as angry lightning bolts flashed from one cloud to another. Distant rumbles of thunder rolled across the Trade Center.

Uptown, the green of Central Park had turned to a mottled shade of brown as the crowd filled all the open spaces. More than two million people filled the park, according to radio reports, but from the extent of the coloring, the estimates were low. Only the quiet blues of the reservoir and the lake remained unchanged.

Still farther south all six lanes of the Brooklyn Bridge were covered with people. A portion of the FDR Drive was visible where the blue tops of city buses gleamed dimly in the failing light. The evacuation was going full swing.

To the east, the view of the bridge and FDR Drive was better. As was the view of the Brooklyn approaches to the bridge. Some of the flashing red lights of the police cars and fire engines that lined the streets of Brooklyn were visible. The combined effect of all the flashing red lights made it appear as though the borough were on fire, so extensive was the illumination. And now, with the failing light, the yellows from the approaching sunset added to the effect as both colors reflected off the windows facing Brooklyn. The very air itself seemed to be on fire.

But the main attraction was to the south. Like flocks of fall geese, waves of helicopters streaked past the windows of the restaurant. They looked close enough to touch. The helmeted heads of the pilots were clearly visible as they flew past.

A strange feeling of optimism grew in the restaurant. It had filled the air ever since the helicopters had appeared. It was as though the cavalry finally arrived. People were actually laughing as they passed from table to table. There was a feeling that someone was taking care of everything. The certainty that Big Brother was indeed watching and wouldn't let anything bad happen. Only the governor's table was gloomy.

Rene watched with a dull sense of amazement. He had seen a lot of bizarre things happen in his restaurant over the years but never the sudden transformation that had taken over this crowd. Didn't they realize that the helicopters couldn't do anything? Or perhaps it was just his limited experience. After all, he was only a maître d'.

"Rene?" A hand tugged at his sleeve. Rene turned angrily. His eyes were icy cold. They softened when he saw who it was.

"Leopold," he said in surprise. He hadn't seen the wine steward since the "cellar" had been depleted. A sad twinge gripped him when he thought of his wonderful Burgundies. "Is something wrong?" Rene maintained his professional poise before the help at all times. It was a matter of pride with him that he never raised his voice to any employee.

"I've been looking all over for you, Rene," Leopold answered.

"Yes? Well, now you've found me. What is it, Leopold?"

The wine steward smiled and produced the graceful shape of a bottle he had been hiding behind his back. He displayed it, label forward, to Rene.

One glance at the shape of the bottle and the color of the wine was enough to tell him. A Rothschild. He saw the year at the top of the label. Vintage. A beautiful bottle of wine. Bouquet like a deep breath of ambrosia. Color of purest amber. Flavor that never bit the tongue, merely rolled off it and slid down the throat smoothly.

"Leopold." He was honored. It was one of the finest bottles of wine ever made. He took the bottle from the wine steward's hands, cradling it as though it were an infant.

"I saved it for you, sir," Leopold explained in a conspiratorial whisper. "It was going to be sold to someone who was half drunk and wouldn't have known it from a port. I couldn't let that happen, so I told him it was already sold."

"Leopold, you shouldn't have." Rene was half scolding and half praising.

"I know it was wrong of me, sir, but I thought that since it was the last bottle in the house you might . . ."

"You know my rules about drinking during working hours, Leopold." Rene tried to sound stern but couldn't tear his eyes off the label.

"I know, sir, but since today is rather unusual . . ."

"You're right," Rene decided suddenly. "Absolutely right. Open it." He handed the bottle back to Leopold.

"Oh no, sir." He gently fended off the proffered bottle. "I wouldn't take that privilege from you." He removed the corkscrew from around his neck and handed it to Rene.

With a sense of excitement that approached sexual

levels, Rene inserted the corkscrew and withdrew the cork with a satisfying plunk. He sniffed the cork. Perfect. He handed it to Leopold, who imitated him, savoring the delicate bouquet.

Leopold then magically produced two clean glasses that they proceeded to polish with clean napkins until they glistened. The two men sat in a corner away from the crowds, unaware of the activity outside the window as they waited for the wine to breathe for exactly seven minutes.

Even the occasional rumble of thunder did not disturb their vigil.

6:45 P.M. *On Board the* SEA MAID

Val's arms bulged with the effort of holding the *Prometheus* on course. He strained against the wheel, trying by the force of his determination alone to bring her back into the center of the channel.

The *Sea Maid* headed directly for the tip of Sandy Hook. Her bow was only yards from the oil-slicked sands, yet he dared not turn away. He pushed her for every inch he could get. The *Prometheus* was headed in just the opposite direction.

"Where is she now?" he shouted out the window.

"Just short of the buoy," Cybil answered from her perch on top of the wheelhouse. She sat there with the Nikon field glasses she had found in one of the cabinets and focused on the stern of the *Prometheus*.

The mammoth tanker had emerged from the white cloud like a tower of ice. At first her hull had been covered by a layer of white, making her almost indistinguishable from the frozen cloud she left behind. As they moved farther into the sunlight, the frost had melted like the morning dew, revealing the angry red-and-black paint of the *Prometheus* rising one hundred feet above the water. Her name glared starkly in white letters.

Cybil had taken the wheel while Val first checked their position. The tanker was off course. She was heading directly for the Sandy Hook shallows. Val checked the charts. The bottom shoaled rapidly. If she grounded there, he'd never be able to pull her off. He cut hard to compensate. Slowly, with the inevitable lag of distance and size, she followed the *Sea Maid* away from the shallows. A mouse pulling an elephant.

Then she headed for the other side of the channel.

It was like trying to land a fish without a fishing rod. The line allowed the maximum amount of freedom and the minimum amount of control. She swerved from side to side, a living creature struggling to avoid capture. She fought the insistent tug of the *Sea Maid*'s line fastened to her hull.

"She's turning!" Cybil yelled.

Val spun the wheel hard to port. The *Sea Maid* bucked and shifted. The view of the beach slid away from Val's window. There was no feeling of motion, only of dislocation as the bow of the tug sought a new position in front of the tanker.

It was a problem of momentum and inertia. He had to pull her hard enough in one direction to begin turning and then quickly shift to a new course to keep her from turning too much. Theoretically a high school student could correctly predict the ideal course for the *Sea Maid* using only a compass and a slide rule. Unfortunately, the high school student couldn't predict the unseen forces of the shifting tides and currents. Neither could Val.

It became a matter of instinct versus the perfidiousness of the seas. A contest of skill and chance. A crap shoot. And Val was shooting blind.

He lined the bow of the tug on the buoy marking the edge of the channel and the beginning of Flynn's Knoll. That should bring her back on course. He hoped. He rubbed his hands against the spokes of the wheel, taking comfort in their solidity and the familiarity of the wheelhouse.

Cybil's head appeared upside down at the window. She was leaning over from her roost.

"How's it going, Captain?" Her face was flushed and her deep brown hair surrounded her like a wave. She had never looked more beautiful.

"You tell me. You've got the view."

The radio squawked cutting off Cybil's reply. *"Apple Tree* to *Sea Maid*. Come in, *Sea Maid*."*

Val picked up the microphone. *"Sea Maid* here."*

"Val, we have a radio call from Washington. The director of N.S.A. I can't transfer it to you because it's on the security line. He wants a message passed to your stowaway. Is she nearby?"

Cybil dropped to the deck and stepped into the wheelhouse. "Right here, Commander. Could you repeat exactly what the director said. His exact words. You have a written copy of his message, I take it."

"Yes. It reads 'Please advise Dep. Sec. Yale of revised weather forecast soonest. Low-pressure areas and thunderstorm are moving into Manhattan. E.T.A. Eighteen hundred thirty hours. Electrical and ancillary effects predicted to be purely local, repeat purely local, in nature. No problem with electrical disturbances in Brooklyn. Repeat, no electrical disturbances in Brooklyn. Other side effects possible. Suggest you plan accordingly. Director N.S.A.' That's the whole message, Professor."

"Thank you, Commander." Cybil returned the mike to Val, who signed off. She looked forward without seeing. Val took the wheel from her hands and steered them back on course. They had drifted a few degrees off while Cybil wasn't watching.

"What is it?" Val asked after a few silent moments passed. "What did he mean about 'plan accordingly'?"

"You have to understand that Dillon's a multileveled person. He never says anything that doesn't have a hidden meaning and he never repeats himself."

"But . . . ?"

"I know. He repeated two parts of the message twice. That means something special is implied."

"But why go to all that trouble? The transmission was on your security line . . ."

"But the transmission from the *Apple Tree* to us wasn't. Dillon must have been trying to tell us something he couldn't say on the open line," Cybil mused aloud. "That means it's something that's too dangerous to let the general public know, yet important enough to call us about."

She paced the wheelhouse, oblivious to her surroundings. Val stroked the wheel, gently maintaining an equilibrium between the tug and the tanker.

"Two," Cybil intoned. "Two messages, twice. That must mean that two things are happening." She stared out the window. "Or possibly that one of two things could happen. First, 'purely local' effects in Manhattan. Second, 'no electrical disturbance in Brooklyn.' Those were the operative phrases. Manhattan and Brooklyn. And a storm. A thunderstorm." She lapsed into silence.

Val watched her as she struggled with the problem. "Well," he suggested, "if you look at it from a sailor's point of view, the most important thing is the storm." He paused. Cybil was listening, her eyes glazed as her thoughts followed his. "And a storm means winds . . ."

"Yes," she agreed, "but he also said that the effects would be purely . . . No," she stopped. "He said the 'electrical' effects would be local. Other effects could be more widespread."

"Yes," Val continued, "and when you have an approaching storm the most noticeable effect is wind."

"Good," Cybil nodded. "Wind certainly is relevant. It determines the speed and direction of the cloud."

"Wind velocity almost always increases before a storm, you can count on that. But direction . . . That's more difficult. Sometimes it blows toward the storm, sometimes away."

"Two choices." Cybil nodded. "That fits. And I'll bet that it's just about even which way it goes. That's what Dillon meant. Manhattan or Brooklyn. Oh, Val," she gasped, "it might be headed for Manhattan. If the wind draws it into Manhattan, the thunderstorm—it'll ignite the cloud. My God, there must be millions . . . all the people from Brooklyn . . ."

"Remember. It could go the other way. The wind could shift one hundred and eighty degrees. I've often seen that happen at sea."

"Right. It could. That would drive the cloud back on itself." She gripped Val's arm. "You know what that means?" The excitement grew in her eyes. "The cloud might be blown out to sea! Don't you see? The entire cloud might just blow away. It can't hurt anybody once it's out at sea. Val!" She threw her arms around his neck. "Val, I know it's only a fifty-fifty chance but . . ."

Her eyes followed the direction of his gaze. The compass, floating in its sealed container of fluid. The black letters SE on the compass card stood out starkly against the background of white.

Southeast.

Cybil looked at the chart, partially unfolded, on the

pilot's desk next to Val. She noticed the star in the right-hand corner. A symbolic compass.

Then it dawned on her. The *Prometheus* was between the *Sea Maid* and Brooklyn. If the cloud reversed direction, it would be headed directly for them.

If it didn't, it would be headed for the center of Manhattan.

6:45 P.M. *Weather Forecast for New York City and Vicinity*

TEMPERATURE:	89° F.	31° C.
HUMIDITY:	100 percent	
WIND:	Variable 3–10 knots	
PRECIPITATION:	100 percent	

SPECIAL CONDITIONS: It is raining in midtown Manhattan. Thundershowers, severe at times, will continue until morning over much of the midtown area. Local temperature anomalies in Brooklyn make other forecasts impossible at this time.

NATIONAL WEATHER SERVICE
NATIONAL CLIMATIC CENTER, ASHEVILLE, NORTH CAROLINA

6:45 P.M. *In a Basement; Somewhere in Brooklyn*

The blackness of the basement wasn't terrifying. No more than the blackness of the street in daylight. To be blind means never to fear the dark. It is a constant companion.

Other senses grow in compensation. Judith's hearing was particularly acute, as was her sense of smell. Her fingers could discern hairline cracks that even the sharpest eye might overlook. Every nerve in her body tried to substitute for her missing eyes. That's why she felt the cold so painfully.

A violent shiver ran up her spine as she stepped into the cold air. Even her ears rang from the cold. She stopped and stood still until she could hear again. Slowly her auditory world expanded.

There was the tapping. Mary's pattern. The rapid knocking of a shoe against a wooden board. A crate probably, Judith guessed, because of the slightly hollow sound it gave off with each rap of a hard rubber heel.

"Mary?" It was a whisper. "Are you there?"

The pattern stopped. A tiny voice cried in the silence. "Judith? Where's Timmy? I was looking for him, but he's lost." A sob wracked the little girl's body, tearing through her with an anguish that her tiny form couldn't contain. Judith could almost feel the muscle spasm of the girl as though she were holding her in her arms.

"Don't cry, Mary." Judith stepped deeper into the basement. The cold lapped up to her calves, causing her entire body to shiver as the heat was drained from her flesh. She took another step and it covered her knees. Another and it stopped. She had reached bottom. Her teeth clenched involuntarily against the cold.

It was cold, but it was not the paralyzing cold of the tunnel. The gas was close but not yet in large quantities, and there was not a ready source of metal that it could use to absorb the heat from the air. It was a cold winter day, not a frigid arctic night.

"Mary? Where are you?"

The tiny voice replied, "I'm cold, Judith. Why is it so cold?"

"I know, Mary." Judith's foot struck concrete. Her toes tingled in the chill. "I'm cold, too. We'll leave in a moment." She slid her foot forward in the direction of Mary's voice.

"Is there any light down here?" Judith asked.

"Yes," Mary answered. "But I thought you couldn't see. Why would you want light, if you can't see?"

"I can't, but you can." Judith slid another foot forward. "You can be my eyes again. Would you like that?"

A swishing sound. It was the gentle rippling of hair against clothes. Mary was nodding.

"Good. Can you see the floor?"

Again the swishing sound, this time reinforced with a small "Yes."

"Is there anything white on the floor? Anything that moves. Like water. Only maybe it floats in the air. Is there anything like that?"

"Yes."

Judith took a deep breath. The smell of her own fear filled her nostrils. She could hear her heart quicken.

"Where is it, Mary? The . . . the thing on the floor. Where is it?"

"Over there." The ripple of an arm being raised. She could almost hear the knuckles bend as the little girl pointed.

"Where, Mary?" she pleaded. "Tell me where."

"I did," Mary protested. "Over there."

"No, Mary. You have to tell me in words. Is it behind me? To my left? Where is it?"

"Behind you."

A new set of chills ran up Judith's spine. The stairs were behind her. "Is . . . is it close to me?"

"No, not too close."

Judith held out her arms. "Can you come to me? Without touching the . . . white thing. Come to me, Mary."

The sound of her tiny shoes striking wood. She was sitting on a crate or possibly a table and hanging her feet against its legs. Her voice came from chest level. Just above the cold.

"But it's so cold," Mary cried.

"I know it's cold, Mary, but we have to go. And since I can't see, you have to help me. Won't you do that, Mary? Won't you help me?"

"Okay." Her voice was resigned.

Her pattern moved. She was moving to the edge of the table or crate. It stopped. A thump. Wood, but more solid. A smaller crate? Her pattern stopped again.

"I can't," Mary cried. "It's cold."

"Yes, you can, Mary," Judith urged. "You can do it."

"No, I can't. I can't," she cried. Her pattern moved back to the other level. She retreated to the higher level. Back to the first box.

"Okay, Mary. I'll come to you and you can ride on my shoulders." Judith's voice trembled from fear and the cold.

"You'll have to guide me, Mary. You'll have to tell me where to walk so I don't step into the thing on the floor. Can you do that, Mary?"

A sniffled "Yes" was her answer.

Judith took one step forward, shuffling her foot against the concrete. "Can I walk straight ahead like this, Mary?"

A rustle of clothes. A nod.

"You'll have to speak to me, Mary." Judith fought to keep her voice calm. "I can't see you when you shake your head. Can I go forward without stepping into the thing on the floor?"

"Yes."

"Okay. I'm going to walk straight ahead until you tell me to stop. Now, Mary, listen to me carefully." She paused. There was no response. No pattern. "Are you listening?"

"Yes."

"Good. I want you to say yes or no before I step. Yes means that there's nothing in front of me. And no means that there is. Do you understand that, Mary?"

"Yes."

"Okay. I'm counting on you to tell me. Ready?"

"I'm cold." She was whining now.

"I know you're cold. I'm cold too. As soon as I get you, we'll get out of here and back outside where we can warm up. Can I step now?"

"Yes."

She slid a foot forward and brought her other one up to meet it.

"Yes."

Another step. The cold grew higher. That meant that more gas was filling the room. Somewhere behind her it was floating out of an open drain or through some crack in the floor, silently filling the basement with its frigid presence.

A trail of yeses led her to Mary. She had no trouble finding the small girl. Her pattern and her tiny crying voice beamed like a verbal beacon in the silence of the basement. Only the silent cold worried Judith.

Her fingers touched the trembling figure. Even to Judith's cold fingers, Mary's skin was cold. The heat was being sucked out of her tiny body at an alarming rate. Her small summer dress was no protection against the chill. She wrapped her arms around Mary and tried to share her warmth. It was all she could do to contain the trembling.

Slowly she pried the tiny arms from around her neck. Goose bumps turned her skin into sandpaper. A small face was buried against her neck and the damp of saline ran moist and cold against her skin.

"Mary," she whispered. "Let go, Mary." The arms refused to relinquish their grasp. The shivering slackened.

"I'm cold," she cried against Judith's neck. "S-S . . . S . . . so cold!"

"I know, Mary. But I need you. I need you to be my eyes again." She ran her fingers through the fine silk threads, feeling them curl and slip through her fingers with the ease of water. "I need you now, Mary." The hand encountered the gentle warmth of the nape of the girl's neck where it was protected by the fall of hair. Even as she touched its smoothness, the rasp of goose bumps appeared underneath her fingertips. Mary shivered violently.

"Okay," Mary said, her teeth chattering so violently Judith could barely make out the words. "I . . . I'll . . . be . . . your eyes."

Judith kissed her lightly against her hair, inhaling the sweet clean smell of youth and savoring it for a moment before turning her around so she rested on the crook of her arm. "Now, Mary. We're going to do the same thing we did when I came to you before. You're going to tell me when it's all right for me to take a step forward. Yes for a step. No means no step. Do you understand?"

The rubbing of silk against her neck meant yes.

"You're going to have to use words, Mary. I can't see, remember. I'm blind and I need you to tell me what you see for me. So remember to use words. Now," she took a deep breath to calm her own trembling. "Now, Mary, is there any of that thing on the floor between us and the stairs?"

"Yes."

Judith's stomach cramped. "Is . . . is there any way to get to the stairs without stepping in . . . it?"

Silk whipped gently against her face. "Yes."

Judith bit her lip. "Which way, Mary? Which way do I turn to get to the stairs without stepping into the thing?"

"Over there . . . to the right."

Judith stepped to her right.

"No. No," Mary shouted. "To the right, I said. To the right."

Judith's heart leaped. Mary was turned around. Her right was Judith's left. "Okay, Mary." She pulled her foot back. "To the right."

Together Judith and Mary inched across the concrete floor. As they moved, the cold crept higher and higher. Mary was leading her around in a circle, Judith knew, trying to circle the cloud. But her concentration was focused on translating the little girl's commands into movement, reversing every right to a left and every left to a right. She soon could not tell where she was, where the stairs were or, worst of all, where the cloud was. She was lost.

She stumbled on the smooth concrete.

"No!" Mary screamed. "Not that way."

Judith froze. Which way? She slowly rotated. Each time she paused, Mary said "No" through clenched teeth. She turned three hundred and sixty degrees.

They were surrounded.

6:50 P.M. *On the Roof; Somewhere in Coney Island*

They had moved Kevin into the sunlight, the weakening rays of the day's dying sun giving him some warmth. His hands rested in makeshift bowls of water. A damp cloth covered his eyes. His skin had the ghastly pallor of wax, a sheen that turned his tan into a parody of healthiness.

He shivered underneath the lightweight thermal blanket that had materialized out of the seemingly endless bottom of Hal's pack. Occasionally he cried out and had to be restrained lest he pull his hands out of the soothing water.

"How's he doing?" Melba asked as Hal leaned over to check the boy's eyes.

Hal let the cloth drop gently back into place. Melba adjusted it more comfortably. She had assigned herself as Kevin's nurse ever since pulling him to safety.

"Tissue damage. Irreversible." He spoke as though he were reading stock quotations. "The hands will have to be amputated. If he's lucky they'll be able to save enough of the arms to allow for the new mechanical ones. They're almost as good as the originals." He barked a short laugh. "I should know. I have some stock in the company that makes them. I once thought I might . . . but never mind.

"It's the eyes that'll be the worst."

"You mean . . ."

"Blind? Yes. At best. Did you take a look at them before we started with the damp cloths?" Hal shook his head. "Frozen. Ice cubes. He'll be lucky if there isn't brain damage as well."

"But how is that possible? He was only in there for a few seconds. It couldn't be that cold."

"It is." Hal stared silently out at the distant peaks of Manhattan, their lights just beginning to glow in warm invitation. The Trade Center towers were totally lit as usual, giving the effect of a geometric Christmas tree. The gracefully arcing lines of the Brooklyn Bridge were dark, since their power came from the Brooklyn side. The majestic tip of the Empire State Building was lost amidst dark thunderclouds and occasional bolts of lightning.

Hal stared silently at the skyline. Then he continued in a whisper. "But if I were you I wouldn't worry that much about Kevin. It doesn't look like any of us will be getting off this fifteen-story tomb."

"What do you mean?" Melba asked.

"Look. At the skyline. There, against the clouds. You can see them coming. The helicopters. Our rescuers."

She stared for a minute and then grabbed his arm. "But that's wonderful!" She threw her arms around his neck, almost dislodging him from his crutches and throwing him to the ground. "That means we're saved. They'll pick us up and . . ."

"Don't be so hasty, Melba," Hal said as he disengaged her arms. "They won't be here for quite a while. If ever. They're coming from the north. We're at the southern tip of Brooklyn. The last to be picked up. If they make it here before that storm does, that is."

Chapter 18

Images of death plagued Faust's uneasy sleep. Gasping for breath he awoke suddenly, drenched in sweat.

He looked around cautiously; it was a ghost town. He didn't know where he was or what had happened. He only knew he was alone.

Off to his right, he caught a faint flicker of motion. He stared south, but the street was empty. Deserted. Shrouded in white. Then the shroud moved.

The cloud! He remembered. The train ride. The crash. The tunnel. The rats. The children.

They had left him. He fell back against the seat, relieved and gasping for breath. Even the slightest exertion was an effort. At least the children had gotten away safely.

Then his blood ran cold. A scream of terror echoed across the silent street. Judith!

The next instant he found himself running. He lurched toward the sound. Pain shot up his calves, stunning him in its intensity. He ignored it.

He staggered toward the storefront, banging heavily into the doorjamb. The plate-glass window with the words EXOTIC TREATS oscillated from the impact. The aroma of the store carried out into the street. Chocolate and spices. A child's wonderland.

The pounding of sneakers caught up to him from behind. "Faust!" Manny put his arm around the motorman's waist to help steady him. "Are you all right?"

"Where's Judith?" Faust gasped, leaning against the youth's shoulder. He took care to avoid jostling the splint.

"I don't know," the boy answered. "I thought she was with you. I went to find Mary and she stayed . . ."

"You mean you lost Mary?"

Manny looked at the floor. "She musta slipped away while Judith and I were talking."

"So they're both lost?"

"I guess so." Manny kept staring at the floor. He had really failed this time. "Unless maybe Judith found Mary."

"Well, Judith's in trouble. Maybe both of them are." Faust shuffled farther into the store. "I heard her scream. I think it was from in here." He straightened up. "Judith! Judith!"

"Elliot?" came the weak reply. She sounded terrified.

"In the basement," Faust directed. Manny helped him over to the stairs and, leaning heavily on the solid metal banister, they descended into the freezing darkness.

The basement was indirectly lit by two dirty windows in the rear. In one corner packing crates were stacked shoulder high. The rest of the basement was filled with burlap bags.

The stairs bisected the basement into two equal portions. Faust and Manny stood silently on the bottom step. Judith was no more than ten feet away. In Faust's prime he might have been able to jump to her side. He was neither in his prime nor willing to try to make the leap.

Separating them was a small pool of white.

It bubbled against the old wooden legs of the stair riser, filling every available space in the basement. It had seeped into the cellar from a set of storm drains only barely visible now as the gas continued to pour in.

Judith stood on a slight rise, elevated above the cloud. Mary shivered in her arms. As Faust watched, Judith completed a circle, standing still on one leg and slowly revolving on the other. Then she stopped, her back to the stairs. From the slump of her shoulders, he could sense her desperation. She was cut off. There was no way to reach the stairs without crossing the white band of death.

"Judith. Don't move." His voice carried a strength and confidence he didn't feel. "Don't move an inch until I tell you."

"Elliot!" She almost wept. "Elliot. You're all right. I was . . ."

"Never mind that now, just do as I tell you. You're about ten feet from the stairs, but the cloud is between us. You can't walk directly to the stairs."

She turned to face the voice, rotating on the balls of her feet, afraid to even shift her weight. "But . . ."

"Just listen, Judith. There's no time to argue. So just listen and do exactly as I say. I want you to turn around. Face directly away from me. Away from the sound of my voice."

She rotated again.

"Now take two steps forward. There are some packing crates directly in front of you. Walk forward until you find them."

"But the cloud . . ."

"Don't worry about the cloud. Just do as I tell you." Faust's voice had the sound of strength and conviction. She leaned on his strength, drawing sustenance from it, and walked forward slowly. The sharp splinters of wood were a welcome pain as they bit into the flesh of her outstretched hand.

"Good. Now get up on the crate," Faust ordered.

Judith boosted Mary to the top of the crate, safely out of the cold, and then followed her onto the wood platform.

"Manny, go upstairs. See if you can find some more crates or possibly a chair, anything wooden. It has to be wood and strong enough to stand on. Hurry."

He turned back to the two girls. Judith was sitting on the edge of the crate. Mary stood beside her, crying quietly. Faust could see the blue tint her skin had assumed. The gas had to be affecting them as well, draining their strength, making them lightheaded. If they passed out, they would be dead. He had to keep them awake.

"Judith, stand up. Stand up."

Judith raised her head and stared sightlessly in his direction. Incomprehension dominated her face.

"Judith," Faust called, his tone almost pleading. "Judith, stand up."

She struggled to rise but could get no higher than her knees. Even there she swayed dangerously on her precarious perch. The gas and cold were getting to her, Faust knew from personal experience. They were robbing her brain of oxygen. Hallucinations first, then sleep or, more precisely, unconsciousness would follow. And then the rippling waves of white would claim them.

"Hurry up with those boxes, Manny," Faust bellowed. "For God's sake, hurry."

White gas covered every inch of the basement floor. It boiled with constant activity, rolling and rippling as internal pressures fought for escape. Like an insistent tide, the waves lapped at the edges of the crate, beating against the foreign body that kept it from covering everything.

Manny had found four crates upstairs, emptied them hurriedly, and tossed them down to Faust. Lining them up, he prepared to rescue Judith. "Hang on, Judith," he called. "I'll be there in a minute."

Like stepping stones, Faust used each crate to move closer to the stranded girls. The first crate was only a foot in front of the stairs. The second, a foot in front of the first. Faust balanced himself delicately on the third and slid the last one into place just short of Judith and the near-frozen Mary, whom she cradled in her arms.

But the crates were thin. The wood, cheap pine, was only a quarter of an inch thick and held together by the shortest of nails. They were not designed to support the weight of a full-grown man, especially one of Faust's stature. Only by distributing his weight across three of the crates could he hope to keep from collapsing one as he went along. This problem forced him to undulate like a snake, making his way across the three crates, carrying the fourth with him.

Faust lay face down on the third crate, the fourth pushed in front of him. Inches from his nose the white cloud bubbled, unseen but not unfelt. Moments before, he had lost all sensation in the skin on his face. It felt as though someone had poured a plaster mold across the skin and it had hardened into an immobile mask. His eyes were squeezed shut against the biting cold. Only his chest retained any feeling. Each breath was liquid fire. He learned to turn his head like a free-style swimmer coming up for air, sucking air through the corner of his mouth. Even that was only partially effective in blocking out the cold that cut painfully into his lungs.

He pushed the last crate ahead another few inches, using his knees to edge himself forward a little more, separating the second crate from the third. The three crates were more or less evenly spaced to bear his two-hundred-plus pounds, but tell-tale creaks warned him of their imminent collapse.

Only a few feet before him, Judith knelt on her packing crate, an island of safety in an ocean of death. The safety was illusory as the white tide slowly rose higher and higher. Mary clung to her like a terrified monkey, wrapping her arms around her neck and burying her head against her chest.

He hunched his body again, drawing his knees closer to his chest. The pine scraped against the frozen floor. He stretched out to his full height, a few inches closer to Judith and Mary. Closer, but not close enough. Manny yelled to him to keep going.

He turned his head for another breath and drew the scalding air into his lungs. He tasted blood as the skin at the corner of his mouth split. He hunched and stretched. Closer. Again. Closer. Again.

It became a rhythm. Three scrapes to a breath. Maybe six inches closer with each inhalation of vaporous death. His head began to spin. Closer. Again.

Bump.

His head snapped up. The crate rested against Judith's. He had made it. Now all they had to do was get back.

Manny called out to Judith. She answered him in a sleepy voice. The gas was affecting her. Faust was too exhausted to speak. He had to rely on Manny to direct them.

An icy finger brushed his hand. He shivered involuntarily. The box beneath his chest groaned at the unnecessary movement. The finger was followed by the cold presence of Judith's hand. Her fingers clasped his. Both hands now. The bridge was complete.

They began the process that he had explained to them earlier. Judith unclasped Mary's hands from about her neck and deposited her on the forward crate. Mary, her body vibrating with the cold, scampered across Faust's back and finally reached Manny's waiting arms as he stood at the anchor position of the chain. Mary was light and the crates barely creaked at her extra weight.

But Judith was another matter.

She weighed too much to pass over Faust the way

Mary had done. Under their combined weight, the crates would collapse. So Faust had to withdraw, pulling himself back the way he had come, leaving the crates behind him for the girl to follow. Only she was blind. And she could only edge her way along, her hands tracing the edges of the wooden crates before progressing.

Faust began withdrawing slowly, reversing the earlier process of pulling his legs forward and bringing his body up with them. Now it was a process of stretching out as far as he could and slowly pressing his body back. Judith's frozen fingers clung to his forearms.

For Judith, the pain was overwhelming. The cold cut deeply into her lungs with every breath as she lowered her body to the first crate. Her only contact was the reassuring pressure of Faust's arms under her near-unfeeling fingertips.

In the distance, Manny called to her, reassuring, warning, and urging her onward. His voice became a beacon, giving her instructions and direction. His voice had a warm timbre that drew her as surely as Faust's strong arms. She crawled forward.

Both Judith and Faust entered that dreamy world of exhaustion brought about by the combination of cold and oxygen starvation. Neither of them could see how high the cloud had risen. Only Manny was aware that it stretched halfway up the crates' sides. Only inches from the fleeing couple. He didn't warn them; they were going as fast as they could. Within minutes Manny was able to grab Faust's extended ankle. It was completely frozen, but the contact allowed him to guide Faust the rest of the way in and take some of the pressure off the crates. He called out words of encouragement.

Finally, Faust reached the stairs. Judith was within reach. Manny extended his hand and guided her the rest of the way. Then she too stood on the stairs.

Spontaneously, arms reached out and encompassed one another. Tears flowed from seeing eyes and ran down unfeeling faces.

"Enough," Faust said finally. "We have to get going." He relinquished his hold on the two teen-agers. They continued to hold one another, Manny's unbroken arm wrapped around Judith's waist, lending his strength as well as his warmth. Faust gave them a gentle shove up the stairs. "Get going, you two." His voice cracked as his parched throat refused to make the necessary sounds.

Manny and Judith tromped up the stairs, their footsteps echoing hollowly in the empty basement. Faust tried to smile. He tasted blood. Feeling the double weight of age and exhaustion, he followed the teen-agers up the stairs. He heard Mary cry happily as she and Judith were reunited.

Faust's feet felt like leaden weights supported by wooden stumps. They dragged against him, threatening to pull him down with each step. The echoes of his feet on the wooden steps rang ominously in his ears. His eyes closed as the effort became overwhelming.

He stumbled.

As he fell forward, the stairs rushed at his face. Reflexively his arms struck out to break his fall as the edge of the steps cut into his knees. His left hand jammed into the stair. His right struck out, seeking support against the wall. Unfeeling fingers found the metal railing.

A bright burst of pain engulfed his right hand, sending tendrils of agony shooting up his arm. He tried to rise, but the pain drove him back to his knees. A howl of agony escaped his lips as he lay there gasping for breath.

He heard the pounding of feet against wood. A set of shoes appeared before his eyes. Sneakers. Manny.

He tried to rise but couldn't. The pain that flooded his body crested and began to ebb. His shoulder began to cramp. He tried to move it but found he could not. His arm was held in a vise.

Pressure against his wrist. He looked up. Manny was pulling against his arm. It was funny but he couldn't feel anything in his fingers as they remained fastened to the white railing.

The railing drew his eyes back. It was the smoky whiteness that he had seen in the tunnel. The tracks in the tunnel looked just like the railing did now. A thin cloud of white vapor circled the railing and sank slowly to the steps. Frost.

The black skin of his hands was covered with the white vapor, obscuring the ebony. His movements brushed the white covering away. The skin below was revealed.

Gone was the familiar black. It was frozen white. The same color as the cloud.

7:05 P.M.   *On Board the* SEA MAID

Drawn between current, tide and tug, the *Prometheus* wandered back and forth across the narrow channel, eluding that delicate point of equilibrium between the three competing forces.

Constant adjustments in the *Sea Maid*'s heading were necessary to keep the tanker from running aground in the shallows on either side. Val made them instinctively, spinning the wheel a few degrees in one direction, holding it there, then, for no discernible reason, flipping it back to its original position again. He had found the "feel" of the tanker and her relationship to the tug. It took only occasional glimpses of the tanker to assure him that they were on course.

Cybil, no longer acting as lookout, stood beside Val, a chart of the harbor spread before her. She marked their progress with a red felt-tipped pen. There was only an inch of red on the chart.

"Too slow," she said as she studied their position. "We'll never make it out of the harbor at this rate. Can't we go any faster?" She looked at the throttle, pushed only halfway to its forward stop.

"I'm pushing it to the limit now," Val answered steadily, his hands resting lightly on the wheel. "Any faster and the *Prometheus* will only swing more and we'll run out of channel."

"I don't understand." She shook her head.

"The towline isn't centered on the *Prometheus*," Val explained. "The more tension on the line, the greater the tendency to veer off course. She has to ride with the tide and the current, not against them."

"But we need more speed," Cybil protested.

"I'm afraid that there are some things that we have to take at their own pace," Val philosophized. "Like the weather." He stared ahead, closely scrutinizing the telltale signs of the sea. The first weathermen were sailors. They had to be, their lives depended on it. The wind could mean life or death in a small boat at sea. Long before computers and satellites, sailors had studied the surface of the oceans for signs of changing weather.

Val edged the wheel over another degree and cut back on the throttle. He pointed to the gray-green expanse before them. "Take a look."

Cybil looked but saw nothing. The ripples that crossed and recrossed the surface of the bay were meaningless to her. "What is it?" she finally asked.

"The wind." He pointed again. "See the whitecaps there and over there. They tell which way the wind's blowing. It's changing."

7:10 P.M. *Mayor's Office; City Hall*

LaSalle stared out the window, lost in thought. He was completely oblivious to the people who still streamed across the nearby Brooklyn Bridge. The blare of horns and the distant shouts of the crowd were inaudible. He was insensitive to all external stimuli.

The world was reduced to a crumpled piece of yellow paper that he still clutched in his hands. It was from Dillon. It was New York's birth certificate. Or, more precisely, an executive pardon. The latest weather forecast.

The wind was changing, the computers finally said, after mulling over the information provided by the myriad satellites, semi-automated remote weather stations, and some firsthand accounts.

The wind had turned.

"Brooklyn," the telex read, "is saved. The cloud is being blown back out to sea. Retracing its path almost perfectly." The reprieve of New York. The savior of the city. The weather.

LaSalle wondered briefly why he didn't feel the elation of victory. He had truly turned the tide of events. He had conquered the foe. It was a greater victory than any he had ever had at the polls, even when his opponent had been overwhelmed. He had won.

But the victory was hollow.

People had died. And he knew but would not yet admit that a borough had died. Brooklyn would never be the same. No one would ever be able to look out over the still waters of the bay and see anything but death. All New

York would bear the stigma. He sighed, savoring the moment of silence. Savoring the greenness and the life that lay before his eyes. This was New York. This, the park, the trees, the silhouette of the bridge, even the squirrels fighting over the first of the fall's nuts, was life as he had known it. Tomorrow would be a different universe. The city would be transformed into an alien sphere, breaking cleanly with the past.

Behind him, he heard the crinkle of cellophane. Newfeld unwrapping a fresh cigar. He could almost smell the familiar odor of imported tobacco. Without turning around, he knew that Newfeld was rolling the brown cylinder between his fingers, testing the quality of the wrapping. "A firm cigar," Newfeld had once said, "is a fine cigar."

"Vince," Newfeld broke the silence. "You know what this means, don't you?"

LaSalle knew. The governor's mansion was his. "I know, Abe," he whispered. "I know."

"You'll be a hero, Vince." The chair creaked as Newfeld leaned back. "A goddamn hero. A true-to-life goddamn hero."

It was true, LaSalle thought. He would be a hero. A national hero. He had saved his city from destruction. No matter that he had had little to do with it. He didn't change the wind. He didn't prevent some unforseen spark from setting the whole damn thing aflame. He didn't do anything that a million others wouldn't have if they had been sitting in his chair. Maybe some of the others would have found some way to save a few thousand more. My God, a few thousand. A few thousand.

"We're saved, goddamnit, Vince," Newfeld growled. "So what's bugging you? You're staring out that damn window like a love-sick teen-ager. Damnit, Vince, stop this," he pleaded. "We have work to do."

LaSalle continued to stare out the slightly smudged windows. In the growing gloom of approaching dusk, the silhouette of the Brooklyn Bridge beckoned.

7:10 P.M.   *On Board the* SEA MAID

They were in the open sea. Ahead lay the choppy waters of the Atlantic. The waves were stronger here, rocking the tug more violently with each passing minute. With her stern weighted down by the mass of the *Prometheus* she couldn't ride the waves like a normal ship and her bow careened under the steady onslaught of the waves. They were hitting the tug slightly to the starboard side, threatening to push them off course. Val couldn't allow that to happen.

They were now going full speed which, when drawing the *Prometheus,* meant about five knots. Each wave had to be exactly countered with thrust and direction. And then the wheel spun back to keep them on course until the next wave arose and had to be met.

It was a tribute to Val's seamanship that he could keep the tug and the tanker on course. The finicky tanker still veered from side to side like a crazed fish fighting a fisherman. The currents still tugged at the mammoth tanker in unpredictable ways, drawing her toward the shallows that lined the sides of the narrow channel. The tide still pushed in contrary ways, guided by the unseen roads of the bay. Val's years of experience conducting ships through the oceans of the world were being sorely tested.

Cybil stared out the windows at Sandy Hook.

She had never really seen the peninsula before. On her earlier trips into the bay on board the *Apple Tree* and even her trip on the *Prometheus* she had ignored the low-lying piece of land. It was uninteresting at first glance. Sand dunes and a sprinkling of sea grass waving in the breeze. A picture that was repeated a million times on any oceanside property where nature had not yet been trampled by the economic concerns of man. Dull. Beautiful, but dull.

The tug skewed, tossed by an unanticipated wave. From the top of the wave her eyes caught the vague impression of motion.

They rose on the crest of the next wave. She scanned the shore for some recurrence of the motion. There was nothing.

Then she saw it again. The whipping of a red line through the air. The line resolved into a fishing rod. A piece of silver flashed brightly in the air near the rod, the lure. That's what she had seen the first time. The flailing of the lure in the air as the yet unseen fisherman sent the artificial bait flying out into the surf.

"Val," Cybil cried.

"What is it?" He grunted as he struggled to keep the bow headed directly out to sea.

"There's someone on Sandy Hook. A fisherman." They rose again, and this time she could see the man. He was wearing a fluorescent orange life jacket over similarly colored wading pants. The lure went spinning over the top of the wave to splash into the water a few dozen yards short of the *Sea Maid*'s path.

"See. There he is."

Val couldn't spare the time to look. They were entering a particularly rough spot between the knoll and the peninsula. The currents eddied in mysterious and ever-changing patterns here. He had his hands full. He merely grunted.

"But he'll be killed," Cybil protested. "The cloud'll be coming over Sandy Hook as soon as we pass. I thought they would have gotten everybody evacuated from there by now."

"I guess they just missed one," Val said absentmindedly. "You can't expect these things to be one hundred percent perfect, you know."

They rose again. This time they were so close to the fisherman that he remained in sight even when they dropped into the trough. He must have heard the sound of their engines as he looked up at that moment. A smile spread across his face. His teeth shone out in his deeply tanned face. He raised an arm in greeting.

Then he saw the *Prometheus*. His mouth dropped open, a dark pink gap. One hand went to his face to shade his eyes against the setting sun. From the deck of the *Sea Maid* the tanker looked like a mountain. Standing hip deep in the surf, she must have looked like the edge of the world as she came silently stern-first toward the open sea. He stumbled back a step as he stared at the approaching tanker. He must have thought it was headed straight for him.

Cybil ran to the wheelhouse door and threw it open. Immediately the droning of the engines grew louder as she abandoned the shelter of the enclosure. She waved to the fisherman. "Get back," she hollered. "Get back." She waved her arms toward the shore. "It's poison. Deadly." But she knew it was no use. There was no way he could hear her over the droning of the tug's engines.

She looked over her shoulder. The tanker rose starkly out of the water. A vertical wall, one hundred feet tall to deck level and another hundred and fifty feet to the top of the superstructure on the stern. She had to lean back to see the top. The cloud surrounded the tanker like a cloak, obscuring the bow and the horizon.

The wind was rising, Cybil saw. It had changed direction; that she and Val had known for five minutes. But now it was affecting the cloud noticeably. The entire length of the plume would be slow to respond to any wind change, partially because it was heavier than the surrounding air and therefore clung to the ground or the water where the wind velocity was less, but more just because it was so huge. At last report the furthermost tip of the cloud was more than five miles from the tanker. And a mile wide.

Cybil stopped waving.

Her eyes caught another flicker of motion on Sandy Hook. It was on the beach behind the lonely fisherman. A drab green jeep was pulled up on the sand, near the sea grass that separated the beach from the dunes. Below the jeep, on a direct line between the fisherman and the vehicle, a column of gray smoke rose slowly in the breeze. It too was headed south. A campfire.

A battered old coffee pot hung over a metal tripod, roasting over the bright yellow flickering flames that fed off the stack of assorted driftwood piled there. It was a strong fire, the type that could warm you after spending hours standing waist deep in the cold waters of the Atlantic. It was the sort of fire that was perfect to sit around and sip coffee after the sun went down.

It was the sort of fire that could ignite the cloud.

Cybil's heart pounded in her chest. She ran back into the wheelhouse and in a few animated sentences made Val understand what was happening.

He took one look over at the fisherman, who was now frantically reeling his line in, and the campfire in the background. Val's face blanched. He forgot the tug completely as the full import of the fire hit him. The tug heeled over as a wave caught her bow. Val grabbed the wheel to bring her back onto course. Cybil threw her arms around him.

"Oh, Val," she sobbed. "This is it."

He put his hand on her head and gently stroked the deep brown hair, feeling it between his fingers like fine strands of thread. He pulled her face close to his chest as he looked over her at the campfire on the shore. The first wisps of cloud were cutting into the beach a few hundred yards away. They had maybe another two minutes, maybe three, before the cloud reached the fire.

"I guess it is, Cybil," Val whispered, calming her with his voice and hands. "I guess it is." A sense of peace settled over him as he felt the inevitability of death approaching. They had been fighting a losing game for almost five hours now, living with the knowledge that the entire cloud could explode at any second. Their lives could be snuffed out without warning, almost before they could realize what was happening. Now at least they knew. They had a minute together before the end. He was thankful for that.

He pulled her close. Her tears dampened the front of his shirt. Her sobbing subsided. She pulled away, wiping the tears with the back of her hand. "I did it again, didn't I? Acting like a woman again." She made no attempt to dry her eyes. "I'm sorry."

"I'm not," Val replied, pulling her back to him again. "I . . . I just wish I could cry at a time like this. Somehow, it seems so . . ."

"Right," she supplied, the word muffled as she spoke into his chest.

"Yes," he agreed. "I guess that's the right word." He lowered his head until his face rested in the brown folds of her hair. He smelled the now familiar essence that he had come to know as Cybil. He inhaled deeply, savoring it. She pulled him closer. He returned the motion. They strained against each other, arms trying to bring their bodies closer than physically possible.

For a moment they stood there, transfixed in anticipation of death. The rest of the world, the *Prometheus*, the cloud, the fisherman and the campfire were obliterated. There was nothing but the two of them. And their love.

The silence was pierced by a high wailing cry. Val pulled Cybil tighter, believing that this was somehow the end.

The cry ended suddenly in a resounding thud. The sound of a fighter smacking a gloved fist into a punching bag. The expected explosion and wave of terminal heat didn't come. Val raised his head.

The cry came again. A banshee wail. The hauntingly familiar sound that he had heard before. It crossed overhead.

Artillery fire.

The thud of fist on leather.

The *Apple Tree* rode a hundred yards off to the port side of the *Sea Maid*. Her forward gun, the one used in the abortive attempt to sink the *Prometheus,* was trained in their direction.

A flash of fire from the muzzle. The shot rose and sailed over the tug. Val traced the sound with his eyes. They were firing at the beach. At the fisherman.

Cybil raised her head. "What?" she muttered as the next shell rang forth. She saw the flash from the *Apple Tree.* "What's he trying to do now?" She turned toward the beach.

The fisherman had dropped his rod and was scrambling as fast as he could through the waves to reach the shore. He thought, as Cybil did, that they were firing at him. The shell impacted on the beach, sending a shower of sand and sea spray flying. They must have been using practice shells because there was no explosion, only the dull leathery thud of the shell burying itself in the sand.

The next shell tore across the bow of the tug. It landed about fifty feet to one side of the campfire. Another banshee scream. Twenty yards short of the fire.

"He's trying to bury the fire," Val yelled. "He's trying to kick up enough sand to put the fire out. By God, I don't believe it." He stopped as the next shell tore across the sky. Twenty yards to the other side of the fire. "He's got it." He gave Cybil a hug that lifted her off the deck. "He's got it bracketed now. I think he'll do it."

The next three shells came in rapid succession, one leaving before the preceding ones had even hit. It was impossible to talk on the *Sea Maid,* but Val's cheers echoed long after the third shell had buried itself in the crater that used to mark the campfire. Cybil confined her enthusiasm to jumping up and down in the circle of Val's arms.

Val reached for the foghorn and gave it a long tug. A salute. He stood there, one arm on the horn, the other wrapped around Cybil, sending his congratulations to the *Apple Tree* in the oldest communication of the sea. The *Apple Tree*'s foghorn cried back to them, acknowledging and accepting the accolade. They were celebrating the victory together.

Suddenly, remembering the tanker behind them, Val released his grip on both Cybil and the horn to grab the wheel. He spun it hard to pull them back into the center of the now-widening channel. Cybil grabbed the rope on the foghorn and gave it a tug. The bass notes of the signal reverberated throughout the cabin.

Of the fisherman there was nothing to be seen, Cybil noted after relinquishing her hold on the foghorn. He had probably run for cover somewhere behind one of the sand dunes. In a way she was glad that he was out of sight. She had no desire to see anyone else die in the clutches of the cloud.

The tug resumed her former battle with the waves, leaving the tip of Sandy Hook behind. Cybil went to the door to watch the cloud silently slip into the pit that once was the campfire. She doubted that any embers were still hot enough to ignite the gas. She was proved correct as the cloud filled the hole with frozen gas and then swept onward, greedily reaching for the sand dunes beyond.

The sea grass turned to brown just before the carpet of white reached them. Then all that was left was the gentle waving of the grass on the top of the highest dunes.

The *Prometheus* was now in the Atlantic.

7:10 P.M.   *In a Basement; Somewhere in Brooklyn*

"Don't touch me," Faust gasped as he struck Manny's hand away. "Stay away." He struggled to his knees. The pain had disappeared; only a numbness remained. His head swam and he could feel the excited thump of his heart as it beat madly in his chest. There was no sensation in his arm, only a faint itch that slowly crept toward his shoulder.

Faust stood erect, backed against the wall of the stairwell. His hand, frozen to the railing in a depressed angle, made his position awkward, forcing him to hunch over the railing.

"Isn't there something we can do?" Manny asked. He stood on the step above, uncomfortably shifting weight from one foot to the other. The step creaked with the regular motion.

"What? What's happening?" Judith asked from the head of the stairs. She extended her arm as if feeling for an obstruction, waving it before her like a broom. "What's wrong? Tell me, Manny, what's wrong?" She reached the top step. Her hand automatically sought the railing to guide her.

"Stop!" Manny shouted.

Judith froze in her tracks, her hand inches from the frosty white railing.

"Don't touch the railing. It's frozen. Faust's already stuck." His voice trembled with fear. "And if you touch it . . ."

Judith pulled her hand back as though burned. "Elliot? Are you all right?"

"I'm . . . I'm not sure, exactly." Faust tried an imitation of a laugh. It sounded more like a gasp. He abandoned the effort. "I just have to get my hand unstuck."

"I don't understand," Judith said. "How are you stuck?"

Manny answered while Faust gathered his strength. "Did you ever touch your tongue to an ice cube right out of the freezer and have it stick?"

"Sure," Judith answered.

"It's just like that, only colder."

"But can't you pull it off? I always did when it happened to me. All you have to do is wait."

Faust grimaced as he strained against the railing. It was like trying to pull against a tree. There was no give, not even the slightest indication of a sway as he pulled with all of his strength. Hampered by the angle of his arm and by the narrowness of the stairwell, he couldn't bring his full weight to bear, but even if he had, there would have been no difference. The hand was there to stay. Unlike the ice cube, there was no way that Faust could just wait until the railing warmed up, releasing his hand. The gas lapping at the base of the railing would keep the railing at subzero temperatures.

He gave up. Falling to his knees, he gasped for breath. Manny reached forward but was stopped by a word from the trainman.

"Manny, you're going to have to go. Leave me behind. There's just not enough time to wait for me to get free. And there's nothing you can do to help me anyway, so you take Judith and Mary and head north."

"But we can't just leave you," Manny protested. Judith echoed his sentiments from the top of the stairs. Even Mary joined in.

"Yes you can, Manny. You too, Judith. You don't have any choice. There's nothing you can do for me. If I get out, it'll be on my own." Faust stopped to catch his breath. For some reason he was having trouble taking a deep breath. His heart was beating rapidly. "You have to go on. I can't take you any farther. You have to do it alone. Remember Mary. She's counting on you to get her to Manhattan. You have to leave and now, before the cloud cuts you off. So hurry!"

Faust twisted his body so he could sit on the stairs. The awkward position would have been very painful if he had had any feeling in his arm. But there was no feeling, only the growing line of white and the faint itching that preceded it up his arm.

Manny knew that Faust was right. But he was torn between the conflicting drives of loyalty and duty. Childhood told him loyalty was more important. This was the man who had saved them; risked his life for them. Duty said he had to bring Judith and Mary to safety. Duty to the species perhaps.

He walked down the final steps that separated him from Faust and extended his hand. Faust took it with his left in a backward handshake. He looked the boy in the eye. "Good luck, Manny. Take good care of them."

"I will, Elliot." He gripped the hand with the sincerity of his duty. "I will."

Judith and Mary were next. They came down the stairs, careful to stay clear of the railing. Mary threw her arms around the man's shoulders and cried into his neck. "I don't want to go. Not if you can't go. Won't you come with us?"

Faust patted her head, stroking the golden hair. "No, Mary. I would, but I can't. I just can't." Manny helped him remove the little girl's arms and set her back on her feet.

Judith was the last to say good-bye. She ran her fingertips across his face, their delicate touch lingering on his lashes and around the curve of his mouth. She bent over and placed a warm kiss on his lips. "Thank you," she whispered. And then she was gone. With Mary in her arms, she raced to the head of the stairs.

"Manny and Judith," Faust called out just before they disappeared from view. They stopped and turned back.

"Yes, Elliot?" Judith asked.

"I just wanted to wish you good luck. And remember, stay away from anything that's heading downhill. Always go up, if you can."

"We'll remember," they promised. Judith gave one wave before she picked up Mary's hand.

Manny did likewise before turning his back on the trainman and his childhood.

Three sets of feet crunched noisily on the broken glass and the strewn remnants of the tea cartons as they headed for the door. Two small steps from Mary for every one of Manny's.

Faust was alone in silence. He sat there wondering whether he should bother trying again. The seal had the feel of permanence to it. Testing it would prove little. Instead he watched the cloud slowly bubble and rise in the basement, climbing the steps toward him. There was no pain, he was surprised to notice. Somehow he had thought it would hurt, but ever since that first contact with the railing he had felt nothing.

His heart began to pound. Perspiration sprang to his brow, despite the cold that filled the stairwell. He felt as though he had a fever. He gasped for breath. The feeling went away.

A slight drowsiness filled him. The approaching lethargy of death, he realized calmly as he felt the strength drain from his limbs. Oxygen starvation was setting in.

This time he welcomed it. There was no struggle, no resistance, no anger. Only the peaceful calm of dark waters closing over his head, shutting out the light and the sounds of life. Peace.

7:20 P.M. *On a Roof; Somewhere in Brooklyn*

Like an avenging angel the helicopter fluttered down from the heavens to hover over the roof. The pilot was looking for a safe landing place. His face was clearly visible through the tiny window on the side of the craft. A white diagonal stripe carried the insignia of the Army Air Force and a small U.S. flag was emblazoned near the rear stabilizer. Hal had never seen anything more beautiful in his life.

The pilot picked a spot on the northern side of the building, as far away from the motor room as possible. His rotors extended over the side of the building. As they lowered, the wind kicked up by the rotors spun dirt and dust around in tiny whirlwinds, temporarily blinding everyone on the roof. When the dust died down, the copter was sitting solidly at the rear of the roof, its door flung open in greeting. A jump-suited airman stood in the doorway waving them to come over. They did.

"Hurry it up, will you? We ain't got a lot of time here, you know." The airman's face was masked by a helmet and oversized goggles. He was noisily cracking gum between his teeth. He couldn't have been more than nineteen at the most.

"We need help," Hal said, looking for some identifying badge of rank. He found none, so he decided to use flattery. "Sergeant, I need you and one of your men to help carry an injured man over to the ship."

"Ain't no men," the gum crackled between his teeth. "Can't he make it himself? There ain't no one here but me and . . ."

"No, Sergeant. He can't. He's unconscious and has to be carried. Don't you have a stretcher or something? I'd do it myself but . . ." He raised the crutches to show his inability to carry a stretcher.

"Right." The airman disappeared into the darkness of the center of the helicopter and reappeared a moment later carrying an aluminum stretcher. "Okay, Pop, show me where he is." He hopped out of the copter with a practiced leap.

Hal pointed to the huddled figure of Melba as she knelt next to her charge. "Over there." The airman nodded and started forward. Hal kept pace.

"Is there someone who can help carry him?" the airman asked as they neared the corner. "I can't carry him all by myself, you know."

"I'll help," Melba said.

"A woman?" The airman snorted. "Rather do it myself. Faster anyway."

But when he got one look at Kevin's face the boy's cockiness disappeared. He blanched visibly when the bandage fell off the blood-soaked eyes. Gingerly, following Melba's concerned instructions, they lifted the still figure onto the stretcher and strapped him in. The airman handled Kevin's hands as though they were eggs as he crossed them on the boy's chest and strapped them in, secure from any accidental blows.

Melba proved to be more than adequate in taking her share of the weight. They were at the side of the copter and in within a minute. The airman slammed the door closed, cutting off all of the light but little of the noise. He plugged his helmet's microphone into the intercom and spoke quickly to the pilot.

The engines revved and the sickening sensation of an elevator rising too quickly grabbed at their stomachs. The airman hunched down next to Hal.

"You're mighty lucky, Pop, you know," the boy said, trying to strike up a conversation.

"How do you mean, lucky?" Hal watched Melba's back as she fussed over Kevin.

"Lucky," the boy repeated as he dropped his rear against the floor and wedged himself against the wall. "We just got the word. We've been ordered back. Seems like there's something about to happen. Least that's what they told us when they canceled the rest of the mission."

"What's going to happen?"

"Don't know," the boy answered, losing interest in the conversation. "They didn't say. Least none too specific. Something 'bout a fire."

Hal's face fell.

"Don't worry none, Pop. This here's *Red Leader*. The best damn ship in the Air Corps. Best pilot." He smiled with genuine pride. "Best crew. You ain't got nothing to worry about, Pop. No little fire's going to stop us."

Chapter 19

7:25 P.M. *On Board the* SEA MAID

"Val, can't we put it on auto pilot and get off? We're beyond Sandy Hook now, so it should be all right, shouldn't it?" Cybil asked. This was the third time they had gone through the same conversation, each time with the same result.

"Not yet, Cybil. Soon," Val said.

In the back of his mind, Val had never given up hope of saving his ship. Ever since they cleared the harbor, that feeling of hope had grown into a certainty. He was convinced that somehow he could save the *Prometheus*. But if he relinquished the wheel, that dream, and the *Prometheus,* would be dead.

"Are you trying to get us killed?" Cybil asked, changing her position so that she stood almost directly in front of him. He couldn't avoid looking at her eyes. "Answer me, will you? Are you trying to get us killed?"

Val shook his head. "Anytime you want to, you can just pick up that mike and call the *Apple Tree*. Commander Wade will be more than happy to pick you up. I just have to stay a little longer until . . ."

"Val, don't you understand? She'll never be out far enough to be perfectly safe. All we need is a sudden change in the wind and the gas could go drifting back toward New York City. Or," she shuddered, "perhaps down the coast toward the refineries. As long as she's afloat, Val, she's a threat. A real danger to the entire East Coast. Val, you have to know that."

They stared at one another for a moment. Their first quarrel. He was wrong and they both knew it. But he'd be damned if he'd be the one to admit it. It wasn't pride; he just couldn't leave the *Prometheus*. She was his ship. His command. He was tied to the tanker by something much stronger than the towline that trailed the *Sea Maid*.

The radio crackled into life. "*Apple Tree* to *Sea Maid*. Come in, *Sea Maid*."

Cybil picked up the mike. "Yes, Commander."

"*Sea Maid*, I have another message for you from Dillon. It reads Code Seven; Condition red."

"What?"

"Shall I repeat the message?"

"No, I know what he means. Commander, bring the *Apple Tree* alongside and prepare to take us off. Immediately."

"Wilco. *Apple Tree* out."

Cybil turned to Val. "Val, now you'll have to listen. You have to leave."

"I'm not going. You can go, but I'm staying with the *Prometheus* until there's no longer a chance to save her. And that's final."

"This is the end, Val. That message from Dillon. Code Seven is the computer identification of a nuclear explosion. It's used in all the N.S.A. war games. Condition red means imminent. Not probable. Imminent. In Dillon's mind that means that it's going to blow any second now."

"I'm sorry, Cybil, but I'm staying. I don't care what Dillon thinks. I don't care what his computers tell him. As long as I'm in charge of the *Prometheus*, I'll be the one who decides whether or not she's abandoned. And so far I don't see or hear," he looked at the radio significantly, "anything that changes my mind."

Cybil's face turned scarlet. "Why you . . ." she sputtered. Her anger was so great she couldn't talk. "You pigheaded, obstinate, irrational . . . sailor." Again her anger overcame her vocal chords. She grabbed the binoculars and stormed out of the wheelhouse in such a fury that she cracked the glass on the door when she slammed it behind her. In a moment, she returned.

"Here, Captain," she emphasized his title angrily, "go see for yourself." She thrust the binoculars at him.

Val accepted the glasses in one hand but continued to hold onto the wheel with the other. "What am I supposed to see with these?"

"The end of the *Prometheus*. Look back at the Jersey shore. You'll see it. If your prejudice doesn't blind you to it, that is. It's seemed to blind you to everything but your damned ship and your so-called responsibility to her.

"I'll even make it easier for you," she continued, her tone losing none of its sharpness. "Just look in the path of the cloud. About half a mile down. There's a refinery, although a damn old one. Look for the tallest smokestack. I think it's painted blue. Coming out of that smokestack you'll see two things. First, one of the worst air pollution violations on the East Coast. And second, if you look very carefully, you'll see a yellow flame flickering in the smoke.

"I know that type of plant. We've put a lot of them out of business in the past few years. They waste a lot of fuel by burning the impurities away. But there's one other thing I forgot to tell you. There's no way to shut off the flame without practically blowing up the joint. Am I making myself clear? There's no way in hell of stopping the cloud from coming into contact with that exhaust flame. None."

She stared at Val. Her body was trembling with emotion. "There's no way of stopping the explosion, Val. It's going to happen in the next ten minutes. And if we're still this close to the *Prometheus*, we're dead."

Val closed his eyes for a second. When he opened them again, there was resignation in them. He handed the glasses back to Cybil. "Here, I don't need them. Your word is enough."

He reached forward and flipped the switch on the automatic pilot.

The wheel jumped out of his hand as the invisible mechanical helmsman took command of the *Sea Maid* and her trailing tanker.

7:25 P.M.   *On the Streets of Brooklyn*

Manny led them in a game of hide-and-seek through the empty streets, trying to avoid the cloud. Whenever they saw even a trace of the white vapor they ran to the nearest building, climbing up the steps until the cloud had passed.

The strength seemed to be seeping from the white substance, Manny noted as they stood in the doorway waiting for the street to clear after one particularly large eruption. Before, it had seemed menacing, creeping forward with an internal pressure of its own. Now it seemed to be fleeing, running for its life as the storm winds cut through it, mixing it with air, diluting it and making it disappear.

Even the biting cold had diminished. Once Manny had accidentally stepped into a gutter where the wispy white gas ran in its frantic procession to the sea. It was cold, but not the crippling cold of the basement. His foot tingled for a few minutes and then was fine.

Helicopters buzzed overhead and he wondered what they were doing. They all seemed to be going south, so he didn't give them another thought. He kept his eyes on the ground.

Judith had fallen silent ever since they left the tea store. She gripped Manny's elbow with a firm hand and held Mary's with the other. Her mind was back in the basement with Faust.

To protect them from the erupting sewers, Manny kept them in the center of the street.

A gentle breeze blew in their faces. In the distance Manny could see the looming thunderclouds of the storm that was breaking over Manhattan. Through occasional breaks in the roofline, the jagged shape of a lightning bolt briefly lit the sky. The delayed booming of thunder gave them background music to walk north.

7:30 P.M.   *In a Helicopter; En Route to Manhattan*

"The skipper says to hold tight," the airman reported. "We're going to have some turbulence, so grab onto something." He passed among the frightened and huddled passengers, spreading the word.

Hal sat staring out of the tiny window that faced south. The plastic was pitted from hard years of flying, and visibility was almost zero. He could make out the curvature of Staten Island and, for a brief instant, the familiar green lady of the harbor flashed by. Already she was fading in the distance.

The repeated crashes of thunder shook the helicopter violently. People huddled together trying to get security from human contact.

Melba crouched over the unmoving Kevin. His skin was burning up. His face was so red that it was visible even in the gloom of the cabin. Hal saw her lips move in prayer as she tended the boy. He wasn't sure whether the prayers were for Kevin or for her lost daughter. The thought surprised him. Melba hadn't said a word about her missing daughter for almost an hour.

The copter veered suddenly as the tail swooped forward, trying to pass the front. The view from Hal's window changed: he was now facing north.

The stark outlines of the World Trade Center rose in front of him, silhouetted by the backdrop of black clouds and storm. A warm yellow light gleamed from every window, welcoming them to safety.

A line of helicopters hovered between them and the sandy plot of ground next to the Trade Center. Slowly they moved forward as helicopters unloaded their cargo of refugees and took off to make room for the next shipment.

7:30 P.M. *Windows on the World; World Trade Center Tower One*

The place was in pandemonium. People shouted at one another, slapping each other on the back as though they were college chums at a winning football game. There was a festive spirit in the air. People pressed against the windows: the morbid curiosity that had gripped them before was replaced by an enthusiasm to be part of the dramatic rescue.

The storm raging on the north side was ignored. It burst over Manhattan with the fury of an avenging angel. Lightning bolts crackled from the sky to strike every tall building. Thunder rumbled continuously: the restaurant sounded like a subway tunnel at rush hour. The seconds of silence were mere interludes in the din.

But the storm inside the restaurant held even more force. Everyone celebrated the news that the cloud had reversed itself. It was now being blown out to sea. The disaster was over, the announcers cried on the radio and television. The disaster was over.

Only two men didn't share in the celebration. They found themselves standing alone staring silently at the storm. Rene didn't notice the other man at first. When he caught sight of him out of the corner of his eye, his first reaction was annoyance. Why wasn't he over with the other revellers watching the show; watching the helicopters land on the Battery Park lot to discharge their passengers? Why did he have to intrude?

Then Rene recognized the face. He was shocked. The man looked as though he had aged twenty years since he had first entered the restaurant two hours before. His face was haggard, torn between grief and joy. Split with conflicting emotions.

Rene noticed the empty glass in the man's hand. He extended a half-full bottle of Burgundy toward the man. "How about a drink, Governor?"

Without a word, Thomas Lowe held out his glass and watched Rene pour a generous helping.

7:30 P.M.   *Mayor's Office; City Hall*

Newfeld was a ball of energy. He had three phone conversations and two cigars going at once. The networks, LaSalle assumed from the nature of the conversations. He was making arrangements for a press conference "as soon as the disaster's over." From the tone in his voice, LaSalle knew that for Newfeld the disaster was already over. The cloud had turned away. It would be totally out of Brooklyn in another ten minutes. Only Coney Island was covered with any appreciable amount of the gas.

Phyllis stuck her head in the door. "Sir?" she asked the

mayor's permission to enter. He waved her in. "I'm sorry. I tried to buzz you, but Mr. Newfeld has tied up all the lines, even the intercom."

LaSalle gave her a weak smile. "Yes, he does seem to do that, doesn't he? Well?" LaSalle tried to snap himself out of the lethargy that threatened to engulf him. He rose out of the chair and walked toward the window. The faint cheering of the crowd could be heard over the hum of the air conditioner. "What now, Phyllis?"

"Director Dillon's on the private line, sir. He said he's been trying to get through on our regular numbers . . ."

LaSalle grabbed for the phone. It was a plain black receiver separate from the rest of City Hall's equipment. It had only two extensions, one at his desk and one at Phyllis's.

"Yes, Dillon?"

"Mr. Mayor, I've been trying to reach you . . ."

"Yes, I know all about that. Now you've reached me. Say what you have to say." LaSalle stood quietly as he listened to the N.S.A. director outline the situation in that mechanical way of his. Straight facts. No interpretation. No emotion. Only the facts.

Newfeld looked up and saw the expression on LaSalle's face. He spoke in the direction of the three phones. "Listen, something's come up. I'll have to call you back."

He dropped the receivers into their cradles just as LaSalle let his slip from his fingers and clatter onto the desk.

"What's happened?" Newfeld demanded. "For God's sake, Vince. Tell me what's happened!"

Chapter 20

Cybil stood close to Val as they watched the shape of the *Prometheus* draw away. The cutter was moving at flank speed, and the salt spray whipped at their faces. She had forgotten just how huge the tanker really was. From the stern she was merely mammoth; a vertical steel wall. In profile, she seemed never-ending. The *Sea Maid* looked like a flea in comparison. It seemed ludicrous to think that the tug could actually tow the tanker out of the harbor. Still, she had done the job.

Val put his arm around Cybil's shoulders. A silent apology for his stubbornness, or perhaps just a desire to be close. Cybil covered his hand on the railing with hers. Together they watched the final moments of the *Prometheus.*

It happened in slow motion. The cloud lingered near the base of the refinery, deterred by an invisible fence that surrounded the compound. Then it crept in, twisting around the pipes and running across the walks toward the center of the refinery. In less than a minute the base of the compound was hidden from view. The white cover was impenetrable.

Then, slowly, a finger of gas was drawn up the smokestack, attacking the black smoke that poured out. Cybil knew that the cloud was being drawn aloft by the convection currents that surrounded all smokestacks; air was heated at the base and rose along the sides until it mingled with the smoke. Even with that knowledge, it still looked as though the cloud were alive and actively seeking the flickering yellow-and-blue flame that perched on top of the stack. A finger of white curled and spiraled its

331

way to the top. A finger of flame whipped around the top of the smokestack, driven by the north wind.

The two fingers met and merged.

The flame grew, feeding on the substance of the cloud. It reared into the sky, a bright yellow beacon. It grew higher and higher, extending into the heavens, cutting through the clouds. It spread downward with equal speed, twisting its way around and around the stack, retracing the cloud's path. A fuse of bright yellow.

The flame touched the body of the cloud, spreading in all directions at once. It was impossible for the eye to follow for those first few seconds. A ball of fire billowed upward. The flames spread across the waters and touched the gas still floating over Coney Island, igniting it immediately.

Simultaneously, flames spread along the arm of the cloud leading to the *Prometheus*. It was the longest run and took more time, perhaps two seconds in all. As they watched, the white cloud disappeared under a blanket of yellow flame.

Cybil gripped Val's arm tightly as the first flickerings touched the tanker. It was the death of his ship. It was his first command. His greatest command.

It was also his last command. They were too close. Far too close, Cybil knew, as she felt the first waves of heat radiating from the flaming tanker. When those tanks went there would be nothing left alive in at least a two-mile radius. The cutter couldn't move fast enough. Fire was much, much faster. And explosion was faster still.

The *Prometheus* was completely encircled now. Only occasional glimpses of steel gray showed that the ship was still there. Flames shot thousands of feet into the air, fed by the exposed LNG in hold number two.

The *Prometheus* was being torn apart. On the surface of her hull, the temperature of the bright flames was two thousand degrees. The LNG was two hundred and sixty degrees below zero. No metal, no matter how strong, could withstand that temperature differential for long. The tanks burst, one after the other, spewing their contents throughout the center of the ship, flooding the passageways, the engine rooms, and every available compartment with the cryogenic liquid. The temperature of the ship dropped to two hundred below in seconds.

Ice within fire. The heart of the flames was frozen. The edges were ablaze

Oxygen was drawn in and trapped in the remnant of the ship. The gas mixed with the air. Fire touched the mixture.

The *Prometheus* exploded.

The shock wave erupted from the tanker with the force of a small atomic bomb, spreading out in all directions.

The nearest thing to the tanker was the *Apple Tree*. It was picked up and thrown over like a child's toy. It crashed into the waters of the Atlantic and broke apart, disappearing beneath the tidal waves that followed.

7:35 P.M.   *Windows on the World; World Trade Center Tower One*

A deathly hush fell over the crowd as the yellow ball grew on the New Jersey coast. It grew until it filled the horizon. A bright flame that turned the impending twilight into a bright afternoon.

Everyone pressed against the windows trying to see what was happening. The festive mood of a few seconds before was forgotten. Curiosity returned. The tanker caught fire with a suddenness that caused those nearest the windows to fall back in fear. They looked at one another and laughed nervously. After all what did they have to worry about? They were miles away.

The glass of the windows was warm to the touch. The radiant heat from the fire, someone explained. They could even feel it on their faces. But the windows became the attraction as people stretched out their hands to feel the reflected heat from a fire five miles away. The crowd edged closer to the windows.

The first explosion ripped the *Prometheus* apart. Flames billowed out in every direction, growing like a nuclear mushroom. Those closer to the windows fell back in fear. Some of the women screamed. Some of the men screamed as well.

Then the windows blew out.

Glass flew everywhere. A vacuum effect, associated with all tall buildings, sucked at the interior of the restaurant. Tables and chairs were pulled toward the windows, only to crash and splinter against the sturdy aluminum frames. The pieces went flying into space.

People were also drawn toward the vacuum. The narrowness of the windows allowed some to grab onto an edge before being drawn out. Some managed to keep their handholds. Others did not. Their screams were mercifully drowned out by the roar of the rising wind.

7:35 P.M.   *On Board* RED LEADER

Red Leader saw the yellow ball of flame rise on the Jersey coast. "Jesus Christ," he whispered as he watched it climb. It looked like it would never stop.

Coming to his senses he opened his command channel and radioed to all units. *"Red Leader* to all units. Get down. On the ground as fast as you can, wherever you can. That thing's going to blow any second. Get down."

The straps of his safety harness cut deeply into his chest and crotch as the helicopter plummeted toward the sandy plot of ground next to the Trade Center. Fortunately they were pretty close to landing, but he felt a moment's pity for those who were still over the river. They would have to ditch in the river. Never a nice prospect. Particularly when other copters were coming down all around you. Pieces of broken rotors would be flying like shrapnel.

He heard a few screams from the passenger compartment, but he quickly dismissed that from his mind. If they didn't get on solid ground fast they would all be dead. A few bumps and bruises, even a few broken bones were worth the price of living.

He braced himself for the landing. It would be a rough one.

7:35 P.M.   *Mayor's Office; City Hall*

LaSalle stood in front of his "thinking" window, staring out at the trees. He couldn't see Brooklyn or the growing fire. All he saw was the bright yellow glare reflected harshly off the sides of the Brooklyn skyline. That was enough to tell him what was happening. He could imagine the rest, as clearly as if he were there. This was his city; he breathed her troubles and knew when she hurt. He shared her agony almost physically.

The explosion caught him by surprise. There was no warning, just the faint rippling of leaves in the park and the momentary terror of the squirrels before the windows broke over him.

He threw up his hands to protect his eyes and twisted away, but the pressure of the wind drove him across the room and slammed him into his desk. He had a moment to worry what this would mean to Manhattan before he slid into unconsciousness.

7:35 P.M. *On the Streets of Brooklyn*

"Look," Mary cried, pointing to the flames that lit the sky.

"What is it?" Judith asked as Mary and Manny stopped to stare.

Manny stood speechless. The flames towered over the southern skyline. It looked as though the sky itself was on fire. "Oh, God . . ." he whispered.

"It's pretty," Mary murmured. Then, as she became aware of Manny's fear, she began to cry.

"What is it, Manny? Tell me," Judith demanded.

"Fire," he answered. "The sky's on fire."

"What do we do, Manny? Will it hurt us? Is it close?" The questions came rapidly.

"I . . . I don't know," he stammered. "I think we'll be all right. It's awfully far away . . ." he added hopefully.

The force of the explosion threw them to the ground before they had a chance to react. Glass shattered and flew about the streets, raining down on them like hailstones.

The noise was overwhelming, a deafening roar that obliterated all other sensations. It was the end of the world.

Behind them a second sun rose in the sky.

Epilogue

Rene picked his way through the debris, helping the state's leaders and businessmen to their feet. He had never seen so much blood in his life. He used tablecloths and napkins to staunch the flow of blood from a multitude of wounds. He vowed to become a vegetarian.

There was no way of telling how many people had fallen to their deaths. He was just thankful that there weren't more. He had seen at least a dozen bodies littering the square below. He had stopped counting then.

The governor was a real help, organizing people and getting them to take care of each other, the slightly maimed helping the permanently damaged. They would all bear the scars of that afternoon for life.

Leopold had learned first aid somewhere in his past and was now administering to the more severely wounded. Rene was his assistant.

The room was unbearably hot, heated by the flames of the yellow column that burned fiercely in the distance. The flames were hypnotic, drawing the eyes of everyone in the restaurant as they worked. Even the most severely injured watched the column of fire. It was a fascination that has plagued man since ancient history, since the days of the caveman.

Leopold told Rene to stop staring at the fire and get to work. A woman was bleeding to death because he hadn't tied the tourniquet tightly enough. Rene apologized and gave the knot another twist, using the knife Leopold showed him how to use.

But his eyes kept returning to the yellow column of flame.

7:50 p.m. *On the Streets of Brooklyn*

Manny slowly rose to his feet, ready to dive back to the safety of the concrete at the first sign of another explosion. Glass crunched beneath his sneakers. Wind plucked at the tatters of his clothing.

Mary was sobbing in the dust. He stooped to pick her up. She was battered and had a few cuts, he discovered, as he removed a sliver of glass from the girl's leg. She was more frightened than anything else. They had been lucky. Unbelievably lucky. If they hadn't been in the center of the street they would certainly all be dead from the flying debris.

After admonishing Mary not to wander away, Manny turned to Judith. Her face was scratched and bloody. Only the handsome outline of her profile showed the promise of the beautiful woman to come. Her clothing was stained with blood. Glass shards covered her chest.

She lay limp against his arm. Manny brushed her clothes clean of glass, feeling the splinters cut into the flesh of his palm. "Judith?" he whispered, shaking her gently. "Judith? Are you all right?"

She lay unmoving. Manny pushed the hair back from her face. He put his lips on hers. There was a faint puff of air as she exhaled. He saw a vein throb in her neck. She was alive.

"Uuuunngh," she groaned. Her hand went to her head. Manny caught it, restraining it gently with his. Her unseeing eyes opened.

"Manny?" She clutched at him. "Manny, is it over?"

Manny looked down the street. It was covered with glass and debris torn from adjacent buildings. One or two whole buildings had fallen into the street, their red bricks littering the pavement. Smoke curled from a dozen different windows as fires began to lap at the exposed wood. To the south the sharp reports of sewer explosions rang out like gunshots. To the north, the street was filled with the red flashing lights of approaching fire engines and ambulances. Coney Island, their home, was in flames. The gas had ignited, turning it into an inferno. As the gas was consumed, it left a legacy of fire behind. A firestorm consumed Brooklyn.

Manny looked down at Judith. "Yes, Judith. It's over." With a sigh she relaxed against him.

The wail of approaching sirens said help was on the way.

7:50 P.M.   *Battery Park City; Manhattan*

The wreckage was a mass of flames and twisted bits of metal. Small globs of aviation fuel burned everywhere, filling the air with clouds of dense, cloying smoke. It was impossible to see anything.

Hal crawled away from the remains of *Red Leader*, dragging his useless legs behind him. His braces lay somewhere in the wreckage, as useful as the broken frame of the helicopter. Other people cried around him, some in pain, but most in fear. Or relief. Or possibly grief. They had been remarkably lucky.

The pilot had brought the copter down just before the explosion. Hal had heard a wheel strut snap with a high pinging sound. The copter lurched, falling toward the broken brace. Then the shock wave hit.

The helicopter was lifted and turned, pushed by the incredible force of the explosion. They were thrown against the chain-link fence that surrounded the open lot. It parted with the sound of a rubberband snapping. A second explosion ripped over them, tumbling the helicopter. It rolled against a steel beam of the West Side Highway and wedged there.

The survivors lay stunned for a moment, amazed that they were alive. Then the smell of smoke crept through the copter and panic set in. There was a stampede to escape. Hal, crippled without his braces, managed to crawl out of the way while the plane emptied.

His next thought was for Melba. She would never leave Kevin. He was certain of that. He crawled through the smoke, heading for the section of the plane where he thought they would be. But everything had been tossed around so that there was no sign of Melba or the stretcher that bore Kevin.

"Melba!" Hal called into the smoke. The crackle of fire covered any response. He called again. No answer. He crawled farther astern.

Melba was lying across the remains of the stretcher. Kevin hadn't had a chance. Strapped into the inflexible stretcher he had been broken like a matchstick when the helicopter smashed into the support. His spine had shattered against the unrelenting steel of the helicopter wall.

She must have tried to use her body to protect his. Hal realized as he viewed the couple locked together in death. Her arms were wrapped around the canvas, her head draped across Kevin's chest.

Hal slowly crawled away as the flames began to lick at the interior of the cabin. The heat and smoke drove him out into the fresh air.

It must have been the smoke that made his eyes tear so much, he thought as he dragged himself away.

7:50 P.M. *Mayor's Office; City Hall*

The office was in shambles. LaGuardia's desk tottered on three legs. Pictures of past mayors littered the floor with disapproving faces. Glass and slivers of wood had been trampled into the rich amber carpet. It would take hours for the workmen to get it clean again. The blood would give them the most difficulty.

LaSalle lay on his leather couch, his face obscured in a blood-soaked towel. He kept trying to take it off and sit up, but Newfeld would have none of it.

"But, Abe . . ." LaSalle protested.

"No, Vince. Just wait for the doctor. There's one on the way."

"It's only a scratch, I tell you. Just a scratch. There's so much to do . . ."

"And there are so many to do it, so relax." Newfeld patted his pockets looking for a cigar. All he found were a few bits of glass. They stung his fingertips. He pulled out a sliver with his teeth and carefully spat it onto the rug. "What you need now is time to relax. To get your thoughts together. Think about what you're going to say at the press conference.

"You know, of course, you're a national hero. The man who saved New York. They're already calling you that on the networks. Your face, without bandages I'd guess. No, wait, maybe with bandages. I like that. It shows that you've suffered as well. Yes, we'll insist that they use a shot of you with the bandages when they put you on the cover of *Time* and *Newsweek*." Newfeld was getting wound up. This was the same type of speech he had given LaSalle five years before when he convinced him to run for mayor.

"It'll be perfect. You'll be governor in a few months, there's no question of that now. Lowe's out of the picture."

"Abe, slow down," LaSalle said, his voice muffled by the towel. "I . . . I have a lot of thinking to do about this. You know I've never wanted to do anything but work in government, don't you, Abe?"

"Of course," Newfeld replied. "And right now you're the hottest thing since F.D.R."

"But now I'm not sure I want to be 'the hottest thing.' I'm not sure I can take it. 'The man who saved New York' you said. Saved? How many people died? One hundred thousand? Two hundred? Three? Christ! All I can think about is my next phone call from that bastard Dillon who'll gleefully tell me that his computers have come up with a new 'death estimate.' Damnit, Abe, if this is what winning is like, I'm not sure I want to play the game. I'm thinking of quitting. Seriously. Just as soon as I get the mess straightened out in the city, I think I'll retire from office."

"Okay, Vince. Okay." Newfeld calmed him. "Look, it's your life, you can do anything you want. I wouldn't think of trying to force you to do anything. Just rest. The doctor will be here soon."

Newfeld leaned back in his chair, glad that LaSalle couldn't see the grin that spread across his face. With an attitude like LaSalle's they could be in the White House in two years. He mentally started composing LaSalle's opening statements to the press, a Cheshire grin cutting his face in half.

7:50 P.M. *In the Water; The Atlantic*

The column of flame rose skyward. Bright yellow along it's length, blue at its base, it was magnificent to look at, elemental, almost possessing a life of its own.

Had it enough to feed on, it would have grown ten times its present size. But, surrounded by a hostile elemental force, water, it could feed only on itself. Still, it would burn for half an hour, giving off more heat than one hundred thousand Hindenburgs.

The temperature was overwhelming. Radiant heat alone was enough to melt glass at five hundred yards. Nothing could live that close to the fire.

Cybil and Val were twice lucky. They had been thrown from the *Apple Tree* when she was flipped over by the explosion. That probably saved their lives as the cutter went down like a stone taking the commander and his crew with her. And they were far enough away to escape the spreading circle of flame. It had stopped slightly more than two thousand yards away.

Cybil had to keep dunking her head to avoid the heat. The stench of scorched hair lingered from the last time she had forgotten. Her face was blistered from staring at the tower of flame, but she couldn't pull her eyes away. Her eyebrows were mere ashes washed away by the Atlantic.

Val stared, not at the tower, but at the base. Somewhere in there lay the wreckage of his ship. The ship wouldn't be recognizable, of course, even if he could penetrate the glare of the flames. But she was there.

He didn't see the scientific beauty or even the esthetic beauty of the fire. To him it was a pyre. The funeral pyre of the *Prometheus*. She went out in glory. A name never to be forgotten. Long after the day's dead were buried and the mourning over, people would talk about that column of fire. It was something to see. The *Prometheus*.

He noticed Cybil's hair was smoldering again and unceremoniously dunked her head in the water. She came up sputtering.

"Hey," she complained.

"Hey," he replied, splashing more water on her face. "Are you trying to get a sunburn or do you just want to go around bald for the next six months or so?" He laughed.

In a second, she joined in. "Who ever heard of a bald bride." She splashed him back. They drifted apart and were pushed back together again by the gentle current of

341

the sea. They met in one another's arms and kissed, the salt of the ocean mixing with their lips, sealing the caress.

They broke apart and turned their backs on the fire. Sandy Hook was less than a mile away. They started swimming.

The column of flames rose into the heavens and disappeared into the clouds, returning the gift so long ago stolen from the gods.

The best
in modern fiction from
BALLANTINE

No one who buys it,
survives it.

THE HOUSE NEXT DOOR

A terrifying novel
by
Anne Rivers Siddons

29330 $2.50

BALLANTINE BOOKS

G-1c

Bestsellers from BALLANTINE